BRIAN ULLMANN

DARWIN'S

"Brian
action-p
crosses
—Stev

DEDICATION:

To my personal base camp: Cindy, Lily, and Jake.

Published 2009 by Medallion Press, Inc.

The MEDALLION PRESS LOGO
is a registered trademark of Medallion Press, Inc.

Names, characters, places, and incidents are the products of the author's imagination or are used fictionally. Any resemblance to actual events, locales, or persons, living or dead, is entirely coincidental.

Typeset in Adobe Garamond Pro
Printed in the United States of America

ISBN:9781934755075

10 9 8 7 6 5 4 3 2 1
First Edition

ACKNOWLEDGMENTS:

The idea for Darwin's Race was born on the mountains of Kilimanjaro in Africa and Aconcagua in Argentina, so a hearty round of thanks goes out to all of my fellow climbers, guides, and support crew.

During the process of committing these experiences to paper, a host of early readers helped shape the manuscript. You know who you are, but a special thanks is due Ken Stevens and the rest of the gang at The Writer's Center for helping this fledgling writer learn the craft. Wanda Haskel took her red pen to an early draft without mercy, and the book is much improved as a result.

To my agent, Ron Goldfarb, who saw something in that early draft of Darwin's Race and took a chance on an unknown author. Your advice and guidance have been invaluable, and I look forward to a long and rewarding relationship together.

Darwin's Race would not have been possible without the generous help of Steve Alten (Meg, Domain, The Loch, Hell's Aquarium). For months, Steve went through each page of the manuscript with the keen eye of a best-selling author. You simply wouldn't be holding this book in your hands without his support. Steve, I owe you one.

Kerry Estevez and the rest of the staff at Medallion Press have been helpful and patient in guiding an admitted novice through the publication process. A writer couldn't hope for a better publishing partner.

And finally, to my family. Your support and encouragement throughout the process of writing has been incredible. This is for you.

PROLOGUE

September 1999

Kuk Sur, Southeastern Tibet
19,492 Feet

Mother Nature was angry.

There are some places, apparently, where she didn't want man to tread. She baked deserts with scorching heat, draining them of all life and water. She churned the seas with towering waves and thundering ocean storms.

But Mother Nature saved her best work for the sorry lot who considered themselves mountain climbers. For reasons she kept to herself, Mother Nature used everything in her extensive arsenal to keep men and women off her majestic peaks.

She sucked the oxygen from the air until it could no longer support life, coated the steep slopes with thick ice, sometimes loosing tons of snow and ice down their flanks, and blasted everything with winds forceful enough to grind down solid rock. And then, her *coup de grace*—bone-chilling cold. No, humans were not built to endure temperatures of 40 degrees below zero. And Mother Nature knew it.

Fortunately for them, mountain climbers are blessed with remarkably poor memories.   If they could recall the curses of high-altitude climbing–paralyzing cold, wet, sleepless nights, bone-deep hunger—climbers would surely never again set booted foot upon another abominable slope.

And yet here I am, Conner Michaels thought. *Too cold to move and too proud to stop.*

Conner could see the summit, a snowcapped peak two thousand vertical feet above his head. Kuk Sur rose sharply from the frozen Tibetan plateau like a giant ice pyramid, its steep summit marking the easternmost peak of the immense Himalayas, the tallest mountain range on planet Earth. Kuk Sur was the most inaccessible of the lot, defended to the east by the world's largest and deepest canyon, the Tsangpo Gorge. America's Grand Canyon would barely climb halfway up the massive chasm.

Though the summit was less than a day's climb away, at that moment nothing seemed farther. Sucking wind at nineteen thousand feet, Conner had lost feeling in his extremities over an hour before. His fingers had long since frozen stiff inside his thick wool mittens, locked in place around a pair of ice axes. Icicles clung to his face, turning his once-brown eyebrows to a dirty white. Ice crystals speckled his three-week-old beard, the mountain version of salt and pepper.

Under the grizzled exterior was a ruggedly handsome thirty-three-year-old, with eyes the color of caramel and legs as thick as the redwoods in his home state of California. But with frozen snot hanging a half inch below his nostrils, Conner looked like he'd been on the losing end of a raging fight with a blizzard. Which, of course, he had been. The twenty-two thousand-foot Kuk Sur was giving Conner a wintry beating.

Still, the mountain summoned Conner and other mountaineers like a beacon. As the highest unclimbed peak in the grand Himalayan range, Kuk Sur represented the challenge of a lifetime. A chance to have your name immortalized alongside such legends as Mallory, Hillary, and Messner. A first ascent is something to which all climbers aspire—and in a rapidly shrinking world, the summit of Kuk Sur embodied one of the last true firsts.

And so Conner found himself high upon Kuk Sur's northwest ridge, chasing a glorious dream and gazing west through the crisp Himalayan air toward Namche Barwa. A ten thousand-foot gash in the earth separated the two towering peaks, carved by the mighty Tsangpo River. From high on Kuk Sur, the Tsangpo was little more than a windy brown trickle, but remembering the fury of the river up close quickened Conner's pulse.

Yes, it was vistas like this that erased the hardships from the minds of alpinists.

Mountaineering had always been like this for Conner.

It was the ultimate rush: red-hot adrenaline pumping through his veins. Others referred to the high as "feeding the rat," but for Conner it was more than that. It was his way of life.

After bitterly frigid days and even colder nights of heavy slogging up high mountain passes, the satisfaction of summiting was as pure an emotion as there could be. It was nature's kind way of saying, "Okay, you made it. You deserve to feel something special."

It was almost enough to make him forget how miserable he felt.

Conner glanced at his wrist computer, a Suunto X6-HR complete with altimeter, barometer, compass, and heart rate monitor, and saw the temperature had dipped to 30 below. With wind chill factored in, minus 40 easy.

"That's all you got?" Conner yelled at the elements through his balaclava.

Of course, that was not all Mother Nature had. Not by a long shot.

Conner lifted his wraparound snow goggles to his forehead and squinted into the falling snow. His brother was perhaps twenty feet ahead, inching along a narrow ridge. Seven years younger, Tucker was wearing a fire-engine red wool cap that stood out in the snowfall like a lighthouse beacon. His brother swore the hat was the warmest he had ever worn, but Conner often joked that no matter how warm he was, it couldn't possibly justify wearing something so hideously ugly. It was certainly hard to miss.

Tucker's jacket flapped in the whipping winds, threatening to knock him from the arête at any moment. The gusts had picked up dramatically over the last two hours, scouring the mountain slopes like frozen sandpaper. Suddenly, Conner wished they had roped up farther down. In these conditions, a safety rope connecting the climbers could mean the difference between a controlled ascent and a fatal fall.

The Michaels brothers had been raised outdoors. With parents who'd kicked the rambunctious pair out the door at first light every morning, Conner and Tucker had delighted in the exploration of the neighborhood forest. They wandered the banks of a nearby brook, navigating toppled tree trunks and tangled roots. Even when they were confined to the house by rain, or more likely, by punishment for overly boisterous behavior, the brothers erected elaborate mountains of pillows and blankets and boxes, then scaled these makeshift peaks until they collapsed under their collective body weight.

As young teenagers, the brothers graduated from mountains of pillows and boxes to the real thing, first in the Shawangunk Mountain Range, the birthplace of so many world-class climbers. Eventually, they moved on to big mountains: Whitney, Shasta, Hood, and eventually and invigoratingly, Rainier.

His brother was all grown up now: a husband and, of all things, a father. They didn't see each other nearly as much as they once had, but these climbs—once a year, at least—kept them as close as brothers could be.

Replacing his goggles, legs like lead weights, Conner trudged up the ridge.

Though Tucker Michaels was barely thirty feet ahead of his older brother, his boots were a full six feet over Conner's head.

Yes, you're a steep one, he thought. *No wonder no one's tamed you yet.*

The ridge was only ten inches across, with steep slopes that fell three hundred feet on either side. The exposed rock was so razor sharp that Tucker couldn't place his heavy boots side by side. Instead, each step had to be a carefully choreographed movement that placed each footfall in front of the other, like a high-wire act. Difficult with clunky size 11 plastic boots.

Tucker's trick to ignoring the wicked elements of high altitude climbing was to think of a happy place, and for the twenty-five-year-old that happy place was a small family home in Charlotte, North Carolina. He had married his childhood sweetheart in an intimate ceremony on the beach, surrounded by friends and family. Less than a year later, Melanie gave birth to Jacob Donald Michaels, a bright-eyed boy with a shock of dark hair atop a perfectly round head. Just before he left for Kuk Sur, Tucker bought his son his first set of tiny hiking boots. The memory of Jake's very first unsteady steps in those boots was enough to make him forget about the blistering winds and piercing cold of Kuk Sur. Almost.

Tucker paused for a breath in the thin air, balanced himself, and turned to check on his brother. Conner was struggling, to be sure, but making steady progress. Up ahead of Tucker, the third partner in their climbing team had stopped, head bowed against the thickening snowfall.

Now what? Tucker thought.

Conner saw that his brother had stopped up ahead and hurried to catch up.

"What gives?" he asked. "Tess, why are we stopping?"

His climbing partner for the past eight years, Tess Chamniss was one of those rare creatures that blended ruggedness with femininity. Her five-foot-five-inch frame was muscular without appearing so. Hard and soft at the same time. She was the type of woman that eschewed makeup, preferring to let her womanly radiance shine naturally. She was a tomboy for sure (no female mountain climber of her caliber wasn't), and yet she somehow managed to look like a woman at all times. Maybe it was her strawberry blonde hair that always looked professionally styled with just a few tussles. Or her piercing blue eyes that stood out in the fields of white snow like an oasis. Whatever it was about her, it had bit Conner from the very first, a chance meeting during a climb of Washington's Rainier.

Maybe he saw in Tess some attributes of himself, because he could also show a softer side. It was pretty common for Conner to lose himself on those high summits, break down, and weep tears of sheer joy. Tess had seen it firsthand, Conner enraptured atop a summit, on more than a dozen climbs, and he supposed that was one of the things that had drawn her to him. On that very first trip to Rainier, Conner stood atop the fourteener and Tess caught his expression as the tears flowed freely down both cheeks. A girl, even a hardened alpinist like Tess, couldn't help but melt for a sensitive men. They had been a couple ever since.

Tess pointed a few feet ahead of their position, and suddenly Conner understood why she had halted their progress. A giant crevasse, twenty-five feet across, yawned open before them. Conner inched forward to gaze into its depths. He couldn't see the bottom.

"Well, this is a problem," Conner said, frowning. "I guess we have to go around."

Tess wiped her snow goggles with the back of her mittens. "What about that snow bridge?" she said. "Cuts right over the crevasse."

The snow bridge didn't look promising to Conner. Though it stretched across the entire gap, it was barely four feet wide. It was solid ice, covered with two inches of fresh snow, and completely unsupported. If it broke away under the weight of the climbers, there would be no recovery.

"I don't know," Conner mumbled. "Does it look solid enough to you?"

"Hasn't collapsed yet," answered Tess. "Must be pretty strong."

"I think we should go around. It'll take a couple extra

hours, but I think it's worth it."

Tess turned to Conner's younger brother and asked, "Tucker, what do you think? Cross the bridge or go around?"

"Man, I just want to get up and get down," he said, stomping his feet to keep warm. "In case you haven't noticed, it's pretty damn cold up here!"

"That baby face of yours getting chilled?" Conner teased. "Maybe if you could grow some facial hair it would keep you a little warmer."

Tucker fingered his hairless chin reflexively and laughed. "Don't hate me for being boyishly handsome. The only reason Tess here settled for you is because I was already taken. Tell him, Tess."

"You two," Tess groaned. "Do I have to listen to this inane brotherly banter all the way up to the top? If so, I suggest we cross the snow bridge and get this over with. I need some peace and quiet."

Just then, the snowfall lightened and Conner could see a break in the cloud cover. Gazing out toward the horizon from this altitude, he could see the actual curve of the earth. He wiped his snow goggles with the sleeve of his North Face jacket for a clearer view. For him, this was one of the highlights of alpine climbing: He felt like he was on the top of the world.

"Uh oh, Tuck. I think we've lost your brother again."

Conner smiled. "Takes too long to get here not to enjoy it," he said.

Tess shrugged. "That's fine and all, but we have to keep moving. We've got maybe four hours left before we need to get back to camp."

"Alright, alright," Conner said, breaking away from the view. "This is a democracy, so majority rules. I think that snow bridge is too risky. I say we go around."

"I'm going to have to disagree with the great Conner Michaels," Tess said. "You may be the three-time Eco-Challenge champ and *Adventure Racing Magazine's* Man of the Year two years running, but I think you're playing this one too close to the vest. I say we go right over. It's silly to go around–we'll waste hours—when there's a perfectly good bridge right in front of us. We can rope up if that'll make you feel better."

Conner turned to his younger brother. "I guess that leaves the decision to you, little brother. What do you want to do, Tuck? Cross the bridge or go around?"

Rubbing his mittened hands together, Tucker surveyed the length of the crevasse and the icy span. "Look, I'm cold. If we cross now, we can make summit in a couple of hours and we can all get the hell off this mountain. I say we take the snow bridge."

Conner frowned at the decision. Tess was always eager to challenge the elements, take the more daring route to test her considerable skills. He could understand her reasons for the crossing, but Tucker was basing his choice on temporary factors like warmth and comfort. Not the best way to make critical decisions, Conner thought.

He prayed it wouldn't come back to haunt them.

Tess went first.

Even with a sixty-pound backpack filled with climbing gear, she was still many pounds lighter than Conner and his brother. She inched out onto the bridge, allowing the span to feel her weight. A safety rope was tied to each of the three climbers, fastened tight to the harness around each waist. Standard equipment for alpinists, the rope served as protection in the event of a fall; the super strong nylon could keep a potentially fatal plunge to a relatively minor twenty-foot fall. Even if the bridge collapsed, the brothers' combined weight would be able to arrest Tess's fall.

Conner and Tucker watched from the edge of the giant crevasse, hands gripped around the safety rope, bracing for a collapse. The ice groaned like a wounded animal and Conner held his breath as Tess finally clambered to the far side. She yelled something back over the crevasse, but the winds carried her words away.

"Go ahead, big brother," Tucker said. "I'll bring up the rear."

Conner waited until Tess picked up the slack on the safety rope before stepping out onto the snow bridge. He followed her snowy footprints, stepping where she had stepped as if the span would be more stable in those tracks. On wobbly knees, Conner resisted the urge to look down into the abyss. It wasn't that he was afraid of heights, but he had heard stories of climbers that experienced debilitating vertigo at the sight of bottomless chasms. It was better not to chance it.

"See? That wasn't so bad, was it?" Tess said, grabbing his arm when he reached the far side. "Piece of cake."

Conner inhaled a couple of deep, calming breaths and waved across the gap to his brother. Tucker waved back, and Conner pulled up the slack. "Alright, little brother. Take it nice and slow now."

Tucker stepped onto the snow bridge.

The snow bridge swooned under Tucker's plastic boots.

"Nothing to see here, folks," he said aloud. "Don't look down. Just move along."

Halfway across, he couldn't resist breaking his own rule. As he leaned out from the bridge, he kicked a small piece of ice off the edge and watched it plummet into the depths. The darkened crevasse gobbled up the piece of ice like a hungry wolf.

Suddenly, Tucker didn't feel so good. He felt lightheaded, like he was going to faint. His head began to spin, wildly enough that he wanted to drop to a knee to regain his balance. But he couldn't move. The sight of the blackened depths of the crevasse had frozen him in place.

His breathing was short and shallow, but he couldn't seem to slow himself down. He was starting to fear that he would hyperventilate. He tried to call out for help but found he couldn't speak.

He closed his eyes and thought of home. Images of his boy—splashing in the bathtub with an armful of rubber duckies, chasing the family dog around the living room—flashed through his mind's eye. God, how he loved that kid.

The mental exercise helped, and Tucker felt his breathing return to normal. He opened his eyes and peered across the snow bridge. He could see the concerned look on Tess's and Conner's faces, so he shot them a little wave of reassurance. With a final steeling breath, Tucker glanced down at his boots and began to take another step.

That's when he saw the crack.

It started on the right side of the snow bridge, outside his right boot. As he watched, the fracture silently snaked its way across the span, directly underneath him, finally connecting to the opposite side. Tucker stood stock-still. He didn't move a muscle, afraid that the least movement would cave in the bridge completely. Slowly, he reached out and grabbed the safety rope with both hands.

And prayed.

"What is he doing?" Conner asked. "Why is he stopping?"

And then everything happened at once.

With a bone-rattling crack that sounded like the felling of a mighty oak tree, the snow bridge collapsed upon itself in a giant V. Fifty tons of ice and snow—and the flailing figure of his helpless brother—plummeted into the crevasse, spewing ashes of snow like a frozen volcano.

Conner yelled over the roar: "BRACE!"

Throwing himself face down onto the ground, Conner thrust his ice axe into the frozen ground over his head with both hands . . . and clung on for dear life. He prayed Tess was doing the same—his own weight would not be enough to break his brother's fall. Waiting for the safety line to snap once Tucker had fallen the length of the slack, Conner clenched his eyes shut. He locked his grip around the buried ice axe.

The slack caught, and Conner felt the full weight of the plunge in his shoulders burning as if he were holding up the entire mountain himself. The sudden jerk wrenched his axe from the icepack as Conner was dragged toward the precipice, his hatchet dredging a jagged gash behind him.

"Conner!"

Flailing for purchase, struggling to grip the axe that was slipping from his hands, Conner vaguely heard Tess's cry. If Tess had assumed her own brace position, his descent would be slowed as soon as the loose rope tightened. Then he would be able to halt himself completely.

Conner felt his feet spill over the edge of the crevasse.

With one final surge of energy, he hoisted the axe into the air and plunged it down into the ice a second time. The force of the blow slashed right through the rim of the crevasse, cleaving off a giant shard of ice that bashed Conner in his raw shoulder before pitching into the blackness below. The ice axe ripped from his hand, trailing the ice shard over the edge in a shower of snowy debris.

Heart leaping into his throat, Conner Michaels fell.

Then the slack caught, and his body jerked to a halt as if his parachute had opened at one hundred miles per hour. He tried to call out to Tess, but the jolt had knocked the breath out of him. Conner stared down into the abyss . . . and saw nothing but darkness.

"Conner!" Tess screamed from above. "Conner, you've got to grab hold of something!"

Conner gasped for breath. "Can't . . . no . . . ice axe." He hoped Tess could hear his panting words.

"Conner! I'm braced, but I can't hold the both of you!"

As if to prove what she was saying was true, Conner dropped a full foot before the slack caught again. He felt like he was in the grip of some wicked puppeteer hell-bent on jerking him around like a marionette.

Conner glanced up into a shower of ice and saw Tess's boots hanging over the cliff. She tried to dig her crampons into the face, but she couldn't do it; the angles were all wrong. She couldn't hang on long; Conner would have to act fast.

Swinging on the safety rope, Conner thrust his crampons into the wall of blue ice inside the crevasse. But the force of the swing tracked in the opposite direction and pulled him free of the ice.

Above, Tess's screams were becoming more urgent. "I can't hold you!" she yelled. "Grab something or cut loose!"

Out of the question. If he cut himself free, both he and his brother would plummet down into the bottomless pit. Not a good plan. He reached down and tugged on the safety rope that connected him to his brother. He could feel his brother's weight on the rope.

"Tucker! Tucker, can you hear me?"

From the blackness below, a faint sound. "Conner . . . I'm hurt, man. Real bad."

"Can you brace yourself? You need to use your axe!"

"Arm's . . . broken. Can't . . . hold—"

"Tucker, can you see the bottom?"

A pause. "No. Too dark. But there's a ledge. If I can swing a little, I may—" His voice trailed off, weakening.

"Okay, Tucker, do it. I'm going to help you swing."

Conner felt the safety rope below him begin to swing, as if he had hooked some giant fish from the murky depths. "Hang on, Tess!" he yelled up. "Just a minute longer!"

"Can't do it!" she screamed back. "The axe is slipping! Jesus Christ, I don't wanna die!"

Conner dropped another six inches; Tess's body was now nearly hanging completely over the edge.

From below, Tucker called up: "Almost . . . One more swing—"

"Cut him loose!" Tess screamed, panicking now. "Please, God! CUT HIM LOOSE!"

"Tucker? Tucker, are you on the ledge? Tess can't hold us much longer!"

No response. Conner held his breath as ice crystals cascaded down into the abyss like frozen rain. Then Tucker's voice from the blackness rose up to him: "Conner, I'm on the ledge. It looks like there's some kind of cave—"

"Tucker? I can't hear you. What was that last part?"

"Conner, something's not right down here," Tucker said, his voice cracking with concern. "Something smells really bad down here."

Above, Tess's screams were reaching a feverish crescendo.

"Tucker, loosen the safety! Take the weight off Tess."

No response.

"Tucker, can you hear me?"

His brother's reply stopped him cold. "Conner, something's down here with me. I can't see it, but I can hear it breathing. The smell . . . *Oh, Jesus—!*"

Tucker's scream rose up from the abyss, echoing off the crevasse walls in a cacophony of terror. The rope beneath Conner swayed violently, swinging him about the crevasse, slamming him into the wall. Above, he heard Tess scream anew, urging him to cut his brother loose. But Conner couldn't hear her words drowned out by the horrifying sounds coming from below.

Dreadful sounds.

Gurgling.

And then the rope went limp.

"Tucker!" Conner screamed, tugging on the now-weightless rope. "Tucker, can you hear me?" When the edge of the safety rope reached him, Conner stared at it in disbelief.

The safety rope, with a tensile strength of over eight hundred pounds, had been torn straight through.

The serrated fiber edges were flecked with blood.

PART ONE

CHAPTER ONE

Rockefeller Center
New York City

If New York City was the media capital of the world, Rockefeller Center represented its epicenter. "The Rock," as it was known within Manhattan, was home to the largest news gathering organization in the world, the Associated Press, as well as the broadcast headquarters of NBC-TV and Radio City Music Hall. But it was perhaps most famous for its flag-lined sunken plaza. During the winter months, the plaza morphed from an outdoor restaurant to a giant ice-skating rink, the site of the famous Rockefeller Christmas tree.

Months before the first chill of winter, the sunken plaza had been converted into a massive stage, a six-foot platform that stretched forty feet across, facing a dozen rows of folding chairs.

On the far side of the plaza, a striking statue sat atop a large fountain. Forged in bronze and covered in gold leaf, it depicted the Greek mythological figure Prometheus stealing fire from the gods as a gift for man, bringing knowledge and arts to the mortals.

Like ravenous rats, reporters swarmed the open courtyard between the stage and the gilded Prometheus. An empty podium sat on top the otherwise bare stage, surrounded by broadcast cameramen and audio techs adjusting microphones, checking levels, and trying nonchalantly to sneak a peak behind the giant curtain hanging at the back of the stage. Two burly security officers positioned on either end of the stage saw to it that none were successful, forcing the media to pacify themselves with live teases and taped stand-ups.

Snatches of their reports could be heard over the clamor.

"*Speculation is rampant,*" a pretty blonde reporter vamped into a video camera, "*as NBC and Discovery Channel are set to announce a joint project shrouded in secrecy.*" The woman gestured to the growing throng of media. "*One of the reasons for all this media attention is the recent press release issued by hotshot producer Terrance Carlton. Yesterday afternoon Carlton, known as the creator of the TV phenomenon* Endure *and the executive producer of the granddaddy of all adventure races, the Eco-Challenge, released the following brief statement.*"

The reporter displayed a piece of paper to the camera

before quoting from it directly: "'*The National Broadcasting Company and Discovery Channel Entertainment in conjunction with Eco Productions cordially invite the esteemed members of the media to a unique program announcement this Thursday at 1 p.m. in Rockefeller Plaza.*'"

The woman waved the piece of paper at the camera. "*That is the extent of the release, but the real buzz started yesterday with an article in* Variety *reporting that NBC had won the broadcast rights to Carlton's new venture after a fierce bidding war with two other networks. The article cited sources within the upper management of General Electric, the parent company of NBC. Apparently, the significant rights fee had to be approved by the parent company due to the, quote, 'explosive nature' of the program's content.*"

The reporter flashed her perfectly white teeth nicely complementing her carefully groomed locks and a smart navy business suit. "*All of our questions will be answered in roughly twenty minutes and CNN will carry the press conference live. For now, reporting live from Rockefeller Center, this is Susan Peretti, CNN, New York City.*"

Terrance Carlton was pacing.

The fifty-fifth-floor office of NBC's vice president of special programming, Horace Alger, was nearly large enough for a full-court basketball game, but Carlton felt like he was suffocating. The office offered clear views of the Plaza, and Carlton distractedly surveyed the activity below. Alger himself was seated on a lush Theodore sofa, and Carlton could feel the weight of the vice president's heavy gaze upon his back as he strode from one side of the office to the other. Carlton counted the steps it took to cover the length of the office. Thirty-six.

"There's nothing to be nervous about," Alger said finally. "Leslie has taken care of everything. The press is here . . . they're practically chomping at the bit to hear our news. Just try to relax."

Carlton stopped mid-stride to consider the plump executive.

Alger had earned his sprawling office after twenty years of loyal service at NBC. He rose up through the ranks, from a fresh-faced production intern for Brokaw's then-fledgling nightly news to the executive producer for NBC's top-rated *Today Show*. But Alger's big coup came when he orchestrated a groundbreaking partnership with Discovery Channel to provide educational children's programming on Saturday mornings. The move saved millions of dollars in production costs and earned NBC kudos for exceeding the new, strict educational programming guidelines set by the FCC. Alger's reward for his pioneering efforts was a fancy title, an envy-inducing office, and almost complete autonomy for special programming. That's why he was the perfect person to approach with Carlton's latest brainchild, a project that promised to eclipse all his other endeavors, even *Endure*. Alger, not surprisingly, jumped at the opportunity.

Carlton knew that their partnership was big news— the combination of two titans. Failure, as they say, was not an option.

"I'm not nervous," Carlton said, resuming his trans-office stroll. "I'm anxious. There's a big difference. There's work to be done. If we want to launch this program for November sweeps . . ."

Alger interrupted. "Not 'want to launch,' Terrance. We *must launch* for sweeps. NBC didn't shell out this kind of money for a summer throwaway. I don't need to remind you of our financial investment, do I?"

He certainly didn't. Though the media had not yet gotten wind of the enormous price tag, the truth was that it would represent one of the most expensive productions in the history of the network. And all for a program for which there was no pilot, no auditions, no cast, and a logistical nightmare that made *Survivor* look like *America's Funniest Home Videos*.

The only thing they had was a site. And even that presented its difficulties.

Carlton ran a hand through his thick brown hair. Standing two inches over six feet, he was an imposing man. Maybe it was his adventure racing background, but he was known in the television community as somewhat of a bully, a do-anything-to-get-the-job-done type. He certainly wasn't shy about throwing his two hundred muscular pounds around if the situation warranted. A boyishly cute face betrayed forty-five years of wisdom, honed from competing in, and later producing, triathlons, Ironman competitions, and then, ultimately, the most grueling adventure race on the planet, the Eco-Challenge. People *died* during these annual ten-day sprints over demanding courses of rivers, mountains, cliffs, and desert. And that responsibility rested solely upon the event's creator and mastermind. Parlaying his success with Eco-Challenge, Carlton launched *Endure*, a game show/reality show hybrid that dropped a dozen men and women in the most inhospitable locations in the world and then, through a series of physical and mental challenges, challenged them to survive in the wild. *Endure* was the biggest primetime hit in CBS's illustrious history and propelled Carlton to a position of power within the entertainment world.

But there were clouds on the horizon. Eager to make the leap from producing fringe adventure races to prime-time programming, Carlton had made a serious miscalculation. A mistake that, despite his rampant success, threatened everything.

With a deep breath, Carlton filled his lungs, puffed his chest, and straightened his shoulders. "Horace, I realize there is pressure for this program. I *relish* the pressure. It's part of what's going to make this the greatest television event of all time. I just want to get this press conference over with, so I can begin working on actually producing the damn thing. I don't have to remind you where we're filming, do I?"

"No one has to remind anyone of anything," Alger

replied.   "We're all aware of the risks and dangers of this
. . . spectacle.   I talked Discovery Channel into a significant
investment in this project, and we have to make this work no
matter what. The green they're putting up for this could finance
two straight months of *Shark Week*."

"*Shark Week*?" Carlton said with a sneer. "Fuck *Shark
Week*. This event will blow that away. After this, *Shark
Week* will be running during overnights." Carlton felt his
confidence surge. "Horace . . . this is beyond television
programming. This is beyond entertainment of any kind.
What we are doing here is nothing short of . . . history."

At that moment, the door to Alger's office opened and
a beautiful woman stepped through. Leslie Dickerson,
NBC's vice president of communications, was all business.
Designer black-rimmed glasses and hair pulled back in a
severe bun did nothing to draw attention away from a flawless face and a pair of long legs more suited to high-fashion
runways than a public relations desk. She made eye contact
with each of the men, as if sizing them up, gauging their
readiness.

"It's time," she said.

The outdoor courtyard exploded with activity as
Carlton and Alger followed Leslie Dickerson onto the
stage. Flashes popped, reporters scrambled to their seats
and camera operators jumped into position, adjusting the

focus and rechecking audio levels. After years of covering mindless press tours of network suites (each one invariably proclaiming the potential of their fall schedule), the prospect of something really interesting happening had invigorated the cynical press corps.

The NBC communications staff had set out nearly one hundred chairs and all were filled. Overflow media filled the aisles on either side, and a few unlucky latecomers were relegated to peering around the phalanx of television cameras in the back of the plaza. A small crowd of passersby ringed the perimeter.

Several yelled out questions, but as the communications chief assumed her position at the podium, the courtyard fell silent. Carlton and Alger assumed their respective positions in director's chairs upon the stage. Leslie paused for a moment, waiting for the signal from the television cameramen to indicate they were rolling.

"Ladies and gentlemen, you are about to bear witness to an historical moment in entertainment. I am pleased to introduce to you the participants in this evening's announcement.

"On my far right, Mr. Terrance Carlton. Creator of *Endure*, today's most innovative and popular television show. Mr. Carlton has also produced a host of other programming, including the Eco-Challenge series and last year's highest-rated documentary, *Mallory and Irvine: The Quest for Everest.*"

She paused as Carlton nodded politely toward the crowd.

"Next to Mr. Carlton is Mr. Horace Alger, vice president of special programming for NBC . . ."

As Dickerson outlined Alger's résumé, Carlton scanned the crowd for familiar faces. He spotted reporters from *Outside* and *National Geographic*—their coverage was a given—and counted the cameras in the back of the plaza. Twenty-two. Not bad.

There was a slight commotion as a rather large man, bearded and bushy-haired, pressed through the rearmost row of chairs. Carlton's eyes followed the bear of a man until he found a seat. Then, staring directly at the producer, the man winked.

Another wave of applause brought Carlton's attention back to the business at hand.

"Mr. Carlton will speak, but first we have a brief video presentation."

Murmurs rose from the crowd, many glancing about the screen-less stage, confused about where to watch. With a low whir, the curtain parted and a giant thirty-foot-wide projection screen rose from below the stage. A single word appeared in white against the black screen.

TIBET

The screen filled with a sweeping aerial image of a towering mountain range. The narrator, baritone-voiced, intoned: "*Tibet. The Land of Snows. A place of magical mountains and spiritual awakenings. A land of unparalleled majesty. And breathless beauty."*

Images of snowy fields, glistening ice, purple mountain flowers flashed across the screen.

"Lying upon the shoulders of the mighty Himalayan Mountains, Tibet is a land on the top of the world. Birthplace of Buddhism and the sacred line of the Dalai Lama, Tibet is as sacred as it is inaccessible. Shielded from the outside world by towering peaks of snow and ice, Tibetans live simple lives, as they have for hundreds of years."

Children playing. Wrinkled elders working the fields. Clothes of sturdy and colorful construction.

"The size of the state of Pennsylvania, Tibet is inhabited by only a few thousand hearty souls. Though the Himalayas have been the traditional site of religious pilgrimage for Buddhist worshippers for many years, most of Tibet remains virtually unexplored."

Images of caves, churning whitewater rivers, steep granite cliffs.

"There is a special place within Tibet that has been completely closed off to man for over a thousand years. Myth and legend have named this place Shangri-la. We know it today as the Tsangpo Gorge. Few have braved this two hundred thousand-acre wilderness of dense jungle, steep gorges, and towering ice mountains, and the Tsangpo Gorge has never been fully explored. There are reaches of the mighty Tsangpo that have eluded man since time began. The River Tsangpo— borne upon the mountain of Mount Kalaish, the legendary site of the grand struggle between the Buddhist yogi Milarepa

and the Bon sorcerer Naro Bonchung for religious supremacy of Tibet—cuts through the gorge like a scythe. In the battle, Milarepa threw the sorcerer from the peak, establishing Buddhism as the primary religion of Tibet and Kalaish as a center of mystical thinking. In the wild Himalayas, Kalaish unleashes the mightiest river the world has ever known."

The screen shifted to a world map, the image zooming in on Asia. Tibet, shaded in gray, stood out in stark contrast to its neighbors, China to the north and east and India to the south and west. The image zoomed again, zeroing in on the remote southeast corner of Tibet.

"Just east of the Tsangpo Gorge lies an area even more remote. Tibetans hold this land sacred and have never ventured into this unknown territory. But they do have a name for it. Kukuranda—The Three Sisters. Three peaks comprise the Kukuranda, with one towering peak at its center. Tibetans know this mountain as Kuk Sur. The Beast. What is known of this mountain, indeed of the entire Kukuranda, is known only through myth and tradition, handed down through generations of Tibetan storytellers."

On the screen, an ancient Tibetan man speaks in hushed tones, surrounded by children in rapt attention, a snowcapped mountain looming in the distance.

"The storytellers speak of a land beyond imagining. Of a land filled with great animals found nowhere else on earth. A place protected by God himself. A place where no man dares to tread. A place, they say, that shall forever be protected from the ravages of man. Even the invading Red Army found the

Kukuranda impenetrable when they pushed into Tibet in 1950. The Dragon lost many troops during their attempt—and as they headquartered their occupation forces in Lhasa—vowed thereafter never again to set foot in the accursed place.

"Kukuranda is perhaps the last great wilderness on our planet, this generation's South Pole. What marvels can be found there? We now know that Kuk Sur is the tallest un-climbed mountain on planet Earth. But will we ever know the true nature of the vast Kukuranda and the fabled Kuk Sur?

"Perhaps the time is drawing near when these questions will finally be answered . . ."

The screen went black and dropped back underneath the stage. Carlton was standing alone at the podium, his black eyes unblinking in the face of a torrent of lightning from camera flashes. Just before he spoke, the corners of his mouth turned upwards, flashing his trademark grin. Half smile, half smirk, it was a mysterious concoction that be-spoke confidence and secrecy. He paused another moment, breathing in the attention he held, the power of the words that were to come.

"Ladies and gentlemen, NBC Universal and Discovery Communications are proud to bring you the greatest expe-dition of all time. It will be a completely unguided journey through the remote Tsangpo Gorge from the western banks of the Tsangpo River to the summit of Kuk Sur. Some of you know that Kuk Sur and the entire Kukaranda Range have been closed for several years now by the Chinese gov-ernment after a series of fatal accidents. I am pleased to announce that they have agreed to lift these restrictions for this race. The opportunity to make a first ascent of Kuk Sur stands before us."

Carlton allowed a dramatic pause to pass before continuing. "Our expedition team will be comprised of six of the greatest adventure racers and mountain climbers in the world. Champions in the field, with more first ascents between them than any other expedition ever staged, these six individuals—four men and two women—will battle the elements with only what they can carry on their backs. No support teams, no relay stations, no first aid. To any member of the team who survives the dangers of the gorge and reaches the summit, a prize of one million dollars, the largest prize in the history of exploration."

Carlton paused, allowing the explosion of camera flashes to subside. He had one more bombshell to drop.

"And you can watch it live. Each team member will wear a small camera on his or her shoulder. For the first time in history, viewers at home will experience the thrill of discovery firsthand. Discovery Channel will cover the team's progress with nightly, prime-time, tape-delayed coverage. NBC will air a two-hour special every Saturday night during the journey and Discovery.com and NBC. com will be webcasting on a twenty-four-hour basis until we have reached the summit. The expedition begins on November 1, exactly thirty days from today."

Pens flew across notebooks, lapping up every word. Broadcast reporters scrambled toward their cameras for live shots.

"Everything will be live," Carlton continued, his voice rising. "The raging rivers. The towering cliffs. You will see, as no one has ever seen before, every challenge that will face these six competitors exactly as they occur. In the coming weeks, we will be announcing the expedition team that will take on this challenge. They are a special breed; hard adventurers, cunning minds that will be able to negotiate a land completely uncharted. The last attempt on Kuk Sur, over six years ago, ended tragically. Now, the chance is at hand for someone to grasp immortality.

"In developing his remarkable theory of evolution, Charles Darwin hit upon a phrase that I believe is entirely appropriate for this endeavor. With respect to the competition of species for scarce resources and ultimately reproductive success, the battle waged would benefit the strong and punish the weak. *Survival of the fittest.* Which is why we are calling this expedition *Darwin's Race.* Because in this expedition, only the strong will survive."

And then, flashing his trademark smile, Carlton announced: "And you'll have to tune in to see what happens."

The media immediately began to shout out questions:

"When will you announce the expedition team?"

"Are you concerned about the danger of the expedition?"

"How did you get China to open its borders for Darwin's Race?*"*

Carlton tried to speak over the surging thunder of questions. "Ladies and gentlemen," he yelled, "*Darwin's Race*, the greatest adventure of our time, will begin in exactly thirty days. Thank you for coming."

With a final flourish of his hands, Carlton pushed away from the podium and bounded off the stage, an adrenaline-powered skip in his step. Alger followed, quickly ushered off the stage by the communications chief, leaving behind the desperate shouts of questions from the gathered reporters.

Terrance Carlton and Leslie Dickerson had carefully orchestrated it all, every detail of the announcement, and it went exactly as planned. There would be no questions from the stage, One-on-one interviews only, and then only if the interviewer passed muster. Local reporters were at the bottom of the list. *Dateline* was already lined up and even competing networks—*60 Minutes*, *Primetime Live*, *20/20*—were clamoring for appearances. And after this press conference, appearances on *Larry King Live*, *Today Show*, and *Jay Leno* were planned.

That's just the way Carlton wanted it. Always leave them wanting more. Never give them too much. If you gave them what they wanted, you would quickly run out of things to give. And where would that leave you? Out in the cold. Shunned and ignored.

And Terrance Carlton wasn't about to let that happen.

CHAPTER TWO

Rockefeller Center
New York City

The reaction was swift.

The very next morning, newspapers across the country were filled with news of *Darwin's Race*. Headlines ran the gamut from "Expedition to Test Tibetan Wilderness" (*Denver Post*), "Journey to Shangri-la" (*Boston Globe*), to "The Last Frontier?" (*San Francisco Chronicle*).

The television coverage was largely positive, though several retired climbers made a joint appearance on *Larry King Live* condemning the expedition as "a dark stain on the grand history of exploration." *The New York Times* elaborated on this criticism, ripping the expedition as "the latest crass invasion of commercially driven propaganda into one of the very few pure pursuits left in this world."

David Broder, writing in *The Washington Post*, felt similarly: "Thank God for Terrance Carlton," he wrote cynically. "We should all be thanking him for bringing us the majesty of exploration in such a tidy, sponsor-wrapped package. Well, no thanks, Mr. Carlton. I like my tales of discovery without your tactless bombardment of advertisements for energy drinks and electronic toothbrushes."

But the recriminations from the press paled in the light of the official denunciation that came from the Royal Geographic Society.

The British forbear of the National Geographic Society, the Royal Geographic Society had supported nearly every major expedition over the past 170 years. The exclusive club was founded in 1830 by a group of armchair voyagers, only later adding genuine explorers such as Livingstone, Wadsworth, and Burton as a means to investing in expeditions to obtain the riches of far-flung locales. The Society had funded Shackleton's arctic voyages, Scott's Discovery voyage to the South Pole, and Burton's search for the source of the Nile in 1856. For years, the Society had been the acknowledged expert on all things mountaineering, all things exploration. For the esteemed Royal Geographic Society to condemn *Darwin's Race* was tantamount to NASA condemning a space shuttle launch.

Just hours after the announcement of *Darwin's Race*, the Society had issued a media advisory. It was not promising. It announced a full-fledged press conference at Society headquarters in London for the following day, but the final line of the missive gave away their position.

"'Purported expedition'?" Horace Alger raved, waving the release in the air. "They're calling it a 'purported expedition'!"

Terrance Carlton listened patiently to his raving colleague, studying the host of treasures from around the world that filled several bookshelves in Alger's Manhattan office. As the head of NBC's documentary division, Alger often evaluated pitches from documentary producers, who frequently bestowed gifts as defacto inducements toward green-lighting their projects. A sixteenth-century gold medallion recovered from the sunken steamship *Santa Celeste*. An ornately carved mask from Borneo used during tribal sacrifice rituals. A French gold coin rumored to be part of the vast legendary treasure called the lost gold of the confederacy.

Carlton grinned as his partner raged. The redness in the executive's puffy face amused him. His grin, the one that made his eyes twinkle mischievously, only made Alger angrier.

"It's obvious, isn't it?" Alger ranted. "They're going to condemn our expedition. Do you know what this means? This damages our relationship with Discovery, hinders our negotiations with sponsors—and as for racers? You can be assured that no career-minded adventure racer would dare to upset the Royal Geographic Society! Why, if they took part in *Darwin's Race*, they would be jeopardizing sponsorship opportunities for all of their future expeditions. We'll be left with half-assed amateurs, lapsed college football stars grabbing for one final taste of glory. We'll be lucky to entice some old competitor out of retirement just so we can have someone who just might have a chance in hell of making it to Kuk Sur!"

"I don't think it will come to that," Carlton said soothingly.

"Then you're a damn fool!" Alger bellowed. "This press conference will be our undoing—mark my words! And on top of everything else we are facing? Need I remind you that we're already behind schedule with the satellite feeds and relay stations? Terrance! Terrance, are you listening to me?"

"I have listened to every, single, ranting, raving word," Carlton replied. "You're being an alarmist. The Society is a relic, living off the grandeur of expeditions over a century ago. When was the last time they were the primary sponsor of any expedition of note?"

"Well," Alger stammered. "I guess I don't really know. But I'm sure there was—"

Carlton waved dismissively, stood, and marched across the office to a large photograph on the far wall. It was a picture of Sir Edmund Hillary, the conqueror of Everest, standing at the peak's fabled base camp. "The Society peaked in 1953 with Hillary's quest for Everest. Now there was a grand journey—epic in its conception and visionary in execution. Judging by today's standards, Hillary tackled Everest wearing little more than sandals and a cardigan sweater. Yet that was its beauty—it was sheer daring. And the Society was at the forefront of that era—the era of exploration."

Carlton was building to something. He turned his back on the photograph to face Alger directly. "But that era has long since passed, my friend. We are now in the age of television. Without television, and the money it generates, there would be no expeditions. Sure, there are still a handful of die-hard adventurers out there who explore for the sheer thrill of discovery, but they are quickly dying out. Pushed out, rather, by the new breed of adventurer. Young. Brash. Vibrant. And media savvy. The new adventurers have all the skills required for exploration, but they also know what makes it all possible. They know how to secure sponsorship. They know how to garner media attention."

Carlton paused a moment, pleased to see the color returning to his colleague's rotund face.

"Remember the old riddle—if a tree falls in the forest and no one is around to hear it, does it really make a sound? For years, people debated the answer. Hell, even researchers at the University of Tennessee attempted—and failed— to devise a scientific method to solve it. When, really, we knew the answer all along."

Alger looked confused. "We did?"

"Yes, we did," Carlton nodded. "If there is an expedition down the Yangtze from source to sea, or a first ascent of the still unclimbed northeast face of Annapurna, and there is no one there to witness it, it may as well never have happened. Hell, remember Mallory and Irvine's summit attempt on Everest in 1924? By all accounts, they were still going strong toward the summit, just a few hundred feet to go. It would have been a first, a truly remarkable accomplishment. Only there was no one around to verify the summit. No cameras to document their feat. To this day, very few people believe they actually reached the summit. Just think, they may have beaten Hillary to the summit by thirty years, but because there was no one there to see it, it simply didn't happen."

Comprehension dawned on Alger's face.

"So, yes, my friend," Carlton said. "We have known the answer for a long time. If there is no one there to hear it, a falling tree makes no sound. When the lucky team reaches the summit of Kuk Sur, our cameras will be rolling—and, oh, what a sound we will make!"

"Quite an ego you have there, Mr. Carlton."

Carlton and Alger spun at the sound of a strange voice. A large, bearish man, dressed smartly in a loose linen suit, stood near the door in the back of Alger's office. Everything about the stranger was extra-large. Standing no less than six feet, six inches, the man was layered with thick muscle, made all the more menacing by a set of thick ridges set over piercing metal-gray eyes. A three-inch gash in the shape of a half-moon scarred his forehead over his right eye. Carlton thought he looked rather like a pirate.

"Who the hell are you?" Alger demanded. "And how did you get in here?"

The man grinned, flashing a set of perfect white teeth through a heavily bearded face. "Is that really what you want to know, Mr. Alger? Or do you want to hear my offer on making *Darwin's Race* a truly monumental enterprise?"

"How dare you?" Alger blustered. "*Darwin's Race* is already—!"

Carlton interrupted the NBC executive with a raised hand. "I recognize you," he said. "You were at yesterday's press conference."

"You put on a good show, Mr. Carlton," the man said, stepping forward and extending his hand. "Pleased to meet you in person. Preston Child."

"Preston Child . . ." Carlton repeated, shaking the man's giant paw. The name rang a bell. "Providence Bank?"

"One of my subsidiary companies, yes, but I would hate to be known solely for some of my more commercial exploits. There are so many other more creditable measures of a man, wouldn't you agree?"

"Providence Bank sponsored last season's *Survivor*," Carlton said to Alger, explaining his sudden familiarity with the large stranger. Then, turning back to Preston, said, "But we never officially met, did we?"

"I generally leave that sort of thing to my very capable staff, so I'm afraid I didn't have the pleasure."

"Yes, now I remember. I had to do a bit of digging to learn more about you. Seems you like staying behind the scenes. Rarely grant interviews. A wizard of Oz type. I did eventually find a business profile on you—*Forbes*, was it?"

"*Fortune*, actually."

"Yes, that's right. Now, stop me if I get some details

wrong. You started with nothing, scraped your way into some land, and then promptly turned a large profit on it. Parlayed that into several more real estate deals, eventually building an empire of companies, from banks to commercial real estate, even a few charitable foundations."

"I'm afraid the president's No Child Left Behind program doesn't quite filter down to some of our more disadvantaged youth. The Child Foundation seeks to rectify the oversight."

"But it was your personal life that dominated the *Fortune* piece. Seems you're a bit of an adventurer yourself. I believe they even gave you a nickname. 'Maverick Man,' was it?"

"It sounds more dashing than the reality, I assure you."

"Horace, he's being modest. At the time of the article, you had already climbed three of the Seven Summits, including Denali, which is a bear. I'm sure you've notched more since then. And wasn't there something about a plane? Some sort of cross-country flight in a glider?"

"I should've left the flying to Branson and Fossett. I'm much better on the ground. I only made it as far as St. Louis out of Baltimore. A record at the time, but woefully short of target."

Carlton paused a moment, pulling additional facts from his memory banks. "And then something happened. You met a woman. On a trek in China, I think?"

Preston didn't correct him.

"Fell in love. And then just dropped out of sight. Left your businesses in the hands of subordinates. A few years later, out of nowhere, you started selling off your businesses one by one. Some said you went crazy, disavowed all your material things and moved into some mud hut to study giant pandas or something."

Preston shook his massive head. "That's why I don't do interviews. The media so rarely gets to the truth."

"Maybe," Carlton said. "You could've cooperated with the *Fortune* piece, but you chose not to. I think that says a lot about you. Either you really despise the media, or you rather enjoy this 'Maverick Man' persona."

"And what do you believe, Mr. Carlton?"

"I think you're a complicated man. It would be foolish to guess at your motivations."

Preston didn't reply. Instead, he locked eyes with Carlton and held them there for a moment. Long enough, in that single instant, for the producer to feel a kinship with the imposing stranger. Whether it was a healthy respect for a fellow businessman or a regard for Preston's adventurous streak, Carlton realized one thing. He instinctively trusted this man.

Horace Alger was apparently not quite as taken.

"Well, I for one would love to know your motives for storming in here," the executive cut in. "Just what is it you want from us?" He reached for the phone on his desk and began dialing security. "And how did you get in here? I left explicit instructions that I was not to be interrupted."

"Mr. Alger, please calm yourself. Your secretary did her job. She intelligently made an exception in my case to let me in."

"And why did she do such a thing?"

"Because I own this building," Preston told him. "And although I value NBC as a wonderful tenant, I seriously doubt the security staff would toss out their own boss."

Alger wasn't giving up. "This building is owned by the Manhattan Development Corporation, and they—"

"— are another one of my subsidiary companies," Preston finished.

Alger's hand fell from the phone, considering the man with a wary eye.

"Well, I'll say this: you have me intrigued," Carlton said. "You mentioned making *Darwin's Race* truly monumental? We think we're already producing an historic expedition."

Preston helped himself to one of Alger's overstuffed chairs. "Yes, yes. You have yourselves a nice little concept here, don't get me wrong. I'm sure the public will thoroughly enjoy the adventure. But I know that you, Mr. Carlton, are hoping for something a bit more. Dare I say, you *need* something big. You see, I know about your business arrangement with a certain competing network for the rights to *Survivor*."

Carlton's jaw dropped. That contract was supposed to be completely leak-proof. He caught Alger, glaring at him for an explanation. *How did—?*

"I see that you know what I'm referring to. The little business about the exclusive rights to the world's top-rated prime-time program being transferred to the network after next season? Bad business move, I'm afraid, but certainly excusable given your exuberance in making the jump from basic cable to playing with the network big dogs."

Alger finally broke his stunned silence. "Is this true, Carlton? You're losing *Survivor*?"

"Your sources must be good," Carlton said to Preston, ignoring the question. "You're right that I need *Darwin's Race* to be a success, and I'll further concede that Alger and I have already set in motion a number of merchandising and licensing deals to ensure it. Certainly, we all have a lot riding on this expedition."

"Then why not raise the stakes?" Preston said. "Why not give the world something to really talk about?"

"I assume you have a proposal."

Preston stood and strode to the window overlooking Rockefeller Plaza, while Carlton and Alger exchanged curious glances. *Get this loon out of here*, Alger mouthed.

"What your expedition lacks is a sense of urgency," Preston said, gazing out at the Manhattan skyline. "An air of competition. If you're going to call this venture *Darwin's Race*, ought it not actually *be* a race?"

Preston turned from the view to face Carlton directly. "I propose a second team," he said. "Comprised of some of the world's best climbers and financed entirely by yours truly. We will make this grand expedition into a race across the gorge to the summit of Kuk Sur. First one to the mountaintop wins a prize of two million dollars."

"Two million?" Alger stammered. "But our prize is only one million. How—?"

"I will put up the difference. Sweeten the pot, jack up the interest."

Carlton's mind was already running with the concept. "Both teams would start in the same place at the same time. With no maps and no relay stations, the teams would most likely follow different routes across the gorge."

"Giving you more action, less down time for your television cameras."

"Let's assume we decide to go for this," Carlton said, waving off Alger's inevitable protests. "What's in it for you? What do you get out of the deal?"

Preston laughed, a deep bellow that shook Alger's office walls. "As you said earlier, sometimes a man's motivations are a mystery, even to himself. But in this case, I simply want to get back in the game. It's been a long time since I enjoyed the thrill of the climb."

Although he had read of Preston's alpine exploits, Carlton still found himself surprised. Men the size of Preston Child just didn't climb mountains. He noticed Preston had drawn a hand up to his forehead, absently fingering the half-moon shaped scar.

"Mountains don't like to be climbed," Preston said. "My little scar here is a gentle reminder from a nasty lady called Annapurna in '84. Despite a layoff of a number of years, I still consider myself a climber. But I can see the concern in both your faces, so let me assure you that I am not proposing to lead the second team. For that, I have someone else in mind."

"And who might that be?" Carlton asked. A few names flew through his brain, climbers considered and dismissed as second-tier for the original expedition team.

"Conner Michaels."

Carlton and Alger threw their hands up simultaneously. "Conner Michaels?" they shouted in unison. "Good luck. Or hadn't you heard? Conner Michaels has been retired for years."

"I am aware of his current status," Preston noted calmly. "But I am also aware that he is perhaps the finest mountain climber in the past fifty years. The only man to climb all seven summits in a single year. The first solo ascent of Nanga Parbat without supplemental oxygen. One of only ten men to summit all fourteen of the world's eight thousand-meter peaks. And that's not to mention his considerable success in the adventure racing field. I believe he won your little race a number of times; didn't he, Mr. Carlton?"

"Three times," Carlton confirmed. "Retired before he had a chance to go for number four. But you're forgetting one thing about the great Conner Michaels."

"Am I?"

"The last mountain Conner ever climbed was Kuk Sur—the very same mountain that now represents the finish line of *Darwin's Race*. The man lost a brother on that mountain, and from what I've heard, he has yet to recover from his death. You'll never get him to set foot on those slopes again."

"Ah, but that's exactly the reason why Conner will not be able to resist my invitation. What climber admits defeat in the face of such a challenge? What climber wouldn't relish the opportunity to conquer the peak that took the life of his beloved brother? Now that the Chinese government has lifted its restrictions on climbing in the Kukuranda, Conner has his first real opportunity to face his demons. You must admit, the concept itself employs a rather divine sense of poetic beauty."

"Conner will never go for it," Carlton said, shaking his head. "We approached him for the original expedition team, but he lives as a recluse somewhere in Virginia. No one knows where exactly. We couldn't even find him."

"I have already located the elusive Conner Michaels."

The diligence of Preston Child surprised Carlton. This Maverick Man really did have good sources. "Even so, I still doubt you could get him to join the race. He left that life behind with his brother on Kuk Sur. I hope you have a backup plan."

Preston smiled knowingly. "If Conner declines my initial invitation, I have other, more persuasive, options at my disposal. Make no mistake, he *will* lead my second team."

Carlton breathed in deeply and met Alger's gaze. "You realize that you have less than a month to put together your team. The first expedition team is already together;

training has already begun."

"I realize my team will be at a competitive disadvantage," Preston conceded. "And I accept this drawback."

Carlton considered his partner, finding Alger's stern expression had dissipated somewhat. Apparently, the bushy stranger had made an impression. Alger gave Carlton a slow, encouraging nod.

"If you can deliver Conner Michaels," Carlton said. "You've got yourself a deal."

"To *Darwin's Race* then," Preston said, extending his hand. "To a truly monumental endeavor."

Carlton shook the man's thick hand, then watched as Alger slapped Preston on the back in congratulations. The hardened VP had apparently warmed to the burly stranger.

Conner Michaels. A second team. A race to the summit.

The possibilities were making Carlton salivate.

CHAPTER THREE

Lake Anna
Spotsylvania County, Virginia

Conner Michaels glided through glass.

The cool fresh water of Lake Anna was flat except for the gentle waves trailing Conner's Perception 3D whitewater kayak. His paddle strokes were smooth and even, honed silky and effortless through years on the water. Like an Olympic diving champion, he sliced each stroke through the water at the perfect angle, causing only the barest ripple across the silky surface.

Conner's shoulders were broad and swelled with muscles from hundreds of thousands of pulls. Though he wore a life vest, he was confident enough to wear only the thinnest model—the Perception Type III. Tufts of wet brown hair stuck out from underneath a well-worn cap-style helmet. Like his shoulders, his arms were well muscled and honey brown, the result of countless barebacked paddles. No protective DryShirts for him. He also eschewed nose plugs, a piece of equipment many considered essential because they blocked water from involuntarily entering the lungs through the nose if a kayak flipped upside down.

Conner Michaels only flipped if he wanted to.

His angular face was striking, with a sharp chin and slightly off-center nose, the result of a mountain biking accident years before. He never had it reset, and now his nose was the only blemish on what many women considered a perfect, strong face.

Conner guided his kayak from the still waters of Lake Anna to the slightly moving waters of Elk Creek. Paddling against the current, the muscles of his shoulders pulled taut across his back. His breathing remained steady. Upstream, perhaps fifty yards, Conner could see his target.

The ten-foot standing wave was wedged between two huge rock outcrops. The otherwise calm creek water crammed together through the chute, down a five-foot drop, and then circled back upon itself, creating what Conner liked to call Old Creeky. Although he had long ago given up on competitive white-water kayaking, he could never stay away from the secluded hydraulic for too long.

Conner breathed in deeply. Inching his way forward, he expertly kept the kayak straight—and with a powerful stroke pushed into the cascading wave.

The crushing weight of five hundred cubic pounds of

water crashed down upon the bow of the kayak threatening to topple the craft. Employing strong bracing strokes, Conner maintained his precarious balance and guided his kayak into position.

When he had the angle just right, he allowed the water to submerge the bow. The butt of the kayak rose out of the water as Conner supported the kayak with strong, lightning-quick paddle strokes. Properly braced, the kayak went perfectly perpendicular, end over end, with his face just inches from the churning white water. Then, with a flick of his paddle, Conner dipped the kayak deep into the cool water, then thrust backwards until the kayak arced free of the water. For a split second, Conner Michaels flew.

Conner relished his time on the water, conducting his intricate water ballet in the quiet solitude of Elk Creek. Usually, he had this entire part of the lake to himself. Which is why he found himself surprised, as he executed another acrobatic hole-riding move, to see a flash of color flicker across his peripheral vision. By the time Conner blasted out of the hole with a perfect roll, a second kayaker had paddled into the fray with a series of end-over-end cartwheels. Flatwheeling was an impressive move, definitely expert level, and Conner paddled into an eddy to watch the show.

The kayaker executed a series of moves—stern squirts, front-enders, whippets—seemingly without tiring. Conner marveled at the proficient display; he was fatigued just observing. With a clean pull through the roiling water, the kayaker lifted the playboat's stern, letting the flow spin him out of the hole like a helicopter. A textbook McTwist.

The kayaker paddled from the hole, pulling the playboat beside Conner's in the wide eddy. As he watched the paddler peel off a white helmet, Conner was genuinely surprised to see a shock of long auburn hair fall below the kayaker's shoulders.

"You look surprised," the female paddler said. "Never seen a girl nail a McTwist?"

Conner smiled. "Sorry. I'm not used to seeing anybody out here. Usually have the place to myself."

"Hole like this is too nice to keep secret," she said, returning the smile.

"Enjoy it," Conner said, pulling out of the eddy. "I've had enough for one day."

He paddled away without looking back, though he could practically feel her gaze on his back as he made his way downstream. By the time Conner paddled back into the serene waters of Lake Anna, his shoulders and arms burned with fatigue. It was the perfect feeling, one of the main reasons he had retreated to his lakeside cottage in Central Virginia four years ago.

But not the only reason . . .

After the death of his brother, Conner returned home, the unbearable weight of grief smothering him like a straightjacket. He tried to forget and when that failed, he turned to others to help him forget. Months of therapy had hammered the stages of bereavement into his skull. Denial had struck first. Without Tucker's body, Conner had refused to believe he was truly dead. For months, he caught himself dialing his brother's phone number to invite him along on his next adventure, only to hear the grief-tinged voice of Tucker's widow.

Then came anger. For Conner, this one was real trouble. At first, he directed a dark self-loathing inward. It was he who had dragged Tucker along to Tibet in the first place. Had he left his kid brother at home in Charlotte with his family, he'd still be playing with baby Jake in the backyard. When Conner's fury had filled every fiber of his being, it exploded outward.

Tess Chamniss was the closest target.

She had returned with Conner to the lake, sticking around as Conner stewed, prodding him to get out and deal with his grief in a more healthy way. When Conner turned on her, in a cruel and barely controlled rage, it was ugly. He blamed her for Tucker's death, reasoning that it was she who forced them to cross that damned snow bridge. If they had just gone around like Conner wanted, everything would still be all right and his nephew would still have a father.

To make matters worse, Tess had been unable to help Conner back down into the crevasse. She claimed exhausted muscles, bad weather, the falling cover of night, but whatever the reason, he hadn't been able to search for his brother. When a Tibetan rescue team explored the crevasse a few days later, they found nothing. And Conner's anger grew.

Tess did not appreciate the attacks, though she must've understood the painful source. "We all deal with grief and guilt in our own way," she had told Conner. She left the next day.

He hadn't heard from her in six years.

The bargaining stage of grief passed quickly into depression. He threw out his television and pulled out his phone lines. He cut off contact with friends, even family members. His two golden retrievers, Jazz and Jambo, were all he needed.

Conner Michaels never quite made it to acceptance.

He quickly pushed the thought aside. Remembrances still came, but were less frequent now. Bitter memories accompanied him almost daily back then, fresh and painful. But slowly, as the days and months passed, his secluded retreat—moonlit nights and sunrises over the lake—worked its magic.

And not a neighbor for miles. There were entire weeks when Conner wouldn't see another soul. And that suited him just fine.

That was why it was so puzzling, as he pulled his kayak from the lake onto the small rocky beach beside his cottage, to see the female kayaker following closely behind.

CHAPTER FOUR

Lake Anna
Spotsylvania County, Virginia

Conner Michaels' lakefront cabin was a two-story cedar rambler that opened from the ground floor onto a wide expanse of green that led down to a private boat slip. Inside, an open living area looked out through floor-to-ceiling windows to the blue lake waters. Decorated to resemble a Colorado mountain lodge, the room featured a stone fireplace and exposed oak beams across the vaulted, twenty-foot ceiling. Pine hardwood floors were covered by rust-colored area rugs placed before a well-worn leather sofa and a high-backed reading chair. Books were piled on a rustic end table; Hemingway's *The Old Man and the Sea* and Steinbeck's *Of Mice and Men* among them.

Conner pulled two Rolling Rock bottles from his

refrigerator, popped the tops, and handed one to his guest. He had changed out of his wet kayak gear, slipping on an old Maryland Terrapins T-shirt and a pair of equally well-worn jeans. His guest had removed her vest, revealing a black athletic-cut swimsuit top and boy-cut shorts.

The woman had pulled her kayak up onto his private beach, a yellow dry bag slung over her shoulder, and asked Conner without hesitation for a cold drink. Taken aback by her directness, he had invited her inside for a beer nonetheless.

"I don't get many visitors," he said. "And I don't believe I caught your name."

"Malika," she said, taking a deep swig from the bottle.

"Just Malika?"

"For now," she said, smiling.

Malika looked good wet, Conner noted as she toweled off. A long, athletic frame, with muscles that didn't quite threaten her soft curves. Her skin was dark, and Conner thought he saw Asian features in her face. Pacific Islander, perhaps. Complemented by her lustrous hair, she was an exotic beauty. Jazz and Jambo took to her instantly and padded excitedly beside the newcomer, eager for attention.

"Sorry about them," Conner said. "They don't see too many strangers around here. My name's Conner."

"I know who you are," Malika said. "That chute was a nice diversion, but I'm really here to see you. An invitation of sorts."

Conner tensed. "Not interested. Look, I live out here for a reason. No outsiders. I don't know how you found me, and I don't really care. You can finish that beer, and then I'm going to walk you very politely to the door."

"You don't even want to hear my offer?"

"Don't have to," Conner said. "Already know the answer is no."

"Is life that horrible after Kuk Sur?"

Conner looked up abruptly at the mention of the Tibetan mountain. Malika was staring, gauging his reaction. He tried to appear nonchalant, but he doubted he was very successful.

He had spent the better part of the last six years forgetting, and he wasn't about to let some stranger—even someone as intoxicating as Malika—dredge up old memories.

"I see you know a little something about me," he said. "But know this: I left that life behind. All of it. The races, the mountain climbing, the competitive whitewater. It was a chapter in my life that I closed years ago." Conner exhaled deeply, as if expelling the remembrances.

"Okay, I'll leave." Malika took a long pull from her bottle, draining it, but made no move toward the door. "So this is the life you want to lead? Cut off from the rest of society? For what? Because your brother died on some mountain thousands of miles away? Don't you think it's time you put your grief behind you?"

"I don't need your advice."

"I don't get it. You had it all. You were on the top of the world. One expedition goes wrong—and you throw it all away? I look around this place, so far from any human contact, and what do I see? Nothing. Where are your trophies from the Eco-Challenge? Where are the rocks from the Seven Summits? Hell, you don't even have any pictures out from *any* of your climbs. This place doesn't feel right. It's not you."

"First, you don't know me," he said, tossing the knapsack at her. "And second, this conversation is over."

"Fine. I just thought you'd be interested in getting back in the game."

"Well, you thought wrong."

"By leading a second team in *Darwin's Race*."

"*Darwin's Race*," Conner said. "Never heard of it."

"That's right, you don't own a television. Don't you read the newspapers?"

"Not if I can help it. You won't find a telephone either."

Malika pressed on, outlining the details of the expedition and the addition of a second team. The reopening of the Kukaranda by the Chinese government, the exclusive race through the fabled Shangri-la, the live television coverage. The two million-dollar prize.

"The whole thing reeks of Terry Carlton," Conner said. "I assume he's behind this?"

"Say what you want—the guy knows how to put together an event. The second team was my father's idea."

"Your father?"

"Preston Child. A bit of a climber himself in his younger days. Now he has enough influence to buy his way into one more adventure. I'll be going up as well. You and me, hotshot. Think you can handle it?"

Conner ignored the bait. "Not interested in one-way tickets, Ms. Child. Twelve people may be going up, but twelve people won't be coming back."

"Ah, but that's the challenge. Everest's been climbed by more than a thousand people. The Seven Summits, the true Seven Summits, have been reached by a few hundred, including a blind guy! The world's been circumnavigated in a hot air balloon, in a rowboat, in a sea kayak, but Kuk Sur's never been touched. It's one of the last firsts out there." Malika paused, allowing her words to linger in the air. "It's also your best chance to deal with the loss of your brother, once and for all."

"Have a nice drive home," he said, walking her to the door.

"Fine, I'll go. But first, a little gift." She pulled her dry bag from her shoulder and began searching for something.

It took a moment for the object to register in Conner's brain, but once it did, the shock made him dizzy.

It was a bright red wool cap.

Identical to the one Tucker had been wearing when he disappeared into the dark crevasse six years earlier.

Conner stared at it as if he saw a ghost.

"Where did you get this?"

"Found it a few years ago on a trek in Tibet. One of those adventure vacation things, *Voyage Through Shan-gri-La* or something like that. We were making our way up from Mt. Kundu, following the Tsangpo River north when we came upon a small Army outpost. A couple of tired-looking Chinese guards come charging out, demanding that we turn around immediately. They were young guys, little more than park rangers with guns, but we had heard about the closing off of some portions of the Tsangpo Gorge and the Kukuranda so we didn't argue much. We were about to turn around when something caught my eye. It was a cave. Not that the cave itself was very exciting—we had seen dozens of them on our climb. The guide said the Himalayas are scattered with them. But there was something just outside the cave. Something red."

Her eyes locked on to the cap.

"It's hard to miss," Conner admitted. "But why did you bother to pick it up, much less haul it back to the States? It must've been completely trashed."

"It was. Soaked through, caked with dirt, all torn up. I don't know why I picked it up. At first I just wanted to see what it was; then I thought that maybe someone from our group had dropped it. I looked around the cave—it was a deep one—but it was too dark to see anything. Anyway, nobody claimed ownership. That's when I noticed the writing on the inside of the cap."

Conner swallowed hard. He already knew what was written there, in Tucker's blocky handwriting, but he flipped the cap inside out anyway. His brother's initials were smudged, faded, but still legible.

"I didn't know what the 'TM' meant, though even then I figured it was somebody's initials. With no other leads to go on, I just packed the cap away, basically forgot about it.

Then, a few weeks ago, I caught a story about *Darwin's Race* on television. The report mentioned the last expedition to attempt Kuk Sur and how a guy named Tucker Michaels died on the mountain. Seemed like a long shot, but I figured the hat may have been your brother's. It took me some time, but I finally tracked you down here. Thought maybe you'd want to have it."

Conner rolled the wool cap over his hands, absently flaking away a piece of dried muck with his fingernail. "You think that coming here today and giving this back to me is going to get me to enter *Darwin's Race*? Is that what you think?"

"I don't pretend to know what's going on inside your head. But I figure, maybe, you've always wondered what happened to your brother down in that crevasse."

"I know what happened," Conner snapped too quickly. "The rope snapped. He fell."

"Okay, okay. If that's how it happened, fine. But I know you never found any trace of him. No gloves, no boots, nothing. I'm not saying there's anything more than that hat to find up in those caves, but if it were me, I think I'd at least have to try."

"Well," Conner said. "You're not me."

"You're right. Look, my father and I want you to lead the second team in *Darwin's Race*. You already know that. Whether or not you take us up on the offer—and whether or not that hat has something to do with your decision— that's up to you."

And that was all. Malika handed Conner her empty beer bottle and was gone.

When she finally disappeared down the road in her dusty pickup, Conner headed back to the kitchen to grab another cold beer. He found a scrap of paper on the counter, Malika's phone number. Underneath the numbers, she had scrawled a short note: *Call me if you change your mind.*

Conner crumpled the paper, tossed it into the kitchen wastebasket and sat down in the middle of the floor. He knocked back half of the Rolling Rock in one long pull. He cursed her silently; not because she had dared to intrude on his privacy, not even because she had dredged up memories that he would rather let lie dormant in his mind, but because her words had cut too close to that still-sensitive bone called truth.

He had managed to get on with his life just fine, thank you. He thought about his brother all the time—he didn't need some woman coming along, drawing out the guilt that still lurked after all these years under a hardened exterior. Thanks, Malika, but no thanks.

But the dam was broken. The reappearance of Tucker's hat unleashed snapshots of his brother that flashed before Conner's mind's eye. He could still hear the awful *crack!* of the snow bridge, the roar of its collapse. Could still feel the weight of Tucker's falling body dragging him toward the precipice of the giant crevasse. Then, the faint voice of his injured brother rising up from the darkness. Conner's face cringed as Tucker's final, horrifying words echoed in his head.

Something smells real bad down here. I think there's something down here with me. I can't see it, but I can hear it breathing. The smell . . . Oh, Jesus—!

And then the terrible gurgling noise.

Jambo padded over and laid his head upon his master's leg. Conner rubbed behind the dog's ear and got a sloppy lick across the cheek in return. "Thank you, boy," he said, fingering Tucker's torn red hat. "I needed that."

CHAPTER FIVE

Royal Geographic Society Headquarters
1 Kensington Gore
London, England

Horace Alger was right about one thing. The Royal Geographic Society did indeed condemn *Darwin's Race*. But, ironically, it was Terrance Carlton who was responsible for their strong recriminations. Though Preston Child had yet to deliver Conner Michaels—or any other member of the second expedition team—Carlton had discreetly leaked word of the second team to a columnist at the *New York Post*. Within a day, Internet newsgroups, climbing clubs, and gossip columns were awash with the news. Even before an official announcement, Carlton had ratcheted up the publicity. Of course, the Royal Geographic Society had heard the news.

Using language that rivaled the rhetoric of a heated political campaign, the Society's executive director, one Dr. William Hillmeade, blasted the race, its creators, even its very concept.

"This so-called race," Dr. Hillmeade had announced, sounding properly aristocratic, "is nothing more than the latest in a string of inane reality programming created by American television. But this one has gone too far."

The reading room of the Royal Geographic Society was quite small, crammed as it was into its townhouse headquarters near Paddington Station. Still the assembled media, a handful of newspaper reporters and two camera crews, found plenty of room to stretch out.

Sitting in high-backed leather chairs around the perimeter of the room were several members of the Society's esteemed governing council. The men were scions of British society, silver-haired, connected, moneyed, aristocratic. Most inherited wealth, some legitimately claimed royal lineage, and all were frowning at the scene before them, as if the distaste of *Darwin's Race* were palpable.

"The very notion that exploration is a race to the finish sullies the reputation of the great explorers of history," Dr. Hillmeade continued, reading from a script. "Livingstone, Speke, Burton. These were men for whom exploration was a way of life. They understood that its essence was the journey itself, not some artificial finish line. Mallory himself, when asked why he wanted to climb Everest, famously replied, 'Because it's there.' He certainly did not say 'Because

I want to be first.' His sentiment represents the true nature of exploration."

He paused a moment, allowing a lone photographer to snap a picture.

"This race—this *Darwin's Race*—is a stain on the history of exploration and goes against everything the Royal Geographic Society has represented for 175 years. Charles Darwin was an esteemed member of this Society, and I assure you he would be appalled that this race has appropriated his good name."

As Dr. Hillmeade finished his comments, several hands raised politely. Media members at the Society were always remarkably well-mannered. Otherwise, a reporter might not be invited back.

"Yes, you in the blue turtleneck. Mr. Thomas, from the *London Times*, I believe."

"Good to see you again, Doctor. My question is this: Given the extreme altitude change inherent in this race, what is the Society's position on the health risks of the racers?"

It was a softball, lobbed gently to Dr. Hillmeade so he could smash it out of the park.

"Quite a good question, Mr. Thomas. As anyone with any mountaineering experience already knows, extreme changes in altitude can have severe consequences. The basic cause of acute mountain sickness is hypoxia, a lack of oxygen. The air is simply too thin in higher elevations to support life. If untreated, this can lead to cerebral edema, which can result in coma or worse. Then there is the risk of pulmonary edema, when fluid accumulates in the lungs. This type of infirmity can happen even with relatively slight changes in elevation. There have been reports of minor pulmonary edema occurring simply by driving up a moderate hillside. To race up this mountain almost begs for serious injury."

The reporter from the *Times* nodded enthusiastically, and Dr. Hillmeade continued.

"The faster one ascends, the more dire the consequences of these conditions. The only way to avoid them completely is to climb slowly, in a controlled environment. This is the classic method espoused by this Society for decades. Given the competitive environment of this race, there is little hope to save a person should he develop this condition."

Dr. Hillmeade shuffled through his papers, apparently searching for something.

"Mr. Thomas' excellent question brings me to what the Society considers the most dangerous condition of *Darwin's Race*. The complete absence of medical supervision. There are no medical doctors on staff at *Darwin's Race* beyond the starting point. Racers are on their own, with no hope of rescue or assistance of any kind. This is completely against the principles the Society developed years ago to safeguard climbers and the reputation of alpine mountaineering. The conditions as set forth for *Darwin's Race* are barbaric."

More hands. "Yes, I can't quite see your face there in the back. In the black shirt."

"Yes, actually I have a few questions," the man said. A murmur rose from the crowd as the gathered media recognized the questioner.

"My first question is really more of a comment," said Terrance Carlton, stepping forward. "Regarding the medical facilities for *Darwin's Race*, we will have a first-tier medical station at the starting point. The facility will have equipment and personnel to treat every possible form of ailment—frostbite, exposure, exhaustion, and, yes, pulmonary and cerebral edema. At great expense, we are transporting each passenger in a state-of-the-art Gamow Bag so we can safely and effectively deal with altitude sickness. And in the case of a true emergency, rescue helicopters can be quickly called up from Lhasa."

"Mr. Carlton, I really . . ." Dr. Hillmeade wanted to move on.

"My second point is a question," Carlton plowed on. "The Society is on the record against *Darwin's Race* for its overt connections with television. You're right on that count. *Darwin's Race* is meant for television—and the millions of people who will be watching from home. Adventure racing is not for everyone, but to the extent that we can bring the experience into the homes of families across the globe, the sport of exploration—a sport that this Society has sworn to promote—will be better off."

The British doctor looked down from the stage at the brash producer with disdain. "Did you, in fact, have a question for the Society?"

"Oh, yes, thank you for reminding me," Carlton grinned. "The Society is against the television coverage of this event?"

The Society's president straightened behind the podium and tugged at his suit jacket. "That's right. It sullies the purity of the expedition."

"And the Society believes exploration should stand on its own, without any media coverage of any kind?"

"Like any great explorer, men and women should explore simply for the joy of it, to gather knowledge. Certainly not for the media attention it may bring." Dr. Hillmeade eyed Carlton warily. His American peer was grinning. Too late, he realized he had just walked into Carlton's trap.

"Well then, my question is this," Carlton turned from the speaker and addressed the media directly. "If television is so bad and so corrupting—then why call this press conference? If the media serves only to "sully"—your word—everything this Society stands for, why invite the media here? Isn't it quite true, that you, Doctor, understand the importance of media very well—and this conference is a rather obvious attempt to legitimize the work of this Society by struggling to reestablish its authority over the field of exploration? Work that has been almost completely insignificant for the better part of a decade? Your conceit is surpassed only by your unbelievable hypocrisy."

The media swung their attention back to the podium, but it was too late. Dr. William Hillmeade had already left the stage.

The exchange was carried on every major television network—including Alger's own network. Carlton had insisted on that.

CHAPTER SIX

Lake Anna
Spotsylvania County, Virginia

Conner wiped down the underbelly of his kayak with a yellow chamois cloth. It was a ritual of sorts, part of his daily routine, no different than the five-mile jog and five hundred pushups he did every morning at daybreak. He'd complete his daily kayak run out on the lake, maybe knock out a couple of donkey flips on Old Creeky, then hoist his kayak into his lakefront boathouse and place it on runners to keep the craft off the ground. Using a fresh cloth, he would wipe down the entire exterior of the 3D, paying particular attention to smoothing out rough areas at the bow and stern. Clean out the interior where water and muck and bugs invariably amassed, then wash off the helmet, wipe down the vest and bent-shaft paddle, and hang everything on hooks to dry.

Conner reached up to set his helmet on its hook and glanced up at a shelf tucked on one of the exposed beams of the boathouse roof. It was a plain box; ordinary cardboard with no distinguishing marks, no writing, but he knew exactly what it contained.

The shelf was nearly twelve feet off the ground; Conner would need a ladder to retrieve anything stored there. That was why he had placed the box there, years ago—to make it difficult to get at.

"Don't do it," Conner told himself. "Leave the box there."

But he had already made his decision. Had made it two days before, in fact, when Malika had shown him Tucker's old wool cap. Though the dust kicked up by her departing truck had dissipated, her words lingered like a bad memory. He managed to stave off the inevitable for almost forty-eight hours.

No longer.

He grabbed a ladder, retrieved the box, and carried it into the cottage. He stoked a fire in his stone fireplace, grabbed a beer from the fridge, and turned his stereo on, selecting a soothing Norah Jones CD. He sat down in front of the fire, Jazz and Jambo collapsing beside him, resting their noses on his leg.

"I know, I know," Conner said looking down at the dogs. "You guys think this is a bad idea, too, huh?" He gave them a quick rub behind the ears, then turned his attention to the task at hand.

The box was taped shut, and he began pulling it away. By the time he was finished, he had a wad of masking tape the size of a bowling ball. "Someone didn't want this box opened," he told the dogs.

The box was half-filled with photographs, magazine clippings, and bib numbers from past endurance races. He pulled out a magazine, *Alpine Journal*, and smiled. The cover photograph was of Conner, on a pair of K2 Super Stinx skis, running a particularly nasty mogul field on Mount Hunter. The caption, in bold block letters read, "Is There Anything This Man Can't Do?"

Conner replaced the magazine in the box and, taking a deep breath, removed a letter-sized envelope. His name was on the front, with no address. It wasn't needed; the letter had simply been left behind when Tess had walked out. How many times had he read those words? Twenty? Thirty? The last time had been years ago, but he could still recall her words with unfaded clarity.

I'm leaving with the knowledge that I've done all I can . . . I no longer have the stomach to watch you crumble apart . . . The only person who can help you now is Conner Michaels.

He cast the envelope to the side and pulled a tattered photograph from the box. Its edges were frayed, the black-and-white image yellowed with age, but Conner recognized the scene immediately.

It had been taken amid the bustle of Lucknow, the

provincial capital of Uttar Pradish in northern India, on the eve of Conner's fateful expedition to Kuk Sur. The picture had been taken by the barkeep in a dank little dive that nonetheless served the beer cold, distinguishing itself from most other Indian joints.

It was a group photo, Conner in the middle, flanked by Tucker on the left, Tess to the right. All three were holding mugs of Kingfisher, a local beer, raised toward the camera. They were toasting, Conner remembered ruefully, to a successful climb.

It was the last picture taken of Tucker alive.

Conner took a long last look, savoring the image of a brother he so sorely missed, then placed the photo back in the box and drained the last of his beer. *Another beer sounds pretty good right about now*, he thought, rising to head toward the kitchen.

Five beers later, Norah Jones just wasn't cutting it anymore. Conner needed something harder, edgier, to go with his warm buzz. He hit eject on the Toshiba disk player and frisbeed the CD across the room. Jazz and Jambo raised their heads off their front paws, alerted to their master's strange behavior.

Conner flipped through his CDs, tossing slipcases aside as he searched. Where was his Stones CD? Where was his *Hotel California*?

Frustrated, Conner hit the tuner button, switching from the CD player to the radio. Though far away from any major city—Washington, D.C. was a good ninety-minute drive—

he could get several radio stations that had enough signal strength to reach Lake Anna. Conner flipped through them until the hard-driving guitars of Metallica's "Enter Sandman" blared out at him. He cranked it up—too loud for the dogs apparently, because they whined and padded out of the living room—as he gulped the last of his sixth Rolling Rock.

The song ended, and the radio host announced it was now one in the morning, time to start the hourly news re-cap. The weather report—"rain clouds headed our way"—sobered Conner up, and he shook his head, disappointed in himself. He began to gather up the empty beer bottles.

"*In Sports News*," the radio announcer reported, "*The producers of* Darwin's Race *announced the six members of the expedition team earlier today in a press conference in New York City. Among the competitors, Cale Anders, the man considered the finest freestyle rock climber in the world, and Blaine Reeves, the reigning Beast of the East champion. Other members include Paul "Hoops" Robeson and Nicki Freyer, both part of the 2001 Mallory and Irvine Research Expedition with a combined forty-one summits. To no one's surprise, the expedition team leader will be veteran climber Wade Stanley. Stanley is best known for smashing the record set by American racer Conner Michaels in last year's Subaru Primal Quest. Stanley will be joined on his team by girlfriend Elizabeth Chamniss. Chamniss is considered the top female mountaineering—*"

The report stopped Conner cold.

So, Tess was competing in *Darwin's Race*. And she

was still with that British blowhard Wade Stanley. Sure, Wade was a capable adventure racer; there was no denying the man's talent, but the radio reporter didn't mention that Wade had beaten Conner's record only after the race organizers had shortened the course by nearly two miles. Even then, Wade had only shaved a few minutes off his time.

Conner spotted his cell phone sitting in its charger beside a clock that read 1:23 a.m. He retrieved the phone but paused before dialing. He walked into the kitchen and reached into the wastebasket.

"Hello?"

From the tone of Malika Child's voice, it almost sounded as if she was expecting his call.

"Okay," Conner said. "I'm in. With two conditions."

"Name them."

"First, I alone select the remaining three members of our team. No interference from you or your father."

"Done."

"The second condition is the most important. I am the captain of this team. Although I generally work democratically, there will be instances when I have to make the final decision. I need ultimate authority on all matters during the race—logistical, personal, whatever. I realize your father is putting up the money, but once we land in Tibet, I am in control of the team. Is that clear?"

"Perfectly," Malika said. "We wouldn't want it any other way."

Conner pulled an old expedition backpack from the

closet in his spare bedroom. It was still packed, a collection of carabiners, chocks, and cams lashed to a series of exterior loops.

"Okay, then just give me a day or so," Conner said, examining his pack for the first time since Kuk Sur. "To pull together my old gear."

"Never mind that stuff; my father has already bought all the latest top-of-the-line equipment. Brand-new boots, harnesses, rope, tents, sleeping bags—you don't need to bring a thing."

Conner ran his fingers over Tucker's cap. A piece of dried mud flaked off and fell to the floor.

"If it's all the same," he said. "I already have everything I need."

CHAPTER SEVEN

Shawangunk Mountain Range
Northern New York

Shandi Davis dunked the fingers of her right hand into the chalk bag at her waist, then crammed her middle and index fingers into a two-inch crack in the rock. Her toes, rather the *tip* of her right big toe, perched precariously on a quarter-inch ledge. Her opposing hand and foot, the entire arm and leg, in fact, now dangled freely sixty-five feet up the one hundred eighty-foot rock face known as Inverted Layback.

Her entire one hundred twenty-pound frame was supported solely by her fingertips and toes.

The Shawangunk Mountains of New York stretched fifty miles from the New Jersey border in a series of parallel rolling ridges. Part of the younger Appalachians, the Gunks were the creation of a violent burst of geological activity—

uplifting, folding, faulting—remaining unchanged since the retreat of the glaciers.

An ecosystem of pitch pine barrens, dwarf pine plains, quartz conglomerate cliffs, slab rock, and virgin hemlock forests, the Shawangunk ridge top was home to some of the nastiest rock faces imaginable—drawing climbers from all over the country. For Shandi, the Gunks were more than a playground; they were home.

She was in the zone. All energies directed to a single task. Find another finger hold. Then, once found, once gripped, another challenge. Find another toehold. Move by move, total concentration—inch by rocky inch.

Layback was not a new route for Shandi, but this particular climb was special.

This part of the Gunks lay in the heart of Minnewaska State Park, an eleven thousand-acre preserve best known as the quarry site for the stone on the base of the Statue of Liberty. But on this cool morning, the small crowd at the base of the pitch had gathered to see a wonder of a different sort.

The fierce crag was in the northeast corner of the Gunks, near her home in Rosendale. Inverted Layback, so dubbed because of its characteristic 5.10 rated overhang, gave even experienced rock climbers fits. It also just happened to be the tallest, most difficult face in the entire system. Only the most experienced climbers even attempted Layback. Shandi had been climbing in the Gunks for years, ever since her father had taken her along to watch her older brother learn to climb. Her brother, it turned out, developed an acute case of acrophobia—a fear of heights. He was now an accountant for an insurance agency in Poughkeepsie; Shandi had been climbing ever since.

Shandi was tackling the route the traditional way, leading without a delay. As she ascended, the twenty-nine year-old placed wedge-shaped metal bolts into narrow cracks. Jammed into the crack, these chocks supported a safety rope, reducing the risk of a long fall. To Shandi, a climbing purist, lead climbing was the only way to go. She largely eschewed top-roping, the practice of fixing an anchor at the top of a pitch, even though it provided a marginally safer climb.

But this climb was anything but ordinary.

"You're almost there, girl! Just a few more feet!"

Shandi didn't have to look down to identify the encouraging voice. Thad Davis had been her climbing partner for nearly five years, her husband for the past two. Like Shandi, he had the lean, sinewy body of an avid rock climber and the rugged face of a devoted outdoorsman. It was during the grueling *Survival of the Shawangunks*, an eight-stage mountain bike, swim, and trail run through the park that Shandi had first laid eyes on her future husband. He was there at the finish line, having completed the course a few minutes earlier, and though she was thoroughly drained by the race, she wasn't so exhausted that she didn't notice the bronze god resting inside the support tent. Attracted to him at first sight, Shandi casually approached Thad, congratulating him on a well-run race, then flipped her blonde hair, hoping her highlights would catch the sunlight, and flashed a wide smile. It worked, and they had been virtually inseparable ever since.

Shandi stole a glance downward. Ten feet below, her husband clung to the rock, her lead rope affixed to his seat harness. He looked up and winked.

She knew Thad loved watching her climb; he was forever telling her that her movements were so fluid, so natural. Thad was confident enough in himself—a trait that Shandi found irresistible—to concede that she was the superior climber. Women often made better rock climbers because, unlike men, they rarely tried to muscle their way up a cliff face. Testosterone-driven men often developed bulging muscles to help pull themselves up a 5.10, only to see a lithe one hundred-pound girl squeak past them as if they were stuck to the crag with glue. Balance, agility, and flexibility—that was the name of this game—and Shandi was a star.

And this was their day.

The crowd that gathered at the foot of Layback had come to witness a record. Shandi and Thad were going to attempt to break the speed record for Layback—from ground to summit in less than thirty minutes. This on a pitch that few short years before many had deemed un-climbable. It was a testament to their skills as climbers, but it was also more than that. It was a spectacle.

A dozen reporters and photographers scribbled and snapped from below. They had come to document the feat, and twenty or so of Shandi and Thad's best friends, climbers mostly, had come to cheer them on.

The park opened promptly at 9 a.m., as usual, and the crowd had amassed at the site by 9:30. Climbing in the morning was preferable, before the rock heated up in the midday sun. At 9:45, Shandi had slid half her left hand into a crack, anchoring it, and pulled her right foot onto a narrow ledge. The record-breaking attempt had begun.

"Ledge two feet to your left!" her husband yelled up to her.

Finding the two-inch-wide outcrop, Shandi maneuvered her foot into place and pushed. Her right hand reached up and found purchase on a small outcrop. Applying counterpressure, she rotated her hips and swept her left foot up the face until she felt another crack. Jamming her toes inside, she pushed up again and searched for the next handhold.

"That's it, baby," Thad encouraged. "Nice and smooth, nice and even. I'm right behind you."

Shandi tried to push all thoughts of the record out of her mind, to concentrate on the experience. She never tired of the feeling; part adrenaline, part total body exhaustion. It felt like every tensed muscle in her body throbbed with adrenaline and electricity, filling her body with a tingly sensation. Thad called it a "Rock O" and Shandi agreed; it wasn't far off from a real, genuine orgasm.

With the growth of adventure racing across the country, Shandi and Thad had been able to kiss off reputable corporate jobs—real estate and nonprofit management, respectively—nearly two years before to take up climbing full-time. As husband and wife, they quickly became known as the First Couple of racing, able to earn a comfortable living on race earnings and sponsorship. Events like this guaranteed exposure in all the right places. She couldn't imagine a better life.

When the top of the pitch came into view, Shandi resisted calling out for a time check. She knew that if both she and Thad reached the top in time to break the record, an official air horn would blow. The desire to hear that horn—the desire to succeed—drove her to dig down and tap into a deep reserve of energy. She scampered up the wall as if she were weightless.

When her hand finally felt the plateau, she pulled herself over so quickly she made herself dizzy. She leaned over the precipice to see Thad only a few feet below.

"You're almost there," she said encouragingly. "Come on; push it!"

Thad swung his leg over the rim and rolled onto his back, his chest heaving with exertion. Shandi collapsed beside him, and for a moment they stared into the blue New York sky.

And then, from 180 feet below, the air horn blared.

The record was theirs.

Shandi, her body glistening with sweat, rolled onto her husband and planted a firm kiss on his mouth. "We did it. We did it."

"Congratulations, honey," Thad said to his wife.

"What a touching scene," a strange voice said suddenly. "Straight out of a Disney movie."

Shandi and Thad bolted upright at the sound. There was no way someone could've reached the top of Inverted Layback before them—they had just set the speed record! With no other way to the top, it was impossible—

Incredibly, a man *was* there, ten feet back from the rim. He was sitting cross-legged, and Shandi saw a small chalk bag fastened to his waist. His hands were flaked with white chalk dust.

She recognized him immediately.

"Conner Michaels," she said, shaking her head. "I can't decide what's more surprising. To see you here in the Gunks or to see you at all."

Conner smiled. "You weren't expecting company?"

"I'm going to forget for a minute that we haven't seen you in over six years, forget that you just dropped off the face of the earth without so much as a phone call. Never mind all that. Because I need to know how you managed to climb Layback, by yourself, beating us to the top. We were the first ones in the park, and we just scaled it in about twenty-seven minutes. Did you hear the horn? That means no one's done it faster."

"It's too bad the reporters didn't get here just a bit sooner," Conner said. "They could've had a real story then."

Thad's mouth gaped open. "But how—?" he stammered.

"You know Lester, the ranger at the main gate? Well,

he and I go back some and I persuaded him to let me into the park a few minutes ahead of you. By the time your little fan club arrived, I was already halfway up. I guess nobody even thought to look up that early in the morning."

"But there's no ropes," Shandi said.

Conner grinned mischievously.

"You free climbed? You free climbed Layback? Layback?" She muttered this several more times, each time hoping it would somehow make sense to her. It didn't.

"And I suppose you clocked yourself," Thad said, pointing to Conner's Suunto expedition watch.

"Yep."

"And?"

"I'm not sure I want to tell you."

"Go on; I don't think anything would surprise me at this point."

"Twenty-nine minutes," Conner said. "Your record stands."

Shandi climbed to her feet and approached her old friend. She had climbed with Conner dozens of times, even tackling the 1998 Borneo Eco-Challenge with him. It wasn't their victory in that race that forged a strong bond; it was the smooth way Conner handled the inevitable quarrels of such a strenuous contest. He was a good man, and Shandi suddenly realized how much she had missed him.

"You know, Conner Michaels," she said. "If it were anyone else up here who just trumped our wonderful new record, I would throw his ass off the top of this ridge and not think twice about it."

Conner climbed to his feet. "But not me?"

"Not you. You, I'm just happy to see again."

They embraced, and Thad soon scrambled to join the reunion. They held on to each other long enough for the air horn to blow again. The crowd below wanted their heroes to return to ground level.

They could wait, Shandi decided. She gave Conner the once-over. He still looked fit—he must've found time for climbing in whatever place he had withdrawn himself to.

"I see the two of you finally got married," Conner said, pointing to their matching rings. "Knowing you two crag-heads, I'm surprised you didn't get hitched on the top of El Capitan."

"It was already booked," Thad joked.

The three old friends spent the next few minutes catching up, reliving some joint climbs, and letting memories of past races rekindle their lapsed friendship. It wasn't long before they were laughing again like old times.

"It's good to see you, Con," Shandi said. "We've both been a little worried about you."

"I appreciate that," Conner said. "But I'm fine. And I've got a little proposition for you."

Conner told them about *Darwin's Race*—which, of course, they already knew all about—and the addition of a second team—which they did not. Shandi's eyes narrowed at the mention of Preston Child and his daughter joining the team.

"Sounds like a bad idea," she said. "This thing sounds too dangerous for beginners."

"I checked them out. Preston has notched some serious mountains: Annapurna, McKinley. Couldn't find much on the daughter, but I saw her whitewater skills firsthand, and I can tell you that girl is a natural athlete."

"If you're comfortable with them," Shandi said, "I'm comfortable with them. I know you; you wouldn't go into battle with novices. My question is why. Why do you want to get into *Darwin's Race*? We thought you were finished with all this."

Shandi saw Conner consider her question carefully, a degree of apprehension behind his deep brown eyes. He was hiding something.

"Hey, I missed you guys," he said. "That's not enough?"

"If you missed us so bad, you could have had us over for dinner. You don't have to drag us all the way to Tibet. Going to the Tsangpo is like going to the moon."

"I guess that's true," Conner said. He squinted up into the morning sun, then back to the climbers. "Look, I've known you two a long time. You're true friends. You know what happened on Kuk Sur, and you know how I . . . well, you know how it affected me. Well, I think it's time to try and get better."

"And you think going back to Tibet is the way to do that?" Thad asked.

"I don't know the answer to that. But the whole living-like-a-recluse thing is getting a little old. It's time to try something different; don't you think? Face my fears and all that babble?"

Shandi and Thad let the question hang in the air.

"Enough of this serious stuff," Conner said loudly, clapping his hands together. "Are you in or what?"

Shandi shot her husband a look. "Do we have a choice?"

Conner grinned. "Of course. But if you bail on me now, I will be forced to climb down there and talk to those reporters about my twenty-nine minute solo climb. I'd hate to spoil your fun."

"You're blackmailing us?" Thad laughed. "That's how you expect to get us into *Darwin's Race?*"

Shandi's mind was racing faster than high water on the Gauley. "When would we leave? What about the rest of the team? Oh my God, I have a thousand questions."

"Hold on a minute there, Shan," Conner said. "You'd only have a couple of weeks to get your gear together—and get yourselves together. It's a big moment, I know, but we'd tackle *Darwin's Race* like any other climb. Make a gear list, pull together a shopping list—food, first aid kit—you know the drill. Preston has offered to buy us whatever we need."

"Whatever we want?" Shandi asked. "This guy really does have money to throw around, doesn't he?"

"I guess so," Conner said, grinning. "And I've got a great way to accommodate him."

Shandi arched her eyebrow. "Conner Michaels, do

you have something up your sleeve?"

"All in due time, Shandi," Conner said, grinning widely. "All in due time."

Thad did a quick calculation. "Okay, let's say—for now—we're in. Plus Preston and his daughter. That makes five. You said a team of six. Who are we missing?"

"Who do you think?"

Shandi exchanged a serious glance with her husband.

"What?" Conner prodded.

"Have you spoken to him yet?" Shandi asked.

"Ian? No, I haven't. I'm driving to West Virginia this afternoon. Plan on catching up with him in the morning. Why are you looking at me like that?"

"Conner, Ian was your best friend. After Kuk Sur, you just disappeared. After all the races, all those climbs together, you just stopped calling. You didn't even return his messages. Ian was hurt. For the longest time, he just moped around in a funk."

"I have some fences to mend," Conner said. "I understand that."

"I just hope Ian is ready to forgive," Shandi said.

The look in Conner's eyes told her that he hoped so too.

"I still can't believe you would blackmail your old friends to get them into this race," Shandi said.

"Oh no," Conner said, trying to look serious. "I expect you to enter the race because it's one of the last, great challenges on earth. The blackmail thing is entirely for fun."

Thad laughed. "Maybe we didn't miss you as much as

we thought we did."

"So are you in or out?" Conner asked excitedly.

"Oh, we're in," Shandi answered for both. "We're *way* in!"

"Darwin's fuckin' Race," Thad said in his usual expletive-laden way. "I can't believe it. We're going to fuckin' Shangri-la."

CHAPTER EIGHT

Summersville Dam
Nicholas County, West Virginia

The small town of Beckley was largely unremarkable. A quiet hamlet nestled in the foothills of central West Virginia, it had the obligatory assortment of country shops, whitewashed homes with large front porches and an air of leisure that could come only from rural living.

Dusty pickups. *Gitter Done* bumper stickers.

From November through April, Beckley sat empty. Sitting at an elevation of just above three thousand feet, the town endured alpine winters with enough snow to close schools for weeks on end. During the winter, even the locals stayed indoors. But as the first rays of warmth started to thaw the frost, something astonishing happened.

People by the hundreds, then by the thousands, drifted

into Beckley like an invasion. They came from as far away as Cleveland and Chicago, south out of Baltimore and DC, north from Charlotte. They filled the campgrounds and hotels and made long lines at fast-food joints all too eager to feed them.

The masses came to Beckley for one reason and one reason only. To run the most intoxicating, exhilarating, and frightening whitewater rapids in the United States.

The New River Gorge cut across Fayette County like a deep gash. And running through it was the furious waters of the New River. Boasting such Class IV and V rapids as Double Z and Lower Keeney, the New drew the bulk of rafters and kayakers during the hot and easy months of summer. When the summer season closed, the rafts slowly disappeared from the river.

Then the action shifted a few miles north. To a river called the Gauley.

Considered the most treacherous of all East Coast rivers, the mighty Gauley once served as the training ground for all expert paddlers. A mistake in this water would be trouble. Monsters known as Sweet Falls and Pillow Rock sounded harmless, but in reality were furious boulder-strewn maelstroms. Undercut rocks and keeper holes lined the twenty-five-mile stretch and for anyone unlucky enough to fall into either, it was Hail Mary time because help was hours away. It was that inaccessible; it was that nasty.

Ian Bjornson straddled his fourteen-foot expedition raft and watched a blue school bus descend from the ridge above the river. A half-dozen identical rafts were lined up beside him along the river's edge, the cold water lapping up against the reinforced rubber hulls. The other guides made themselves busy by strapping down extra gear in water-resistant dry bags.

Ian had been a river guide for three years now, one on the Gauley. He had run the New, too, dozens of times, but preferred the violence of the Gauley. He had guided on Africa's mighty Zambezi for a full season, too, but there was precious little rock climbing—his other passion—in Zimbabwe so he had returned to Ace Adventures to pursue both.

Twenty-nine years young, Ian couldn't conceive of a better life. Spent the day on the river, the nights drinking at the Red Rooster, days off on the rocks. He entered adventure races now and again—his competitive streak still very much alive—though it had been a few years since his last major event.

The time outdoors showed on his face. He was tanned enough to retain a healthy glow even in the winter, and his bright blue eyes attracted the ladies as much as his shoulder-length, sun-streaked hair. There were always a few young women in the group looking for a good time, all too friendly with such a good-humored and handsome guide. Another great perk of his life.

He watched the bus come to a stop and spill forth a torrent of paddle-wielding rafters, all eager smiles and adrenaline-fueled energy.

Wait until they hit Initiation, the first rapid, he thought.

That oughta put a damper on all that enthusiasm.

He waited for his rafters to be directed to him before he began his standard pre-trip speech. "Okay, good morning. My name is Ian, and I'll be your guide today." Smiles and bright eyes stared back at him, the rafters looking faintly ridiculous in their mismatched rented wetsuits and life vests.

"Welcome to the Gauley, the greatest ride on earth. As you may know, the Gauley is runnable only in the fall when the Summersville Dam is released. When they open up that dam, the Summersville reservoir empties down this riverbed and turns this river upside down. That's why you're here, and that's why I'm here. I promise you we're going to have some fun today."

Ian quickly counted his group; came up one short. He called over to the team leader, "Hey, Pete, missing one here." A clipboard-toting guide waved back and pointed to a late arrival. Their sixth member strode over to join them.

"Welcome to the Gauley," Ian began again, "the greatest ride—"

"Hello, Ian," Conner Michaels said.

He didn't say a word. What could he say? It was like seeing a ghost.

Ian stood up and stormed over to Pete. "I need to switch out. Grab someone from Brodie's boat and send 'em over. I can't take this guy."

The group leader frowned. "The other rafts are already putting in. We all have people in our boats we don't like.

Whatever your issues are with that guy, deal with it. I expect you in the water in five minutes."

Sulking, Ian made his way back to the raft. Five faces now looked concerned, and he could feel the weighty gaze of the sixth. He shoved the raft into the gentle flow of the river.

"Okay, the Gauley is no place for beginners, so I'm going to assume you know what to do out here. But I need to say a few words about safety." Ian held up his paddle. "This is your lifeline. Keep the paddle in the water, and it will keep you in the boat. The water will help brace you during the rough stretches. Take the paddle out of the water," he flailed the paddle in the air, "and you are assured of a nice swim. And you better be able to hold your breath. Because these waters will suck you under and if they do, you're looking at thirty to forty seconds of down time. That might not sound like a lot, but it's more than enough to take your life."

The concerned faces now looked positively horrified.

"Don't worry. Keep your paddle in the water, and you'll be fine."

Ian paddled the raft into the center of the river. The waters picked up speed.

"Boys and girls, pay attention now," Ian said, smiling. "We've got an extra-big treat today. Allow me to introduce to you the great Conner Michaels." He waved dramatically toward his old friend. "Conner and I go way back. Years and years. I haven't seen him in a long time, but it's good to have him back. Some of you may even recognize him as a three-time Eco-Challenge champion."

Murmurs of awe drifted up from the others.

"Well, we're in for a special treat today, because Conner is going to do something that's never been done before on the Gauley."

"I am?" Conner mouthed.

Ian reached over and grabbed Conner's paddle and flung it into the river. It drifted away into an eddy. "Conner is going to go down this river without a paddle."

One of the concerned faces, a twenty-something girl, spoke up. "But you said that was too dangerous. Without a paddle, he'll get sucked under the water for sure. That's what you said."

"I'm afraid Conner has insisted, and I'm here only to make sure each of you has a great time. I wouldn't want to get in the way of his good time."

Conner stared at him. "Is this what it's going to take then? To have you forgive me?"

Ian glanced downriver. The roar of the first rapid was upon them.

"It's a good start," he said. "Now, everybody, we're going to the right of that boulder, so I need all paddles in the water."

The same girl spoke up again. "But all the other rafts are going left."

Ian smiled. "They're going the safe way," he said. "To the right is a sucking vortex that most guides try to avoid. But I'm sensing that you are a good group, so I think it's worth a go."

Conner caught his eye and nodded. He had accepted his penance, as suicidal as it may be. His old friend was nothing if not honorable.

Ian screamed, "Now forward, forward, forward!"

The raft shot out over a three-foot ledge and slammed into a towering standing wave. The bow shot straight up into the air and, for one fleeting instant, threatened to flip. But the group, muscles no doubt pumping with sheer terror, powered through it. They emerged into the pool below the rapid and counted their blessings.

"Man overboard!"

One of the rafters stood and pointed back to the rapid. Ian looked back just in time to see a black helmet slip beneath the waves.

Conner.

"All stop," he ordered. "Let's back it up."

He maneuvered the raft into an eddy and waited.

Conner's helmet bubbled to the surface, then was sucked back down again.

"Oh my God," somebody cried. "He's trapped."

Ian scrambled to loose the throw line from his dry bag. He tossed the heavy end towards the boiling water. His aim was good, and it landed next to the bobbing helmet. But Conner made no move to grab the rope.

Something was wrong.

And then the helmet jerked free of the rapid. It bobbed down the river, caught lazily in the flow. As it passed, Ian reached down and plucked it from the water.

"Oh my God, he's gone! That guy is gone! He got sucked down into that hole. He's probably trapped. He's probably dead!"

Ian felt a fist constrict around his heart. The frantic girl was right. The force of the whitewater had ripped Conner's helmet from his head.

A full minute of silence passed. The girl sniffled, fighting back tears.

Jesus, what have I done?

A splash on the starboard side broke the quiet. Ian glanced over in time to see two arms emerge from the water and clutch the bowline. A second later, Conner Michaels' head broke the surface.

He was smiling.

"You bastard!" Ian yelled. "You fucking bastard! I thought you were dead; I thought I killed you!"

"So we're even now? Am I forgiven?"

A hearty laugh of relief spilled from Ian's mouth. "Damn straight you're forgiven," he said. "Now get your ass back in the raft. We've got a river to run."

By the time Ian pulled the rafter over to the take-out, he and his friend had waged a monstrous war of white water. The five original group members literally sprinted for the relative safety of the waiting bus. Conner and Ian had taken turns with the lone remaining paddle, aiming for the most treacherous stretches of the river in crazy attempts to knock each other out of the raft. Each had swum a half-dozen nasty rapids, and each had laughed the whole time through. The rafters must've thought these two men were out of their minds—and they wouldn't be far from the truth.

For Ian, he was just glad to see his old friend again.

"Help me get this thing on the truck," Ian said, lifting one end of the raft. Conner quickly picked up the rear.

"Do we need to talk about what happened?" Conner asked.

"That's up to you. You want to talk; I want to listen. But I know the deal. I know about what happened with Tucker, and I've got a pretty good idea of how that almost destroyed you."

"But . . .?"

"No buts. You didn't call me. You didn't return my messages. I can understand that too. But it bothered me, you know. It hurt. I thought we were better friends than that."

"No excuses," Conner said. "I should've called. At least to tell you that I needed to go it alone."

They hoisted the raft over their heads and handed it to a pair of guides on the back of a flatbed who guided it onto the other deflated rafts.

"Go it alone?" Ian said, putting a hand on his friend's shoulder. "There is nothing in this world that you need to do alone."

Conner nodded. "I know you're right. It took me awhile, but now I know you're right. And that's why I'm here. I want you to enter a race with me."

"Alright, I'll do it."

Conner looked surprised. "Wait, don't you even want to know what it is?"

"*Darwin's Race.* Second team. Tsangpo Gorge. Kuk Sur. I got it."

"But how—?"

"Thad and Shandi called me last night, told me all about it. Told me you were coming to see me."

"So all that business at the put-in, trying to get me thrown off the raft, making me swim Initiation? That was all for show?"

"Not for show," Ian replied. "That was real. That was for being an asshole six years ago."

"And now?"

"And now, we're good."

"You're a good friend, Ian. And I promise I won't let you down again. We've only got three weeks to get ready for this race, so I needed a team I could trust."

"But what about the other two, Preston and his daughter? You trust them?"

"Not yet. But when we all get together in Tibet before the start of the race, we'll get our plans in order. Then we'll see how they mesh with the rest of us. We've got a lot to—" Conner cut himself off. "Why are you smiling like that?"

Ian slapped him on the back. "It's good to have you back, buddy."

"Good to hear," Conner said. "But not nearly as good as it feels to actually *be* back."

CHAPTER NINE

Dulles International Airport
25 Miles West of Washington, DC

A small mountain of duffel bags, climbing gear, and sleeping pads sat beside the Lufthansa check-in counter at Dulles International Airport. A small team of *Darwin's Race* producers hovered around two airline staff members, clutching a sheaf of paperwork and airline tickets. The airline personnel had just summoned extra security to wand the race crew. Conner was glad not to have to negotiate the new security precautions set in place in airports nationwide. With its proximity to the Nation's Capital, Dulles International was particularly stringent about procedure. This was going to take awhile.

Conner leaned back against his tattered duffel, propped a sleeping pad under his head, and pulled out a well-thumbed paperback. The other racers had scattered throughout the terminal, picking up last-minute snacks and reading material for the long flight ahead. Preston and Malika were huddled with the Lufthansa security team, insisting they be allowed to carry on their trekking poles. Apparently, the dagger-like ends of the poles worried the airline, and Conner didn't blame them. He wondered why Preston and his daughter didn't just check the gear like everyone else.

Team North Face, as Wade Stanley's team was now officially named, was there too, killing time until boarding. Conner had to hand it to Terrance Carlton—the producer had certainly pulled together a world-class expedition team.

Stanley, Conner's erstwhile racing rival, was standing beside the mountain of gear, chatting up another expedition member. Wade was undoubtedly the star of the adventure racing circuit. With soap opera actor good looks—shoulder-length blonde hair carefully groomed to look unkempt, piercing green eyes, and the bronzed skin of someone who spent a great deal of time outside—Wade was recognized everywhere he went. His likeness was plastered all over, advertising campaigns for adventure gear of all sorts—kayaks, sleeping bags, even children's trekking boots. But the man backed up the swagger, too. He won races so regularly that most competitions were mere battles for second place—a boast he was all too eager to express to anyone within earshot. Hailing from London, he hardly needed the accent to sound like a pompous ass.

Standing beside Wade was Nicki Freyer, known to her friends as Powder for her uncanny resemblance to the fitness guru. Powder was hard as nails, short and wiry, with a shock of platinum blonde hair cropped close to her scalp. Conner liked her, had even spent some time with her during a forced bivouac in the Andes, but knew she had a bit of a short fuse. Powder Keg may have been a more apt nickname.

A few steps away from Wade and Powder, Cale Anders, Blaine Reeves, and Paul Robeson lounged along a row of chairs. Conner knew Paul as Hoops, a moniker hung on the tall, thin man after four years of college ball at some Division III college. His considerable height contained an unmatched store of stamina; Hoops was a good man to have on any team.

Conner knew less of Cale and Blaine, other than what he had gleaned from the press materials he had read. Part of the younger set that was rapidly taking over the outdoor sports world, Cale was known for his pure rock-climbing skills while Blaine was an accomplished peak-bagger. The official race biographies breathlessly detailed one of Blaine's high altitude exploits.

In 2001, Blaine had been guiding a group of middle-aged business types up the relatively gentle slopes of Mount Elbrus when disaster had struck. As the tallest mountain in Europe, Elbrus qualified as one of the Seven Summits, but the peak, located in Russia's Caucasus, was easy enough for most fit people to attain.

But this group had not been fit. Two members of the group, burly Germans with thick, bratwurst-swelled bellies, began tiring just before the summit. They refused to turn back so close to their goal, forcing Blaine to nearly drag them up the final two hundred feet. Photographs from the summit showed the severely fatigued Germans, pale and gasping for air.

On the way down, it began to snow, and the Germans finally broke down completely. Their legs had turned to jelly; their breaths little more than ragged wheezes. Hallucinations set in. One believed he was back in his childhood home in Dresden. Blaine made a quick triage and decided the hallucinating German had to be taken down first.

With a strength belied by his lean 160-pound frame, Blaine lifted the hefty man over his shoulders and carried him two miles down to base camp. Then, barely pausing for a drink of warm water, he marched right back up to the summit to retrieve the second stricken climber. A half inch layer of fresh snow had caked onto the climber's face by the time Blaine reached him.

For a second time, he lifted the climber over his shoulders and began the delicate down-climb. It took nearly four hours of hard climbing, but Blaine safely delivered both stricken men to base camp before nightfall.

"They were my climbers," Blaine replied when asked why he didn't just radio for assistance. "They were my responsibility."

In today's climbing world, such selfless acts were increasingly rare. Conner reminded himself to find some time with young Blaine Reeves.

Conner scanned the terminal for any sign of Tess Chamniss. Though all of the other racers were present and accounted for, she was nowhere to be seen. He fought the urge to search the entire airport, issue an all-points-bulletin, file a missing persons report. That would appear desperate, right? He wondered if perhaps she was avoiding him altogether, then on second thought realized that was giving him more credit than he deserved. It didn't really matter either way, as they would be sharing the same airplane soon. He was excited about the pending reunion; he just didn't want to look like he was.

Conner's own team was now known officially as Team Providence. It was Preston's money, after all, that was financing the entire deal, so Conner supposed it was his right to name it after one of his own companies. He actually liked the name. The idea that history did not proceed randomly, that it was instead somehow purposeful, progressive, appealed to him. Not a particularly religious sort, Conner found poetry in the idea of a higher power—whether you called that power God or Nature or something else entirely.

The American Honda Motor Company supported Shandi and Thad Davis year-round, and the couple had to negotiate special dispensation to allow them to compete under another corporate banner. Preston had generously allowed the car maker to emblazon all expedition back-packs with Honda's trademark logo and to provide power generators for base camp. It was all a little much for Conner, who preferred to concentrate on the task at hand, rather than haggle over financial technicalities. Still, he recognized the need for financial support of major expeditions and he rather enjoyed the television commercials featuring his famous teammates.

Honda had built an entire marketing campaign around Shandi and Thad to advertise their minivan, the Odyssey. The television commercials had been running for a few months now, featuring rapid clips of Shandi rock climbing. At the end of the spot, Shandi and Thad climbed into the minivan (Shandi in the driver's seat), throwing a mountain of gear into the spacious interior. The camera zoomed in on Shandi, who intoned: "What? You think you need kids to drive a minivan?"

The campaign was Honda's attempt to reach out beyond the yuppie soccer mom crowd to a new pool of potential consumers, and it provided Shandi's teammates endless opportunities to poke fun. Both Conner and Ian now referred to Shandi as "Mommy" almost exclusively, much to her bemused chagrin.

"I'm not boarding that plane without my trekking poles!"

Preston's bellowing voice echoed down the busy terminal, drawing stares from passersby. Conner could see that Lufthansa had called in a suit to handle the agitated big man, but it seemed only to infuriate Preston further. He was brandishing his trekking pole wildly, poking it into the belly of the Lufthansa rep.

Preston had proved to be a promotional machine in the weeks leading up to the departure. Appearances on *60 Minutes* and *20/20* had cemented his reputation as a pistol. He had gone so far as to describe himself to Ed Bradley as "King Kong with crampons." But Preston was also sincerely deferential to the leadership of Conner Michaels, happily reciting Conner's résumé at every media opportunity. If people turned on *Darwin's Race* to watch the burly business tycoon, Conner thought, so much the better. He didn't really like the idea of being watched around the clock by those shoulder-mounted cameras anyway.

But the hype in *Darwin's Race* was already ratcheting up.

There were numerous reports out of Las Vegas noting that oddsmakers had made the Wade Stanley-Tess Chamniss team clear favorites. It was the first time Vegas had placed odds on an adventure race, a testament to the growing public interest in *Darwin's Race*. On a more sobering note, the best bet on the board—even money—was that no one would reach the summit.

A report on CNN detailed the rise of dozens of clubs dedicated to watching *Darwin's Race*. These groups had pledged to watch every minute of the coverage, round the clock, on Discovery.com and NBC.com, nightly on Discovery Channel, and weekly on NBC.

Cameras from *Darwin's Race* were already rolling

inside Dulles, though Conner didn't think shots of twelve adventure racers lounging around an airport would prove very interesting to anyone.   They were NBC cameras, capitalizing on the exclusive relationship Alger had forged with Carlton. One of the benefits of the monster media deal with the peacock network was that it virtually ensured *Darwin's Race* comprehensive coverage. It was a positive catch-22. NBC signed on to capitalize on the media hype that was sure to surround *Darwin's Race* . . . and thus *Darwin's Race* enjoyed massive exposure . . . on NBC.

Though he tried, Conner found it difficult to avoid the promotional machine set forth by Carlton. When he spotted Wade Stanley being interviewed on *The Today Show* one morning, he couldn't turn the channel. The British racer had been in rare form. The piece started out with a report on the most recent attempt to pass through the Tsangpo Gorge. An attempt that ended in tragedy.

Conner knew the story well. It was a story he didn't want to hear again, so he tuned the report out. The Tsangpo Gorge held enough bad memories for a lifetime.

It was the last time, the reporter breathlessly announced, that anyone dared to test the mighty Tsangpo. Conner was glad they didn't mention his own attempt on Kuk Sur. But since he had not passed through the Tsangpo Gorge back then—choosing to approach the climb from India in the south instead—the report moved right on to the interview with Wade Stanley.

"Of course we know the Tsangpo Gorge is virtually

unknown," Wade had said. "It's probably the last great un-explored region on earth. I mean, we're talking about the fabled Shangri-la. A place of absolute mystery."

The British climber was laying it on thick.

"But that's the beauty of *Darwin's Race*. The producers could've started the race anywhere—India in the south, farther east into China—but no, they decided to take it up a notch. Start from the west, forcing the racers to pass through the gorge to get to Kuk Sur. Genius, I say. And a hell of a challenge for all of us."

He was then asked what victory in *Darwin's Race* would mean to him.

"When I won last year's Eco-Challenge, I thought I had accomplished everything there was to accomplish in adventure racing. The only man to win Eco, Beast of the East, and Subaru in a single year. The record holder in four major races. I remember smashing Conner Michaels' sup-posed unbreakable time in the Subaru. No adventure racer past or present has a higher completion rate, raised more sponsorship dollars, in short, done more for this sport than Wade Stanley."

He paused a moment, allowing his credentials to sink in, measuring his words for digestible sound bites. "British explorers have been roaming the four corners of this great earth for hundreds of years. Like those who have gone be-fore me, I now willingly yet modestly accept the torch they have passed on to me. Though a burden, I am supremely confident in my abilities to carry this mantle and to once again prove the British superiority in this endeavor."

Wade visibly blanched as the interviewer asked about Conner Michaels. He rolled his neck slowly before answering, a gesture Conner immediately recognized. The Brit often rolled his neck when he felt the rising tide of pressure in his spine. In poker, it would be an obvious tell.

Since Carlton had announced the second team would be led by the reclusive star, Conner was a hot topic. As if the mysterious location, unexplored terrain, unprecedented round-the-clock television coverage, and unsupported format of this event wasn't enough, now there was a human face to *Darwin's Race*. The prodigal son returning to battle the beast of the Tsangpo Gorge and Kuk Sur.

"My only competition is myself," Wade answered after his neck was sufficiently limber. "The other competitors are nameless and faceless. Mother Nature will provide her fair share of challenge, I'm sure, but given my career achievements, there is no one on this stage that I view with any sort of apprehension.

"All of the other racers, if they like, may have a rollicking good battle for second place. I rather doubt I'll even see the other team after the first day, so either way I really don't care."

All in all, Conner thought Wade had come off like the arrogant prick he was. But then again, he had thought of Wade as an ass for years now. He supposed some people, some naïve people, may find Wade charmingly confident. *Tess must see something in the guy,* Conner thought. There was no accounting for some people's taste.

Just then, a young production assistant tapped him on the shoulder, rescuing Conner from his train of thought.

"Okay, Mr. Michaels, here's your ticket. You can now go on ahead to Gate 36, but please make sure you have your passport ready for inspection."

Conner thanked the assistant, and the eager young man bounded toward another racer.

"Hey, wait a minute," he called after him.

"Yes, Mr. Michaels?"

"The scene over there with Preston and Malika. Is Lufthansa going to let them carry on those trekking poles?"

"Yes, sir. Mr. Child made a few phone calls, and apparently everything has worked out."

Conner gathered up his carry-on bag, the paperback tucked inside, and made his way to the gate. Preston and Malika were already there, striding calmly through the metal detectors with their precious trekking poles, setting off alarms that clamored throughout the entire terminal.

CHAPTER TEN

United Airlines Flight 325
Over the Atlantic Ocean

United Flight 325 to Frankfurt, Germany, had reached its cruising altitude of forty thousand feet. The cast and crew of *Darwin's Race* occupied over half of the giant 747, and everyone was settling in for a long trip. The flight would last just over seven hours, followed by a two-hour layover, then a second flight, direct to Kathmandu, Nepal. And that was not the end of their journey. From Kathmandu, buses had been chartered to transport them overland to Lhasa, Tibet's capital city, and the jumping off point for dozens of Himalayan treks each year. Most of the two hundred-plus people associated with *Darwin's Race* were nestling in for as much sleep as they could; it would be in short supply over the coming weeks.

The members of each team shared a row, but several rows separated North Face from Providence. It was just as well, as they had little desire for camaraderie—most of the competitors had switched on their game faces once they'd lifted off from Dulles International Airport.

Conner and his teammates were seated toward the back of the plane, occupying the middle bank of seats. Good view of the movie screen, though Conner frowned at the flight's offerings. Kiddie movies; he shrugged. Airlines were always so sensitive about what they show onboard, invariably choosing films made for children. Ian had already assumed his sleeping position beside Shandi and Thad, who had decided to endure *Shrek the Third*.

Conner couldn't sleep. Even with the cabin darkened, his eyes were wide with restlessness. Already through his own copy of Matthiessen's *The Snow Leopard*, he had borrowed Ian's paperback of *The Worst Journey in the World*—the tragic account of Scott's pursuit of the South Pole. Conner had read it years ago, a grim reminder of the price some men pay in the pursuit of being first. The author, Aspley Cherry-Garrard, had written of icebound exploration: "Exploration is at once the clearest and most isolated way of having a bad time which has ever been devised."

Conner thought Cherry-Garrard must've been a pretty perceptive guy.

Tess Chamniss was seated seven rows in front of Conner. Although he could see only the back of her head, he knew it was Tess by the way she pulled her hair in a ponytail through the gap in the back of her red baseball cap. He recognized the cap she was wearing—University of Maryland—because he had given it to her, a memento of his alma mater. Even the fleeting glimpse from behind was enough to quicken Conner's pulse. Surely the Terps hat was a good signal, right?

Wade Stanley was nowhere in sight—probably asleep somewhere in first class—so Conner unbuckled his seatbelt and made his way up to Tess's row. She noticed his approach and smiled. Warmly, Conner thought. That was a good sign. It felt like his heart was going to burst out of his chest.

Drawing in a deep breath, Conner said, "You'd think it would be easier to approach a woman you spent nearly four years of your life with."

A blanket-covered shape shifted restlessly beside Tess, obviously annoyed at the conversation. "Hoops," Tess whispered, gesturing to her seat neighbor. "Let's go to the front, where we can talk."

Once they were standing at the flight attendant's station, there was an awkward silence. Should they hug? Shake hands? What's the proper etiquette for reacquainted lovers?

"Didn't get a chance to talk to you earlier," Tess said finally. "Left some luggage in the hotel and had to go all the way back to town. But now that I see you here, live and in the flesh, I can hardly believe it. Conner Michaels, competing again. I thought you had given all this up."

"Things change," Conner replied simply.

"Lots of things change."

"You haven't changed. Still as beautiful as ever. I like your hat."

"It fits," she said, absently running her hand across its brim. "You look good, too. Lake life agrees with you."

"Look, Tess. I know things didn't . . . the way things ended . . ."

She held up a hand to stop him. "There's no reason to go there right now. People change, feelings change. We grew apart—same drama, different actors. I don't hold any grudges." She let that sink in for a moment. "What I really want to know is why you decided to compete in this damn race. After all this time. And this mountain."

Conner could've asked her the same question. For six years, a single question burned inside him, begging to be asked. She was surely smart enough not to give him the standard answer: *Climbing is an inherently dangerous sport. It's a risk we all assume knowingly, even willingly.* As if Tucker's acceptance of the perils of mountaineering made his death somehow more palatable, easier to cope with, easier to move on from.

Conner wanted a real answer. What had she done that allowed her to move on, seemingly so effortlessly? What was her secret? He wanted a real answer because he was still searching for his.

But the time for these questions was not now. She was still wary around him, he could sense it in the way she avoided direct eye contact, shrunk from his touch. For now, it was best to keep things casual, nonthreatening.

"I just figured it was time to get back in the game."

"Maybe face some demons while you're at it?"

Conner looked away. "Maybe, but I have to admit I was bitten by this crazy concept. A live race through unexplored territory, finishing on an unclimbed mountain? The adventurer in me could hardly resist."

"And here I thought the adventurer in you had gone someplace far, far away," Tess said. "Glad to have you back."

Conner wanted to tell her the truth but hesitated. He was feeling vulnerable, as if his skin were covered with raw nerves, delicate to the slightest touch. Looking at her now, the enormity of how much he missed her surprised him. He missed the way she burned the coffee in the morning (*who burns coffee?*). Missed the way she sometimes wore mismatched socks (and didn't care). The way she wrestled with Jazz and Jambo. The way she nuzzled into his chest on Sunday mornings.

After almost six years apart from the woman he had once loved, Conner felt his hands trembling.

But if he didn't tell her now, when? Once they hit the ground, the race preparations would take over. They would be surrounded by crew and other team members round-the-clock. And one thing Conner had promised himself was this: *Don't waste an opportunity to tell her how you feel.* He had committed that sin once and wasn't about to do it again.

"Tess," he said, grabbing her arm. "There's something I want to say—"

"Well, well, well. What have we here?"

Wade Stanley materialized, seemingly out of nowhere, beside Tess.

"A long-lost reunion? How quaint." Conner dropped her arm as Wade placed his hands on her shoulders. "Well, don't let me stop you. I'd love to catch up with one of history's greatest competitors. It's like 'Where are they now?' on ESPN. Classic. Where is Conner Michaels now?"

Whether it was the condescending tone in Wade's voice or the fact that he had interrupted at precisely the most inopportune moment, Conner found himself supremely annoyed.

"Hello, Wade," Conner said, trying to keep his anger in check. "I figured you'd be up in first class, flirting with the flight attendants. What brings you back to the cheap seats?"

"Ah, Conner," Wade smiled mirthlessly. "I see you haven't lost your rapier-sharp American wit. I am, in fact, seated in first class—compliments of the airline—but accepted only because of my knee injury. You remember the one. I hurt it in Subaru last year. Still throbs from time to time."

The reference to last year's Subaru Primal Quest, the race where Wade broke Conner's record, was meant as bait, and Conner didn't just nibble—he devoured. "Yeah, I did catch that race. Shaved a whole five minutes off my record. Of course, the race directors were kind enough to knock almost five klicks off the course. Would have been hard *not* to break my record with that kind of accommodation."

"Why squabble about past races?" Wade said, "when we have *Darwin's Race* to look forward to. I'm not sure what compelled you to come out of retirement for this, but all the better, I say. The playing field is as level as it can be—we'll just see who the better man is, won't we?"

"It's a team sport," Conner pointed out. "Or had you forgotten?"

"How could I forget?" Wade grinned, tightening his grip around Tess. "When I've got my very own girlfriend on my team. We make a great team, wouldn't you agree?"

Tess squirmed, looking uncomfortable, so Conner decided to back off. "I think there are two great teams in this race. Twelve able competitors. I'm just looking forward to getting started. See what's left in these old bones."

"Yes, you should get some sleep," Wade said. "You'll need to be well rested for the actual race. There's bound to be some rather nasty snow bridges up there, eh?"

The comment hung in the air, as if Wade had just pulled the pin of a grenade and they were all waiting for it to explode. Conner knew he was being goaded into a confrontation, but he also knew the remark—and its obvious allusion to his brother—could not stand unchallenged.

"You know, Wade," Conner said, stepping closer, nose to nose. "You're a prick. And you've always been a prick. If you ever even *think* about my brother again, I will personally tear the life out of you."

"How poignant," Wade grinned. "I think perhaps you overstep your bounds."

"Just try me." Conner's stare bore a whole through Wade's forehead.

"It appears that your brother's death still haunts you. I don't think you're in any shape to take on a race of this—"

"You better stop now," Conner interrupted.

"Or what?"

They were standing nose to nose; boxers in a pre-fight stare-down. The commotion had stirred some of the other passengers, who were now murmuring nervously and looking about for a member of the flight crew. A fight at forty two thousand feet in a post-9/11 security-conscious world would almost certainly force an emergency landing.

"Alright, boys. That's enough," Tess said, squeezing her way between them. "Look what you've done now. The stewardess is on the phone to the pilot. I'll calm her down, but this is going to be a long flight. No more confrontations."

Conner finally stepped back. Out of the corner of his eye, he saw the pissed-off stewardess storming down the aisle from first class. Tess shoved Wade up the aisle to intercept. She looked over her shoulder, the warmth in her eyes now frozen over with contempt. "Go back to your seat," she ordered. "I think it's best if you just stay away."

"But Tess, are you going to let him talk about Tucker like that?" Conner protested.

"Grow up, Con. You sound like a child. I will take care of him," she said. "Now go back to your seat. And don't come within ten feet of either of us for the rest of the trip. I won't stand for it."

The look on her face told Conner that resistance would be futile. He wanted to wipe that smirk off Wade's face—wanted to *bash* it off—but instead he straightened his shirt, nodded to Tess, and retreated slowly toward the back of the plane.

"What the hell was that all about?" asked Malika as Conner slumped back into his seat.

"Nothing," he said. "Nothing but some unfinished business."

CHAPTER ELEVEN

Tsangpo Gorge
Gompo Ne, Tibet

The cold was penetrating two levels of fleece and a thick set of thermal underwear, laying a field of purple goose bumps along Bill Greenback's spine. It wasn't raining exactly, but a continuous mist—from the clouds or the river, he couldn't determine—had soaked him to the bone.

"Waterproof, my ass," he spat, tugging at his two-hundred-buck REI rain parka. "Piece of shit."

Dispatched three weeks ago to Timbuk-fuckin'-tu, the chief engineer for *Darwin's Race* was not a happy man. Those suits at NBC expected him to lay cable, build relay towers, and construct a state-of-the-art television control studio. By Thursday. All in a place where electricity was as hard to find as a bar of soap.

No, Bill Greenback was not a happy man.

The simple beauty of Gompo Ne was utterly wasted on him. And he definitely didn't have time for the children that huddled around him like white on rice, tugging on him for candy and god-knows-what-else. He had shooed them off hours ago. He didn't have time to pause and pray at the sacred stone-and-mud *chorten* on a small rise overlooking the half dozen dilapidated structures in Gompo Ne. A series of mud-brick homes with corrugated tin roofs that rattled in the rain dotted the cheerlessly brown landscape, fronting a mud track that led up to his newly constructed tower. He paid the homes no mind.

He didn't even have time to glance east to the Confluence, the maelstrom that was the meeting place of the Po Tsangpo from the north and the Yarlung Tsangpo from the west. Though the sound of the collision between these two great and massive rivers roared with a never-ending ferocity over the village, Greenback did not have time to notice.

He had time for only one thing. Getting this relay station operable.

It was giving him fits and the cold and the rain, or whatever the hell it was, were not helping matters. His team had built the tower standing over the village like a steel sentinel and he and Eric Hill, his assistant engineer, had installed a wireless relay station. The station, one of a dozen erected throughout the inhabited reaches of the gorge, would serve to relay the signals from the racers' shoulder-mounted cameras to the control studio. Although most of his seventy-five-person crew were assembling the control studio at the starting line in Tumbatse, nearly thirty miles west, and planning for a forward production center on the flanks of Kuk Sur, Greenback was forced to troubleshoot.

His assistant engineer had just informed him, over a static-filled walkie-talkie, that this relay station was little more than a steel hunk of garbage. The dish was receiving the images; they could see them on the small black and white monitor installed at its base. But back in the control studio, Hill wasn't seeing shit. The relay station was anything but.

"What's a relay station that doesn't actually relay anything?" Greenback yelled into the walkie talkie. "It's a piece of shit!" *Just like this damn parka,* he didn't add. He didn't have to; his partner had already heard all about it.

"Have to go back to the truck," he mumbled to himself once he had climbed down the ladder to the ground. He held a scorched RG-6 cable, used to connect the antennae to the small computer at the base of the structure. "Look for something to replace this cheap piece of Japanese crap."

Pulling the hood over his already-drenched head, the chief engineer headed toward his Land Rover, parked below because it could not negotiate the hilltop perch of the relay tower. As he trudged into the muddy and eerily silent settlement, the curious faces of the dispersed children peered out from their windows. He pulled his hood tighter and walked on.

He quickly found a six-foot replacement cable in the back of the truck and pulled it from his gear bag, tossing the scorched one to the side. As he made his way back, he heard a voice call him out from a mud-and-wattle home along the dirt road. An ancient man, hunched and shriveled, was waving him over. The man looked to be over a hundred years old, with wrinkles crisscrossing his face like animal tracks.

In a hurry, Greenback would've ignored the old man but for what he held in his bony hands: a large ceramic cup, steam rising from it invitingly. Didn't know if it was tea or just steaming hot water; it really didn't matter; he needed something to warm him.

He approached cautiously. Stepped inside the man's home.

A small fire was burning in an open stone hearth in the corner of the small hut, flickering shadows against the dark walls. The warmth was astonishing and Greenback pulled off his hood. He accepted the steaming cup, thick yak milk flavored with sugar as it turned out, and sipped eagerly. The hot liquid coursed down his throat, through his chest and into his belly. Breathing in deeply, he felt revived.

The dwelling was sparse, just a simple wood table and chair upon a bare dirt floor. A white tapestry hung on the wall above the fire. A polished bronze prayer wheel sat beside the hearth. A low hatchway led to a second room, where Greenback could see a bundle of wool blankets piled on the floor.

The old man watched intently as the engineer stepped closer to the tapestry. It wasn't a rug, he realized. It didn't appear to be woven at all. In fact, it looked more like a pelt than anything. He couldn't be sure; he wasn't much of a hunter himself. He pointed at it. "Snow leopard?"

The man showed no sign of comprehension. Greenback gestured to the pelt again. "Animal?" he asked slowly.

The old man smiled, revealing a row of cracked, blackened teeth. "*Meh-toh*," the man croaked, pointing out the window, south toward the gorge. "*Kang-mi meh-toh*."

"I don't understand," Greenback said slowly, shrugging his shoulders. "*Kang-mi*? I don't know what that means."

"Grandfather is crazy."

Greenback started as a young man emerged from the back room. *Jesus Christ, where did he come from?* The boy appeared to be about ten, but it was so hard to be certain out here where the faces of the children were so weatherworn. He was barefooted, and he pulled a wool blanket around his shoulders.

"He is an old man with crazy thoughts," the boy continued. "He has been in the jungle too much."

"He's your grandfather?"

The boy nodded. The old man had fallen silent, shrinking into one of the room's shadowy recesses.

"You speak English?" Greenback asked.

"I not live here. I from Lhasa. Learn English there."

"Then maybe you can tell me about this. Is it some kind of animal?"

Just then, the old man unleashed a barrage of agitated speech, prattling at such a rapid pace Greenback couldn't tell when one word ended and another began. The old man was practically screeching. It took the boy a full minute to calm his grandfather.

"What was that all about?" the engineer asked.

"Do not listen. He crazy."

"Did he say where this pelt is from? What kind of animal?"

The boy paused a beat before answering. "He say it from the mountains. From a secret place."

"From the mountains? Snow leopard?"

The boy considered the engineer with large brown eyes that glistened in the firelight. "No leopard. This animal live in cave, move in darkness. Walk on two legs. Growls. Whistles."

As if he understood what his grandson was saying, the old man began to growl, an inhuman snarl meant to imitate the animal. The sound made Greenback shudder.

"Your grandfather said *metoh. Kang-mi metoh.* What does that mean?"

The boy shook his head. "He not speak well. *Metoh* is man-bear and *kang-mi* means snow. He say this is bear from the snows of the mountain. But there is no bears here. Grandfather is confused."

The old man emerged from the shadows and drew to within a few inches of the engineer. He extended a bony forefinger toward the white pelt.

"*Kang-mi,*" he whispered. "*Meh-toh.*"

The old man began to laugh, a creepy, haunting cackle that had Greenback inching toward the door. The boy intercepted his grandfather, hushing him and trying to usher the frenzied old man into the back room. The man's voice rose to a shrill, and Greenback stepped backwards out of the dwelling, keeping a constant watch upon the strange pair. Outside, he turned and marched hurriedly toward the broken relay tower.

What a loon, he said to himself. This place is filled with crazy. Then again, you'd have to be crazy to live way out here in the jungle, wouldn't you?

"*Kang-mi,*" the old man's voice lifted from the hut, following the retreating engineer like a curse. "*Kang-mi. Meh-toh! MEH-TOH!*"

The chief engineer walked on, never once looking back over his shoulder to the old man, whose disturbing cackle echoed through the deserted village of Gompo Ne like a warning siren.

CHAPTER TWELVE

Darwin's Race Base Camp
Tumbatse, Tibet

Eric Bailey would be turning over in his grave.

In 1913, the young botanist journeyed through Tibet, landing for a time in the village of Tumbatse. At twelve thousand feet, amidst a towering fir grove, Tumbatse proved to be a perfect base of operations for Bailey and his fellow travelers. The climate was more moderate than some of the villages east and south, and the alpine meadows that surrounded the village were bursting with spring flowers. It was a botanist's dream.

On a crisp summer afternoon, after hours of riding bareback over tough Tibetan terrain, Bailey collected a strange and beautiful poppy in a place called Nyima La, a series of grassy areas just outside Tumbatse. His journal entry for the day, in part, read, "Among the flowers were blue poppies I had not seen before."

Although notably brief in his expedition journal, Bailey had just discovered a completely new plant. On subsequent expeditions to Tibet explorers collected seedlings for *Meconopsis baileyi*, and upon their return to Britain the flower became a huge sensation. Eric Bailey became famous as its discoverer and *M. baileyi* earned awards from botanical societies across Europe. Its seedlings were sold for a record five pounds apiece at the 1927 Chelsea Garden Show.

Bailey's fields of blue poppies were no longer faring quite so well.

Three massive tents, each measuring forty feet long by twenty feet wide, were staked out amongst the fields. Without protective flooring inside the tents, the parade of boots of the *Darwin's Race* crew, support teams, producers, cameramen, and racers had long since smashed the delicate blue flowers into the thick Tibetan mud.

The thickly canvassed tents were rimmed with dozens of smaller tents for all sorts of race support: medical, facilities, gear storage, crew accommodations, sponsor tents, dining, restrooms, showers.

Trails of boot prints created muddy crisscrosses between the tents. The production tent, the largest structure on Bailey's field, sat on the north side of Tumbatse, on a small rise overlooking the crude tent village. A giant satellite dish, nearly twenty feet across, had been erected beside the makeshift studio. It pointed at the southern skies like a rocket ship, a bizarre attraction for the bewildered villagers.

A few miles away, the snowcapped peak of Gyala Peri jabbed over 23,000 feet into the air. Farther east loomed Namche Barwa, at 25,446 feet the highest peak in the eastern Himalayas. Buddhists believed the twin peaks formed the breasts of the Diamond Sow, the embodiment of the Dorje Pagmo, the Buddha's consort. The Tsangpo River, squeezed between the mountains, represented the spine of the great goddess.

Against this backdrop of man and nature, Conner Michaels leaned back in a collapsible camp chair, stretched his legs, and yawned. The tent for Team Providence had been set up like the others, gear to one side, tables of finger snacks on the other. Scattered throughout was an array of tables and chairs and cots for team meetings, interviews, and napping. A whiteboard stood in the corner. Someone had scrawled "Welcome to Tibet" across the top. Underneath, someone had added, "Where's the shit tent?"

The rest of the gear was gathered in a single, unmanageable pile, waiting to be sorted. Conner scooped a handful of trail mix from the snack table and shoveled it into his mouth. The raisins were frozen, and he let them thaw before chewing. The other members of his team shuffled about, keeping busy without actually accomplishing much of anything.

It was the calm before the storm.

The team had spent the first afternoon resting. The overland journey from Lhasa had been a bear, even for hardened racers accustomed to rough terrain. Now Conner could see their nervous energy bubbling to the surface. Everyone was eager for the start of the race. He, on the other hand, was eager for a nap. He tipped an Australian bush hat over his closed eyes and tried to relax. He felt himself drifting off when something nudged his chair.

He peeked up under the brim of his hat to see Shandi standing there, hands on hips. Her brow was furrowed in a half-worry, half-angry grimace. She looked like she had some serious questions to ask.

Along with Tess and Ian, Shandi and Thad had been teammates on Conner's final Eco-Challenge championship in 1999. The pair were intense competitors, fierce spirits fused with a carefree streak that managed to lighten even the most dire situations. Conner found the combination refreshing, and more than once had been pulled along by their seemingly bottomless supply of optimistic desire. They were perfect teammates.

Now, seeing the concern on Shandi's freckled face, Conner knew what was coming. His teammates had yet to ask about the altercation with Wade Stanley, and he certainly was in no mood to bring it up. But with the race poised to begin the next morning, clearing the air seemed inevitable.

"Shandi?" Conner said, stretching his arms over his head. "Got something on your mind?"

She waited a beat, staring at him as if the question was obvious.

"You want to talk about it?" she asked. "That scene on

the plane?"

"What about it?"

"Come on, Con. You know what I'm talking about. You haven't said word one about it since we landed. Don't you think you owe us an explanation? Or are we all supposed to just forget you almost punched Wade in the face?"

"But I didn't." The words sounded pitiful, even to Conner, so he quickly added, "He said something about Tucker. Something I didn't appreciate."

"Didn't appreciate, eh?" Her tone indicated that she didn't appreciate Conner's answer.

"What?"

"Do I have to say it? You're gonna make me spell it out? We're concerned about you. First, you hand out some bullshit about your reasons for entering the race. You want to keep that to yourself, fine. I can accept that. I hope it has something to do with Tucker, but that's your business. But that fight on the plane? That affects all of us." Shandi paused a moment, exhaling deeply. "I guess we just want to know that your head is completely in this race."

"You're speaking for the group?" he asked.

She nodded. "We've all seen it. You don't seem yourself."

Resigned to offering an explanation, Conner stood. "Then I'm going to say this once, and I want you to pass it along to the others. This shouldn't become a bigger issue than it needs to be."

In the end, Conner told her the truth. Mostly, at least.

Shandi already knew, of course, about Tucker's death and the effect it had had on him. She had joined the chorus of supporters telling him that it was just one of those things. A freak accident. Not his fault. So he told Shandi about his feelings of deep guilt, though he hardly needed to.

He told her how much his brother's death still played upon his conscience—how many times he had searched his mind for anything he could've done differently, how he wished he had been more insistent about going around that damn snow bridge. How he would do anything if it would just make everything better, told her that six years of feeling sorry for himself seemed like enough, that it was simply time to try something new, even told her that the re-opening of Kuk Sur by the Chinese government felt like karma, like the planets had aligned at just the right moment to spur him to action. He told her all of this in a burst of emotion that felt like his soul spilling forth—and when he was done, he was done. And he was ready.

Ready for the dense jungle, biting insects, blistering Himalayan winds. And finally, four years after leaving behind his brother's body somewhere on that mountain, he was ready to face his guilt on the very same icy slopes upon which it was born.

What he did not tell Shandi—and would not, if he could help it—was Malika's discovery of Tucker's wool cap. The same torn cap now stowed away inside Conner's backpack. Nor did he share his lingering suspicions of what really happened to his brother down in the dark crevasse.

Something's down here with me. I can't see it, but I can hear it breathing. The smell . . . Oh, Jesus—!

Some things would have to remain hidden.

After his conversation with Shandi, Conner called together the entire squad. Everyone scrambled to attention, eager to get started. Preston was there, his scruffy hair tucked into a gray wool cap that had seen better days. *Still carrying around his precious trekking poles,* Conner noted. Malika grabbed a seat right next to her father, dressed in well-worn trekking gear. Another sign she was no novice.

"Time to get this pile in shape," Conner said, pointing to the team equipment. "Since we have some new members on our little team here, I think it's time to go over our basic philosophy."

"Should I be taking notes?" Malika asked, smiling.

"Will this be on the test?" Thad teased.

Ian's arm shot up. "Mr. Michaels? Can I have a hall pass? I have to go to the bathroom."

"*Ian . . .*" Conner-as-professor admonished. He waited for the snickering to subside before continuing. "Alright, alright. My basic philosophy hasn't changed. Prepare your gear for every situation you can think of, and then prepare your mind for everything else. There's no way to anticipate what we're gonna run into out there, but we need to be ready for the unexpected."

"Uh, Mr. Michaels?" Ian said. "Isn't it true that you stole your sacred philosophy from the Boy Scouts? 'Be prepared,' right?"

"Hey, I never claimed originality." Conner knelt down beside the gear. "We'll each be carrying sixty or seventy pounds on our backs, so let's see if we can distribute the gear as evenly and fairly as possible."

According to the rules of *Darwin's Race*—now there was an oxymoron—each competitor could take whatever he or she wished. There were no restrictions other than the outright ban of maps or GPS devices. But unlike other races that allowed additional gear to be stored at strategic checkpoints throughout the course, all competitors had to carry all of their own gear from day one. Every team would have to be completely self-sustaining.

Each member sorted his or her personal items. Because *Darwin's Race* involved summiting the twenty-two thousand-foot Kuk Sur, everyone would have to haul some serious mountaineering equipment. Each person of Team Providence packed a polypropylene top and pants, a fleece layer, wool cap, headlamp, Gore-Tex waterproof down jacket, waterproof pants, Gore-Tex gloves, snow goggles, and a sturdy pair of plastic boots to fit over hiking boots once they encountered snow and ice. The gear list also included a sleeping bag, toothbrush, lip balm, compass, climbing harness, avalanche beacon, and extra socks.

To preserve precious space, the team would carry extra gear in pairs. Conner and Ian paired up, as did Thad and

Shandi and Preston and Malika. One of each pair would carry a first aid kit, a white-gas stove, and extra fuel, while the other hauled two eighty-foot lengths of rope, flares, and the food.

The fare was somewhat less than gourmet, consisting mainly of freeze-dried meals. They were largely tasteless, filling enough but, more importantly, lightweight. Without knowing how long this race was going to last—there was absolutely no reference for such an unsupported trek into unknown territory—the racers would carry ten of these packets, providing enough food for two full weeks. If the race lasted longer than that, food and water would have to be gathered along the way. Baggies of trail mix, protein bars, and other snacks were stowed away to complement the primary food.

In addition, trekking poles and an assortment of cara-biners, ascenders, chocks, and cams were lashed to each pack, along with a set of crampons. Conner and Preston would carry the extra weight of two heavy-duty tents.

Once all the gear had been checked, double-checked, and stowed, the backpacks were weighed. Shandi, Thad, Ian, and Malika would be carrying seventy-five pounds; Conner and Preston, five pounds more. Heavy for sure—heavier than any of them had ever carried into a race. And Conner's load was about to swell by exactly twelve pounds.

He had a secret weapon.

CHAPTER THIRTEEN

Darwin's Race Base Camp
Tumbatse, Tibet

"A raft?"

Conner looked around him at a sea of wide eyes and raised eyebrows. Ian's skeptical tone seemed to reflect what everyone else was thinking.

Conner had dragged a fully inflated whitewater raft into the Team Providence tent. It was large—a sixteen-foot self-bailing expedition model—with flip line and a series of tie-down straps around the perimeter of the raft. Two removable thwarts wedged tightly across the bottom. The skin was made of thick nylon, durable enough to glance off sharp rocks without puncturing.

"We'll each carry a collapsible paddle," Conner explained. "But with the strong current of the Tsangpo, we'll really only need them to steer."

His teammates looked at Conner like he had just announced they were paddling to Antarctica. Ian massaged
his temples as if he had a sudden migraine. Shandi and
Thad exchanged glances of disbelief. Only Preston and
Malika seemed nonplussed.

Conner sensed their apprehension. "What?"

"Uh, have you gone mad, man?" Ian asked.

"What do you mean?"

"The Tsangpo has a 'strong current,' huh?" he said, the
sarcasm dripping from his words like melting ice cream. "I
guess Everest is a 'bit high.' And the Pacific is 'kinda deep.'"

Shandi spoke up next. "The Tsangpo is virtually unrunnable. No one has ever done it. It's just too wild. And
Conner, you know me—I'm up for a good stretch of whitewater any day of the week, but come on. If Wick Walker
and his team couldn't make it—" Her voice trailed off, the
mood suddenly turning somber.

It had been in the fall of 1998. At the close of the
twentieth century, an end-to-end descent of the Tsangpo
River fired the imaginations of some of the best boaters in
the world, who saw in the foam and fury of the rapids the
ultimate whitewater challenge.

Five American whitewater experts, Wick Walker,
Doug Gordon, Tom and Jamie McEwan and Roger Zbel,
descended deep into the Tsangpo Gorge to the banks of
what many had dubbed "the Everest of rivers."

Swollen to three times the size they had expected,

the Tsangpo lived up to its fearsome reputation. Tossed, flipped, and generally manhandled, the team pressed forward. On day twelve of their expedition, Doug Gordon launched off an eight-foot waterfall and flipped. He and his overturned kayak spilled into the heart of the thunderous river and were swept downstream, never to be seen again.

The expedition was over.

"They didn't even make it to Gyala," Thad said. "They paddled maybe thirty miles of the, what, one hundred and forty-mile gorge? Plus, they had to portage huge chunks that were just too nasty to run. Now *we're* gonna do it? Come on, Conner. It's suicide."

"I read Wick's book," Shandi said. "That river is one nasty bitch. Whirlpools sucked the kayaks into giant holes. Some of them got flipped so fast they didn't even remember going over. Angle your body in the wrong place, and you tear all the muscles in your arm. That's how strong the current is."

Murmurs of assent rose from the others.

"I hear you, I hear you," Conner said. "Let me explain to you why I think it will work. Come on, everyone, get in the raft."

Tentatively, they did as they were told, assuming positions within the raft.

"First off, this raft is infinitely more stable than the play boats those guys were using. Look, there's room in here for all six of us. Comfortably. Plus plenty of room for our packs. It's like on the Gauley during high water, after the dam is released. The only safe way to run it is with a heavy fourteen-foot raft. With that many people, that much weight, it's almost impossible to flip."

His teammates looked unconvinced, so Conner moved on to point number two. "Wick and the rest of his team put in at Pe. They wanted to hit the rough stuff between Pe and Gyala. That was why they had come to Tsangpo in the first place."

"But that's not what we're doing?" Shandi asked cautiously.

"No. Here, take a look at this." Conner climbed out of the raft and moved to the whiteboard. He quickly erased the gear checklist and drew what looked like a steep bell curve across the board. In the center of the curve, under the hump, he sketched a triangle and labeled it "NB." A second triangle, this one marked "KS," was added along the right side of the descending bell curve.

"This line is the river. It starts out here at Pe, then heads north past Gyala, up to the Confluence where it meets the Po River, doubling its flow. Then it heads south, down through Gande, right past Kuk Sur."

"What's the triangle there in the middle?" Shandi asked.

"Namche Barwa. But I'll come back to that. So instead of putting in at Pe, like Wick, we'll overland from Tumbatse to Pe, then up past Gyala. We'll put in just after Pemakochung. That way, we'll miss all the real nasty stuff. We'll raft up to the Confluence on relatively calm waters. If we can keep going, we keep going. If it gets too rough, we ferry. If we have to portage sections, we portage. Believe me: safety is my primary concern here. But this is the fastest way to get to the base of Kuk Sur."

"How can you be so sure?" Shandi asked.

"Good question. For the past two weeks, I've pored over all the maps and guides I could find about the Tsangpo Gorge. I read Baker's journals, Bailey's field notes. I even got my hands on some satellite images that show the topography pretty clearly. And I kept coming back to the same conclusion."

"Are you going to share?" Ian asked.

"The gorge is almost impenetrable. The jungle is just too thick. There's a reason the Tibetans steer clear. We could spend days hacking through there and advance only a few miles. It would take us weeks to get all the way through."

"You're not exactly inspiring confidence here," Thad said.

"If there's one thing I've learned from adventure racing—and some of you can back me up on this—it's that the terrain dictates the course. If the gorge is as nasty as I think it is, there may be only one navigable route through it."

Conner could practically see the light bulb illuminate above Ian's head. "That means we'll be up Wade's ass the whole way."

"That's right," Conner nodded. "The terrain will almost certainly force the teams together. We'll never spread out enough to get a lead. That's why the river is a better option. The other team won't even think to run Tsangpo—"

"Because they're not out to kill themselves!" interrupted Thad.

"They won't run it," Conner continued. "They'll overland to Pe, because by now we all know there's a rope bridge there. Then they'll trek out overland again, cutting through the gorge. But that means they'll run straight into Namche Barwa. The mountain will slow them down. If we raft from Pemakochung all the way down to Kuk Sur, we can get there way before North Face. And once we hit the flanks of Kuk Sur, it's anybody's game. The key is to get started solving the mountain before Wade and the others do."

Ian studied Conner's crude map. "But rafting from Pema to the Confluence means we'll have to shoot Rainbow Falls!"

"Not to mention Hidden Falls," Thad interjected.

Ian continued, nodding. "That's not even possible, is it? I mean, those rapids are killers! Twenty clicks of foam and drops. And who knows what's beyond Hidden? It could get even worse. You know the legends."

Indeed, Conner did. The legends of a waterfall hidden deep within the gorge were well known in the exploring community. Whispers of a waterfall greater than Niagara's one hundred sixty-seven feet, greater even than Africa's three hundred-feet Victoria Falls, had echoed for generations.

Explorers had searched for Hidden Falls for centuries. The existence of the legendary falls had been presumed through simple mathematics. The one hundred fifty-mile stretch between the Pemakochung Monastery to where the Tsangpo emptied into the Brahampotan plains in northern India dropped over nine thousand feet, thirty times steeper than the Grand Canyon. An altitude drop of such magnitude could only be attained with a series of cascades. But for decades, no one had ever laid eyes upon a single waterfall.

In 1885, celebrated plant hunter Francis Kingdon-Ward set out to solve what he called the "riddle" of the Tsangpo: How could it lose so much elevation so rapidly if not for a major waterfall? After two weeks of hiking in miserable conditions, Kingdon-Ward discovered what later came to be called Rainbow Falls. Gazing up at the seventy-five-foot cascade, Kingdon-Ward scribbled his assessment into his journal: *"Worthy, but certainly inferior to the falls that must lie below."*

Mudslides and an outbreak of malaria in his crew forced Kingdon-Ward to turn back, but he remained convinced of the existence of the so-called Hidden Falls. *"The source of the Nile has been determined,"* he wrote in his memoirs. *"The Poles have been achieved. The search for the Hidden Falls of the Tsangpo must be the last great romance of geography."*

For almost a century, the river valley remained virtually impenetrable. In 1967, an intrepid explorer named Ian Baker picked up the search for mystical waterfall. Leading a group of hearty trekkers, Baker pushed past Rainbow Falls and on one quiet afternoon spotted the telltale spray of a large waterfall.

Baker inched out along a steep cliff to peer down the valley. From his precarious vantage point, he could just make out a sliver of the river where it dropped from view. The force of the falls resulted in a heavy mist that rose well above the rainforest canopy. Attempting to push on, Baker did not make it far. The jungles were impassably dense, and the cliffs on either side of the river were as sheer as ice. Baker snapped a photograph of his waterfall but could move no farther into the valley.

Ultimately, Baker declared his waterfall the Hidden Falls of legend. He also came away believing that the waterfall represented a portal to the gorge's innermost secret realm.

But the realm was destined to remain secret. After haggling and credit-taking (a Chinese team of scientists also claimed to have discovered Hidden Falls a year earlier), China grew tired of the controversy and closed the gorge at the same time they closed the Kukuranda. The gorge below Hidden Falls would remain terra incognita. A blank spot on the map. A place of myth.

Yes, Conner Michaels knew the legends.

"If we encounter falls we can't run," Conner said, "we'll just go around. And if we can't skirt around, we'll just dump the raft and continue overland. No harm, no foul."

"If that happens, we'll be stranded miles north of the other team," noted Thad. "North Face will be cutting directly across. We'll have given them a huge head start.

"It's true we will ultimately travel farther," Conner

conceded. "But if we can stay in the raft—and I believe we can—we'll be traveling faster and without these eighty-pound loads on our backs. By the time we reach Kuk Sur, we'll be fresher than the others."

Conner looked at his teammates and still saw a lineup of hesitant faces. Preston was studying the makeshift map intensely, tracing the path of the river in the air with his thick finger. He whispered something to Malika, who nodded.

"I think this is going to work," Conner said. "But I want to hear what you think, too."

Preston stood and climbed out of the raft. "I knew I had made the right choice for captain of this team," he said. "I think this plan is brilliant. It's like a highway right to the mountain. While the other team toils away through the thick jungle, we can follow the river directly to Kuk Sur. I think I speak for everyone here when I say: we trust the judgment of our captain."

Conner studied the others. "Is everyone in agreement then? We'll put in at Pema? Give this old raft a try?"

Ian was the first, but eventually, all nodded agreement. Conner knew his team well enough to see that they had worked through their anxiety and would commit them-selves totally to the plan. All traces of apprehension would be gone once the race began.

Or so he hoped.

All twelve racers, along with the support crew and several dozen members of the production staff, gathered in the communal mess tent for a final send-off dinner. The carb-loaded spaghetti dinner with plenty of meatballs and garlic bread doubled as an excuse for another press conference and tripled as a final equipment check.

Terrance Carlton and his crew had banked *Darwin's Race* on the capabilities of twelve shoulder-mounted cameras, a dozen relay stations, and a satellite uplink that had required a team of engineers working around-the-clock to assemble. Now that the cameras had been tested, and a trial broadcast had been transmitted successfully back to NBC headquarters in New York, Carlton wanted to make sure his production didn't come crumbling down because of operator error.

The cameras were manufactured behind the concept of "no operator needed," a marvel of miniature engineering, contained entirely in a sturdy four-inch-long weatherproof casing with ultra low light capabilities for nighttime imaging. The apparatus was mounted to a harness easily worn around a competitor's right shoulder like a holster. Flat batteries, specially made for *Darwin's Race* by Duracell—another sponsor eager to cash in on the event—lined the harness, but they were needed only for backup. The top of the camera was a solar panel that would provide power during daylight hours. To prevent energy depletion—and monotonous video imaging during downtimes—each device was also outfitted with a motion sensor. Any movement within the range of the motion detector—roughly fifty meters— would activate the camera. A tiny antenna built into the mounting apparatus would automatically beam the image out into the sky, where it would be picked up by one of the relay stations in the gorge. The station would then enhance the image and relay it to production control in Tumbatse, then up to a satellite orbiting hundreds of miles above the earth, where it could be broadcast directly into the homes of 250 million Americans and countless millions more watching worldwide.

All in a matter of seconds.

Carlton held one of the cameras in his hand and was displaying it to those gathered in the tent. First to the media, making sure they got their requisite close-ups, then to the racers, who didn't much care.

"I can't stress this point enough," he said. "The camera apparatus must be worn at all times. Failure to wear the camera will result in a team's automatic and irrevocable elimination. In fact, the Chinese government has made it a requirement for entrance into the gorge."

Conner looked up at this. *Vintage Carlton,* he thought. *Get the Chinese government to mandate the use of cameras for your own benefit. Clever.* As if to accentuate Carlton's point, four soldiers from the Chinese Red Army armed with automatic rifles were patrolling the perimeter of the tent. Utterly unnecessary but compelling visuals for the television cameras.

"As you can see, the camera is small, lightweight—it weighs less than eight ounces—and I think you will all rather get used to it after the first day or so."

"What if it breaks?" asked Cale Anders from Team North Face. "Are we supposed to fix the damn thing?"

"They will not break," Carlton answered. "We have tested these things under all sorts of nasty conditions. We tested a prototype at Muddy Buddy last April. No problems whatsoever."

The racers still looked unconvinced.

"However, I do realize that the terrain you all will be heading into tomorrow morning is largely uncharted," Carlton conceded. "Therefore, each team captain will carry one spare camera on them at all times." Groans filled the tent. "Now, now. A few more ounces is surely not going to hinder anyone's progress. I don't believe the outcome of this race will hinge upon a tiny extra camera."

"Is it waterproof?" asked Ian, who immediately regretted the question. He didn't want to betray Team Providence's plan to spend much of the race running the mighty Tsangpo. "We will have to do some river crossings," he added, attempting subterfuge.

Carlton nodded. "Absolutely waterproof. To a depth of thirty meters."

Someone else asked, "What about audio? How does that work?"

"Here," Carlton said, pointing to a pinhole microphone.

"We did have to sacrifice audio quality to maintain the camera's small size, but we will enhance it anyway once we downlink the feed. But just in case, if there's something important you need to relay to us, make sure you write it down. In the snow, in the dirt, it doesn't matter. That way, we won't have to worry about faulty audio."

Conner tuned out as the executive producer ran through some of the other technical details and basic camera troubleshooting. Tess was seated a few rows away, surrounded by her North Face teammates. This would be the last time he would see her before the start of the race. The final opportunity to apologize for the scene on the plane.

She was listening to Carlton, eyes and ears focused squarely on the producer in the center of the tent. In profile, the lines of her face appeared as if painted by a Renaissance master. The intricate brush strokes of blonde hair dangling just in front of her eyes. The porcelain-perfect skin of her forehead. The gentle slope to a dimpled nose. The deep gray-blue in her eyes that shone even in the relative darkness of the cool Tibetan evening. Her mouth was perfect, her lips rose red, full and supple, and they glistened in the overhead light. Botticelli would have been proud.

Christ, Conner. Get your head into the game here.

She must have felt the weight of his stare, for she glanced instinctively toward Conner. Embarrassed for a moment, he maintained a steady gaze. Her eyes met his, and for a moment, lingered.

He moved his lips soundlessly, mouthing, "Can we

talk?" She glanced down at her hands in her lap. She was fidgeting, Conner noticed, nervous. With a quick glance toward Wade, who was sitting beside her, she once again met Conner's look. Slowly, she shook her head. *I don't think that's a good idea*, she mouthed.

He wanted to continue their silent conversation, but she had refocused her attention on Carlton. Conner stared at her, hoping she could sense him. He cleared his throat. Then again, louder. Others glanced his way, but Tess did not turn.

It sounded like Carlton was finishing up.

"If you require anything from the medical tent, I suggest you stock up tonight," he was saying. "Final gear check will be made by the producers first thing in the morning. After that, you won't be able to add anything. That's all for tonight."

He turned from the competitors to the media cameras huddled in one corner of the mess tent. "*Darwin's Race* will begin promptly at eight tomorrow morning. All teams will be available for final interviews beginning at seven. Competitors are to be locked, loaded, and ready for a gear check at half past six. Breakfast will be served here beginning at six—if you think you can keep the food down." He laughed at his own joke. Adventure racers were notorious for regurgitating their pre-race food. Even rock-hard competitors felt the flutter of butterflies before an event.

"I suggest that all of you get some sleep," Carlton concluded. "Tonight may be your last chance. Good night."

Conner tried to push his way through the crowd to Tess without making it obvious, but Ian intercepted him immediately. "Con, we need to head over to see the doc. I want to load up on some Cipro and grab a few bottles of Diamox. I don't know about this Tibetan water. There's a lot of yak roaming around up here around the stream."

Conner ignored the joke, and instead scanned the room for Tess. She had gone, vanishing into the crowd. What was most likely his final opportunity to speak to her had passed. After all, there wasn't much chance they would run into each other in the million-acre Tsangpo Gorge. He tried to push her from his mind; focus on the task at hand.

"Okay," he said, turning back to Ian. "Let's go see the doc."

That night, Conner did not sleep. And the fading din from the camp was not the sole culprit. Next to him, Ian was breathing heavily. Shandi and Thad had bunked out in a private tent, relishing one final night alone together. Father and daughter Preston and Malika had retreated to separate bunks. Everyone knew it would be their last chance to sleep alone without sharing cramped tent space with a partner's muddy boots, grubby backpack and loud altitude-induced snoring.

Usually able to sleep even under atrocious conditions—hell, Conner once endured a forced bivouac on an

icy six-inch ledge on Annapurna for three stormy nights—
slumber would not come this evening. Whether it was the
situation with Tess or something else, Conner's eyes would
not close. On his back, he stared at the top of his tent.

He tried to think about the two million-dollar prize.
Melanie and Jake could sure use the money. As for himself,
he didn't really care one way or the other. He'd give most
of it to them—maybe keeping some to fix a swath of loose
planks on his dock. The money was not the reason he had
returned to face Kuk Sur.

He tried to think about the prospect of an historic first
ascent. It would certainly ensure his name on a short list
of alpine legends. But neither the prize nor the glory had
drawn him back to Kuk Sur, and it failed again to occupy
his attention for very long.

The truth was that he needed *Darwin's Race*. In 1985,
during his first ascent of Rainier, Conner had experienced a
full-bore mystical illumination. Standing atop the mountain, a wave of certainty had washed over his entire body.
Later, he told friends the ascent had given him "a basis for
proceeding." Somehow, the experience had stripped away
the superfluous refuse of life, crystallizing what was important. Conner had read about this phenomenon. It had
something to do with oxygen depletion and brain waves
and how the body adapted to harsh conditions by shutting
down everything that wasn't absolutely vital.

Conner wasn't sure about the science bit, but he knew
for sure it was a feeling he was utterly unable to duplicate

anywhere near sea level. After the accident on Kuk Sur, Conner had felt rudderless. Returning to the mountains, Conner hoped for another glimpse inside himself.

So what then was this strange feeling, like a thick knot in the pit of his stomach, keeping him awake on the eve of the greatest adventure race in history? It was a feeling he had not experienced before and the more Conner stared at the roof of his tent, the more the knot tightened, like a boa constrictor around its prey.

It felt like dread.

"Hello, stranger."

Conner turned at the sound of the voice, surprised to see Malika standing there beside him. She was dressed in a snug layer of thin fleece that highlighted her curves. He was struck anew by her natural beauty.

"Malika?"

"I see I'm not the only one who can't sleep."

Conner made some room on his cot. "Sit down. Your dad's snoring finally get to you?"

She smiled widely, a cute dimpled thing. "Just pre-race jitters, I guess. What's your excuse?"

He considered lying to her, avoiding the subject, diverting her attention to something else more pleasant. But he decided on a more straightforward approach. Truth.

"Thinking of my brother," he said. "Melanie and Jake. His wife and son. Did you know he had a family?"

Malika nodded. "Yes. I can't imagine what that must've been like for them. Or you."

Conner weighed his next words carefully. "Why did you lie to me about how you found Tucker's cap?"

He watched her carefully for a reaction. For a fleeting moment, Malika looked away. Swallowed hard. But just as quickly, she regained her composure. "How did you know?"

"You said you were part of a tour group trekking up the Tsangpo near the Kukuranda. The Chinese government requires a licensed guide to enter that area, and there's only one outfit with the credentials. Yak Tail Treks. The owner just happens to be an old buddy of mine so I called him up to check you out. He had no record of you on any of his treks."

"If you knew all this, why didn't you bring it up sooner?"

"I was hoping you would beat me to it."

"You knew I had lied, but you're still here. Why?"

"Because the hat definitely belonged to Tucker. You must have found it somewhere. At the time, that was good enough for me."

"And now?"

"Now I'd like to know the truth."

Malika exhaled. "I did find the hat in a cave, just like I told you. You have to believe that. But I wasn't trekking with a tour group. I was with my father."

"Go on."

"And we weren't south of the Kukuranda. We were in the middle of them."

"That's impossible. That area is restricted, guarded by

Chinese soldiers."

"My father knows his way around these mountains. We slipped past the outposts."

A dozen questions swam inside Conner's head. *How does Preston know his way around the Kukuranda? Why hadn't he mentioned that fact earlier? And if he had already explored the region, why had he been so insistent on getting Conner to captain the second race team?*

Another question occurred to him. "Why the Kukuranda? There are plenty of other treks in the Himalayas. Why risk getting caught?"

Malika didn't answer immediately. Conner felt her shift nervously beside him, once again turning away from his gaze. *What was she hiding?*

"Malika?"

"You sure do ask a lot of questions."

"I just want to know the truth. I think you owe me that much."

She paused a full moment before speaking again. "My father and I had spent a lot of time in Tibet. We even trekked to Everest base camp. But we had always honored the sanctity of the Kukuranda. Then, one day he just decided he had to see it—experience it—for himself."

Because it's there, Conner thought. It was the same reason he'd been drawn to Kuk Sur six years earlier. The fact that he could relate to Preston's reason gave it the ring of truth.

"Where exactly was this cave? The one where you

found Tucker's hat?"

"You want to see it."

"I think I need to."

"It's in the northern foothills of Kuk Sur, around fifteen thousand. My father thinks it was a drainage point for a larger system. There were signs of water erosion all over the entrance of that cave. Your brother's hat probably washed down from some other cave farther up into the mountain."

For a few moments, neither said a word.

Malika rose from the cot. "Conner, I'm sorry about what happened to your brother. I hope I made the right decision by bringing you the cap. I didn't mean to bring up such a painful subject."

Conner managed a thin smile. "I know that," he said. "Now you'd better get back to your own cot. Race starts in a few hours."

Before she left, Malika leaned close and kissed Conner's cheek. Her lips were soft and warm against his skin. She left without another word, leaving Conner to toss and turn without sleep.

A few hours later, daylight peeked into Conner's tent.

CHAPTER FOURTEEN

Darwin's Race Base Camp
Tumbatse, Tibet

Tumbatse was a whirlwind.

A banner arced over the starting line, black block letters proclaiming "The Race Is On," decorated with balloons and sponsor logos. Underneath, media, crew members, support teams, and cameramen scurried about for last-minute interviews, preparations, and live shots.

It was 7:30 in the morning. Thirty minutes before the start of *Darwin's Race*.

Conner Michaels squinted through his wraparound sunglasses into the already bright Tibetan sun and breathed in the cool, crisp Himalayan air. He wore black trekking pants, wool cap, boots, and a long-sleeved gray micro-fiber shirt, pulled tightly across his muscular frame. The hiking gear was mostly misdirection, of course. If all went as planned, Team Providence would change into river wear in a few hours once they reached Pemakochung.

Conner's teammates were dressed similarly, light and comfortable for the relatively temperate climate of the lower elevations. As they pushed up Kuk Sur, they would start layering up.

A reporter rushed up to Conner, brandishing a microphone. A television camera materialized behind the young, smartly dressed woman.

"Conner Michaels, what do you think of your chances against Team North Face?" she asked. "As you know, Wade Stanley is the early favorite."

Conner grinned. "There are no favorites out here," he said. "I'm pretty sure Mother Nature will treat us all just about the same. If I were a betting man, I'd put my money on Her."

"Does that mean you don't think anyone will complete this race?" the reporter pressed.

"Let's put it this way: the only way any of these teams will finish is if the elements allow us to finish. Our team realizes that we are at the mercy of this valley and that mountain." He pointed east, toward the distant peak of Kuk Sur. "If we reach the top, it will be because we adapted to what nature threw at us. But being prepared is not enough, nowhere near enough. We'll need a fair bit of luck as well."

The reporter was about to ask another question, but

Conner dismissed her with a polite "thank you" and walked on toward Team Providence's pre-designated starting position.

Ian jogged to catch up. "Is that supposed to be some kind of a pep talk?" he asked loudly. "We need luck to win? Can't win without luck?" He shook his head in mock exasperation. "What happened to all that 'be prepared' stuff?"

A disembodied voice echoed in the air over a blaring loudspeaker. "Racers, please assume your starting positions. *Darwin's Race* will begin in three minutes."

The starting line cleared a bit, as the twelve competitors gathered together. Game faces on, the teams did not mingle, even though they were only a few meters apart. Teammates, if they spoke at all, did so under their breaths.

Terrance Carlton appeared, flanked by the television host of *Darwin's Race*, a smooth-faced guy who looked vaguely familiar.

"Ladies and gentleman," the host announced dramatically. "Welcome to *Darwin's Race*. In a few minutes, twelve of the most daring and experienced adventure racers on the planet will embark on a journey through a Tibetan gorge that is virtually unexplored. If all goes well, these two teams will emerge on the other end of the gorge and begin their assault on the mountain known as Kuk Sur. This mountain, towering at over twenty-two thousand feet, has never been summited. The rules of *Darwin's Race* are simple: there are none. The first team to reach the summit of Kuk Sur will be named the winner of *Darwin's Race,* and I will personally present them with a check in the amount of two million dollars!"

A roar of approval from the racers forced a pause. He turned to face a television camera. "And now, to officially get this race underway, here is the producer of *Darwin's Race*, Mr. Terrance Carlton!"

Carlton nodded to the host and took the microphone. "*Darwin's Race* is a race for these twelve men and women," he said, gesturing to the gathered teams. "But ultimately it is more than that. It is a contest against nature itself. Since the beginning of time, man has battled the elements, attempting to conquer the unconquerable. *Darwin's Race* represents nothing less than the penultimate challenge of a fight that has waged for eons. Man versus nature.

"Adventure racing is the greatest sport on this planet— and these adventurers are the best this discipline has to offer. We are in for one hell of a ride—and I'm just as anxious to watch it as the millions watching around the world. So, without further ado, let's get this race started. Racers, please gear up!"

The individual team members hoisted their packs upon their backs, aided by support crew. After a six-year layoff, Conner realized his eighty-pound pack felt more like seven hundred.

"Racers, approach the starting line!"

The expedition teams approached the starting line, toeing yellow duct tape stuck to the dusty Tibetan ground. Conner grinned at the scene. *Darwin's Race* would take days to complete—even if they survived their "end-around" gamble on the Tsangpo—and here were twelve intelligent adults, inching their toes forward as close to the yellow line as possible as if a half-inch at the beginning would somehow translate into victory at the finish.

Carlton bellowed into the microphone, and his voice echoed over base camp.

"Racers, on your marks!"

Conner looked down the line, searching for Tess. It could be the last time he saw her. The gorge was a large place with plenty of hiding places. He just wanted to catch her eye one last time.

"Get set!"

Wade Stanley was blocking his view. Apparently grasping what Conner was trying to do, Wade leaned forward, obliterating any hope he had of catching a final glimpse. Resisting the urge to knock that damned grin right off his manicured face, Conner instead dropped his head to stare at the starting line.

Time to get focused, he told himself. *You have a race to complete. Just put her out of your mind.*

Terrance Carlton's voice echoed over the loudspeakers. *"GO!"*

PART TWO

CHAPTER FIFTEEN

Team Providence
Tsangpo Gorge

Team Providence's introduction to the foothills of the Himalaya was a surprising one. As they descended toward the gorge, the racers found themselves in an unexpectedly lush valley.

The dense underbrush of the Tsangpo Gorge was a veritable horticultural omnibus of the Himalaya, remnants of tropical rain forest yielding stands of rhododendron and magnolia with scatterings of exotic trees completely foreign to American eyes. The understory was a thorny thicket of wild rose and Asian barberry and mayapple. Hundreds of feet over their heads, creepers, vines, and lianas formed a green canopy that cast the forest floor in muted shadow.

After four hours of heavy slogging from Tumbatse

over the pass at Nyima La down to the steep banks of the Tsangpo, Conner ordered an early rest stop beside the bamboo footbridge that spanned the river at Pe. Team Providence munched on some granola and watched Wade Stanley and the rest of Team North Face march across the bridge. Just before disappearing into the jungle on the far side, Wade looked back with a smirk.

Go right ahead, Conner thought. *Asshole.*

God, how he wished he could be there to see the look on Wade's face when he realized Team Providence was pulling an end-around on the river. From his vantage point atop a rocky bluff, he peered across the valley. When it came to orienteering, his mind was already clicking through standard terrain assessments. Difficulty of mountains, possibilities of portage, distance and elevation, soils, annual rainfall, drainage, the predominant flora and fauna, availability of forage, presence of minerals, proximity of salt, date the river would close with ice and the date it would open anew in the spring. Most racers never approached this level of detail in their planning—certainly not the new breed of blind adventurers who found pleasure in jumping into a foreign environment unaware—but to Conner the knowledge was invaluable. Besides, after years of competitive racing, it was the only way he knew.

Sticking to their plan, Team Providence slipped north, following the Tsangpo toward Gyala. They were trekking along the same stretch of river where Doug Gordon had given his life in 1998, and each of them was more than happy to be bypassing this death zone from the safety of solid ground.

Just outside Gyala, Conner climbed a flat boulder that afforded views of the river valley below. It was early afternoon, and it had been hours since he'd lost sight of North Face.

"What do you think, Ian?" he asked.

In addition to being a seasoned adventure racer, Ian was the resident rafting expert. He had served as a whitewater guide on the Gauley for years and for Shearwater on the mighty Zambezi for a full season, rafting by day, drinking African Tusker by night. He had experienced high water and low and was convinced he would never again see whitewater as ferocious as the African monster.

The look on Ian's face as he surveyed the river told Conner everything he needed to know. Astonished at the sight of six-foot standing waves, eight-foot ledges, and swirling holes into which water—and anything else— disappeared, never to reappear again, Ian was clearly reevaluating the plan to run the river. Judging from this stretch of water, it would be sheer madness.

"Jesus-H-Christ," he said, shaking his head. "Suddenly, the Zambezi at high water is looking pretty tame. Paddle or no paddle, we're in for some swimming."

Conner's confidence was rarely shaken; still he tried never to let pure bravado lead him into poor decisions. The river would be rough, but he had faith in his team, and the raft itself was sturdy.

"It looks bad; I'll give you that. But it'll look different

once we get closer."

Ian laughed. "Yeah, it'll look ten times worse!"

They passed through Gyala without stopping. The villagers paid them little mind—as if the sight of six strangely dressed white people tramping through their village were an everyday occurrence. A few hours later, Team Providence gazed upon the majestic—and deserted—Pemakochung monastery.

The monastery was a shadow of its former grandeur.

In 1950, the most powerful earthquake of the twentieth century rocked the gorge. The Assam Earthquake registered a magnitude of 8.6 and crumbled the monastery, once an important center of Buddhism. A decade and a half later, the destruction of the monastery was completed by the invading Red Army of China. It had sat empty ever since.

The dilapidated building, paint peeling on towering spires, sat at an elevation of eighty-five hundred feet. The small village that surrounded the monastery enjoyed a relatively mild climate. Several village children, swathed in broad robes made of handwoven wool and fastened about their waists with brightly colored cloth belts, ran out to meet their guests.

Two boys approached Conner, tugging on his sleeve, running grubby hands over his backpack.

"What do they want, Con?" Ian asked.

"Pens, candy bars, anything really. Wish I had something to give them."

"How about a shiny new raft? It's not too late to call off our little river trip, you know."

Conner chuckled. "It's not like you to be scared, Ian."

"Not scared. Just trying to spare us some unnecessary swimming."

A crowd of children had gathered around Malika. Conner watched as she playfully tussled their hair, and was struck at how easily she seemed to blend in with them. The boys and girls surrounded her like bees to honey, talking rapidly in a language Conner didn't recognize.

Then his jaw dropped.

Malika began to talk back—without a hint of accent. The children jabbered excitedly around her. She pointed toward the river, prompting another animated exchange.

Ian, whose own mouth was also agape, tapped Conner on the shoulder. "That beautiful, with a body like that, *and* she speaks fluent Chinese? Where'd you find this girl?"

Conner waited for Malika to extricate herself from her young friends before approaching. "What was that all about?" Conner asked. "You didn't tell me you knew Chinese."

"Actually, it's a Tibetan dialect unique to the gorge," she corrected. "But, yes, I speak Chinese as well."

"You're full of surprises. Any other hidden talents I should know about?"

Malika smiled coyly. "None that will do us any good out here."

"So, what were they saying?" Ian asked.

"It's interesting," Malika said. "They were asking where we were going, so I told them that we were going to go down the river. Well, they seemed shocked at this.

Started calling the river by a word I'm not familiar with. *Beyul*. Any ideas what that means?"

Conner nodded. "I know the word from some books I've read about the Himalaya. It means 'sacred place.' There's a tradition that tells of dozens of hidden valleys throughout the mountains, scattered by the Indian yogin who brought Buddhism to Tibet in the eighth century. Anyway, some of these ancient Buddhist texts tell of these *beyul*, places of mystical retreat, pilgrimage, and refuge during times of great strife. Only a *terton*, a 'treasure finder,' can find and open a genuine *beyul*. Supposedly, some of these hidden valleys are still hidden. The local people believe that their discovery awaits the proper time. Neat little story, huh?"

Malika shrugged. "Myth or not, these kids really believe we are headed for trouble. I guess they don't consider us real 'treasure finders.'"

Suddenly, the children exploded with excitement, climbing all over the expedition team, jabbering wildly. Even Malika was having trouble keeping up. The children pointed to the river below and Conner followed their line of vision toward the Tsangpo.

Something was on the river. From this distance, it was little more than a black speck upon raging whiteness. But Conner knew what it was.

"No—" he breathed.

❀ ❀ ❀

Team North Face
Tsangpo Gorge

"Hold on!"

The River Tsangpo bucked Team North Face's raft like
an angry bull. Wade's pleas were drowned out by five thousand pounds of liquid fury, but it hardly mattered. Tess,
Blaine, Cale, Hoops, and Powder already grasped the rope
supports as if their lives depended on it.

And they just might, Tess thought. A wave smashed to
starboard. She gripped the ropes tighter and clenched her
eyes shut.

Team North Face had put in at Pe as soon as Team
Providence was out of sight. Wade Stanley had come up
with the idea of rafting the Tsangpo, and convincing the
others had been little more than a simple matter of inform-
ing them about his plan. His team was not a democracy.

In any event, the others had eagerly agreed. The
raft was sound, solid, and strong at sixteen feet, and each
team member had rafted big rivers before. It seemed like
a logical—and fast—route to the base of Kuk Sur and for
the first mile or so, they enjoyed paddling over the various
Class III and IV rapids, laughing and generally enjoying
the swift ride.

The river's profile, they discovered, was classic pool-

and-drop. Every few miles a large rapid appeared, followed by a flat but quick-flowing section of water. At the beginning, the drops were steep but runnable—all in the three to four feet range—and the raft easily managed to stay upright.

They had avoided even a single portage, the dreaded task of dragging the raft around a rapid, often over slippery and sharp rocks. The water would have to be particularly gnarly to incite a portage, as kayakers and rafters universally detested them. They swore that more injuries occurred during these walkabouts than on the water itself, and they were often right. Sprained ankles and bloody feet were common—and, in rare instances, there were even broken bones.

Halfway between Pe and Gyala, the ride had turned treacherous.

Each member knew the river was turning steeper, the horizon line advancing rapidly as the river shot down the canyon. Even Wade felt uncomfortable at being blind on such a churning waterway; he started to roll his neck muscles. Tess knew from experience that meant he was nervous.

But there were no options. The embankments on either side were thick with vegetation, and portages were all but impossible. There was no stopping now.

The six members of Team North Face held on and prayed.

"Here we go!" Wade warned.

The raft slammed into a ten-foot standing wave, the water at once crashing forward and then churning back under itself creating a perpetual keeper hole. Seated in the bow, Tess could see down into the hole twelve feet below. As they rode the crest, the back of the boat lifted clear of the river, threatening to nosedive into the roiling abyss. Tess slipped forward, her entire upper body dangling overboard. In an effort to regain balance, she swiped at the water with her paddle. She met nothing but air. Clenching her eyes shut, she braced for the plunge.

Miraculously, the back of the boat flattened at the last second and the raft squirted over the churning hole. A smaller craft—a kayak playboat for instance—would've certainly been stuck in the hole, regurgitating itself over and over and over.

Team North Face exhaled a collective sigh of relief as their boat drifted in the pool that followed the drop.

"Maybe it's time to take a breather," Blaine suggested. "This is some pretty wild stuff. What do you say, Wade?"

But Wade Stanley was not listening. His eyes were wide and fixed firmly on the river before them, his facial muscles tighter than ever.

"Too late," he said. "Ladies and gentlemen, I suggest you hold on."

In an instant, all six members of Team North Face knew they were in trouble. They scrambled to latch onto the rope lining along the perimeter of the raft as Wade screamed again, "Hang on!"

Riding a collapsing wave, the next thirty meters of the Tsangpo opened up before them in all its raging glory. The lush vegetation lining the banks suddenly gave way to steep rock channels as the waterway narrowed to a mere fifteen meters. Like a squeezed water hose creating greater water pressure, the constricted channel drove the mighty river forward like a shot. In an instant, the river doubled its already enormous speed, hurtling the raft through the gap.

There was no place to stop, no way to paddle. The steep walls of the canyon were like prison bars.

As the raft propelled forward, Tess watched slack jawed as the churning water dropped out of sight completely just a few meters ahead. A white vapor cloud hung overhead like a rain cloud. She knew instantly what it was.

"Waterfall!" she yelled.

Unable to stop or steer, they hurled over the falls like a slingshot. For a moment, the raft seemed suspended in midair as they shot free of the ledge. In that instant, Tess could see the stretch of river that lay ahead—and below.

The raft tipped nose first—and the bottom fell out.

The raft plunged.

Down, down, Team North Face careened toward the churning hole below. One of the packs came loose and bounced around inside the boat, smashing into the back of Tess's skull. The raft was near vertical—and still they dropped, the back of the vessel threatening to overtake its bow.

They crashed nose first into the hole, shooting six feet beneath the surface. As the raft battled the water for buoyancy, the current ripped the paddle from Tess's clenched fists. It smacked her in the head before disappearing into the watery whirlwind.

For what seemed an eternity, the raft bounced like a ball in a pinball machine amid the raging towback, emerging briefly from the hole only to have the crushing weight of the waterfall thrust it back down. Tess swallowed a mouthful of water, gagging.

Suddenly, the hole released them, and the raft sprung out into the calmer pool below the falls. Tess hacked some water out of her lungs and looked about the raft, counting teammates.

. . . three . . . four . . . five . . .

One short.

Blaine Reeves was not in the boat. She turned back in horror toward the hole to see his helmeted head disappear beneath the water.

"Blaine!"

Wade and Cale spotted their fallen teammate and were already turning the raft back toward the falls. Careful not to be sucked into the vortex, they paddled until the heavy spray threatened to swamp the raft.

Tess spotted the top of Blaine's head. "There!"

Miraculously, the stricken racer was still clinging to his paddle. Then he was gone again, sucked down into the hole.

Just as quickly, Blaine was back up, churning inside the giant washing machine. His paddle was gone, his arms no longer flailing. He was quickly losing energy fighting to keep his head above the water. He would not last long.

"Do something!" yelled Tess. "He's drowning in

there!" Wade and Cale looked at Hoops and Powder stupidly, unsure of what to do. Any closer and the raft would be sucked in on top of Blaine.

From nowhere, a thick orange rope fell into the water beside the hole.

Tess looked up. *What the hell—?*

Conner Michaels scrambled down the steep canyon wall, kicking dust and pebbles into the valley below. Holding one end of a thick climbing rope, Conner prayed the other end would find its mark before it was too late.

From two hundred feet above the river, Conner had watched as the Tsangpo battered North Face's hapless raft. His initial thought—*Damn that Wade Stanley for thinking of rafting the river*—was quickly pushed aside by the second: *Tess*.

Dropping his pack, Conner charged down a narrow path that plunged toward the river below. The sight of the giant falls spurred him ever faster, and he ignored the treacherous footing on the inches-wide trail.

He held his breath as Tess and the raft plunged over the falls, breathing again only when the raft reappeared. It wasn't until North Face turned back toward the falls that he realized something was wrong. A knot formed in his throat as Blaine Reeves bobbed like a cork in the tempest.

Conner heaved the rope toward the hole, hoping

against hope that Blaine would be able to see the orange fiber and grab hold.

But the drowning racer made no move toward the rope. Blaine slipped under a crashing wave.

He's going to die, Conner thought dourly.

Tess simultaneously saw the rope plunge into the water, Conner on the cliff above with the other end, and Blaine Reeves sink under another crashing wave. Time for action. She stood upright in the raft, swatting away the hands of her teammates—

—and dove headfirst into the churning river.

The cold burned her skin. Her head popped out and she gasped for air. Wade and the others were screaming at her from the raft, but she couldn't make out what they were saying over the roar of the falls. Holding her breath, Tess kicked toward the hole. The orange rope floated just a few meters out of reach.

Suddenly, the hole was sucking her in. Tugging at her legs, the current whipped her around until she was facing back toward the raft. The last thing she saw before the hole dragged her under was a horrified look on Wade Stanley's face.

Tess was held fast under the water, her eyes wide open in a combination of shock and panic. The bright line of orange floated over her head. She reached for it, but her fingers fell inches short. The pull of the hole was growing stronger. She was being dragged deeper. Her lungs felt like they were about to implode.

She kicked violently with her legs—*push, push*—until her head cracked the surface. She gulped in a mouthful of air and slipped two fingers around the rope just before being sucked back down into the vortex. Exhausted, she willed herself to relax, allowing the hole to pull her down, down. Then, as the hole regurgitated itself, Tess shot up out of the water. She was right next to Blaine!

He wasn't moving.

Tess quickly slipped the rope around Blaine's waist. He was no longer fighting, dead weight. At that instant they were both pulled under again. Tess's lungs burned; she was out of air and swallowing huge quantities of water.

Then, as the great roiling water tugged at her feet, she felt the rope jerk. She clung to Blaine's body with all her might, feeling like she was being pulled in opposite directions by two galloping horses.

The hole unclenched its watery fist and released them. Free, out of breath and out of energy, Tess felt herself being pulled toward the shoreline.

Through the roar, someone was yelling.

But it sounded so far away—

"Tess! Tess!" Conner yelled. "Say something!"

Preston had yanked her through the current to a narrow ledge beside the river, but she didn't look good. Her face was purplish, and her eyes were shut tight. Conner dropped to his knees beside her prostrate body and felt her skin. Ice cold.

Eyes still shut, she drew her knees up to her chest, her stomach spasming violently.

He tilted her to her side, slapping her hard on her upper back.

"Come on, Tess. Don't do this to me."

A second passed, and then Tess's body lurched. She coughed and spewed brackish water in a warm gush. Even as she vomited, Tess struggled to speak.

"Help . . . Blaine . . ."

Conner gripped her hand. "We're on it."

Ian and Thad had already pulled Blaine from the water onto the same narrow ledge, working feverishly to revive the racer. No response. Blaine's skin was a darkening shade of purple.

"He's not breathing!" Shandi yelled. "Should we do CPR?"

Malika shook her head. "He's got too much water in his lungs. We've got to get that water out first. Roll him onto his side."

"Did that already!" Ian shouted. "Didn't work!"

"Jesus Christ! We have to do something!"

Conner sprung into action. Bounding across the ledge, he flung his leg over the lifeless body, straddling it, and began pushing down on Blaine's chest with both hands. He pumped, hard, pushing faster than one per second. Thirty seconds passed. Sixty.

Conner pumped harder.

When the water finally gushed from Blaine's mouth, it exploded like a geyser. It shot up into Conner's face, warm and smelling of bile. Blaine coughed, gagged, then finally inhaled a ragged breath of air. As life-saving oxygen filled his lungs, he coughed again, spit up some more water, and rolled over onto his side, water flowing from the corner of his mouth.

"Sit him up," Malika ordered.

Conner and Preston pulled Blaine up, just as Team North Face paddled their raft to the banks and spilled out, splashing toward their stricken teammates. Wade headed for Tess; Cale and the others headed toward Blaine.

"Elizabeth!" Wade called out. "My God, Elizabeth, what were you thinking? You could've drowned!"

Tess pointed toward Blaine, now breathing more steadily. "He *was* drowning. I had to do something."

"I'm fine; I'm fine," Blaine spluttered. "What happened?" He turned to Conner. "Where the hell did you guys come from?"

"We saw you from the monastery at Pemakochung," Ian answered. "We saw you headed right for the drop. From up there, it didn't look like much. But that shit must be fifty feet! I think you just survived Kintup-fuckin-Falls!"

For a moment, everyone turned up to gaze at the falls. An awed silence hung in the air like the mist from the cascade.

"Lucky for us you were there," Tess said to Conner. "I

hate to think what would've happened if you hadn't thrown that rope."

"The hole would've released him," Wade protested. "I've been in a number of them myself and the best thing to do is just curl yourself up in a ball and wait it out. It'll spit you out eventually."

Conner fought to restrain himself. *Was this guy actually justifying his inaction?*

"And I've seen men *never* come out of a hole like that," he said, purposely inflecting his voice with spite. "They don't call them keepers for nothing. I'm just glad we were in the right place at the right time."

"The heroes of the day," Tess said.

Blaine struggled to his feet, wobbly but at least now under his own power. He extended a cold hand to Conner. "Thanks, man. I'm not quite sure how I'm going to repay this one."

"I heard what you did on Elbrus. You already earned this one."

Conner barely had time to take the proffered hand, when Wade abruptly cut between them. "Yes, yes. Well, everyone is safe and sound now. We're all very glad that Elizabeth braved the waters."

"And Conner," Blaine said. "If it hadn't been for his quick thinking with his rope, I'm not sure I'd be standing here right now."

"Ah, the rope, yes. Well, I believe that Conner's valuable rope is about to slip into the river."

Conner turned in the direction of Wade's pointed finger to see his rope being pulled into the flowing water. Blaine, closest to the retreating nylon, made a move to grab the end, but Wade interceded again. "We've got a race to run," he said. "Let them get their own rope."

Conner scrambled down to the edge of the whitewater and plucked the end of the rope just as it was pulled off the ledge. He looked up just in time to see Wade grin mischievously.

"So you're running the river too, huh?" Thad asked Tess. "And here we thought we had stumbled onto an original idea."

"It was actually Wade's idea," she replied. "But the river's a little rougher than we thought. Hopefully it flattens out between here and Rainbow Falls."

Conner wasn't about to divulge his own team's plans. But planting a seed of doubt in the minds of Team North Face? Now that was a splendid idea.

"Rainbow's not the only problem. Right after that you got Hidden Falls too. You know the stretch below Hidden has never been rafted, right?" he said.

Wade's reply dripped with disdain. "Well, *I* haven't attempted it. I doubt we'll have much difficulty. But for you, I suggest another, safer route."

Safer route? Conner didn't know if he was reading too much into the comment, but it felt like another jab at his brother. He swallowed hard and stepped toward Wade.

Blaine, perhaps sensing what was about to happen, began to shiver. "If it's all the same to everyone else, I'd love to get out of these wet clothes."

A moment of silence passed, the tension palpable. Conner stared down Wade's beady eyes until the British captain turned away.

"We'll have to climb out of the gorge," Tess said finally. "Unless we can get above it, the spray from the falls will keep everything drenched."

"There's a way up from here, steep but doable," Shandi pointed out. "I think all of us could use some rest. Let's take what we need for tonight and get ourselves warmed up."

Decision made, Team Providence began to gather up their packs. Wade and Cale lashed their raft to a large boulder while the others followed Shandi up the narrow trail.

Conner had left his pack at the top when he had first spotted the errant raft, so he turned to Tess and offered to carry her pack. She whispered her thanks as he flipped her pack onto his shoulders.

As they began their delicate ascent over a series of slippery ledges, Conner could feel Wade's eyes burning a hole into his back.

CHAPTER SIXTEEN

Base Camp
Tumbatse, Tibet

Seated in a director's chair, his name stenciled in bold letters across the back, Terrance Carlton studied a bank of thirty-two-inch color LCD monitors. Each screen displayed the feed from each individual racer. From his chair, Carlton could watch every thrilling second.

The production control studio for *Darwin's Race* was a marvel of engineering. Inside the large canvas tent, the facility was nearly indistinguishable from a fully-equipped soundstage back at NBC headquarters. Switchboards, character generators, monitors, computers, and miles of cabling filled the fifteen thousand-square-foot facility. Two broadcast-quality cameras and a set of klieg lights were arranged around a small set for post-race interviews and commentary segments by the host and Carlton himself. A backdrop of the majestic snow-covered Himalayas loomed over the set.

The mere fact that such a facility existed in the remote Tibetan wilderness, a place where electricity was as rare as a McDonald's Quarter Pounder, was a miracle. Carlton allowed himself a moment of pride at the feat he had orchestrated. Thick black cables, taped down with gray duct tape, crisscrossed the entire facility; but outside the studio was largely wireless. A small army of Ninja Eight 180-horsepower generators powered the entire operation, including a large satellite receiver erected on a small rise nearby. The receiver picked up the signals from the relay stations in and around the gorge, pumping the images from the racers' shoulder-mounted cameras into the switcher and onto the wall of monitors.

Carlton watched as, one by one, the monitors went dark as each competitor fell asleep and the cameras slipped into power-save mode. The slightest movement would trigger the camera back on, ensuring that the producer, and millions of viewers back home, wouldn't miss a thing.

The debut of *Darwin's Race*, the television program, had smashed Discovery Channel records for a debut show. The feat was all the more remarkable because it hadn't included any actual race footage. The twelve million viewers who tuned in to the two-hour program were treated only to pre-race footage, interview segments, and a special report on poisonous snakes of southeastern Asia. Not until the final fifteen minutes of the broadcast did viewers actually witness the live start of *Darwin's Race*.

With a ten-hour time difference between Tibet and the U.S. East Coast, Carlton and his team of editors would use the next few hours to splice together the footage from Day One for the next show. *And then we'll really see big numbers*, Carlton thought. Online viewers, of course, could see the footage earlier, but even those feeds were on a two-hour delay. Carlton liked the added control the delay provided.

But the majority of Americans would no doubt be transfixed by the near-tragedy at the foot of Kintup's Falls. The footage from the cameras mounted on each competitor's shoulder was shaky—but that made it all the more exciting. The heroic rescue of Blaine Reeves by teammate Tess Chamniss and fellow competitor Conner Michaels would have viewers literally holding their breath; Carlton was sure of it. He would devote nearly half of the 120-minute program developing the storyline of the obvious tension between Team Providence and Team North Face, the Conner-Tess-Wade triangle.

Carlton could hardly wait to begin the editing process.

A flashback segment of previous adventure races was already in the can, showing Conner and Tess as a couple, fresh from a one-two finish in San Francisco's Alcatraz Triathlon. Happy and content and holding hands like they would be together forever.

"But there was trouble lurking underneath this seemingly perfect relationship," the narrator in the piece intoned. It

was melodramatic, and the program never actually divulged what the trouble was. "Let the viewers wonder," Carlton had ordered during editing. "Let the story unfold slowly."

Carlton loved the next part of voiceover. *"And now, deep in the unforgiving jungles of Tibet, Conner Michaels must face not only the challenges of this unprecedented race, but the heartache of competing with the love of his life and her new man, the captain of Team North Face, Wade Stanley."*

Over the top, for sure, but the audience would eat it up.

In his mind, Carlton replayed the program's close with a dramatic, slow-motion action shot of Conner, Tess, and Wade. *"In the delicate balance between life and death in the Tsangpo Gorge, a bitter rivalry rears its ugly head. A brewing love triangle between three great adventure racers threatens to push the strained teams to the brink."*

Yes, that sounded perfect. Carlton leaned back in his chair, folding his hands contentedly behind his head.

Everything was proceeding splendidly.

Tsangpo Gorge
Gompo Ne, Tibet

Bill Greenback steered his muddy Land Rover around a bend in the dirt road. The SUV bounced roughly over every rock, jostling the chief engineer like a pinball. He was pushing twenty miles an hour, fast for the unpaved, pitted track. The rough ride did little to improve his mood.

"Goddamned piece of shit," he grumbled.

It was the relay station he cursed. The very same relay station that had given him trouble before the race had even started. Burned out cable last time, and he figured it was the same thing this time around. Must have a short somewhere in the patch panel. You'd think that being chief engineer meant being able to order some lowly technician to drive out here to get the thing fixed. But his entire staff was already stretched thin just maintaining the production facility.

That left him. That's why he was driving himself down the worst road in the world, through the most desolate stretch of land in Asia, his ass cheeks red and chapped from the hard leather seats.

Greenback turned off the dirt track across an open field and shuddered as the tiny village of Gompe Ne came into view. He could still hear the awful cackle of that crazy old man echo inside his brain. *Steer clear of him*, the engineer reminded himself.

Grabbing his duffel filled with cables, switches, and audio cards, he climbed out of the Land Rover and began the slow trudge through the mud up to the relay tower.

That's when he noticed something was different about Gompe Ne.

It was completely deserted.

Where there had once been tiny faces peeking from clapboard windows, now there was nothing. A breeze blew through the decrepit huts, blowing loose reeds from the angled rooftops. Otherwise, the place was utterly still. Laundry hung untended along battered fencing. He listened for sounds of life.

Nothing.

Gompe Ne had become a ghost town.

He continued on, increasing his pace as he passed by the old man's home. A thin line of smoke rose from the place, then, as Greenback watched, wafted out. He waited a moment for it to reappear, but apparently the old man wasn't tending to his fire. Greenback shrugged and continued on up the hill, thankful to leave the desolate village behind him.

A quick examination of the patch panel confirmed his suspicions. Burnt fuse. Greenback extracted a replacement and quickly made the adjustment. *Goddamned three-hour drive for a two-minute fix.*

He turned back to the village. Despite himself, Greenback found himself unnerved. Where were the people? They hadn't exactly rolled out the welcome wagon last time he'd visited, but at least there had been signs of life. Now the emptiness was creeping him out.

Greenback hurried down the hill toward the truck. The fire was still out at the old man's place. And there was something else, too. Something that stopped him in his tracks.

The front door was demolished. It leaned askew across the frame, splintered apart along the hinge side. Greenback stepped tentatively closer.

"Hello?"

No response.

He approached the door, peered beyond. The inky darkness was impossible to penetrate.

A strange odor drifted from somewhere inside. Like spoiled food.

"Is anybody there?"

Again, no reply.

Greenback moved the door to the side, careful to keep it from crumbling completely apart. He stepped inside. The stench was stronger here, strong enough for Greenback to cover his nose with a cupped hand.

It took a moment for his eyes to adjust to the darkness in the living room. The only light emanated from a few smoldering embers in the black stove. As details came into focus, Greenback could see the room was empty. The bronze prayer wheel was upturned in the corner. He glanced to the doorway on the far side of the room.

A noise was coming from beyond.

It was a gurgling, a slurping. Something wet. Like a ravenous dog devouring a meal. The engineer realized he was trembling.

Keep it together, Bill. Keep it together.

Greenback shuddered and stepped into the doorway.

The first thing he saw was the blood. It was sprayed all over the sparse room, running in gristly streaks down the clay walls. Soaking into the dirt floor in pools of crimson.

The body of the old man lay awkwardly in the corner of the room, his torso ripped open from shoulder to pelvis.

A bloody tangle of intestines, bone, and gristle spilled out in a gush. A chunk of flesh had been removed from the man's thigh down to the bone. Greenback gagged on a thick line of bile at the back of his throat.

What in God's name—?

From the opposite corner of the room, something gurgled. Greenback jumped. He peered into the shadows. He couldn't see anything in the darkness. He reminded himself to breathe, something he hadn't done since stepping into the room.

Something stepped out of the shadows.

Greenback stumbled backwards, searching for an escape route that didn't exist. His back hit the wall. He was shaking uncontrollably now, his body wracked with terror. A whispered prayer fell from his trembling lips.

Our Father, who art in heaven, hallowed be thy name.

The thing was enormous, towering over the tremulous engineer.

Thy kingdom come, thy will be done.

Its mouth was covered in blood and flesh and bits of viscera.

On earth as it is in heaven—

Greenback couldn't finish the prayer. The horrifying realization of what had happened forced his knees to give way. He collapsed to the floor in a disheveled heap.

The thing had been feasting upon the old man.

It was upon him before he could scream.

CHAPTER SEVENTEEN

Team North Face/Team Providence
Kintup's Falls

The morning brought misty rain and a silver sky. The members of Team North Face and Team Providence, uneasy allies, broke camp quickly and silently. Sipping hot water flavored with lemon-lime Gatorade warmed them only slightly.

Conner's lower back had stiffened thanks to the hard Tibetan ground, and he tried in vain to stretch out the tenderness. It had been a long night at the shared campsite. Perched atop a ridge overlooking Kintup's Falls, the tents and backpacks from North Face and Providence had been covered with a cold wet spray that left them shivering in the dark. They had shared a pit fire but little else, opting for separate food, opposite sides of the flames, and hushed conversations.

Conner stewed most of the evening, barely concealing his feelings at the sight of Tess and Wade snuggling beside the fire. He would've gone straight to bed if not for the planning he had to do for the next day.

By the end of the evening, stars filled the sky as the teams agreed to run the Tsangpo together until Rainbow and Hidden Falls, then help one another get through the anticipated rappel-portage. Then they would shake hands and go their separate ways. At that point, the race would be back on.

As Wade and Tess made their way to their tent, Conner couldn't help but think back on the countless nights he had spent with her, huddled close inside a single sleeping bag. How Tess would slip her hand down his pants while at the same time slipping off her own. She always told him how she enjoyed lovemaking inside a tent. It was liberating and exciting and out in the wilderness she could scream at the top of her lungs if she wanted. And she often did.

As Wade zipped them into their small tent, the memory burned inside Conner's brain. Just about the only consolation came when, a few minutes later, Blaine slipped into the same tent. There would be no screaming tonight. Still, Conner couldn't shake the image and slept fitfully.

Now, in the early light of morning, Wade darted through camp purposefully, descending quickly down the trail toward the river's edge. His teammates, Tess included, followed closely behind.

Team Providence gathered their gear and slowly made

their way down the steep cliff. When they arrived at their lashed raft, Wade was already tying down his team's backpacks.

There was something halting and abrupt about the way Wade worked, like he was mad at something, and Conner couldn't help but think that there were still sore feelings from his emasculation the day before. Wade would no doubt be eager to reassert his alpha male status.

Sure enough, when Wade strode over to Team Providence's raft, his tone was that of a commanding general.

"Gentlemen, we have quite a mission ahead of us this morning. There are two choices here. We can run the main channel—right down the middle—riding the deepest water. That way we can simply slip right over any submerged rocks. Or, we can stick to the side, eddy jump, avoiding the really big stuff. We'll be more controlled, but we'll be in shallower water and more likely to encounter some nasty holes."

Interpreting the pause as an invitation to offer a suggestion, Conner dived right in. "Even the edges of this river are big—Colorado big. That main channel is just too—"

"Anyway, I've decided we should run the main channel."

"—dangerous," Conner finished, apparently pointlessly.

Wade ignored the comment. "It's fast, and if we stick together we'll be able to provide important safeties for each other. Team North Face will go first; make sure everything is safe. Of course, I'll only point positive; show you the way."

"How nice of you," Conner said. "You must've slept well?"

Wade smiled. "I always sleep well in the company of a

beautiful woman."

Touché, thought Conner. Wade was really pushing it this morning, and Conner fought the impulse to instigate round two with a left hook into his smirking jaw. Though Conner loathed to admit it, Wade's words stung. The idea of Tess keeping that British prick warm at night churned Conner's guts.

Fortunately, Ian Bjornson took that precise moment to make his first appearance of the morning.

He descended from the cliff-top campsite wearing his black zip front flotation vest and battered whitewater helmet. And nothing else.

"Good morning everyone!" Ian announced cheerily. "Mighty fine weather for a day on the river, I'd say." He threw his pack into the Team Providence raft and squatted to lash it down. Conner tried to avert his eyes from the horrific sight.

Malika and Shandi, arriving on the wrong side of the naked squat, squealed like schoolgirls. Preston roared, his baritone laughter echoing off the canyon walls like thunder. Wade just shook his head as if he didn't understand American humor. Like Benny Hill hadn't done the same bit hundreds of times before.

"What?" the naked Ian asked, deadpan, looking around the area as if searching for a missing piece of equipment. "Did I forget something?"

"Yeah, you forgot what a man's genitalia do in cold weather," Malika quipped, struggling to contain her laughter.

"With a package like that, you really ought to put on some pants."

Suddenly embarrassed, Ian covered himself with cupped hands. "Okay, okay," he said, reaching for his clothes. "Let's keep it civil. Just trying to lighten the mood around here. I think we all understand that what you see before you is not the real me."

"It better not be," Shandi retorted. "Otherwise, you've got one *very* unhappy girlfriend back home."

As Ian dressed and the others recovered, Conner surveyed the river ahead. He would've enjoyed nothing more than to disagree with Wade's assessment of the whitewater, but Wade's plan of attack was sound. He might be an asshole, but he wasn't an idiot.

Their gear fastened tight, the teams shoved off. A brief pool of flat water allowed them to get their bearings. Cliffs rose nearly ninety feet on either side, steep and smooth and impenetrable. Lush jungle spilled over the rims.

A solitary black-necked crane swung lazily over the river. According to local belief, the birds were considered sacred, reincarnated beings that came back to the world to help other souls to enlightenment. Conner, strangely calmed by the sight of the crane, held his raft back, allowing North Face to assume the lead. His teammates paddled smoothly from their perches upon the rim of the raft—Shandi and Thad in front, Preston and Malika amidships. Conner and Ian, the most experienced paddlers, anchored the rear.

Wade called out to Conner, repeating the plan to run the main channel, then, without waiting for an answer, paddled his raft into the current.

Team Providence followed at a respectable distance. The first set of riffles rocked the lead raft, but they passed with little trouble. As Conner and the others paddled over the Class III waves, he saw Wade skirt to the right, around a half-submerged boulder. Conner probably would've seen the boulder in time, but there was no warning, no instruction from Wade.

So that's how it's gonna be, thought Conner. Team co-operation had not lasted very long.

The current quickened. Digging into position, Conner maintained balance by keeping his paddle in the water. Experienced kayakers, his fellow team members did not need coaching. Even Preston, his chest bulging beneath his flotation vest, looked comfortable in the rapids. They moved in unison, their strokes crisp and strong.

A wave crashed over the bow as the raft smashed through a wall of water.

"Forward!" Conner yelled. They plowed through the wave, only to be met by another crash of foam. Then a third. The boat was beginning to fill with water; the drain holes in the bottom were quickly being overwhelmed.

The raft bucked violently over a rapid. The stern of the boat was taking the worst of it, and Conner and Ian wedged their feet under the thwarts for leverage. The river was hurtling now, chugging along with a foamy fury, rocketing the raft along like a runaway roller coaster. The water was filled with deep troughs and crests so high that Conner had difficulty reaching the water beneath the raft with his paddle.

A giant wave crashed over the starboard side. The backwash knocked Malika into the center of the raft. Preston nearly toppled over into the river, only managing to regain balance by clinging to the flip line. With an uneven load now on the port side, the raft began to list. Another wave to starboard would certainly flip them. Seeing this, Conner leaped across the raft to balance the load. He managed to flatten the raft . . . but now the raft began to spin like a top in the rapids.

Not good.

"Left forward!" Conner yelled.

Rafts are most sturdy from front to back. Rarely does one flip end over end. But enter a hole or plow into a wave *sideways* and you're almost always toast.

Now Team Providence was doing exactly that.

A monster standing wave lay dead ahead. "Hard left!"

There was no time for Malika to scramble back into position. She ducked, bracing herself.

"Hang on!"

The raft shot down a three-foot chute like a freight train. Maybe their run-up speed and the force of the current would be enough to propel Providence over the wave. For a brief instant, Conner thought they were going to make it.

He was wrong.

The raft smashed into the wave side-first. It was like running into a concrete wall. Whitewater kayakers called these kinds of waves "stoppers" because if you hit one, that's exactly what it did. The monster halted Team Providence dead in their tracks. Caught in the maelstrom between the collapsing wave and the furious chute, the raft edged closer to the hole. In this fury, Conner knew this hole was a keeper. If they went in, they weren't coming out.

The raft, starboard side to the wave, began to roll.

"Forward!" Conner yelled.

They dug their paddles into the roil. Trapped on either side by the hole and the standing wave, Providence strained to skirt out the side. Grunting with exertion, they couldn't budge the raft.

They were lilting so badly now, the strokes only sliced through the top of the wave. The giant hole gaped open to the port side, the power of the vortex so strong it nearly ripped Conner's paddle from his hands.

"Forward!"

Conner thrust his paddle into the water . . . and found nothing but air. The raft was perched on its side! Somebody screamed—

—and the raft flipped!

Conner plunged into the ice-cold water, air sucked from his lungs. The hole swallowed him down like he was wearing two hundred-pound ankle weights. He kicked, scrambling for the raft just over his head. His fingers found the flip line, and he hauled himself up. His head finally, mercifully, broke the surface in the hollow space under the raft. As he gulped air, he could hear muffled shouts, panic.

Suddenly, he felt a lifting sensation. Clinging to the flip line with one hand, Conner shot out of the water as the starboard side of the raft freed itself from the hole! The raft had done a complete side-over-side somersault! Foamy water crashed over him, and his fingers began to slip from the line. As he grappled for purchase, the chute poured over the port side, threatening to roll the raft again.

His finger slipped from the rope—

—just as a hand locked down on the back of Conner's vest. He was hauled into the raft, landing roughly on the floor of the raft. Preston loomed over him. Somehow, the burly man had managed to stay in the raft as it flipped. In fact, they were all in the raft: Malika, Ian, Shandi, and Thad—all soaked to the skin. Each of them eyed Conner like he had returned from the dead.

"Not the best time for a swim," Preston said in his gravelly voice.

Conner coughed up some water and scrambled into position. Realizing he had lost his paddle somewhere in the hole, Conner braced himself on the swamped floor.

"Forward!"

With one desperately deep stroke, the five members of Team Providence left with paddles pulled hard into the crashing waves. The raft moved, just a little, but enough to spark some hope.

Digging their paddles into the water, they pulled again. Preston roared like a wild animal.

The river let them go. They exploded out of the hole into a side channel, and after a few more exhausted paddles, they mercifully came to rest in a large eddy.

They collapsed into the center of the raft, utterly spent. Muscles burning, lungs gasping for air, minds only now catching up with what had just happened.

Something bumped into the raft, and Conner looked over the side. His paddle. He reached over and plucked it from the river. And he began to laugh.

The others were momentarily puzzled by his outburst. Then, one by one, the terror that gripped their bodies lifted. They laughed so hard they began to cough—they had all ingested an unhealthy amount of the mighty Tsangpo. The laughing subsided—as they all took deep, calming breaths.

Then they heard someone screaming over the roar of the river.

Conner straightened and stared downstream toward the sound of the call.

It was Cale Anders, standing in the North Face raft, waving wildly. And though the crash of the whitewater was nearly deafening, Conner could just make out his words.

"Come on, you guys! We've found Rainbow Falls!"

The ghosts of Francis Kingdon-Ward and Ian Baker

seemed to hang over the misty precipice of Rainbow Falls. From Conner's perch atop a rock outcropping—the rafts safely lashed to the rocky shore—he envisioned he was following in the explorers' footprints at the exhilarating moment of discovery.

The falls careened over the edge in furious waves, plunging nearly eight stories to a boiling hole below. The river cut out of sight around some large rocks. A quarter mile farther on was Hidden Falls. No one had ever glimpsed what lay beyond that legendary cataract. The idea that they were on the verge of discovery quickened his pulse. As the others tended to the gear, he relished a moment of sheer awe. When he turned to help with the rafts, Conner felt better than he had in months.

"We obviously can't raft the thing," he announced. "We'll have to lower the rafts to the pool below."

"Who says we can't raft it?" Wade smirked. "I've routinely steepcreeked falls higher than that with no problem."

"In a playboat, not a raft." Conner could hardly believe he was arguing with this guy. Was he seriously considering running Rainbow Falls?

"Take your team the safe way then. By the time you lower your gear and your people down to the pool, we'll be miles down the river."

"Don't be an asshole, Wade. It's eighty feet down. That hydraulic will crush your raft like a taco. You'll be trapped in that hole, with no way out."

"The backwash will spit us right out into that pool."

"If the hole is deep enough."

"It's deep enough. I'd estimate that it's at least thirty feet deep."

"Except for the boulders that are certainly down there too."

"If the boulders were there, we'd be able to see them from here."

"Go on then. It'll be a nice treat to see the water snap your neck like a matchstick."

Tess stepped between the two captains. "Nobody's shooting the falls," she said with an exasperated sigh. "I'm going to get into my climbing harness and rappel down. There's a shelf down there, just wide enough for me to stand on and untie the rafts as you lower them down." Wade started to protest, but she stilled him with a raised hand. She pulled her harness from her backpack and stepped into it. "Once the rafts are down, the rest of you can use the same ropes to follow me down."

Conner cursed under his breath. He had let his rivalry with Wade cloud his judgment. Instead of figuring out how to get to the pool below on his own, he was only concerned with shooting down Wade's idea. Lapses like that could be costly. He admonished himself for sinking to his rival's petty level.

"I'll tie off your safety," he said to Tess meekly.

Wade stepped forward, rope already in hand. "I'll do it," he said curtly. "I'll take care of my own team, thanks."

Conner backed off, hands up in surrender. "Suit yourself. We'll start tying off the rafts."

CHAPTER EIGHTEEN

Base Camp
Tumbatse, Tibet

"Three . . . take three. Ready on seven . . . take seven."

Terrance Carlton watched the bank of monitors with an unflinching eye. The action from the racers was unfolding quickly—faster even than he had anticipated.

The monitors—twelve in all, one for each competitor—displayed in real-time whatever that racer's camera was capturing at that moment. To switch shots, Carlton only had to call out a camera number and an assistant director would switch the image.

The main image—the broadcast image—was displayed on a sixty-four-inch digital Trinitron plasma screen that hung over the bank of monitors. An array of digital recorders captured every frame from every camera so Carlton could splice the footage together during postproduction.

Carlton would ordinarily leave such hands-on work to a technical director, but this was no ordinary show. Too much was riding on the success of *Darwin's Race*. His entire career hung in the balance, and he wasn't about to turn that over to anyone.

"Going to North Face," Carlton said. "Twelve . . . take twelve. Ready with Chyron . . . dissolve . . . good. Dissolve out."

A two-person team of production assistants was assigned to each bank of six screens, representing a single team. If something interesting popped up, the PA would yell it out to the director. The producer would cast an expert eye on the footage—and if he liked what was happening, he'd put the feed "on-deck" and then switch to the broadcast feed when the timing was appropriate.

With twelve live cameras feeding continuous footage, the control tent was a cacophony of sound.

"I got a good angle of the falls on Seven!"

"Blisters on Five and Six. And man are they nasty!"

"Come to me; come to me! I've got Two in a shouting match with Four!"

Before *Darwin's Race*, Carlton thought he had seen it all. He had produced eight Eco-Challenges in some of the world's most inhospitable places. Helmet cams, crowd reaction shots, commentary booths—the Challenge had been a logistical nightmare, with hundreds of cameras strewn across dozens of venues. But at least they were broadcasting within an easy drive of a major city. Cities that were blessed with an abundance of camera operators, control technicians, engineers—and electricity.

But this was something altogether different.

Three weeks ago, this area had been little more than a stark field of dried mud. Oh, there had been a few purple flowers up where the teams' tents had been erected, but they had been quickly trampled by the support crews.

They brought in generators, miles of fiber, switchers, fuses, and plugs. A crew of eighty had been flown in and were working shifts of twelve hours on, twelve hours off. With so little to do outside the race village, they often milled about the control room, tracking the action. A few of the more enterprising crew members had even started a pool. Fifty bucks a pop; a crew member would pick a date and time and name his team. If his team reached the summit at the predicted hour, the money was his. The pot was up to eight hundred bucks.

Back home, this kind of gambling was strictly verboten. Out here, in an isolated village hundreds of miles from a working toilet, Carlton let it slide. Lord knows there was nothing else to pass the time. In any event, it was no different than the hundreds of similar bets being placed all over the United States right now. Hell, even Las Vegas had posted odds. In just a few days, *Darwin's Race* had become a national obsession.

The race was a goldmine. And Terrance Carlton controlled it all.

Although he answered only to himself, the executive producer often solicited opinions from the crew. Apart from the occasional "Let's focus on Tess Chamniss," they kept their distance. The trust in the producer's ability was complete—Carlton would not miss anything of importance.

As he directed the live action, Carlton simultaneously eyed the playback on a small monitor next to his chair. It was the final edit of the show that had aired the previous evening back home. He had finished it early that morning—at some ungodly hour like 4 a.m.—and had immediately ordered the uplink. It was good stuff, tempered only because of the lack of prep time. He would've liked some more wide shots of the terrain; the stock landscape footage had already worn thin. But that wasn't what people wanted anyway.

No, the viewers tuned in for the human drama. And action. The incident at Kintup's Falls conveniently provided both.

The Web site control team monitored fan interest by studying hourly Web reports from Discovery.com. With each site visitor able to choose whatever camera they wanted from any competitor (with the two-hour delay), it was clear who people were logging on to watch.

At first, the team was puzzled as to why so few of the viewers were accessing the cameras of Conner, Tess, or Wade. But the producers quickly learned that viewers chose other cameras so they could get clearer views of the three burgeoning stars of *Darwin's Race*.

The final frame of the program rolled past, and Carlton

turned to his assistant. "Remind me to spend more time on Shandi Davis next time," he said. "I think she's a comer." His assistant nodded and scurried off on an errand. "And don't forget to tell them about the music bed," he called after her. "I want something with more zip!"

Leslie Dickerson, the NBC communication chief, entered the tent, grinning widely, waving a sheet of paper in her hands. "Nineteen million," she said, shoving the paper into Carlton's hands. "Nineteen million viewers last night! Bigger than *Dinosaur*, bigger than anything Discovery had ever done! And the Web traffic is swamping Discovery's computers—they've had to add a tenth server just to handle the demand. And now NBC wants to push up their special to tomorrow night."

Carlton was anticipating good news, but this surpassed even his expectations. "Jumping on the bandwagon, huh? Well, we'll give 'em something good; that's for sure."

"We're going to set up some interviews with the morning shows. You'll need to be ready to go live tonight at nine."

"Fine, fine. Nineteen million, huh?" *Just wait until we hit the major network,* he thought. Those numbers will go through the roof. Suddenly, his career trajectory was trending way up. "Have you seen Greenback? We had a little bet on the numbers, and he needs to pay up."

"He left a few hours ago. Something about a problem with one of the relay stations."

"He's not back yet? It was supposed to be an easy fix.

There's a flicker from some of the feeds. Imperceptible to most, but I want these images to be crystal clear. Give him another hour; then send out a search party. I need him here to revel in our success."

"With these numbers," Leslie said. "I hope it takes them all year to get to Kuk Sur."

"Not likely," said Carlton. "Their little river trip is moving right along. If it hadn't been for Rainbow Falls, they'd be at the mountain by now."

"Ah, yes, the river," Leslie said. "And how are our teams managing the mighty falls?"

"See for yourself," replied Carlton, pointing at the monitors. "We're live on them right now."

CHAPTER NINETEEN

Team North Face/Team Providence
Tsangpo River

The teams had successfully portaged Rainbow Falls, descending the cliff beside the cascade to the pool below. The view from the river confirmed Conner's earlier assessment of the falls. Unrunnable. Tess had probably saved lives by insisting on the portage. *Too bad,* he thought. He would've loved to see Wade make the doomed attempt.

They had paddled barely fifteen minutes in the swift current before the horizon line suddenly dropped away like a ski jump. A giant spray erupted continuously beyond the edge of the water. A roar as loud as jet engines echoed inside the rock canyon. There was no mistaking their location.

Hidden Falls.

This time, the sight of the massive hydraulic, over one

hundred feet of furious energy, made any debate pointless. They would have to do a second portage.

Lengths of brightly colored nylon dangled down a steep face of granite. Tess Chamniss, attached to the ropes with a high-ply seat harness, scampered down the rock like a spider. Watching her rappel, Conner found himself holding his breath. Tess was a capable climber, but something about descending a slab the size of a fifteen-story building with a giant waterfall crashing nearby, drenching the rock in a slippery cold mist, gave him pause. Only when Tess reached the narrow ledge below did he allow himself to relax.

Preston hauled up the ropes, and the others busily lashed a raft to the line. As they had done at Rainbow, they would lower the gear once both rafts were in the water. Tess would prevent them from drifting off in the current until everyone had the chance to descend.

It took nearly three hours, and by the time Conner rappelled down, belayed by Ian and Preston from the Providence raft, everyone was itching to get moving again. Especially Wade. He ordered the North Face raft away even before Conner had stepped out of his harness.

They paddled out into a relatively calm stretch of water. Conner's team took turns paddling, so everyone stayed relatively fresh. A relaxed routine developed, the racers lapsing into silence as the jungle-choked canyon drifted past.

Conner, wary of Wade's diligent watch over his girlfriend, tried to avoid even glancing in Tess's direction. He kept his mind on the task at hand, paddling a surprisingly easy stretch of flatwater. With every stroke, the racers probed ever deeper into unknown territory.

The canyon here was lined with towering cornices and high spires, some forested, most slabbed with sheer rock. There was no bank here, nowhere to pull ashore if the water grew perilous. But though the water moved quickly, it was notably level, almost tranquil.

"There's something strange about this river," said Preston, breaking a long silence. "It's too calm."

"Knock on wood," Shandi said. "I've had just about enough of those monster rapids."

"That's what doesn't make sense. The river literally hurls itself over the first fifty miles or so—and now it's all calm and flat. Look, the water is barely moving."

Conner had been thinking the same thing. All six of them had to paddle just to keep up a decent speed. The only reason for a river to slow down like this would be—

Suddenly, Malika stood upright in the raft, letting her paddle drop. *"My God—"*

Ahead, a mountain of stone and rubble lay collapsed across the width of the river. The wall of detritus stretched between the steep canyon walls on either side, forming an immense dam three stories tall.

That was the reason the water was no longer flowing. It had nowhere to go.

Wade Stanley quickly pulled his team's raft to the banks of the rubble, and Team Providence followed suit.

Once on the stony banks, the racers clambered up its steep and rocky slope. Breathing hard by the time they reached the top, they surveyed the far side with astonishment.

The Tsangpo had dried up to a shallow trickle. Unimaginably, the mighty river was no deeper than a rain puddle, revealing a brackish, muddy bottom. The water had spilled out into a broad lake, flooding into the surrounding jungle. As far as the eye could see, the forest floor had been submerged.

"There's something you don't see every day," Ian said.

"This I didn't expect," Conner agreed.

"How did this happen?" Shandi asked. "There must be tons of rock here."

"Obviously a landslide," Wade answered. "It happens naturally all the time, I'm afraid."

"I don't think there's anything natural about this." The sound of Preston's commanding voice drew stares.

"What is that supposed to mean?" someone asked.

The Maverick Man hesitated, as if he preferred not to elaborate, but a lineup of anxious eyes convinced him. "Landslides do occur naturally," he said, "but they're mostly caused by erratic weather patterns. Thunderstorms, lightning, something like that."

Wade asked, "So how do you know that didn't cause this one?"

"This slide is only a few days old. Look up at the cliff. See those old avalanche chutes, how smooth they are? This one is still jagged and dusty. It's barely had a chance to settle."

"So?" Wade was growing impatient.

"So, we've been here for four days now. Have you heard any thunderstorms?"

At this, Wade remained silent.

"If not lightning," Conner asked, "what then?"

"You mean you haven't heard it?" Preston asked.

"No. Heard what?"

Preston raised a thick finger. "Listen."

Everyone fell silent as the stillness of the canyon settled over them, broken only by the gentle lapping of water against the rubble pile. Then, Conner heard something. It sounded far in the distance. A drumming. Deep. Heavy. Like the footsteps of a giant.

The others must've heard it, too, because they all turned back to Preston for an explanation.

"The Chinese," he said. "Outside Zedang. They are drilling for uranium, iron ore, other minerals. I've heard it all afternoon."

"But Zedang is a hundred miles from here," Ian pointed out.

"Sound travels better through rock than air. The entire Himalaya is one giant sound transmitter. Since the Chinese invaded Tibet back in the fifties, they've decimated almost half of the country's arable land. Huge deforestation. Massive mining. Some believe as much as 60 percent of Tibet's trees have been steamrolled by Chinese trucks. The yaks the Tibetans rely on for sustenance have become endangered. Thousands of them have been killed by the deforestation. Nature's balance has been thrown off."

"But what does that have to do with the landslide?"

"Back in 1970, an earthquake off the coast of Peru started a landslide hundreds of miles away. Killed over eighteen thousand people. The Chinese are basically simulating mini-quakes all over this province. The more they drill, the more land they clear, the more dire the consequences will be. Like this landslide."

Conner pondered this a moment. "I had no idea. How do you know all this?"

Before Preston could answer, Wade promptly announced he had seen enough. "Our little rafting excursion is over," he said, scampering back down the side. "Time to start walking." Team North Face closed ranks at their raft, speaking in secretive tones Conner couldn't make out.

"What gives?" Ian asked. "We've got to walk now?"

"Looks that way," Conner said. "The river's barely flowing on the other side. Definitely not enough to raft. We'll have to leave it here and hoof it the rest of the way."

Thad looked up. "Time to cut through the jungle, boys and girls," he said, pulling his hiking boots from his pack.

"You didn't really think it would be that easy, did you?" Conner teased, pulling his own pack from the raft. "At least we're closer to Kuk Sur now. Fifteen, twenty miles maybe. Without a map, it'll be tough going, but I say we cut through the jungle. We could follow the river, but it takes us north before turning south. Out of the way. Could be faster though."

"Through the jungle," Ian said, the others nodding in agreement. "I say we head straight for it."

Wade Stanley chose that precise moment to stride over, directly through the huddled Team Providence. "I'm afraid you won't be able to ride our coattails any longer."

"Hey, I think you got that backwards, slick," Malika spat back. "Conner's the one who saved your team's ass at Rainbow." Conner was surprised to see her speak up so vociferously. *Where did that come from?*

"Careful, young lady. You would do better to mind your place."

Malika's face turned red. "My *place*? Oh, I get it. You're one of those little-dick guys that can't handle strong, independent women. You surround yourself with mindless yes-men—and women—to make yourself feel better about yourself. Well, knock yourself out. Just don't ever speak to me that way again."

Now it was Tess's turn to get angry. "Hey, you don't know Wade Stanley. And you don't know the rest of us. So just keep your nasty little comments to yourself."

Malika mumbled something under her breath that Conner didn't catch.

"What was that?" Tess said, stepping forward aggressively. "If you've got something to say, speak up now."

This time, Malika spoke up loud enough for all of the stunned racers to hear. "I said, 'Why don't you just cut and run? That seems to be your forte.'"

"And what's that supposed to mean?"

"I think you know exactly what I mean."

The two women had stepped close enough to each other that their breath clouds collided.

Conner decided that was enough. "Alright, let's keep this civil," he said, stepping between them. "Step back, both of you. Take a deep breath."

Reluctantly, Tess and Malika retreated to their own teams. Now, Team Providence and Team North Face faced off atop the landslide like they were about to rumble. It looked like Malika was ready—*eager*, even—to enter the fray. She was a scrappy one, Conner decided.

"We're wasting time here," he said. "We need to gear back up and get moving." Malika still looked like she was about to pounce. "*Now*, Malika."

She finally relaxed, retreating slowly with the rest of the team to the foot of the rubble.

Conner looked up to see Team North Face scramble up the landslide, fully loaded, and disappear over the far side. Just before vanishing from view, Tess looked back over her shoulder. She didn't say anything, and he couldn't read her expression like he used to, but for that one single, fleeting instant, Conner thought she was hoping they would follow.

"Looks like they're going to follow the river," said Ian.

"Good riddance," Malika added.

"Geez, they didn't even say goodbye," Shandi added with mock hurt.

"I guess that means the race is back on," Conner said. "Come on, let's get geared up. We move out in five."

✦ ✦ ✦

Team Providence
Tsangpo Gorge

The jungle of the Tsangpo was alive with sound and movement. Home to over four hundred endemic bird species, the rainforest echoed with the distinctive *quiok-quiok* of the Himalayan grouse and the musical call of yellow-banded warblers. Tipula spiders and armies of stag beetles skittered across the soggy ground, eyed hungrily by black-eyed marmots crouching in the canopy above.

Conner rubbed the perspiration from the back of his neck with a soaked bandana, took a pull from his water bottle, and listened to the symphony. He knew there was no other place on earth where he could hear the distinctive sonata of these jungles. Because of its unique landforms, wide gaps in altitude, and varied types of climate, about a quarter of the species found in Tibet were unique to the region. There were animals here found nowhere else on earth.

Conner was alone in his admiration of his surroundings. For the others, it was their first break after six hours scything through thick walls of bamboo, hemlock, spruce, and brown fir. They had all slid down near-vertical cuts of eroded dirt, climbed by clinging to damp roots, and now all they wanted to do was peel off their sodden boots and expose their bare feet to some fresh air. It helped ward off blisters and sore spots. Preston and Malika devoured baggies of trail mix while resting on the carcass of an uprooted tree. Its exposed roots were wet and oily and teemed with grubs. A troop of long-tailed monkeys chattered in the canopy overhead. No one except the team captain seemed to notice.

"We've been going all morning, and we've barely covered ten miles," Ian grumbled.

"We're doing all right," Conner said, surveying ahead. A few miles to the south, the exposed moon-like flanks of Namche Barwa rose out of the dense jungle. "I figure we can traverse the lower slopes of Namche; they should be a little less wooded. Should make for easier going."

"And fewer bugs," added Shandi. "These flies are driving me insane."

"Me, too," echoed Thad, waving at a swarm hovering near his head. "Hey, shouldn't we keep moving anyway? I mean, this is a race, right?"

"It's a race alright," Conner answered. "But it's not a sprint. I figured it would take three days to reach Kuk Sur, then another three to summit. And that's only if everything goes smoothly. So the best thing to do is to take everything nice and steady. Stay hydrated, and stay focused."

"I sure hope we made the right decision at the landslide," Ian said. "I hated losing sight of the other team."

Conner silently agreed. He could do without the smarmy grin of Wade Stanley, but the separation from Tess was more difficult to accept. She was a grown woman, more than capable of taking care of herself, yet he felt much more comfortable when he was close enough to watch over her. Now the distance made him restless.

Preston leaned his trekking poles against a tree and climbed atop a large boulder. He peered through a pair of binoculars north toward the river. "Can't see anything," he said. "But it does look better to the southeast." The others dropped their trail mix baggies and gathered on the boulder for a look. Across the gorge, the snow-covered mountains of the Kukuranda were jammed together shoulder to shoulder. Even at this distance, they looked massive, unyielding.

Conner took the opportunity to examine Preston's poles. The guy was certainly attached to them. They were thick, heavy. Solid black with no markings on the shaft or grip. Must be some new prototype.

"Hey, Preston, where did you get these poles? I've never seen them before."

Preston's eyes widened at the sight of his precious poles in Conner's hands. He clambered down from the boulder, bounding to Conner in three lopping strides. He snatched the poles back. A little too roughly.

Preston must've recognized his own erratic reaction and tried a feeble smile. "Sorry, I'm protective of these babies. But to answer your question, yes, they are a sort of prototype. I constructed them myself."

"Off the shelf not good enough for you?"

"These are special," he replied seriously. "For a special occasion."

Before Conner could press him about their unusual heft, a piercing yell stopped him cold.

It was Shandi, standing stock still, pointing back to where the team had dropped their packs.   A small horde of leaf monkeys had descended upon their rest site and was greedily consuming the trail mix!

"Monkey bastards!"

Ian led the charge from the boulder, screaming curses as they sprinted back to the bags, arms flailing to scare off the invaders. Shandi and Thad arrived first, just in time to see the little primates grab their precious protein bars and scamper into a grove of rhododendrons. The monkeys stopped on a chest-high branch, just out of reach, and quietly continued to munch on their snack—watching the strange humans with bemused curiosity.

"Goddamned monkeys," Ian mumbled, kicking his empty baggie. "Don't you know that we're more evolved than you?" He picked up a rock and was about to hurl it toward the closest monkey when he realized the absurdity of it all. Instead of throwing something, he sat down and began to laugh.

Conner joined him, then Shandi and Malika. Preston's distinctive bellowing soon added to the laughter. The sound shook the vegetation.

"What the fuck is so funny?" Thad demanded, without a flicker of amusement in his tone. "Those monkeys just made off with our food. You think that's funny?"

Conner settled himself with a deep breath. "You want

to know why I'm laughing? Let me tell you a story. There was a guy I knew, an old friend of mine. He was traveling through the Cordillera Blanca in Peru back in the mid-nineties. Anyway, he and his group were trekking near Huascaran, and it was nasty going. Four days, nothing but rain and mud and Peruvian leeches. One day, cold rain still pounding, he came across a log that had fallen across the trail. It was chest-high, no way under or around it. Had to go over. So he takes a running start, jumps, and smacks right into it. Stomach first. He picks himself up and tries again, this time landing in a mud puddle on the other side. Gets up cussing the log, the mud, Peru—you name it, he cursed it."

"What does this have to do with our food?" asked Thad, exasperated.

"So, this guy decides to hide in the bushes on the other side of the log, to see how his fellow travelers handle the hurdle. One of the team's porters comes sloshing up the trail, ankle deep in mud. He sees the log, takes a running start, jumps—and slams smack into the log, knocking him on his ass. So my friend fully expects the guy to start ranting and raving, right? Only, he doesn't. Lying there in the mud, the porter starts laughing—giant belly laughs. He tries again . . . and again . . . and on the fourth time, he manages to slide over. Completely covered with grime, the porter stands up, brushes himself off, and lovingly pats the log as if it were a dear friend, then proceeds up the trail, smiling the whole way."

"Oh, I see the point now," Thad said sarcastically.

"My friend told me that it was at that very moment that he had an epiphany. It became obvious that it wasn't the external world that was his problem, but how he chose to perceive it. He could experience life as a helpless victim, blaming everything around him—the log, the rain—or he could assume a positive attitude about his own experience. Once he had figured all this out, he gained a tremendous sense of control and freedom. 'Adventure is not outside, man,' he told me; 'it is within.' It was the secret to enduring the Peruvian jungle."

Thad didn't seem sold on Conner's spiritual theory. "So you think, what, that all we have to do is think happy thoughts and those little fuckers will bring back our Clif Bars?" He plopped down on the fallen tree in disgust.

"Listen to me," Conner said, addressing the entire team. "*Darwin's Race* is not for the fainthearted. There will be days when we don't feel like going on. This is just the second day. It may rain from here to the summit of Kuk Sur. We can't control that—but we can control our attitude. And I think a positive attitude will make the difference. If we can laugh off the tough parts, we'll all be better off. Now come on; let's get our packs back on. We'll go until we reach the other side of Namche Barwa—then we'll eat a hot dinner and get some sleep."

The speech seemed to have its desired effect. Shandi, Preston, and Malika pulled on their packs without complaint, though the entire team could hear the rumbling from Thad's stomach.

"Monkey bastards," he muttered.

Team Providence pushed on through the jungle, slicing through the verdant undergrowth of the gorge. They eventually climbed free of the foliage, ascending onto the lower flanks of Namche Barwa. Thousands of feet over their heads, a plume of snow billowed like a smokestack from the arrowhead-shaped summit. From the pass, the plateau curved slowly downwards toward the lower branch of the Tsangpo. They could see the flanks of Kuk Sur rising steeply to an ice-capped peak on the far side of the river.

The sight buoyed everyone's spirits. Tired and hungry, Ian Bjornson adjusted his pack straps for the hundredth time, trying to relieve the weight on his raw shoulders. Still days away, the finish line for *Darwin's Race* finally seemed within reach.

Though once a pilgrimage route, the pass was now strewn with sharp rocks and other detritus that clogged the ancient path. Hunters from the scattered villages within the gorge made only infrequent visits to these high meadows, to hunt *takin*, dog-like creatures that roamed easily over the terrain, searching out Tibetan wooly hares. The valley below was home to the few remaining Tibetan tigers, though just south across the border Indian tigers were still plentiful. The presence of these man-eating hunters surely helped keep visitation to a minimum.

After a few hours, Team Providence once again descended into the wet valley. The hard slog behind them, they stopped beside a shallow creek to fill their Nalgene bottles. The trickling water was clear and cold, and they drank freely without adding purification tablets.

"Hey, I got to take a potty break," Ian announced.

"Just do it downstream," Thad chided. "Better yet, stay away from the stream altogether, will ya?"

Ian plunged through a thick rhododendron grove until he had some privacy. While he went about his business, he looked toward the treetops. An amateur bird watcher—a fact he rarely copped to within hard-nosed adventure racing circles—Ian often searched for colorful birds in the rainforest. Yesterday, he had spotted a Himalayan monal and this morning as they first entered the jungle, he had heard the distinctive call of the satyr tragopan.

So his senses were attuned to the movements and sounds of the forest when he heard a sound he couldn't place.

It was a whistle-like sound—a high-pitched *wee-whir*. He tried to shrug it off. There were hundreds, perhaps thousands of birdcalls he couldn't identify. But this one troubled him.

It sounded . . . human.

Something splashed just downstream. Though the creek disappeared into the thick bush, Ian could hear the movement clearly. It was coming closer.

"Thad?" he called out. "Thad, is that you? Dude, what

are you doing down there? You're freaking me out . . . Jesus H. Christ."

It wasn't Thad.

Three women materialized like evil spirits from the jungle. Their ancient faces were streaked black, with what Ian hoped was just mud. The women were dressed in rags, stained robes that hung in tatters across their shoulders down to bare feet. All three had gnarled noses and black hair, matted and stringy as if they had been in the jungle a very long time. They smelled of rotted fruit.

Ian guessed they were native Tibetans, their faces bearing the familiar half-Asian, half-Indian look of the villagers he had encountered at Tumbatse. As they drew closer, one of the women beckoned to him with gnarled fingers.

"Hello," Ian said politely in broken Tibetan. "My name is Ian." Met with blank stares, he suddenly wished he had studied a bit more of the language.

The beckoning woman with the crooked fingers carried a small woven bag. She slowly reached into the bag and removed what appeared to be a piece of fruit.

"*Mgyogs po shog*," she croaked, holding it out for him. "*Shog, shog.*"

Bowing his head in thanks, Ian accepted the piece of fruit and turned it over in his hands. It wasn't a fruit, but a mushroom—about the size and shape of a portobello. He loved portobello mushrooms. Tender and flavorful, they were a staple of his diet—substituting admirably for steak or even hamburgers. Tired of the freeze-dried horseshit he had been forcing down, Ian felt his taste buds start to dance.

The women gestured for him to eat. "*Za ba, za ba . . .*"

"Thank you," Ian said, smiling. He lifted the mushroom to his lips. He could smell its sweet fresh aroma. He was practically drooling.

"Stop!"

Ian whirled at the sound just as Thad and Preston barreled through the jungle, their arms waving frantically in the air.

"Drop it. Drop it right there," Preston ordered.

The three gypsies began jabbering excitedly, flailing their hands in the air. They were obviously agitated.

"You don't want that," Preston said, shooting a steely glare at the women. "That is a poisonous mushroom. And it will kill you."

"What the hell are you talking about?" Ian asked, suddenly confused. "How do you know that? You haven't even seen what kind it is."

"I don't have to," Preston replied. "I know these women."

"But how—?"

"They are *dugmas*—members of a jungle cult who roam the forest offering poisoned food or drinks to anyone they encounter."

Ian's jaw dropped. "Poison?" he asked dumbly. "That's the craziest thing I've ever heard. That can't be right."

"I assure you that it is. These women—and dozens more like them—believe that they gain merit by doing away with unsuspecting victims. Pilgrims, monks, their own husbands and children—it doesn't matter to them. If you were better read you would know that Kingdon-Ward himself encountered a pack of *dugmas* during his first mission into the gorge. One of his team accepted a cold drink from one of the women and broke out in a terrible rash all over his body. Started puking blood. They had to carry him twenty-five miles to Marpung. The poor guy began to hallucinate—seeing monsters and angels, even God himself. The doctor did not arrive in time, and the man died on a straw bed."

"Jesus Christ, I almost ate this damn thing," Ian yelled. "Why didn't you tell us sooner?"

"I never thought we'd encounter a *dugma*," Preston said. By the tone in his voice, he seemed almost glad he had. "Fascinating. They're just as Kingdon-Ward described. These women grow poisonous mushrooms, then paint their faces black, braid one side of the hair and under the light of a full moon, swear to use the poison. If their intended victim becomes suspicious, they may try the food or drink first, then add the poison afterward by hiding it under a fingernail—or even by administering the poison in the night by scratching the person while he sleeps. I even heard a rumor that the wife of Tenzing Norgay—you know the guy who climbed Everest with Hillary?—that she was killed by the poison of a *dugma*."

The jabbering women hobbled closer—pointing to the mushroom still clenched in Ian's hand. He dropped it like a hot potato and watched it roll into the creek. The women squawked as they scrambled to retrieve the root.

"Let's get the hell out of here," Ian said, warily stepping away from the madwomen. "We need to keep a large distance between ourselves and these wackos."

Preston led Ian and Thad back through the jungle, quickly returning to the spot along the creek where they had refilled their bottles. Conner and Malika were still drinking directly from the stream.

"What was all the commotion?" Conner asked. "Sounded like a party."

"Hardly," Thad replied. He relayed the story quickly, adding that if Ian had eaten the mushroom, there'd be more protein bars for everyone else.

"Very funny," Ian said. "Joke all you want, but better keep an eye open when you go to sleep tonight. I might just invite my new friends over tonight."

"Hey, where's Shandi?" Thad asked, suddenly realizing his wife was nowhere to be found. "She's missing all the fun."

"Bathroom break," Malika said.

"You guys just let her go off by herself?" her husband asked. "With crazed poison-wielding women roaming the jungle?"

"Contrary to popular belief, we women don't always go to the bathroom together."

Ian smiled. "But you do have pillow fights in your bra and panties, right? Please don't tell me that's a myth, too?"

"Uh huh. And we videotape the whole thing, too," Malika joked. Then, turning back to Thad, she said, "Don't worry. She'll be back in a minute."

Everyone packed up, topping off their bottles with fresh water and waited for Shandi to return. A minute passed. Five minutes. No Shandi.

Then, despite the increasingly frantic calls into the jungle, ten minutes passed without any sign of her.

It was as if the jungle had swallowed her whole.

CHAPTER TWENTY

Team North Face
Tsangpo Gorge

The decision to break away from Team Providence to follow the now-dried path of the Tsangpo had turned out to be an unfortunate one.

Though the riverbed was clear of the jungle's thick brush, it was hopelessly clogged with a diabolical combination of holes, mires, and rotted tree stumps. After a few hours of valiant effort wading through thigh-deep muck, all six racers were exhausted and pissed.

All of them were wondering the same thing: Had Team Providence discovered an easier path?

Wade decided on a change of tactics. As soon as he found a route out of the channel, he led the climb up to the edge of the jungle. Hacking through a thorny thicket,

Team North Face stumbled onto a cypress-choked swamp. It made for slow going, each step a battle against the sucking dark waters. They may as well have stayed in the riverbed, Wade groused.

The bottled-up Tsangpo had flooded the tributaries that crisscrossed the gorge, spilling over into the swamp. When North Face finally emerged from the boggy terrain onto higher ground, everyone was soaked to the skin from the waist down.

The jungle here was suffocatingly dense, clogged with big-leafed *Butea* trees, thorny *Zizyphus* bushes and *Carissa opaca*, shrubs with cave-like hollows that often served as cool shelters for napping tigers.

Tess sat down on a rotted trunk and pulled off her boots and socks. "Shit," she said. "Leeches."

Her feet and ankles were covered with the slugs, swollen with blood; three or four deep in places, each jockeying for position near the thick veins on her heels. Though it was a common enough sight for adventure racers, the squishy creatures still made her stomach roil.

It had only been a matter of time, of course; no jungle was free of leeches. The little buggers, about the size and shape of garden slugs, waited patiently on leaves and bushes in the forest until some unsuspecting creature passed by. Using hundreds of sticky fibers on its belly, the leech would then attach itself and make its way to a cozy spot; on humans, they loved the warm, sweaty spot just inside wool socks. The leech would then proceed to bite through the skin; a small amount of anesthetic numbing the spot first, keeping the prey completely oblivious to the parasite.

Once in place, the leech would suck the prey's blood until it swelled with blood to nearly four times its original size. So strongly were the slugs attached that they could only be removed in two ways. Burn them off—they released their bite and curled up when touched with a lighted match—or sprinkle salt on them. Option two worked best—just like the garden-variety slugs back home—but adventure racers rarely carried salt.

Blaine tossed over a book of wet-start matches.

"Thanks, dude," Tess said, striking the match. "This looks like a five- or six-match job." She initiated the procedure for removal. Identify it, burn it, pull it, and throw it away. She threw the first one toward Powder. "Don't you want to join the fun?"

Powder looked at her own still-booted feet. "I'm sure I'm just as bad off as you. I'm just dreading taking a look."

Tess burned through five matches, clearing a blood-streaked calf, only to discover another cluster on the back of her knee. She didn't quite have the heart to look any higher. Her count had passed forty-five leeches two matches ago.

Except for Powder, the others had gathered up enough courage to look at their own feet—and were not at all astonished to see bunches of the ink-black parasites covering their skin.

"We could be here all day," Blaine mumbled.

Tess stood abruptly. "Screw it."

"Are you offering something to the entire team?" Blaine asked, grinning.

"Let's not waste any more time," she said. "Let the little suckers do their thing. We've got a race to win—and I'll be damned if I'll let a few leeches slow me down." She pulled on a pair of dry socks, right over the suckers, and laced up her boots. "I'll get 'em when we stop for the night."

"Ugh, just the thought of them squishing around down there makes me sick," Cale protested, frantically pulling off as many as he could. "But you're right—nobody ever died from too many leeches . . . did they?"

Wade had already pulled his boots back on. "Nope, no deaths. In fact, some people here in Tibet still believe bloodletting has the power to heal the sick. Maybe there's something to it—maybe we'll all feel even better if we leave them on."

Tess felt one of the leeches squish under her heel. "Well, if nothing else, all those people watching this on television are getting a pretty good picture of what it's like out here. No makeup and special effects needed out here, that's for sure."

Once everyone had laced back up, Team North Face continued their march through the jungle, trying to ignore the slippery sensation inside their boots. After a few hours, they climbed out of the lush forest onto a broad meadow dotted with colorful alpine flowers. For the first time in hours, Tess felt the sun's warmth upon her face.

"We're stopping here for food," Wade announced, facing Cale's shoulder-mounted camera. Blaine caught Powder's attention and rolled his eyes. Over the past two days, the team captain had developed the annoying habit of performing for the cameras. Instead of looking, for instance, into Tess's eyes during a conversation, his gaze often drifted to the apparatus on her shoulder, as he spoke directly to the presumably millions of viewers back home. Tess supposed it was essentially harmless; heaven knows she had long ago become accustomed to Wade's propensity for attention. For her boyfriend, it wasn't enough to compete and win; he had to look good doing it. That's why he was not only the sport's most successful athlete, but the most recognizable as well.

"It's been tough going," Wade continued. "But we've been going all day without food or drink. Fatigue is setting in."

Cale took note of Wade's obvious posturing. "Dude, you sound like you're narrating a nature documentary," he chided.

Tess ignored the ensuing banter and slipped back into the trees for a bathroom break. Out here, you had to take advantage of privacy when you could get it.

She didn't bother to remove her pack. Instead, she just dropped her trekking trousers around her ankles and used the pack to prop herself against a damp tree. It had rained intermittently throughout the morning, and the trail was caked with mud. By the time she was finished, her boots had sunk three inches into the muck.

Tess pulled her pants back up—after wiping with a handful of large green leaves—and hoisted her pack back on her shoulders.

That's when she saw it.

It looked like a footprint of some kind, impressed into the mud right beside her. It couldn't have been hers. The size was all wrong.

She knelt beside the print, allowing her pack to drop to the ground beside her. The depression was huge—twice the width of her hand—and deep. Something heavy had made the print. And recently too. Rain had yet to accumulate inside the print.

Tess immediately thought it resembled a human foot-print. It was plantigrade—whatever had left the track had placed all five toes in the mud—unlike a tiger or dog that uses only four. It was difficult to make out the details in the seeping mud, but wasn't that a heel? There, in the back of the foot, where it seemed a little deeper than the rest of the imprint? And there, on the opposite side, didn't that look like a series of smaller depressions? Toes?

Tess scanned the ground, but found no other prints. If it was a footprint, where were the other tracks?

"What are you doing?"

The sound of Wade's voice startled her. As she whirled around, her elbow brushed against her pack. It happened too fast to stop it. The sixty-five pound pack toppled over—and landed with a thud directly on top of the strange print.

"Damn it, Wade!" She tugged the pack upright, but it

didn't matter. Whatever had been there was now obscured in the larger impression of a North Face alpine backpack.

"What's gotten into you?" Wade asked. "Surely you're not upset at soiling your pack?"

"There was a print here. A footprint. Can you see it? Right here, see this depression?"

Wade looked at her like she was seeing ghosts.

"You don't believe me?"

"No, no. I believe you. But there are hundreds of prints in the jungle. Thousands even. What surprises me is your shock at discovering one."

"This one was different. It was huge!" She held her hands a few feet apart to signify size. "And I think I saw toes, too."

"Like a human foot?"

The image of the print was already fading in her mind. There were toes right? Right there, at the top of the print? Five indentions, as if Tess's own toes had pressed into the mud. But there was something different about them, wasn't there?

It was the shape of the impressions. Not round and even like a human digit, but sharp, angular, more like a gash in the mud. As if it had been left, not by a soft toe, but more like—

— a claw.

"Tess? Was it a human footprint? It may not seem like it, but there are tribes that live here in the gorge. It is not unheard of to postulate a barefoot man—okay, a *large* barefoot man out here in the jungle. But if it was a man, where are the other prints?"

Wade answered himself. "Maybe he climbed this tree here," he said, slapping the large larch tree. "Or maybe, just maybe, it wasn't a footprint at all. The human mind is spectacularly adept at recognizing patterns in natural formations. Bunny rabbits in clouds, faces in rock formations. Tess, isn't it at least possible that maybe you mistook a natural depression in the mud for something else? Or do you choose to believe that a giant, one-legged man is hopping about the gorge?"

Tess looked meekly up into Wade's face, a slightly embarrassed smile cracking across her mouth. "You must think I'm being silly."

"I think you are lovely and, like the rest of us, tired and hungry. If it was a print of some kind, your camera there undoubtedly picked it up. When we get back down to base camp, after we win this race, we can ask them to identify it. But that's for later. Come now, it's time to get back to the others. We've got a race to run."

Team Providence
Tsangpo Gorge

"Shandi!"

Conner listened to Thad's increasingly frantic calls for his wife and frowned. After dispatching the poisonous gypsies, Team Providence had combed the jungle in search of their missing teammate. After ten minutes, Thad began to show concern. After twenty, he was edging toward full-on alarm. It was not like Shandi to wander off during a hike, much less a high-stakes adventure race. Something was not right.

Conner wiped his brow with the back of his wrist—for the tenth time in the past sixty seconds—and called out into the jungle. His voice didn't carry far. The thick under-growth swallowed his words right out of the air.

Then, something. A sound. Distant.

He called again, this time in the direction of the noise. He yelled for everyone to be quiet, then strained his ears to the jungle.

The birds and insects and leaves and wind paid no mind to Conner's call for silence, but he quickly tuned out the natural sounds of the valley. Senses on full alert, he filtered out a chattering troop of macaques and listened.

There it was again, faint and weak.

A woman's voice.

Conner sprinted toward the sound. Calling for the others to follow, he dashed for twenty yards through the undergrowth, ignoring the branches that sliced across his face, and spilled into a clearing. Thad quickly emerged from the jungle and stood beside him, followed by the others. Then the clearing went quiet again.

"Shandi!" Thad called.

Then, closer now, a voice. *"Thad?"*

"Shandi! Where are you?"

"*Over here. Follow my voice.*"

Conner and Thad sprinted across the clearing, plunging once again into the dense brush. When the racers emerged from the jungle Shandi Davis stood alone in the center of another clearing. They were surrounded by weeping pines, thick and lush and immense. A bed of fragrant red needles covered the ground.

Shandi's pack lay upon the needles and she looked up at her teammates, wide-eyed. She looked confused. Jumpy. Her eyes darted around the canopy, searching for something no one could see.

Thad rushed to her side and ran his hands over her body, searching for injuries and apparently finding none. "Shan, you had us worried sick. Why did you wander off?"

Before Shandi could reply, Conner saw the body.

It was partially concealed by the underbrush, leaves and dirt and grime. Bloody entrails spilled over the ground. Whatever it was, it was no longer alive.

"Jesus God," breathed Ian. "What the hell is that?"

It had been ripped to shreds. Long gouges crisscrossed a broad back, exposing the white of bone. Skin had been slashed from the bones, hanging in jagged strips on the ground. It was some kind of animal, but otherwise unidentifiable.

Conner slowly approached the ravaged carcass.

"I heard strange noises," Shandi said. "Like a growling sound. I decided to follow. I know I shouldn't have—but I tried to call to you guys, but you didn't hear."

"Yeah, this jungle kills sound," Ian said.

"It was just so loud, I guess my curiosity got the best of me," Shandi continued. "I figured I could catch up to you guys later. So I followed the growling for a while. All of a sudden, the sounds just stopped. Gone. That's when I stumbled onto this . . . thing." She gazed down at the body. "I'm afraid to touch it."

Preston stepped forward, past Conner, and prodded the carcass with his trekking pole. "Whatever it was, it's not likely to hurt us now," he said.

The head was folded grotesquely under the body. Preston tried to push the body over for a better look. It was thick and heavy and didn't budge. It looked to be the size of a good-sized bear.

"Lift up some of that skin," Conner suggested. "Maybe we can tell what it is by its skin."

Preston speared a flap of limp skin with his pole and slowly flipped it over. Conner immediately recognized the jagged stripes of orange and brown. The pattern was unmistakable.

"Tiger," Preston whispered, shaking his head. "Big one, too."

"Wow," said Ian, stepping closer. "A goddamned tiger. But what in the hell could do that to a tiger?"

Something growled behind them.

Turning slowly toward the sound, Conner held his breath. Whatever was behind them was probably the same thing that had flayed this tiger. And he wasn't eager to face whatever monstrosity that was.

At first, he could see nothing. The edge of the clearing was a wall of green foliage.

A head poked through the dense brush.

"Shit," Conner breathed.

The second tiger emerged like doom from the hard-scrabble forest. A massive head hung low to the ground, legs crouched. Stalking. The sight of the animal was almost beautiful. Even close to the ground, the tiger was nearly five feet tall, with a full, muscular body that Conner pegged at six hundred pounds. The marauder coat was nearly red with jagged black stripes as if branded by lightning strikes. The tiger radiated pure menace. It stared with black eyes directly at the six fear-stricken members of Team Providence. Its ears were pinned back against its skull. Hunting.

Menace crackled.

"What do we do?" whispered Shandi.

"Don't make a move," Conner replied. "Let's just see what she wants to do."

Something rustled in the jungle, momentarily drawing the tiger's hungry gaze. Then, all was silent. Above, the macaques fled in a burst of chatter.

The tiger stepped forward.

"Let's just start screaming," Ian suggested. "Maybe she doesn't like loud noises."

For a full minute, nobody made a move, nobody made a sound. There was always the chance the tiger was only deciding which of them to attack first. Any sound just might cinch her decision.

The animal's jaw dropped, revealing a mouth filled with knife-sharp fangs. They dripped with saliva.

"Okay," Thad said, inhaling deeply. "I'll start it."

He opened his mouth, poised to scream, when a gravelly voice silenced him.

"Scream, and you will die."

Preston stepped forward, moving away from the tiger carcass, and circled slowly toward the stalking cat. Conner saw that the giant man had changed his demeanor completely. This was a meaner, more intense Preston Child.

Since the expedition had begun, the millionaire businessman had largely kept to himself, except for a few hushed conversations with Malika. He had been pleasant enough, regaling the others with sordid tales of the high-stakes world of big business. Through it all, Preston had impressed Conner with his self-deprecating, easygoing manner. It couldn't have been easy for such an obviously successful leader to take a secondary position in such a vast undertaking, but Preston had slipped into the role without issue.

But now, the Preston Child that stepped forward, closer to the stalking tiger, was different. Harder. More focused. His eyes narrowed to slits, the thick ridges above his eyes furrowed menacingly. He looked downright terrifying. The Maverick Man was back.

Preston raised one of his trekking poles to his shoulder, pointing it at the cat like a rifle. It looked as though he was about to spear the great feline.

"If she feels threatened," Preston said, eyes never leaving their stalker, "she will strike."

"What then?" Ian asked.

"Pray," Preston replied. "Pray she just decides to leave."

Just as Conner was about to ask if that was likely, something blurred.

The tiger shot forward.

Moving. Moving fast. Running. Behind the force of two muscular hind legs that pumped like machine pistons, the tiger closed the gap in a blur of motion. Conner heard a scream—it may have been his own—and braced for the impact.

The tiger leaped directly for him.

And then something happened that really surprised him.

It was a second blur of motion. For a split second, Conner didn't trust his own eyes.

Preston hurled himself directly into the tiger's path.

Moving with a quickness that belied his bulky frame, Preston launched himself against the thick flanks of the beast. The collision rocked the jungle.

Preston bounced off the tiger as though he had hit a brick wall, the charging animal momentarily thrown off balance. Springing back off the ground with the nimbleness of a cat, Preston squatted on his haunches. The tiger roared in fury and swiped a paw of razor-sharp claws across Preston's chest, drawing blood. The animal swiped again, but this time Preston was quicker. He nimbly jerked away.

Conner would've never believed it if he weren't watching with his own two eyes, but burly Preston was lightning quick. With every enraged attack of the tiger's muscular body, he managed to evade each strike.

But how long could he keep this up? Sweat was already pouring from his brow—surely the tiger could outlast the burly man.

Preston brandished the trekking pole at his side.

The tiger roared again. And attacked.

In two loping strides, the animal was upon him. Preston maneuvered deftly to one side, evading the brunt of the charge. As the tiger barreled past, he jabbed the metal tip of his trekking pole into the back of the animal's neck. Something crackled loudly. Preston was thrown backwards.

The tiger collapsed to the ground, jerking in a series of involuntary spasms. Then, stillness.

Preston took a few deep breaths and then stood over the animal's apparently lifeless body. His shirt was soaked with sweat. He wiped his brow with the back of his hand, leaving a grimy smear of blood across his forehead.

Preston eyed his teammates warily, as if he had just revealed something deep and dark about himself. He stared at the camera mounted on Conner's shoulder, suddenly looking embarrassed.

Ian rushed to Preston's side. "Holy shit! That was fuckin' crazy!" he gushed. "You're fuckin' Superman!"

Immediately, Shandi and Thad enveloped Preston,

slapping him on the back in adulation. Malika dabbed her sleeve to a gash on her father's broad chest where the tiger had been a bit too fast. The cut was not deep.

Preston shrugged them off. "The tiger is not dead," he said. "Merely unconscious. We need to move now before she awakens."

"What did you do?" asked Ian.

Preston held up his trekking pole. "It's a taser, developed by one of my labs. Pressing this button here sends a high-voltage electrical pulse through the metal tip. Delivers a fifty thousand-volt electric shock, enough to shut down our little friend's nervous system. But not for long. We have fifteen minutes before she regains consciousness."

"That's what was setting off the airport security alarms," Conner said. "And you brought that weapon along why? The odds of running into a tiger are one hundred to one."

Preston ignored the question, pressed past his bewildered teammates, and knelt beside the first tiger carcass. He calmly continued his examination of the beast now, probing its flesh with his bare fingers. He lifted a shred of its pelt and pulled something from the innards. Conner couldn't see what had been removed, but it looked like a large tooth or a piece of bone. Whatever it was disappeared into Preston's pants pocket.

He finally stood and approached Conner close enough for the team captain to feel the man's hot breath on his cheeks. "Hundred to one, huh?" he said. "Tigers are territorial creatures. They've been known to slay their own."

"Is that what happened here?"

Preston stared hard into his captain's eyes. "What else could it be?"

By the faint light of dusk, Team Providence marched on through the jungle. Preston's display of preternatural strength and courage had rendered everyone silent. Even Conner couldn't summon up any conversation. How could they talk about food or movies or even the upcoming elections when they had just witnessed a man snap the neck of a ferocious tiger?

But something about the encounter unsettled Conner. He wasn't buying Preston's theory about the first dead tiger. From what he knew, tigers didn't generally attack their own kind. In dense, forested regions, predators tend to be more scattered. But merely the presence of two tigers in the same area didn't necessarily mean that one had slaughtered the other. And another thought nagged at Conner's brain—something that didn't quite add up. Tigers usually kill only when they're hungry. If the second tiger had feasted on the first—and there was no doubt that something had—it would have gorged itself to the point where another meal wouldn't have been necessary for at least a few days. But Conner had looked into the black eyes of that stalking tiger. Had seen what lurked there. Hunger. Whatever had consumed the first tiger, it hadn't been the second. Preston seemed convinced, but Conner was not so sure.

But what else could slay a tiger so ferociously?

And why had Preston been so insistent on bringing along his electric trekking pole in the first place? It was not, he was certain, for encounters with tigers.

For the rest of the day, Conner started at every crack and groan of the jungle.

That's why, when darkness finally fell, he found a campsite free of the dense foliage that could conceal a stalking bloodthirsty creature. They quickly erected the tents on a small hill that rose out of the jungle. Preston and Malika started a fire for a hot meal as the rest of the crew collapsed inside the camp, grateful to ease the eighty-pound burdens from sore shoulders.

The team spoke in hushed tones, still stunned by the day's events. Conner slipped away into the jungle, backtracking alone to a small creek to fill his water bottle. He dropped to his knees and eagerly scooped the water to his mouth with cupped hands. Then he poured some over his head, relishing the coolness on his overheated body.

"That looks good," said a voice from behind.

CHAPTER TWENTY-ONE

Team North Face
Tsangpo Gorge

From his perch atop a small promontory that skirted the edge of the jungle, Wade Stanley watched the sun set over the pass at Doshong La. It was a picturesque site for camp, and the rest of his team huddled around a small fire bookended by a pair of heavy canvas tents.

To the east, the flanks of Kuk Sur were just visible in the purple skies. They would reach the first gentle rises of the mountain in the morning. Surely Conner couldn't possibly arrive any sooner. There had been no sign of Team Providence since they had split ways at the landslide. *Probably lost in the jungle,* Wade thought, smiling to himself.

"What's so funny?" asked Tess. She had changed out of her dirty trekking pants into warm, dry fleece.

Wade pointed to Kuk Sur. "Seeing the finish line makes me happy."

Tess wrapped her arms about his waist and squeezed. "Well, I'll bet a warm dinner would make you even happier. It should be ready soon."

"Sounds good. Shall we?"

"Meet you there," she said, pulling away. "I've got to get some water first."

"Don't be long."

Tess waved her empty Nalgene bottle at him, and disappeared into the jungle. Wade watched her go, amazed how good she looked in a simple pair of fleece pants. They hadn't been together that long—six, seven months—but it was enough to know this was no ordinary relationship. He had been with dozens of women over the years, but they were easily dismissed and even more easily forgotten. Elizabeth was different. He was drawn to her in a way he hadn't experienced before. Wade didn't consider himself a romantic, but the time was rapidly approaching for a more serious commitment. They hadn't actually discussed an engagement, but weren't things going well? Perhaps he would celebrate their inevitable victory in *Darwin's Race* with a nice, big diamond ring.

Yes, Wade decided, things were definitely going well.

He rejoined his teammates with a wide grin plastered across his face.

"What's for dinner?" Hoops was asking, dramatically rubbing his stomach. "I'm starved."

"Don't look at me," Cale said quickly. "I cooked last night."

"Yeah, how could we forget?" Hoops teased. "Undercooked rice and beans. Mmm mmm good. My ass has been paying the price of your sorry cooking all day."

"Well, I'll be very excited about what you make for us tonight in these conditions. And please don't mention your ass again. I have to sleep next to you tonight, and I could do without the visual."

"Oh no, I cooked at Doshong La. I think it's Powder's turn."

Their female teammate emerged from the tent just in time to hear her name. "Water's already boiling, boys. Just give me a few minutes, and we'll get some yummy spag-bol in your tummies."

"Spaghetti Bolognese," Hoops said dreamily. "See, it takes a woman to really cook up a nice meal."

Powder threw a boot at her teammate, smacking him in the shoulder. "I'm not sure whether to be flattered or outraged," she said. "So I hit you just in case."

Though amused by his teammates' banter, Wade didn't partake. He was staring into the jungle. Tess had not yet returned.

❁ ❁ ❁

"That looks good."

By the light of the half moon diffused through a low-hanging bank of cloud, Conner identified his surprise nocturnal visitor.

"Well, well, well. Tess Chamniss. And here I thought we had left you in the dust back at the landslide. How did you manage to catch up?"

Tess chuckled. "Ha. I think it's you guys that did the catching up. We've been here for hours."

"You're camped out around here?"

"Just through the trees."

"Wade has the entire Tsangpo Gorge to find a campsite and he has to intrude on our space? That's not very nice."

"Hey, we were here first!"

"I guess it's not that surprising. I told my guys before the race that the terrain in the gorge was almost impassable. Good adventure racers go where the land allows them to go. We were bound to run into each other again." Warmth surged within Conner, like the feeling he got when he returned home after a long trip. Something like tranquility. It was amazing how easy, how comfortable, it was to talk to Tess. When it was just the two of them.

"Well, I see you've got an empty Nalgene," he said. "Come on and fill up. The water's great."

"I'm actually glad I found you," Tess said, dipping her bottle into the stream. "Alone."

Conner's heart skipped a beat. "Oh yeah? I thought it was pretty clear from your boyfriend over there that he didn't appreciate much contact between us."

When Tess didn't answer immediately, Conner bit his

tongue. *Don't mess this up. Just shut up and let her talk.* Tess was looking up to the peak of Kuk Sur, faintly luminous. Its icy flanks looked like they were glowing in the dark. Conner let the silence linger for a moment, drawing a deep breath to quell his nerves. He glanced furtively in the direction of North Face's camp, expecting Wade to emerge at any moment.

"I feel this distance between us," she said, her voice slow and deliberate. "And I've been trying to figure out what it is. To see you after all this time, it's brought back memories of what happened up there." She nodded toward the mountain.

"Tess, I—"

"No, wait. Let me finish." She turned to face him directly, placing a hand upon his arm. "I know you blame yourself for what happened on Kuk Sur; that's pretty obvious. And I also know that you blame me."

Conner tried to interrupt, but she stopped him.

"I accept the blame. Don't think I don't question myself every single day. Did I do the right thing? Could I have done more to save Tucker? Every day I ask myself these questions, and every day I get no answer. In those first few months back, I saw you were going through the same thing. And I wanted to get over it together, help each other deal with the grief and the guilt. But you just pushed me away. You just pulled yourself inward and cut off all contact with the world. And with me." She paused to look Conner in the eyes. "You never even considered that I might need you, too."

A breeze whistled through the canopy, sounding vaguely like a scream. Conner trained his headlamp into the trees, but when nothing emerged, she continued.

"That hurt, Conner. That really hurt me. We were supposed to be a team. Supposed to be able to work through anything. But you just cut me out of your life. Do you know we would spend entire evenings without speaking? I'm not sure if you even realized what you were doing to us. I begged you to enter the Lake Anna Half Ironman—just to get your mind on something else. But nothing would rouse you."

"I was responsible for my brother," Conner said quietly.

"No," Tess said with a forcefulness that surprised him. "He was responsible for himself."

"I should've insisted on going around."

"Tucker knew the risks—and he accepted them. The collapse of the snow bridge? That was an accident, pure and simple. Tragic, yes, but an *accident*."

"He was in no condition—"

"You don't know that," Tess said, cutting Conner off. "Tucker was an experienced climber, Con. If he felt he couldn't go on, he would've said so."

Conner shook his head. "Do you know what it was like to have to call Tucker's wife? To tell her that her husband wouldn't be coming home? That the father of her baby boy was dead? Do you know how hard that was?"

"I do know," Tess said. "Because I saw how it tore you

up inside. And I wanted to be there beside you to help you get through it. To help you get better."

"But you left me," Conner said. It sounded harsher than he intended.

"You left me no choice. I'm sure it was difficult, and my heart goes out to Melanie and Jake every day. But you can't control Mother Nature—there's nothing either of us could've done."

"We could've kept searching. He might've survived down there."

"The Tibetans searched for days, Con. They didn't find anything. If they found nothing, surely the two of us wouldn't have done any better."

"We were right there," Conner said. "The search party didn't get there until the next morning. We might've found something." Even as the words slipped from his lips, he realized the utter pointlessness of it all. Here they were, estranged lovers, arguing about something four years in the past. What Conner really wanted to do was move forward—that's why he was out here.

But wasn't the future tied explicitly to the past? One could not exist without the other. Conner's own future was born in his past, his childhood, his loves, his friends, his races.

This very mountain.

It hurt—God, how it hurt—but Conner knew to embrace his future; he had to reconcile with this past. A past that included Tess Chamniss.

"You may be a Superman, Conner Michaels. But you aren't all-powerful. Even out here in the gorge, do you really think you are prepared for everything? What about that landslide? Who expected that the mighty Tsangpo would be bottled up like that? Not me, not you, not any of us. What more proof do you need that we are not in control out here?"

"Do you think I tried to control you?"

Tess seemed taken aback by the sudden question, but Conner didn't care. He knew sometimes the only way to ask the tough questions was to just blurt them out, see what happens.

"You wanted me to sit idly by and watch you turn into a hermit," she answered. "I couldn't do that. I tried to engage you in something, anything. But I'm not a miracle worker—you had to fix yourself. I couldn't just waste my life away. So I left. It broke my heart, but I wasn't helping you anymore. I thought leaving would maybe snap you out of it, but that didn't happen either. Conner, it's been almost four years since we've spoken."

One thousand three hundred and ninety-four days to be exact, Conner thought. *And not a single one passed without me hoping you would return.*

"I was so happy to see you at the press conference in DC—you have no idea," she continued. "Finally, I thought, you have broken through whatever it was you were going through. Maybe it was the sheer audacity of this race—the chance to do something no one has ever done before. I don't know. I'm just glad you're here now. I guess I wanted you to know that."

It suddenly occurred to Conner that maybe he wasn't the only one trying to reconcile with the past. He thought back to Tucker's cap, still tucked away in his pack. He had never shared with Tess what he'd heard down in that crevasse.

Conner, something's down here with me.

Maybe it was time for the truth.

"Do you know why I'm here?" he asked after a deep breath. "Do you want to know why I entered *Darwin's Race*?"

They both started at a rustling noise behind them. Flashing his headlamp through the trees, Conner glimpsed a set of piercing eyes blinking in the blackness. He felt one of Tess's hands clamp down on his arm as a sense of utter dread washed over his body. Images of the slain tiger, the blood, swam inside Conner's head. The mysterious jungle predator had finally tracked them down. And this time, Preston was not around to save them.

Then, with another rustle of leaves, Wade Stanley emerged from the jungle, shielding his eyes from the glare of Conner's headlamp.

"Elizabeth, darling. What did I tell you about cavorting with the enemy?" Wade tried to deliver the line with a touch of sarcastic humor, but his tone suggested bitterness and anger just beneath the surface.

"Conner Michaels, I'm surprised to see you here. I figured that your ragtag team would be well behind by now. I commend your efforts."

"We've actually been moving a bit slower than anticipated," Conner lied. "We had a bit of an encounter with a tiger a ways back. What's your excuse?"

Seeing the stunned look on Tess and Wade's faces, Conner told them about the first tiger carcass and Preston's astonishing slaying of the second cat. When he was finished, Tess still looked amazed, but her boyfriend was already dismissing the entire episode with that stupid sardonic grin of his.

"Well, that is a nice bedtime story, Conner. Thank you for that," Wade said. "As for us, darling, you really must come back to camp. Your dinner is getting cold. You need to eat so we can get all tucked inside our sleeping bags tonight. Tomorrow will be an early start."

Conner brooded as the pair slipped back through the trees, Wade's arm wrapped around Tess's shoulders. He suddenly felt sick to his stomach as he turned back toward his own camp. It felt like someone had just punched him hard in the gut.

Conner returned to camp, finding it quiet and still. Shandi, Thad, Ian, and Preston sat around a small fire, warming themselves in the cool night air. They looked up at his approach but quickly went back to their own private conversations.

"Is everything alright?" Malika asked, handing him an empty bowl. "You don't look so hot."

He scooped a bowlful of rice from the pot over the fire and began to eat with his bare fingers. "It's nothing," he mumbled.

"Nothing, huh? Well, that chip on your shoulder isn't nothing."

"That obvious?"

"Big as a boulder."

Conner considered Malika. She seemed eager to listen.

"Team North Face is camped just over there. I ran into them when I was getting some water."

"Let me guess. Tess?"

"Wade, too. Look, Malika. I'm not sure I'm ready to talk to you about this. I barely know you."

"Sometimes it's easier to talk to someone you don't know."

Conner remembered his lineup of anonymous therapists and psychologists. "I tried that," he said. "Didn't help."

Malika stood, brushing dirt off her pant legs. "I'm not going to pretend to know what's going on with you, knowing that you're about to climb Kuk Sur again. The memories of your brother must be rattling around like crazy in that head of yours. I know it's hard. You feel powerless, like the world around you is swirling out of control and you can't do anything to slow it down. I know because I know about loss, too."

Conner looked up from his empty bowl.

"My mother," she said quietly.

Malika stared across camp to her father. Preston was sitting alone by the fire, absently adding sticks to the flame.

"I'm sorry. I didn't know."

"She was everything to him," she said, still gazing at

her father. Abruptly, she turned back to Conner. "The two of you are alike in so many ways. So strong, so independent. Always thinking you can deal with everything on your own. But there are times when everyone needs someone. There are some things you can't do alone."

"Your father—he reached out to you?" Conner asked.

Malika smiled, the flickering light of the fire dancing across her face. "Let's just say we reached out to each other," she said. "Everyone faces their demons in different ways."

They stared into the fire for a moment.

"Have you heard of Milarepa?" Malika asked. "He was a Sherpa poet at the turn of the millennium."

Conner shook his head.

"He wrote something that I always found insightful. He said, 'What appears as a monster, what is called a monster, what is recognized as a monster, exists within a human being himself. And disappears with him.'"

"What's that supposed to mean? That there are no monsters out there?"

"Oh, there are monsters out there," she said. "But they're nothing compared to the ones inside."

With that, Malika moved away, taking a seat next to her father and placing her head upon his broad shoulder. Conner watched them through the flames, envying their easy familiarity. No doubt the loss of a wife and mother had drawn the two of them together, in an era when so many families splintered after a loss. There wasn't anyone there for him after Tucker's death. Melanie and Jake lived hundreds of miles away, and they had lives to pull together. Calls from his mother slowly dwindled over the months, in all likelihood the result of an unresponsive son. And then there was Tess. He had pushed her away, too.

Maybe there *had* been people around. Maybe he just hadn't let them get close enough to help.

Conner gazed at Preston and Malika, wondering what their monsters looked like.

CHAPTER TWENTY-TWO

Team North Face
Tsangpo Gorge

A few hours later, under a black Tibetan sky, the bellies of the members of Team North Face were filled with half-cooked spaghetti—the burners had run out of fuel—and the pots were cleaned and stowed. The racers had completed their final bathroom breaks for the evening. This was vital because it was a royal pain in the ass to climb out of the tent once everyone was tucked inside cozy sleeping bags. One person getting up invariably disrupted the sleep of everyone present, so as a general rule it was better to empty the bladder just before turning in for the night.

Wade Stanley stretched out atop his mummy bag, staring into the inky darkness. Inside the tent, the body warmth emanating from Tess and Blaine made the sleeping bags unnecessary. Not for long though. Once the ascent of Kuk Sur commenced, Wade knew the frigid cold would chase them inside their restrictive bags. Better to enjoy the freedom while he could.

One of Tess's hands was resting on his leg, and he slowly removed it and rolled to his side. He hadn't been happy to discover her alone in the jungle with her old boyfriend, but she had apologized profusely, saying she had no idea Providence had camped anywhere in the vicinity. Sounded reasonable, but the scene of the two of them huddled beside the creek still disturbed him. It wasn't that he didn't trust her. He did. Completely. But the lure of old love was a frighteningly strong current, and Conner Michaels, Wade was loathe to admit, was not a man without charm.

Wade closed his eyes, tried to push the thought from his mind.

Something scratched outside the tent.

By now, Wade had grown accustomed to the night sounds of the Tibetan jungle. The campsite practically *squirmed* with activity; nocturnal creatures skittering about in search of food. But this noise was different, more solid.

Closer.

Suddenly alert, Wade pitched himself up on his elbows and trained his ear to the sounds of the jungle. Beside him, Tess stirred.

"What are you doing?" she asked groggily.

"I thought I heard something."

A light breeze wafted through the half-open tent flap,

crafting an almost musical whine. Wade moved quickly to zip up the tent flap. The whistling stopped.

"Is that what you heard?" asked Tess.

"I didn't think so." He waited another moment, assuring himself, then settled back onto his bag. "I guess it was nothing."

Suddenly an ear-splitting roar shook the tent upon its stakes. It sounded like an airplane was about to land on their tent—it was that close, that loud.

But this sound was animal.

The growl of something wild.

Blaine jolted awake. "What the hell was that?" he asked, bug-eyed.

"Something that needs to be scared off," Wade said.

The sound seemed to come from everywhere, all around them, but Wade couldn't tell if it was the roar of a single animal or an entire pack. He scrambled to retrieve his headlamp from his backpack.

"Don't go out there," Tess protested. "What if it's another tiger?"

The growling outside the tent faded to silence.

Holding his headlamp like a flashlight, Wade slipped out of the tent. The jungle greeted him with a blast of frigid air. The night was pitch dark, lit only dimly with faded starlight. Across the way, Hoops and Cale were peeking out of their own tent.

"What the hell was that?" Hoops asked. "Sounded like a goddamned grizzly bear."

"I'll take care of it," Wade said, waving them off. "Go back to bed." He flipped on the headlamp and squinted into the murk.

Darting the narrow beam across the area, he could see nothing but leaves swinging gently in the night breezes. He scanned the ground, looking for tracks. Nothing. But the light from the headlamp was weak. Easy to miss something. He turned back toward the tent.

"Well, I'd just like to thank my brave teammates for their courage and valor in the face of the unknown," Wade quipped, slipping back inside the tent. "I guess I can always count on you guys to get my back."

"I would've been out there in a flash had anything tried to attack," Blaine assured the team leader.

"I'll just bet," Wade said. "In any event, your courage will not be tested this night. I found nothing."

"Well, something made that sound," Blaine said.

"A marmot most likely," Wade said. "A grouse, perhaps. Either way, it's gone now. I suggest we all go back to sleep."

By the gently snoring sounds filling the tent a few minutes later, Wade knew Tess and Blaine had heeded his advice. But he could not fall asleep quite so easily. For another full hour, Wade remained acutely attuned to the stiff wind—and to the memory of the ferocious growl just outside his tent.

✸ ✸ ✸

Team Providence
Tsangpo Gorge

He was the last to turn in. While the rest of the team nestled snugly inside down sleeping bags, Conner watched the last of the campfire die out before making his way toward his tent, leaving only fading crimson embers in the pit.

He slipped inside the darkened tent, leaving the flap open behind him, and pulled off his boots. Sliding into his sleeping bag, Conner detected Ian Bjornson's telltale shock of blonde hair peeking out from the far sleeping bag. He glanced at the second bag and was surprised to see Malika Child lying beside him.

That was strange. They must've switched with Shandi and Thad, Conner realized. *But why?*

Malika shifted in her bag, moving closer. Conner could sense the warmth of her body as she pressed up against him. She was still sleeping, her rhythmic breathing soothing and peaceful. He was surprised at how much he enjoyed the closeness. It had been years since Tess had left—a long time without the warmth of a woman. It felt good.

He had left behind his solitary life in rural Virginia to travel thousands of miles to the most remote tract of terrain in the world in an effort to confront his past, to face his guilt over the death of his brother, and, hopefully, to put together the pieces of a future. It now seemed pretty clear that Tess was not going to be a part of his new life, but for the first time in a long time, Conner didn't feel that all-too-familiar sense of loss. That feeling that something was missing, that he was somehow incomplete without her.

Malika shifted again, her face now close enough for Conner to feel her breath on his face. He didn't move away.

Maybe he could build a life without Tess after all.

CHAPTER TWENTY-THREE

Team Providence
Tsangpo Gorge

Conner was the first to rise, slipping silently from the tent without disturbing the others. He would have to wake them soon enough, but he needed a moment for himself first. Wisps of clouds hovered lazily in the azure sky like frayed cotton balls. It was going to be a clear day.

Someone stirred inside the second tent, and Conner moved to pull together breakfast. It would be an eat-on-the-run affair: trail mix and lukewarm tea.

Malika was the first to emerge, already dressed in her trekking pants and a tight-fitting microfiber top. Conner handed her a cup. "It's not that hot," he apologized. "I want to break camp quickly."

"Suits me," she said, taking a sip. "If we move, we

should be able to reach the mountain before nightfall."

"Malika?" Conner waited until her eyes met his. "Thanks for last night. It may not seem like it, but I do appreciate it."

"You're welcome," she said. "Sometimes it means a lot just to have someone listen."

"I was surprised to see you had switched tents."

"Surprised and sad, or surprised and glad?"

Preston and Ian spilled out of their tent, clambering over each other to get at the food. Malika smiled conspiratorially. "Ah, saved by the peanut gallery."

"I don't need saving. The answer is surprised and glad."

They held each other's gaze for a full moment before turning back to the work at hand.

Fifteen minutes later, Team Providence had broken camp, packed away their gear, and were hacking along an overgrown trail that snaked its way east toward Kuk Sur. The terrain was a massive crumple zone, with dense valleys and clear plateaus that afforded 360-degree views of the surrounding countryside. After a few hours, Conner noticed a gap in the tree line a few miles ahead.

"There's the river," he announced. "Or what's left of it. Preston thinks there's a bridge there, but if the river is still dammed up, we may be able to cross along the bottom."

The ground angled down steeply back into the jungle, and Preston took the lead, hacking a path with his tree trunk arms. The foliage ended abruptly, and Team

Providence found themselves along the steep banks of what was once the mighty Tsangpo River. The precipice fell almost vertically down to the riverbed, forty feet below. The landslide was apparently still holding. The riverbed was little more than a muddy quagmire.

"It looks awfully mucky down there," Conner said. "I think we'd better look for the bridge."

Ian followed the course of the river. "But which way?" he asked. "How do we know the bridge isn't back in the other direction?"

"We don't," Conner admitted. "But we ought to continue on in a direct line toward the finish line; don't you think?"

"I agree," Preston said. "The river has many curves. Maybe our bridge is just around that bend there."

"From your mouth to God's ears," Shandi said. "Somehow I don't think we'll be so lucky."

Shandi was right. The bridge was not just around the bend. Nor the second. Or the third. Skirting the river, Team Providence negotiated no fewer than seven major twists and turns. Conner began to mull the other option— a wet and dirty crossing of the riverbed. It was hardly an enticing proposition.

After the eighth bend, Team Providence's good fortune finally arrived. Preston saw the bridge first, and he excitedly pointed to the distant span as if he had discovered a burger joint. To Conner it looked like a thin strand of a spider's web stretching across an impossibly vast chasm. It was only when they approached the bridge that they could make out the details—and the scale—of the bridge.

It was a narrow and rickety looking thing made of a series of rotted planks fastened to a few strands of frayed rope. There were no railings of any kind, only a length of worn rope stretched three hundred feet to the far side of the river. *I guess that's what passes for a railing,* Conner thought, shaking his head. *We hiked all this way just for that?*

The high-water scour was etched across the canyon rock like a bathtub ring—nearly seventy-five feet up. Under ordinary conditions, the bridge would've cleared the roiling water by barely five feet. That, at least, was good news.

"Dude, that thing is a deathtrap," Ian said, yanking on the guide rope. "That's an eighty-foot drop to the bottom—and there ain't enough water down there to break my fall. I say we backtrack down to the river bottom and cross down there where it's safe."

Conner studied the threadbare bridge. "Anyone else?"

"I'm with Ian," Thad said. "We'll lose some time, but I sure would feel better about it." Preston seemed anxious to test the bridge, but Malika and Shandi were nodding in agreement with Ian and Thad.

Conner surveyed the narrow trail that led down the riverside. It was passable enough, but the steep bank that descended down the mucky floor looked treacherous. They would have to rope up.

"Alright," Conner announced. "Let's move out."

"Hold up," Ian said, pointing downriver. "Looks like we're about to get some company."

Conner followed his line of vision. Snaking along the riverbed below, Wade Stanley led Team North Face in their direction. Even at a distance, Conner could see Wade's shit-eating grin.

Jesus Christ. Will we ever get rid of this guy?

Arriving at the bridge, Wade surveyed the span with the indulgent appraisal of an explorer gazing upon a newly discovered waterfall. He glanced back down to the river floor, obviously weighing his options. As his teammates arrived, he took a few tentative steps out onto the bridge.

"Jump up and down a little," Ian said. "I think you should really test it."

A wry smile cracked across Wade's mouth. "Ian"— his British accent turned *Ian* into something that sounded more like *Eeen*—"how I adore your wit. So predictable."

Conner took a few steps down the trail. "Come on, team. Let's get out of here."

"Yes, why don't you fellows follow the leader and back-track?" Wade called after them. "By the time you reach the base of Kuk Sur, we'll be halfway to the summit. My team will be crossing by bridge—it's quite sturdy. Come now, one at a time—I'll go first to show you how strong it is."

"Shouldn't you wait for the rest of your team?" Thad asked. He pointed down the trail.

There, seated riverside on a flat boulder, was Powder. She appeared to be tending to a blistered foot.

"She's a big girl," Wade said. "She'll catch up."

Conner looked to Tess for help, but she looked away.

Crossing the bridge was the wrong move, although he knew he would certainly enjoy watching a few of those planks cave in under Wade's over-priced Italian boots. But it wasn't North Face's team captain that he was concerned about.

He moved closer to Tess, following Wade's progress as he made his way toward the center of the bridge. "You know better," he said, pulling her aside. "That bridge isn't safe. Look how it's buckling under his weight. It's going to snap."

Tess looked out toward Wade and pulled her arm from Conner's grasp. "It's a team sport," she said curtly. "I'm sticking with the team."

"What about Powder? Isn't she part of the team?"

"Let it go, Con," she said. "Worry about your own team."

A shout interrupted the exchange. Wade had made it across and was calling and waving the others across. Despite the successful crossing, the members of North Face did not look particularly eager to follow. Tess moved forward, arms stretched out at her sides for balance, and stepped onto the bridge.

"Jeez, Con," said Ian. "If they make it across, maybe we oughta follow. It held Wade."

"That doesn't make it the right move," Conner said, keeping a watchful gaze upon Tess. She looked so small and vulnerable in the middle of the giant chasm. With the flanks of Kuk Sur looming on the far side of the valley, she looked very small indeed.

Something drew Conner's eyes to the riverbed, eighty feet below. Something different, out of place. Something that wasn't right. Something he couldn't place.

Keep moving, Tess. Keep moving.

Powder's feet did not look pretty. The condition of her soles would've given an ordinary person the dry heaves. An array of blisters—some ruptured, some still bulging with pus—covered her heel. Dead skin hung in dried flaps from the pads of both feet.

She worked methodically, puncturing each blister with the blade of her Leatherman. She cut away the dead skin, leaving behind raw pink patches that burned like hell. Pulling blister pads from a first aid kit, she covered each raw spot, wincing in pain.

That ass, Wade, didn't even have the courtesy to wait, she grumbled. *He couldn't hold up for ten minutes?* Powder shook her head in exasperation. Vintage Wade Stanley. No concept of cooperation.

"There is no Wade Stanley in T-E-A-M," she said aloud. The joke made her feel better, good enough to stand and test her sore feet. They stung a bit, but she could continue. The day she let a few blisters stop her was the day she stopped climbing mountains. Today wasn't going to be that day.

Above, Tess Chamniss had crossed the dodgy bridge, joining her boyfriend on the far side. Cale Anders was now inching his way across the bridge. He was moving faster, more confident now that the others had passed. By the time she reached the bridge, her team would be well ahead of her.

"Gee, guys, thanks for waiting."

Powder pondered her options. The riverbed below looked muddy, but definitely passable. If she hurried, she could cross and scramble up the far side to rejoin the others before they got too far ahead.

Decision made, she hoisted her pack upon her shoulders and gingerly stepped onto the steep bank that fell away to the river floor.

※ ※ ※

After watching the members of North Face make successful crossings, Conner's own team stared at him with urgent eyes.

"What?"

"Come on, Con. The bridge held all of them," Ian said.

"Just weakened it that much more for us," Conner replied, only half-joking.

"Then we should've gone first," Shandi interjected. "Is this really how you want to play this?"

Maybe they were right. The bridge *had* held. And no, that was not how he wanted to play things. He didn't come to Tibet to play it too close to the vest.

"Okay," he said. "Let's go. One at a time."

Team Providence crossed in single file, spaced out conservatively—Malika, Shandi, Thad, and Ian making it to the far side without incident. Preston was the happiest of the bunch, literally bounding across the span as if it were his personal jungle gym. Despite himself, Conner smiled. If the bridge could hold Preston's bulk . . .

Conner inched out onto the bridge, surprised at the solidity of the obviously decayed planks. He strode confidently to the center of the bridge and paused to glance upriver. The absence of the roiling waters of the Tsangpo River was still shocking to him, although at this precise moment, Conner was more than happy that the massive current was not swirling under the flimsy bridge.

That's when he heard the roar.

His first instinct was to look up the mountain, expecting to see the gut-wrenching sight of a furious avalanche. But Kuk Sur was calm, and the roar was growing louder. He looked down.

That's when he knew.

The thing that had nagged him about the riverbed. *Movement.*

The water level was rising.

"No—" he breathed.

The Tsangpo had broken through the landslide.

CHAPTER TWENTY-FOUR

Team North Face
Tsangpo Gorge

Eighty feet below the bridge, Powder was mildly surprised to see the water rise over her ankles. She quickly started the slog, cursing the inevitability of soaked boots. And just after she had dried out too. Three hundred feet away, a massive slab of granite rose up on the far side. She could see Tess standing atop the rock.

At least someone was waiting.

Passage was exhausting. With each step, Powder pulled her boots from the thick mud with a loud sucking sound. *Thwuck, thwuck. Thwuck, thwuck.*

She felt something rumble under her feet.

Feels like an earthquake, she thought. She looked to the far bank, searching for her teammate. Tess was still there, still alone. Only now she was waving her arms wildly.

And screaming.

Conner froze.

A lump formed in his throat the size of a boulder. He was short of breath. He tried to swallow and couldn't. He knew exactly what was coming—and still found himself hopelessly paralyzed, utterly unable to move.

He could imagine the scene: Miles upstream, on the far side of the landslide, the water level of the Tsangpo rose. At first, a thin stream of water trickled over the top of the rubble, cascading like a baby waterfall. As the flow increased, the topmost layer of dirt and rock ground away from the pile. As more rubble fell away, the flow strengthened. Until it grew to a torrent. Finally bursting through the landslide like an unleashed beast.

The mighty Tsangpo had awakened.

Someone screamed.

A towering wall of water churned around the river bend into view, barreling down the valley. Conner stared at a liquid wall six stories high. The water looked furious, as if upset at having been bottled up, roiling with mud and rocks and tree limbs. It thundered like a locomotive down the riverbed, consuming everything in its path.

Conner was trapped. There wasn't enough time to reach either side of the bridge. Quickly breathing a prayer, he dropped to his knees and looped the guide rope around his wrists. He faced upriver toward the churning waters, clenched his eyes shut, and braced for the impact.

"Conner! CONNER!"

His eyes popped open and searched the far bank for his teammates. They were there, huddled with Tess and the other members of Team North Face. They were all pointing to the riverbed below him.

Conner leaned over and saw what they were screaming about. Eighty feet below him, frozen in place, was Powder.

The roiling river was two hundred yards away—gaining speed, gaining force. Ordinarily, the Tsangpo hurled through the gorge at speeds approaching forty miles per hour. Unleashed from its rocky prison, the mighty river now roared even faster.

Conner knew the impact of the water would literally tear Powder apart.

Acting quickly, Conner loosed his wrists and ripped his rock climbing rope from his pack. It was standard half-inch rappelling rope, and like all good climbing rope, it had a little give to it. Nothing like a bungee cord, but enough to soften a fall.

Conner hoped it would be enough.

"Powder! Don't move!" he yelled down to her.

The roar of the water swallowed his words whole.

Looping the rope over the railing, he tied it off and wrapped the free end around his waist harness. He peered off the edge of the bridge and prayed he had estimated the right length of rope. The water was less than a hundred yards upstream.

Conner inhaled deeply—

— and jumped.

Powder was a goner.

The wall of water barreled down upon her like a tsunami, tearing up the riverbed, lifting and obliterating giant boulders like they were kernels of popcorn. There wasn't even enough time for her life to flash before her eyes.

When the tempest was less than fifty yards from her, she drew her arms up to her face as if she could somehow ward off what was coming. She could feel the spray of the water on her face, cold and brutal.

From above, something plunged into view.

As he plummeted toward Powder, Conner saw her eyes widen with shock. The slack in his rope shrunk rapidly as he fell toward the riverbed.

Twenty feet.

Just a little bit more.

Ten feet.

If Conner had given himself too much rope, he would smash into the ground at full force and the massive waters of the Tsangpo would no longer matter. He would already be dead.

Three feet.

The rope caught. Conner's body jerked violently, knocking the breath from his lungs. He dangled on the rope inches above the muddy ground.

He thrust a carabiner towards Powder. "Clip this to your harness!" he screamed.

"But—?"

Cold water drenched his back. He dared not turn to face the crashing river.

"Do it now, or we're both dead."

Powder snapped the heavy-duty carabiner onto her harness and looked up at Conner.

"Now hold on!"

The river slammed into them like a hammer blow. Powder screamed as the river propelled them forward with the force of a tidal wave. They exploded downstream, rising with the water level. The rope caught again seventy feet downriver, and suddenly Powder and Conner found themselves clipped together at the waist, being thrashed by thousands of pounds of furious whitewater.

They struggled for air.

The reawakened waters of the mighty Tsangpo twisted like a chained attack dog beneath them. Its jaws snapped at their bodies, desperate to pull them under.

"Hang on!" Conner yelled.

Powerless to help Powder, Conner gripped his climbing

rope with both hands. Fingers burning, he pulled both of them towards the bridge. Inch by inch. Battling the dog.

A few feet from the bridge, Powder was suddenly sucked under the freezing whitewater.

"Powder!" screamed Conner.

She struggled to the surface, gasping air into starved lungs. She was weakening, too; Conner could see it in her eyes.

She didn't have much time left.

Conner heaved mightily and reached up. The river thrashed just about two feet under the bridge. His fingers grazed the sodden planks . . . and slipped free.

He could feel Powder now, her weight dragging him down. Dead weight. She had stopped struggling.

With a reserve of energy he didn't think he had, Conner lunged for the bridge . . . and found purchase.

He hauled himself up and threw a leg onto the bridge. Thus braced, he pulled hard to drag Powder from the roiling waters.

Her face was ice blue. But she was breathing.

They both collapsed, utterly spent.

Through the roar, Conner heard more shouts from the far riverbank. He looked over to see Ian pointing upriver and waving frantically.

What now?

As if angered by the pair's escape from its watery fist, a giant wave had formed *on top* of the churning river! It was twenty feet high at least and now loomed *over* the bridge. It curled toward them like a hooked finger of death.

"Hold on!" Conner yelled again. He grabbed hold of Powder's shoulder straps with his free hand. She tightened her grip around his waist.

The wave smashed into the bridge, rattling its precarious moorings.

With a sickening *snap!* of rotted wood, the bridge tore away.

The floorboards splintered to pieces, crashing against Conner's body. One slammed into his skull, momentarily blinding him. Somehow, one side of the rope bridge was still holding.

The force of the river swung them toward the rocky shore.

The waters raged anew. And this time, Conner had no fight left.

The others on shore also saw what was happening, and they scrambled to the spot where the helpless racers were going to hit. Through the waters, between gasps for air, Conner saw Preston and Ian lead the charge down the slope to the still-rising water line.

Conner and Powder slammed into the granite wall, the impact jarring his grip from her shoulder straps. He clamped both hands around the rope connecting them to the bridge. Their lifeline. If that snapped, both of them would disappear under the Tsangpo forever.

A surge of energy was born with that realization.

"One more second!" he yelled to Powder. "I've got you!"

Through the tumult, he could vaguely make out darkened

shapes scrambling down to the riverbanks.

"Grab her!" he screamed. "Grab her!"

His muscles screamed, burning, cramping until he could no longer feel his hands or arms. Through the bubbling waters, he saw three of his teammates form a human ladder, extending from the banks into the churning water. At the edge, his boots held by Preston, Ian plunged into the water, reaching. He stretched for Powder, his fingers grazing her right ankle.

Conner roared as a fresh cramp squeezed the muscles in his forearms. Although he clutched as hard as he could, his muscles were no longer paying attention, and he felt his fingers slowly peel back from the guide rope. The water pummeled him mercilessly.

And then Powder's harness tore away.

She shot down the river like a bullet, plunging beneath the waves—

—bobbing to the surface ten meters farther down.

And then she disappeared again, crashing over a two-foot ledge into a watery chasm. Her familiar platinum blonde hair slipped beneath the surface. Even as Conner felt a pair of hands upon his numbed arms, he scanned the river below, waiting for her to reemerge.

She didn't. And in that sickening instant, Conner knew the mighty Tsangpo had claimed another victim.

He had only a vague sense of being lifted free of the water. Before he blacked out, Conner blinked his eyes open to see Preston looming over him, screaming for him to breathe.

CHAPTER TWENTY-FIVE

Team Providence
Kuk Sur

When Conner Michaels finally blinked his eyes open, his body screamed at him. His torso was frozen solid, despite the blankets that his teammates had apparently used to warm him. His right shoulder felt like it had popped out of it socket, and his hands burned like hell. Still, only one thought occurred to him.

He immediately hacked up a lungful of brackish river water. "Powder?"

His teammates helped him to his feet as the members of North Face watched intently from a short distance.

The looks on the faces of the others gave him his answer. She was gone.

Ian said, "She never came back up."

"You did everything you could," someone else said. Conner didn't look up to see who.

Conner lungs burned with each breath. "We have to find her."

Ian shook his head. "Not likely. The river is moving too fast, too hard. Water like that is not likely to give her up."

Conner knew his friend was right. Even rivers half as ferocious could hide their victims for months amidst roiling holes and regurgitating hydraulics. He reminded himself that Doug Gordon's body had never been recovered. And that had been years ago.

"Give him some room to breathe," Shandi shouted.

"I'm fine; I'm fine. Just give me a moment."

Despite the blankets, he felt himself shivering uncontrollably.

"Let's get him some warm clothes," Shandi ordered.

As Ian and Thad rummaged through their packs for dry clothes, Conner felt a tap on his shoulder. It was Tess. Her eyes were red.

"You okay?" Conner asked.

"Never mind me," she said. "You know that you did everything you could to save her, right?"

"Are you looking out for me?"

"Come on, Con. You know what I mean. You almost died trying to save her."

He waited a moment before answering. "I know that. If she only could've hung on for a few more seconds."

Wade Stanley abruptly stepped between them. "Her

harness split. There was nothing any of us could've done."

Conner must've hurt his head more than he thought. Was this Wade Stanley offering encouraging words? He shook his head lest he was dreaming.

"We just couldn't get to her in time."

All of the racers stared at their boots in awkward silence.

Wade seemed to sense the tension. "Look, we're all professionals here. We know this is part of the risk of adventure racing. But Powder was an able competitor and a good friend to some of us. If it's okay with the rest of you, I suggest we take some time now to remember her."

Ian looked as surprised as Conner felt. "You mean some kind of service? A vigil?"

"Whatever you want to call it, I think the race can wait for a few hours. And then, after we've said our piece, we can honor her by fighting like hell for the remainder of this race."

Conner studied Wade's face for any sign of disingenuousness. He found none. For the first time since he'd met him, Conner saw a human side to the man. Wade was genuinely upset about Powder's death. He had not expected that. *Win at all costs* had always been Wade's mantra. Or had it only seemed that way?

For years, Conner had hated Wade Stanley. Now he found himself wavering. Was it possible that his own competitive streak had blinded him to Wade's decent side?

Conner climbed to his feet and strode over to Wade. His rival eyed him warily. And then Conner extended his hand. "Thank you, Wade. You could've used this as an opportunity to gain a huge lead, but you didn't. I think a vigil for Powder is an extremely thoughtful—though unexpected—gesture. Thank you."

Wade took the proffered hand, shook it. "No matter what you believe of me, I am not an evil man. I've seen friends die, too."

The two teams started a fire and shared a hot meal. Preston and Thad boiled some river water to make some tea. Together, the teams gathered armfuls of rocks and assembled a small cairn beside the river. To the stones, they each fastened an item of clothing from their packs. A makeshift prayer flag display. They each paused a moment beside the stones, then, one by one, turned back to the fire.

Conner lingered. He stared at the rocks until darkness descended. From the rock bed beside the river, he gathered up a large stone and wiped it clean. He placed it atop the cairn.

"Goodbye, Powder."

Only when he began to shiver anew did he break away from the makeshift memorial and head back to camp.

As the others occupied themselves with camp work, Conner found his pack and slipped away looking for a secluded spot to change into a dry set of clothes.

He found a rock outcrop and quickly stripped down to bare skin. Free of his fast-freezing clothes, he even felt warmer in the cool air. He grabbed his large PackTowl and rubbed out the sore spots along his body. The friction felt good—and his limbs started to feel normal again.

A sound behind him startled him. Conner looked up to see Malika standing there, leaning against the rock with a steaming cup in her hand and a warm smile plastered across her face. Conner quickly moved to cover his nakedness with his towel.

"Don't cover up on my account," she said.

Conner smiled. "Very cold water."

"You look fine to me," she said, glancing down. "I wish we had more time to make sure everything's still working properly," she said, smiling playfully. "But instead, I brought you something hot to drink. Your insides need to warm up, too."

"Thank you."

"You were very brave back there. Everybody knows that."

"Not that it did much good."

Malika stepped closer. "Conner, you can't save everyone all the time."

Conner looked up into her eyes. "I'd settle for just one," he said.

In a soft voice, Malika asked, "And who's going to save you?"

She left a steaming cup atop the rocks and drifted back toward the others without glancing back. Conner watched her go, the curves of her body swaying with each stride, and something began to stir.

Everything, he happily noted, was still working properly.

Base Camp
Tumbatse, Tibet

Watching the entire sequence unfold on the bank of monitors, Terrance Carlton realized he had been holding his breath. From the safety of base camp, he felt detached, like he was watching a TV show, which, in a way, he was. Yet the action on those screens drew him in just as surely as if he had been on that bridge himself.

The crew had gathered behind the executive producer. There were gasps as the cameras picked up the first glimpses of the wall of water barreling down the riverbed, then stunned silence as Conner Michaels dove from the bridge, swept Powder into his arms, and swung back toward the bridge.

A hush fell over the tent as they watched Nicki "Powder" Freyer slip from Conner's waist and disappear into the roiling waters of the Tsangpo. After a few moments, it was obvious she would not survive the plunge down the river.

Carlton had dealt with death before. In one of his earlier Eco-Challenges, in the unforgiving terrain of British Columbia, a competitor by the name of Nicholas Adamson was struck in the head by a falling boulder. It was the first death in worldwide adventure racing, and Carlton had halted the race immediately.

But that had been a mistake.

In the days following the tragic accident, racers and staff almost unanimously told the race organizer that Nick would not have wanted the race cancelled. A week later, Carlton took a call from Nick's wife, Kathy. With a voice that ached with heartbreak, she told him that she hoped Carlton would begin a new race as soon as possible. Adventure racers were a different breed, she said. They would honor Nick's memory in the only way they knew. They would race.

Within six months, Carlton pulled together another adventure race. It quickly sold out, three hundred competitors in all, and he donated the proceeds to a foundation established in Nicholas Adamson's name. By any measure, the race was a success.

This time, Carlton would take it a step further. This time, he would use the accident to his advantage. Risk was an inherent part of adventure racing. The best anyone could do was accept that as fact, a part of reality, and move on.

Carlton went a step further. He decided to take advantage of it.

It was a home run. Audiences back home would go nuts for this kind of action. The human drama of life and death. Juxtaposed against the frantic images of the rescue attempt, the fire-lit footage of the silent vigil along the banks of the Tsangpo would make for inspiring television. The episode would almost certainly be Emmy-worthy. He would have to clean up the footage from Conner's camera—Powder's camera had torn away early in the deluge—but the footage was salvageable. He immediately ordered a new series of promos into production.

"I want them on the air right now," he yelled after a small army of scampering assistants. "The morning shows start in an hour! Let's give 'em what they want!"

He hardly needed to worry. All four networks were scrambling for footage, though NBC and Discovery held the best stuff for their exclusive broadcasts. NBC had exercised their contractual option to air nightly specials and, though the move would certainly hurt their broadcast partner, Discovery would still be earning record ratings. And more importantly, record advertising revenue.

It was going better than even he had imagined. NBC executives were literally getting drunk back in New York as sponsors scooped up commercial spots in droves, pushing thirty-second commercials from five hundred thousand to seven hundred thousand, finally topping out at an even one million dollars. *Darwin's Race* was already outpulling *Survivor*, Carlton's darling. And he knew that when all of the advertising time had been sold—it was a finite quantity, damn it—sponsors would lavish money on Discovery. And still they cried for more opportunities. Merchandise, Web site sponsorship, product tie-ins, and offers of spin-off projects were pouring in. Alger was already drawing up plans for a sequel.

It was official: *Darwin's Race* was a smash hit.

Reports of watching parties poured into base camp. Apparently these groups were cropping up all over the country. It was even reported that a few people had actually quit their jobs so they could watch *Darwin's Race* twenty-four hours on the Internet. That sounded suspiciously like an NBC public relations setup, but no matter. Just more gristle for the giant network promotion machine.

And all this was *before* the fatal accident at the rope bridge. Just wait till they get a load of that. And the thing with the tiger? There was almost *too much* compelling action. He would have to call Alger and secure an extra hour of the prime-time schedule.

"Are those the numbers?"

Carlton turned at the sound of the voice. It was Leslie. She gestured at the computer on Carlton's lap.

"We're killing," he said, displaying the screen for her to see. Numbers filled the screen, in columns labeled "quarter-hour rating" and "time spent watching."

"And these are just the beginning. After what happened today, there won't be a television set in America not tuned in to *Darwin's Race*."

"Unbelievable," Leslie said, shaking her head. "We'll want to do something for Powder's family, of course."

"Do whatever you think is necessary. Start a foundation, whatever." Carlton scanned the bank of monitors along the long wall of the production tent. "Looks like everyone's settling in for the night. Both teams made it up to about seventeen thousand. Conner was still dragging a bit, so Providence is lagging behind by a couple hundred feet. The fact that he's even alive is a miracle. This is still anyone's race."

"There is more bad news," Leslie said. "It's Greenback. He

hasn't come back yet. And the search team found nothing."

"Did they find his truck?"

"Let me get them. You can question them yourself."

A minute later, Leslie escorted a pair of tired-looking men into the control tent. Carlton recognized them as members of Greenback's engineering team.

"Jon Krobot and Jamie Haskel," Leslie said, introducing them. "Go on; tell him what you found."

The one she called Jon shuffled forward. "Well, we went out to the relay station, just like you asked. We found Bill's truck parked along the side of the road. But no sign of him. So we walked up to the tower. The control panel door was open; the wind I guess. But we could tell he had been there. The wiring had been fixed."

"But he never went back to his truck?"

"It doesn't look like it," Jamie said. "The keys were just sitting there, still in the ignition."

"Did you take a look around?"

The pair nodded. "We did. But it was weird. All of the little huts in the village were deserted. We didn't see another soul the whole time we were there."

"Like the villagers had just packed up and left?"

"That was the strange part," Jamie said. "They didn't even bother to pack up."

Carlton frowned. "What do you mean?"

"I mean, they didn't take anything with them when they left. We found clothes and stuff all over the place. In one hut, we even found food still on the table. Swarming with bugs by then. But it was as if everyone just disappeared."

"Who the hell knows what the natives were thinking," Carlton said derisively. "Probably one of their rain gods or some such shit told them to go somewhere else. Greenback must've gotten swept up in the exodus."

"That doesn't sound like him," Jamie said cautiously.

"Christ, I don't need this right now. What I need is working relay towers."

"Well, like I said, it's working now. Bill fixed it, all right."

"Okay then, if he doesn't turn up by dawn, take three of the trucks and search the surrounding villages."

He dismissed the assistant engineers, who seemed all too happy to escape Carlton's growing wrath. A production assistant approached Carlton, waving a printout in the air. He thought her name might be Brenda, but wasn't sure. There were so many production assistants here at base camp, he couldn't keep them all straight. "Mr. Carlton," she said. "I was told to bring this to you immediately." She handed over the printout.

Carlton scanned the paper and frowned. "Thank you; keep me informed," he said, dismissing her. He balled up the paper and threw it toward a cardboard trash can, missing.

"Well?" Leslie asked. "What was that all about?"

"Weather report," Carlton said, staring at the monitors. "Our racers are about to get hit by a snowstorm."

CHAPTER TWENTY-SIX

Team North Face
Kuk Sur: 17, 453 Feet

Morning broke clear and cold across the Tsangpo Gorge. The sky looked like lava: red streaked with the black remnants of cloud. The wind was still, and a fresh eight inches of hard snow clung to the ground. The entire mountainside was eerily silent.

Wade Stanley stepped out of his tent, cursed the cold, and set some water atop the white-gas stove. Kuk Sur loomed like a giant ice pyramid five thousand feet over his head. There was movement in the camp of Team Providence just down the slope a few hundred yards. Wade would have to light a fire under the others if he wanted his team to maintain their lead.

After the incident during the river crossing, he had felt

it was important to push on—take his teammates' minds off the loss of Powder. It had worked. Team North Face had pushed up the lower slopes of Kuk Sur in silence, until the last vestiges of flora gave way to a landscape of exposed rock and bitingly cold wind. It looked—and felt—like the face of the moon.

When the storm began to rage the night before, they had little choice but to retreat to their tents. As night fell, they found some protection from the elements in the shadow of a giant rock wall. The size of a ten-story building, the wall was oddly misplaced. It was as if the years of erosion that had created the scree field had miraculously passed over the rock wall, leaving it as an impregnable fortress on the mountainside.

Wade felt a rush of adrenaline as he surveyed the peak. Although he already had a half-dozen first ascents under his belt—including Darwa Parnung, less than a hundred miles west—the thrill as he poised to tackle another challenge never failed him. Years ago, he had read a climber's account of this phenomenon. The author wrote of a feeling of weightlessness, both of body and soul. A freeing of one's spirit. *That's exactly right,* Wade thought. That's exactly how it felt.

That writer, Wade suddenly realized, had been Conner Michaels. He was struck by their shared concept of the spirituality of mountain climbing.

Perhaps he and his erstwhile rival were not so different after all.

✿ ✿ ✿

Cale Anders emerged from his tent and shivered. He checked his Suunto. Altitude: 17,453 feet. Temperature: minus five centigrade. Five thousand vertical feet below the summit, the temperature had already dropped below freezing.

Now the hard part begins, thought Cale.

Team North Face was entering the Zone, a deadly area notorious for harsh conditions and little oxygen.

One by one, the racers emerged from the relative warmth of the tents, all now donning high-altitude gear. Layering up, Tess and Blaine topped their outfits off with thick, lightweight down jackets, while Hoops opted for the less bulky microfiber shells over a double layer of insulating fleece. Wade was sporting a state-of-the-art North Face parka, lined with heated wires. It was a prototype model, the team captain acting as the guinea pig for his big-name sponsor. He certainly looked warm enough.

Cale preferred to climb light. That meant no down for him. He was blessed with an abnormally high body temperature and rarely got cold. Even in temperatures of fifteen below, Cale managed just fine.

Their packs lighter, their bodies warmer, Team North Face broke camp and began traversing the base of the giant rock wall, searching for a gap.

The terrain was pure scree, a climber's nightmare. A field of loose rock, some round enough to slip on, others sharp enough to cut right through boots, scree was the evil source of nasty falls for mountaineers around the world. Trying to ascend a scree slope, feet often slipped back, like they were walking up a water slide. Two steps up, one step back.

Descending was even worse. With already treacherous balance, if climbers made the mistake of leaning backwards, the rocks often rolled out from under their feet, resulting in a tumble that could take them on a hard ride right down the mountain. Some climbers, when faced with a downhill scree slope, opted simply to sprint down the hill, using momentum and gravity to counteract the unstable terrain.

North Face followed the base of the immense slab for the better part of an hour, shivering in its shadow, until the ground abruptly fell away. A deep, glaciated valley yawned open before them. Going down would be nearly impossible. It was practically vertical. It looked like a dead end.

"We could rope up and try a rappel," Wade said. "Or backtrack in the other direction."

"Go down?" Blaine said. "That doesn't make much sense. We *have* to turn around."

"If we go back, we'll have wasted the whole morning," complained Hoops.

"And Providence will be well ahead of us," Blaine acknowledged.

That prospect brought a frown to the team captain's face. He rolled his head, stretching his neck muscles. He looked stressed.

Cale stared up the face of the rock. "I say we go right

up this thing," he said, slapping the rock with a gloved hand. "It doesn't look so tough, five-one, tops. I've got the equipment."

"It wouldn't be that difficult with proper climbing clothes," Blaine countered. "But in this thick stuff we're wearing, a free climb doesn't seem very smart."

"Do we even have enough rope?" asked Tess.

Cale stripped off his jacket and peeled off his plastic boots. "I'll lead. I've got enough chocks and 'biners to set a fixed rope for the rest of you."

It would be a hundred-foot free climb at seventeen thousand feet in thick alpine gear, on half-frozen rock. His teammates looked at him dubiously.

"What? The holds are there," Cale said, stretching his hamstrings. "I'll fix a safety once I'm topside and belay you from there. Not a problem."

"In those boots?" Tess pointed to Cale's bulky hiking boots.

Cale shrugged. "Not ideal. But like my man Spike Lee used to say, 'It ain't about the shoes.'"

"Actually, I think Spike said 'It's got to be the shoes.'"

"Whatever."

"I'm sure there's no talking you out of it," Wade said, bringing the debate to a conclusion. "I think we should give it a shot. I'm not particularly keen on giving up ground to the other team. So have at it. Just be quick about it—we're going to get cold real fast waiting around for you."

"I'm on the job, Cap."

Stripped to his fleece layer, Cale stepped to the pitch, running his hands over the rock. Within seconds, his expert eye had mapped out a route up the first twenty feet. The rest he would have to improvise. He looped two sixty-foot coils of rope to his seat harness and reached for the first crack.

The first hold was luxurious, a two-inch ledge that angled down into the rock, providing much needed resistance. Two moves later, his feet were perched on the same ledge.

As he moved up the face, his body warmed, his muscles straining with each reach and pull. He climbed gloveless, and though the rock was streaked with ice, his fingers somehow remained warm and tacky.

He climbed quickly, settling into a nice rhythm, and had to force himself to slow down to place wedge chocks into the rock. Once he had threaded the rope through the loop at the end of the chock, he moved up another ten feet and repeated the process.

He could hear vague cries of encouragement from below but didn't look down. It wasn't that he was afraid of heights; he just didn't want to be distracted. His mind was fixed on one thing and one thing only. The next hold.

He continued, moving across the rock like he was stuck to it. At one moment, he clung to the rock with just a few fingers and toes; the next, he had moved effortlessly to a layback position beside a large crack.

Jamming both hands into the crack a few feet over his head, Cale swung his feet away from the ledge. The tip of his boots glided against the rock, feeling for a ledge, finding one, then resting.

He paused to catch his breath.

Inside the crack, something slithered across his fingers.

Startled, Cale yanked back his hand as if he had touched hot coals. In that instant, he knew he had made a mistake. Though his toehold was strong, his balance was gone. He felt his body lean back from the rock, gravity pulling his torso out into space.

Cale fell.

His left hand reached for the crevasse and just as his right toehold gave way to nothingness his fingers found purchase. He groaned as his body weight bore down upon the bones of his fingers. He could hear the gasps from below. He swung out from the rock on unsteady fingertips.

"Left foot five inches up!" Wade yelled from below. The team captain was identifying possible ledges for Cale, now hopelessly blind to anything below his waist. The climber managed to slow his motion, bracing his left foot against the slab. Feeling with the other, he found what felt like a thin ledge. He tested its strength with a bit of body weight. It held, and he shifted his whole weight to his right foot. Leaning his chest into the rock for balance, Cale extracted his crushed hands from the crack. He stretched them out, mercifully relieving his cramped hand muscles. He sighed in relief.

He peered into the crack for whatever insect had skittered over his fingers. He found nothing.

"You're a regular Spider Man up there!" yelled Hoops. "Get it together, and get a move on—it's fucking cold as hell down here!"

Breathing deeply, Cale reached up for the next crack.

In a few minutes, he had made it. At the top, a nice boulder was ideally placed for a safety. Cale tied it off, looped a second rope around it, and threw the ropes to the ground. "Safety on!" he called down. Only after Tess fastened the rope to her harness ring did Cale take a good look around. He was met with a nearly 360-degree view, obstructed only in the north by the ice-capped south face of Kuk Sur.

The finish line.

To the west, Cale could see their old campsite, but there was no sign of Team Providence. Probably trying to figure out a way around this monster. There weren't six or seven climbers on the planet that could've scaled this pitch in these conditions. Certainly no one on Team Providence, though he didn't really know anything about that hottie Malika or her pirate-looking father. How did a wild looking guy like that have a daughter as beautiful as her anyway?

Cale felt a tug on the safety rope. Tess was already on the pitch. It would take all four remaining members an hour or so to get up, but it was by far the fastest, most direct route.

They were making great time.

Team Providence
Kuk Sur: 17,111 Feet

Team Providence had huddled inside their tents until daybreak. Only at first light did the storm abate enough for Conner to venture back outside, test the elements. The night had left behind a hard layer of ice that froze over the tent zipper. From here on out, it would be below freezing. The only question was how far below zero it would drop.

Powder's death hung over the team like a pall. In the moments of silence beside the river, they had all dealt with the loss in their own personal way. Conner struggled more than the others, but he hadn't come all the way to Tibet to turn back before he reached his goal. He had pressed on in silence for the rest of the day.

Now, Providence moved quickly, stomping blood into stiff limbs. In a matter of minutes, camp was broken and they were climbing north along the rock- and ice-strewn flanks of Kuk Sur. Though Conner knew it was there—he could feel it looming—the summit was obstructed from view by an enormous rock wall. Wade Stanley would've most likely led North Face south, so he had decided to try an opposite direction. Put some much needed space between the teams. The disaster at the bridge had done little to cut the tension between the teams. For all of Wade's genuine comments, this was still a race. It was a harsh reality—but the Tsangpo Gorge and Kuk Sur were harsh places. If they didn't focus on the race, Powder wouldn't be the only fatal accident.

After a few hours, Conner discovered a wind-scoured footpath along the rock wall. They followed it, thankful for the opportunity to avoid the nasty scree slopes, until a flicker of movement caught his eye.

Fifteen yards ahead, just off the trail, a spider web of multicolored flags was strung from eight-foot poles, flapping loudly in the mountain winds. A veteran of more than a dozen Himalayan climbs, Conner recognized the display of prayer flags immediately.

For centuries Tibetan Buddhists had planted colorful flags outside their homes and places of spiritual practice for the wind to carry the beneficent vibrations across the countryside. Prayer flags, inscribed with symbols, invocations, prayers, and mantras, were said to bring happiness, long life, and prosperity to the flag planter and those in the vicinity.

This pass must've been used many years earlier, providing passage from Lhasa into southern China, before the Red Army declared the Kukuranda a restricted area. Now, the flags were little more than dusty tatters, witnesses to the empty vastness of the largest mountain range on earth.

Conner pulled a yellow bandanna from his pack and approached the display. There were hundreds of flags fastened vertically from long wooden poles. Sets of five colored flags—yellow, green, red, white, and blue—represented the elements: earth, water, fire, cloud, and sky. Tying his flag to the line, Conner prayed silently with the others for prosperity and good luck for the duration of their journey. And they prayed again for their fallen friend.

Conner, for one, was glad they had found the monument of flags. Although he had tied one off in Lhasa, and another at the starting line in Tumbatse, a look to the heavens told him Team Providence could use all the good fortune the gods could bestow.

The skies above had grown menacingly dark.

The snow began to fall as they pressed up the foothills of the mountain. As they ascended, the scrub disappeared altogether, the air grew colder, and the terrain turned rock hard. Here, the Tibetan mud that had plagued them down in the valley of the gorge had frozen into permafrost. With each footfall upon the frozen tundra, the climbers risked turned ankles and sprained knees.

As they climbed past eighteen thousand feet, the environment became more desolate. They passed through cloud cover, restricting views to a few feet. The ground was covered in a sheer layer of snow and ice. The climbers strapped on crampons, but each step was still dangerously precarious. A fall now would result in a hundred-foot slide down the slopes. With no chance of recovery.

But it wasn't the ice that worried Conner the most. It was the wind.

Out of the protective cover of the forest below, the climbers were now left utterly exposed to the wind gusts. And the vaunted Himalayan weather was living up to its ferocious reputation. The snow now fell in suffocating sheets. Blasts of freezing air whipped over the slopes, swirling the flakes in midair vortexes that threatened to swallow them whole. Shouting over the roar of the storm, Conner ordered the team to rope up in groups of three.

Shandi fell first. Head bowed against the driving blizzard, Thad reached down to help her to her feet. Conner saw her rise wobbly, shake her head. He looked up. The dark clouds had descended to just a few dozen feet over their heads. They were entering the eye of the thunderhead.

Through the whiteout, he could detect the faint outline of a rock wall that extended up through the cloud cover. He pulled his balaclava off his face and shouted over the din, "We need to get out of this. Make camp. Over there by the rock."

They moved quickly, battling the wind gusts to erect the pair of tents beside the wall. Conner watched Preston, Shandi, and Thad disappear into one tent, lugging their packs inside with them. He followed Ian and Malika into the second tent, zipping the flap behind him. With three people and three large backpacks, the tent was cramped. But anything was better than the roaring elements outside.

Conner and Ian braced the packs against the tent poles. Tried to find some space for their exhausted and wet bodies. Stripped off ice-crusted boots. The combined body warmth compelled them to shed snow pants and down jackets, too.

"So now that we're here," Malika said. "How will we

pass the time?" She shot a mischievous look in Conner's direction that Ian caught.

"Why do I suddenly feel like a third wheel in here?" he asked.

"No third wheel," Conner said. "And to answer your question, Malika, I think I have a deck of cards here somewhere."

"Exactly what I had in mind," she said sarcastically.

Suddenly, a spark of light shot up through the aluminum tent pole.

"Whoa," they said in unison.

"It's the thunderhead," Conner said. "We're in the middle of an electrical storm."

The supports flashed again, arcing and pulsing with bursts of orange and red.

"Enjoy the show, but don't touch. There's a big jolt in those things."

Conner felt Malika inch closer. He moved to make a comfortable nook between his shoulder and his chest for her head.

The display of lights crackled overhead.

CHAPTER
TWENTY-SEVEN

Cale Anders couldn't sleep.

He lay flat on his back, his entire body except for his face enveloped in a down mummy bag, and stared at the roof of his tent. Hoops was asleep beside him; he could hear his ragged, rhythmic breath in the silence.

It was bitingly cold, even inside the tent. Cold enough that a crust of frost had formed on the tent's plastic frame. He exhaled and watched his breath vapor freeze, falling back onto his face in hard droplets.

After Cale's ascent of the rock face, Team North Face had pushed up a ridge that cut southwest from the peak of Kuk Sur. As they climbed, the snow and ice thickened and hardened until only patches of weather-beaten rock protruded through the whiteness. They reached nineteen thousand feet quickly.

Then the snow stormed in.

The winds whipped to gale force, blasting the climbers, threatening to topple them over the steep ridge. Snow fell in piercing sheets that stung exposed skin like razor-sharp grains of sand.

When it became obvious that attempts to progress would be futile, Wade had ordered the tents up beside an ice-streaked slab of granite. The elements forced North Face into two self-sufficient sub-teams—Cale and Hoops were camped in this tent and Wade, Tess, and Blaine in a second tent nearby—and ate their meals separately. When the conditions improved—if they did—they would reunite to continue the push. But for now, they were staying put.

Cale's bladder was about to burst. He had been holding it for three hours now—literally pressing his hand to his abdomen—but he was weakening. He certainly couldn't sleep with the fire in his groin. He was going to have to venture outside.

Into the storm.

Cale and his teammates had relieved themselves earlier, before settling into their bags, but he had consumed an extra liter of water before bedtime in an effort to ward off an approaching altitude headache.

The sudden elevation gain—in Team North Face's case, nearly two thousand vertical feet—had wreaked havoc with Cale's innards, forcing him to down the extra fluids. Now, in the middle of the goddamned night, his throbbing temples had relaxed, but the pressure in his loins seemed worse.

An easy enough cure, to be sure, but the cure was *out there*. In the freezing, numbing cold.

Swirling winds howled outside, and ice pellets pounded against the tent. It did not sound very welcoming.

Cale cursed under his breath.

It didn't have to be like this. Seasoned climbers quickly developed a habit of carrying a spare water bottle for just this sort of dire situation. Cale was certainly no different. It was far easier to piss into a five hundred-milliliter bottle from the relative warmth of a sleeping bag and dump it out in the morning than to venture out into the sub-freezing cold. Even ten steps is a long way in a Himalayan blizzard. Sleeping with a bottle full of urine to keep it from freezing was an acceptable, if mildly repulsive, irritation.

"Goddamned piss bottle," he grumbled.

His spare Nalgene bottle had cracked earlier that morning when he'd fallen hard on the scree slopes. When he heard the crack, he knew instantly what had happened and the harsh ramifications the shattered bottle would incur. Breaking a bone in his arm would've almost been better—at least he could splint that up and continue on. Breaking your piss bottle meant freezing your ass off on the side of a treacherous mountain in the middle of the dark night. Cale was not happy.

Cale felt for his boots in the dark. He pulled them on, along with his camera holster, and grabbed his headlamp.

He heard the soft *whir* of his shoulder-mounted camera stirring to life with his movements.

"Watch this, America," he whispered. "This is real adventure racing—taking a leak in a snowstorm."

He poked his head outside and was greeted with a blast of icy snow. Cursing louder now, Cale extricated his entire body from the tent and zipped it back up quickly. No need to let the cold air disturb his teammates.

Pacing a few meters from the tent site—it wasn't proper form to pee next to the tent—Cale flipped on his headlamp. The light reflected against an almost complete whiteout. He couldn't see more than two feet in front of his face.

"Oh yeah, this is fun," he said.

Putting his back to the wind gusts, Cale relieved himself into a deep snowdrift. He stomped his feet to keep warm. The storm roared so loudly he could barely hear the thumping of his own boots. He wondered idly if anyone ever suffered frostbite of the dick. He could already feel a burning down there and was relieved to finish up and tuck everything back where it was warmer.

Suddenly, Cale felt like he was being watched.

It wasn't that he could actually see anything—the blizzard conditions were getting worse, if anything. No, it was that strangely unsettling feeling of a presence. The same feeling you get when someone puts a hand near your face. Even with your eyes clenched shut, you just know something is there.

Cale could sense he was not alone.

"Hoops? That you?"

He squinted into the night, but could see nothing in the whiteout. He flipped off his headlamp and allowed his eyes to adjust to the ghostly darkness. The visibility didn't improve much, so he flipped his headlamp back on. The wind picked up, sounding eerily like high-pitched—

—breathing.

He stilled his own stomping boots to listen.

But the sounds of thumping footsteps did not stop.

They were muffled at first. Distant. Then, louder. Faster. Like someone was running.

When the impact came, it seemed to come from nowhere. One moment Cale was standing there, ears and eyes perked like an attentive dog, and the next he was lifted completely off his feet, hurtling over the frozen ground. He crashed into a hard-packed drift.

Cale felt something snap in his shoulder. He struggled to his feet, moaning in pain.

The second blow—from something large and rock-hard—crashed into the small of his back, knocking him face first into the snow.

"Owwww . . . ahhh!" he groaned.

Concussed, Cale barely was able to lift his head. He spit up bits of ice and frozen dirt. Warm blood trickled down his face to his lips.

Something snatched his ankles.

"No . . . please . . . NO!"

And suddenly Cale found himself being dragged roughly across the ground.

He flailed his arms, searching for anything to grab, his fingers gouging deep ruts in the ground. He was facing away from whatever clamped down on him, and he struggled to catch a fleeting glimpse of his assailant. He couldn't see anything.

But that smell—

He was lifted off his feet.

His body crashed into a large boulder, his head and neck smacking against bare rock. He screamed in agony as his collarbone shattered like glass. The impact smashed his headlamp, and the mountainside slipped into utter blackness.

For a moment, Cale didn't move. His wide eyes darted around the darkness, searching, searching. His breaths were ragged gasps for air. His broken limbs screamed in agony.

The wind shrieked and he jumped, anticipating another attack. Nothing came.

"Oh God . . . please . . . please," he prayed.

In the ghostly light of the night, Cale could see the rock wall looming just a few feet away. He needed to escape. He needed to *climb*. With a deep, steeling breath, he made a break for it.

His shoulder felt like it was on fire as he sprinted to the wall. There was something wrong with his right knee, too. Dislocated, probably. But his fear—as palpable as the blood streaming into his mouth—was pumping pure adrenaline through his body. He pushed aside the pain and reached for the rock.

He climbed blind, sliding his hands along the face, searching for cracks, ledges, holds. He closed his eyes—they were useless anyway—and let his instincts take over. He found a rhythm, ascending quickly, his breathing evening out. Whatever had attacked him, Cale was now more than thirty feet out of reach. He paused a moment to take a deep breath.

Thank God.

That's when he felt hot breath on his neck.

Slowly, he turned his head—

Something sharp gripped Cale on the nape of his neck and lifted him from the rock face. Then he felt himself swinging forward, as helpless as a rag doll. He smashed head first into the rock, the bridge of his nose cracking, his right cheekbone shattering. He smashed into the rock again. And again. And again. Cale fought oncoming unconsciousness, hearing only the sounds of his skull cracking apart, puncturing his delirium.

And then he was falling, plunging toward the ground. All went black before impact.

Base Camp
Tumbatse, Tibet

Brenda Dawson was mad.

She had drawn the graveyard shift. Again. As a lowly production assistant, Brenda had been scheduled the 3 a.m. shift two nights running and wasn't at all happy about it. She glanced at the wall of monitors, found them all black. *What the hell else would they be?* she grumbled. *It's the middle of the goddamned night.*

The field cameras had long ago slipped into sleep mode as the racers had all turned in for the night to escape the furious snowstorm. The rest of the control room was silent. Her on-duty producer, Mike Fiebig, was napping quietly on a cot. He left instructions to wake him if anything interesting happened.

"What a joke," Brenda muttered. "Nothing interesting ever happens from three to five."

She was right. For the first couple of nights, both teams had slept during her entire boring shift. When the skies began to lighten outside—generally just after five— that's when the activity began. And that's when Brenda relieved her duties to the next shift.

"This is what I went to film school for?" she asked aloud. "To stare at blank televisions in the middle of the night? Oh, yes, my folks would be so proud. Daddy, your money was certainly well spent."

She hadn't even been able to help with the setup of the forward production control facility currently being constructed at the base of Kuk Sur. With both teams now beginning their ascent, a facility closer to the action was required to pick up the signals from the cameras. The engineering crew had left earlier in the day with two cargo helicopters full of equipment, headed to the camp location. By morning, they would have a second production facility up and operational.

And Brenda didn't have a damn thing to do with any of it.

She had volunteered for the move, but Carlton had insisted she stay here. *To monitor fifteen blank screens*, she thought dourly. *Thanks a lot.*

She closed her eyes and rubbed her temples. Thoughts of frantic whitewater escapes and rock climbing exploits filled her head. Why couldn't something like that happen on her watch? Didn't Carlton know she had given up a steady job as assistant director for the NBC affiliate in Washington, D.C. for this? Didn't he realize that he was wasting her enormous talent by scheduling her at this ungodly hour? Wouldn't it be better if—

Brenda's eyes popped open—just in time to catch a glimpse of movement on one of the monitors. It was a fleeting look—and then the monitor filled with static.

A piece of white tape had been affixed to the bottom edge of the monitor, number eight. It read: Cale Anders.

"Okay, Cale Anders," Brenda said. "What are you up to out there?"

The first thing the young production assistant did was to scan the monitors for the rest of Team North Face. She engaged the manual override on Blaine Reeves' camera. Though it was dark, three members of the team appeared to be resting comfortably. As comfortable as minus thirty allowed, anyway.

Brenda switched to the camera on Paul Robeson—Hoops, everyone called him—and scanned the second tent. Studying the grainy image, she could see a snatch of Cale's sleeping bag. It was empty.

"Okay, Cale, where have you wandered off to? A little bathroom break?"

Checking the connections at her control board, Brenda tried to employ the override on Cale's camera. No response. The monitor was still filled with static, and she quickly re-routed another camera feed to the monitor. Blaine's camera image popped onto monitor eight, confirming that the monitor was working properly. Definitely a camera problem.

Brenda turned to her console and activated a tracking program called LinkAware. The program checked camera status by sending a transmission from the nearest receiving tower. A module on the camera would then relay operational details back to the computer. Camera malfunctions had happened before—usually returning messages such as "low power" or "focus adjustment." Brenda hit the *transmit* button and waited for the pulse to return the information. She realized she was actually enjoying herself. Finally something to do. A beep signaled the information had been collected, and Brenda quickly called up the data.

Only there was no data. Only a two-word message, one that Brenda Dawson had never seen before.

FATAL ERROR.

Something was really wrong here. She jumped from the console and hurried over to where her producer was napping. He woke with a start.

"It's Cale Anders; his camera is completely dead."

Brenda escorted Fiebig to her console and showed him the error message.

"That can't be good," he said. "Have you run playback?"

"Not yet," Brenda said, silently reproaching herself for not thinking of it. Every second of every camera was recorded digitally using an array of industrial servers in the back of the control facility. That way, everything was available for editing for the television broadcast. She could've checked the feed by simply calling up Cale's camera and entering the appropriate time code.

She punched the numbers into her computer, setting a playback for ten minutes earlier.

"Put it on the big screen," Fiebig ordered.

The large monitor flickered to life, showing a grainy image of the interior of a tent. Brenda recognized Hoops huddled inside his mummy bag.

Then, movement.

"There he goes," Brenda said. "I think he's going out for a bathroom break."

The image brightened as Cale flipped on his headlamp. Though its reflection shone off the driving snowstorm, it was clear what Cale was doing. The camera angle dipped sufficiently to see a pale yellow arc streaming into the snow bank.

What happened next took just eleven seconds. The image jerked wildly. A flash of sky, then face down into the snowpack. Then the image lifted and moved quickly, as if Cale was looking for something in the night. The image jerked again, violently. The entire sequence was little more than a blur. Then nothing. The picture flickered to life nine seconds later, but it was difficult to make out the image.

"What's he doing?" Brenda asked. "Climbing? In the middle of the storm?"

"I don't think he's doing it for kicks," Fiebig replied. "It looks like he's trying to get away from something."

The picture jerked again, then went dark. Brenda let the tape roll, but there was nothing more.

"Play it back again," he ordered. "This time at half speed."

The image was even blurrier in frame-by-frame mode, but Brenda managed to get a sense of what had happened. She didn't want to accept what her own eyes were telling her, but it looked like something had attacked Cale, knocked him flat, then lifted him and smashed him into a giant boulder. Then it appeared that Cale—unbelievably—was climbing, actually scaling the ice-strewn pitch in the dark.

Then blackness.

Brenda rolled back the tape to the final frames and paused it, freezing the blurry image. She could see the rock face, one of Cale's bare hands just visible in the lower right-hand corner. Large dark blotches splattered the lens.

"What is that?" Brenda asked, turning to her producer. "What are those dark spots?"

"It looks like—" he stammered, a quiver in his voice.

"Like what?"

"Like blood," he said. "Somebody wake up Carlton. We've got a big problem."

PART THREE

CHAPTER TWENTY-EIGHT

Forward Base Camp
17,483 Feet

Terrance Carlton didn't want to believe his own eyes. He had just watched the raw footage from Cale's camera, and the first thing he said was "Fuck."

The second thing he said was "Kill the feeds. The last thing we need to do is get the folks back home all riled up before we know what's happened."

Thanks to that bit of quick thinking—and the rapid response of his overnight production team back in Tumbatse—the live feed from Cale's camera had been cut off within the two-hour delay. Thousands of those rabid online viewers would be spared the blood-splattered sequence.

Awakened by a production assistant in the middle of the night, Carlton had spent the past two hours gulping down black coffee and watching the live feeds from Team North Face, waiting for them to awaken. As the rest of the crew gathered sullenly around the monitors, Carlton had watched—two, three, four times—the playback of the apparent attack on Cale Anders.

Like the others, he was shocked by what he saw.

Serving as executive producer was like walking a high wire, Carlton often said. Success was generally a straightforward matter of controlling variables, ensuring that the correct personnel and equipment were in the right place at the precise time. For *Darwin's Race*, this meant managing the construction of a sprawling production facility in Tumbatse—with its requisite satellite dishes, miles of cable, monitors, and crew—as well as a second facility on the lower slopes of Kuk Sur.

Forward base camp was similar to the setup in Tumbatse. The canvas tent was thicker, to ward off the colder mountain air, and smaller, though still large enough to house a bank of monitors, computer editing equipment, computers, digital recorders, and switchers. Outside, the crew had erected a tent village with shelters for the crew, medical personnel, and competitors. With Greenback still missing—Carlton had sent a small team out to the transmitter to track him down—the producer himself had managed the construction of the production facility in less than twenty-four hours.

But that intricate high wire act could be disrupted by the smallest disturbance.

Cale Anders' apparent death now threatened everything.

Nearly all of the thirty-person crew crowded inside the main tent, anxiously staring at the monitors. It was almost daybreak. Wade and Tess and the rest of Team North Face were about to discover one of their own was missing.

"Terrance, we have to get word to Providence."

Carlton heard Leslie Dickerson, his communications chief, loud and clear. But he didn't reply. Everything had been going so well. Millions were watching the nightly broadcasts on Discovery and NBC. Hundreds of thousands more watched twenty-four/seven online. Advertising revenue had exceeded all expectations, netting over one hundred million dollars for the networks. Just hours before, Carlton had gone to bed thinking that nothing could go wrong. He had dreamed of *Darwin's Race II*.

"We do not tell Providence," Carlton announced forcefully. "We have one missing racer; that's all. Shit, we had entire teams go missing during Eco-Challenge. Remember Patagonia? We couldn't find Team REI for almost four hours."

Leslie shook her head. "First of all, we already lost one racer. Powder. Remember? Cale makes two. And he's already been missing for *six* hours," Leslie said. "Jesus, Terrance, this is different. You saw the blood same as I did. Something has gone wrong up there, and we owe it to Providence to tell them what's going on."

Carlton glared back. "No," he said forcefully. "*Darwin's Race* will go on. But since you've got yourself all worked up about this, go ahead and get Norgay in Lhasa on the radio. Order up a rescue helicopter. That make you feel better?"

"A little. But Terry, we have to consider the consequences of our actions. The media—"

"That's my decision," Carlton said, cutting her off. "It's a goddamn race, Leslie. Injuries are part of the deal. We don't know what happened to Cale Anders, but we're sure as hell not going to find him in the dark now. A full-scale helicopter search in the morning; that's the best we can do."

"A chopper is next to worthless." Leslie said. "The air's too thin. He'll be lucky to get to eighteen thousand feet. Cale disappeared at nineteen-five."

Carlton dismissed the notion with a wave of his hand. "A chopper got to twenty on Everest in 1996. I think they'll be able to handle a little trip to nineteen thousand. End of discussion."

The crew scattered, and Carlton slumped back into his director's chair. Leslie retreated quickly. He stared, bleary-eyed, at the bank of monitors. All the screens were dark gray, only heavily shadowed shapes discernible in the night. The camera worn by Paul Robeson was aimed directly at Cale's empty sleeping bag. The sight made Carlton's stomach roll. He ordered one of the PAs to bring him a bottle of Rolaids.

He glanced at each of the other monitors, noting in turn the sprawled bodies of each of the other racers. Team Providence slept blissfully unaware of what was going on just a few hundred feet away. If they were to find out,

Conner Michaels would definitely pull his team out of the race. And where would that leave Carlton? Clinging to the tatters of a costly television production in one hand, the remnants of his career in the other.

I've made the right decision, Carlton told himself. *I have to balance the well-being of my racers with a multimillion-dollar production.* Nobody held a gun to anyone's head. They had all signed legally defensible waivers of liability. Everyone knew the inherent risks of *Darwin's Race*—the racers knew what they were in for.

But that wasn't entirely true, was it?

These twelve men and women had signed up for an adventure race; they expected biting insects, below-freezing temperatures, even avalanches. But this? Carlton had watched the footage nearly a dozen times, and he still couldn't see exactly what had happened to Cale Anders. Had he been attacked? Had he fallen? The only thing Carlton knew for sure was that one of his racers had gone out in the middle of a storm to take a piss and had ended up . . . well, missing. Something unexpected had happened.

Something bad.

It was no accident. This wasn't like Powder. The bloody images told him that. Something had attacked one of his racers, savagely enough to splatter the camera with blood.

The search party will find Cale, he told himself. There was still a chance he was alive. The producer wanted to believe that, *longed* to believe that, but deep down knew better. *No one survives a frigid Himalayan night without shelter.*

Carlton was about to turn away from the monitors, to speak to the chopper crew personally, when he noticed something. Monitor number four. Shandi Davis' camera.

The image was stock-still; she was sleeping easily. The camera attached to her shoulder displayed a dark, but clear image of the rest of the tent. Her husband was there, mouth open, wrapped tightly inside his mummy bag. It looked like he was snoring.

There had apparently been a change in the team's sleeping arrangements. Malika was now sharing a tent with Conner. A possible love connection? That, the producer determined, would bear watching.

But it was the other sleeping bag that drew Carlton's attention.

It was empty.

Preston Child was gone.

Team North Face
Kuk Sur: 19,449 Feet

At first, no one even noticed Cale Anders was missing.

When Wade Stanley roused himself from his warm mummy bag, his tent mates were still sleeping soundly. He would allow Tess and Blaine to rest a few moments more, partly because they needed it and partly because his own bones ached. He didn't want the others to see how stiff and sore he was. It wouldn't do for his teammates to see the captain limping around camp.

But there was no denying this pain. Three days of dashing through the jungle, and now below-freezing temperatures had taken their toll. Luckily for Wade, the ache would dissipate as soon as his muscles warmed up and the adrenaline started to flow again. He hoped so, anyway.

He crawled out of the tent, rubbing the cramps from his thighs. He felt the tightness in his calves loosen somewhat as he shoveled some snow into a pot and set it upon a white-gas burner. In these temperatures, it would take nearly thirty minutes to bring the snow to a boil. They didn't have that kind of time—his team would have to settle for lukewarm.

The sun was a perfect red circle hovering over the horizon—it would be clear for the first day of their assault on Kuk Sur. With any luck, they could ascend to twenty thousand feet before dark. The final push to the summit—and the two million-dollar prize—would begin the following morning. He was almost there. A victory here would finally allow him to step from the large shadow of Conner Michaels once and for all. Conner would sulk away to wherever it was he had come from, out of adventure racing—and out of Elizabeth's life—for good. The prospect buoyed Wade's spirit, a boyish elation bubbling through his veins.

Time to wake the others. He detected a rustling in

his own tent; Tess and Blaine were stirring already. Wade turned his attention to the second tent. Time to have some fun with Cale and Hoops.

He placed his ear against the tent, heard gentle snoring from inside. Sleeping like babies.

Wade cupped his hands around his mouth and screamed into the tent at the top of his lungs—

"AVALANCHE!"

Hoops exploded out of the tent like it was on fire, spilling onto the ground on all fours, scrambling frantically for his boots. A look of utter terror was plastered over Hoops' face. His sleeping bag was still caught around his ankles, and he tripped as he scrambled to escape.

Then he heard Wade's laughter echo over the mountain.

"A joke? This is a joke?" said Hoops, not smiling. "You bastard!"

"Whoever said I don't have a well-honed sense of humor?" Wade said, grinning mischievously.

"Oh, that's a good game," Hoops said, flipping Wade the bird. "Make up life-threatening situations to scare the shit out of others—that's great fun."

The earnest anger only goaded Wade into louder rolls of laughter.

The commotion drew Tess and Blaine out of their tent. "What's going on out here?" Tess asked. "What did we miss?"

"Oh, just Wade being an ass," Hoops said. "Nothing

new there."

Blaine pointed to Hoops' sleeping bag, still wrapped around his ankles. "Are you planning on wearing that today during the ascent?"

Tess was the first to notice that someone was absent. "Where's Cale?" she asked. "He's missing all the fun."

"Don't look at me," Hoops replied. "He wasn't in the tent when Wade decided to play his little joke. He's not out here making breakfast?"

"I was the first up," Wade said, his grin dissolving quickly. "I haven't seen him."

"Taking his morning constitutional?" Tess suggested.

"Uh, guys?" Hoops was kneeling just inside the tent. She held up Cale's clothes. "His heavy gear is still here. Wherever he is, he's only wearing his fleece layer."

"It's got to be near zero out here," Blaine said. "What the hell is he thinking?"

"That guy doesn't get cold," Hoops said, feigning optimism. "I'm sure he'll be right back."

They sat around the gas burner in silence, watching the water not boil. A suffocating sense of dread had descended.

"Guys, this is a problem," Tess said.

"Did anyone hear him go out?" Wade asked. "Any idea how long he's been gone?"

No one had any answers.

"We need to find him now," Wade said. He reached for his trekking pole. "Right now. Elizabeth, you come with me. Blaine, take Hoops and search up toward the wall. If Cale's been out here more than a few minutes, he may be in trouble. Let's get moving."

The fresh snowfall had obliterated any hope of finding footprints, so the searchers were relegated to combing the slope in a semi-organized sweep. The wind was mercifully calm, the sky clear. As the sun rose over the peak, the air warmed—twenty degrees by Wade's Suunto. *Warm,* Wade thought. *But not warm enough.*

Then, a voice broke the silence.

"I've got something!"

The sound of alarm in Blaine's voice jolted Wade into a sprint to his side. Blaine was kneeling near a rock outcrop, Hoops standing over him. A small object, dark and small, protruded from a large snowdrift.

"Dig it out," Wade ordered. "Dig it out now."

Blaine began shoveling handfuls of snow from around the dark object. It emerged quickly.

Cale's camera.

It had been snapped off at the base and cracked across the top of its waterproof housing. There was a large dent in the casing, as if it had been smashed with something heavy. The lens was shattered completely.

Tess pointed to the snow and ice encrusted on the broken apparatus. "This has been out here awhile," she said.

"Oh, *fuck*—" Hoops whispered.

"Now's not the time to panic," Wade said. "But we need to move fast. We have to assume that Cale's been out here all night. Elizabeth, go move the burner inside the tent. We'll need someplace warm to revive Cale."

Even as he spoke those words, Wade felt a sinking feeling in his stomach. He willed himself to stay positive. Surviving a Himalayan night without shelter was tough, but not impossible. Wade himself had lived through a forced bivouac on the storm-ravaged slopes of Nanda Devi just a few years earlier. Of course, he had been wearing a down jacket. But survival was at least still possible.

Hoops and Blaine moved away, scanning the slope as it fell away from the ridge. Wade turned his attention to the rocky crag. It jutted up from the ridge, stretching twenty feet above his head. Could a large rock have fallen on Cale's camera, knocking him out in the process? A second thought occurred to him, though he didn't want to acknowledge it. It was possible that Cale had simply walked off the steep cliff nearby. It was certainly not unheard of on dark mountains, particularly in whiteout conditions.

But that can't be it. It doesn't explain the busted camera.

Sunlight began to creep down the west-facing rock. Snow and ice had begun to melt, dripping down the face in thin streams. Lulled by the slow trickle of water, Wade was momentarily transfixed.

The trickle had turned *red*.

He followed the trickle up . . .

Shit.

Seven feet above the ground, a large splash of blood marred the rock. Like someone had thrown a can of bright red paint against the face. Wade stretched a finger to the rock. When he drew it back, his fingertip was wet. A second splash was there, several feet above the first. More streaks of blood, interspersed with bits of something glistening and gray-colored.

A thin rivulet of blood trickled down to the ground at the foot of the rock face. Scanning the ground hastily, Wade discovered several drops of blood leading across the ground.

A few feet away, he found another spray of red. And something else.

Poking out from the snow, a single blue glove.

Wade sprinted across the ground and dropped to his knees. "I'm going to need some help here!" he yelled.

He began to dig. The others quickly joined him, frantically scooping snow with bare hands. If Cale was down there, somehow buried in the snow, he could still be alive.

"Oh, God, please," someone prayed.

Pockets of air often formed in snowdrifts—countless avalanche survivors could attest to that fact. These pockets would even serve to insulate anyone trapped inside—Eskimos built homes from ice and snow based on the concept.

But air was a precious quantity. And in an underground pocket, a finite one. If Wade and the others were to extricate Cale's body in time, they would have to dig deep. Perhaps six feet deep. That was going to eat up precious time. Time Cale Anders didn't have.

But they didn't labor long. They didn't dig deep. They didn't have to.

There was no body.

Only the glove.

Wade pulled it free of the snow. Cale must've lost it in the dark.

"Damn it," he muttered.

The glove felt strangely heavy.

Forcing down a line of bile in his throat, he turned it over in his hand. A jagged edge of bone jutted from the opening, wrapped with bloody tendrils frozen in place like red icicles.

A cry escaped from Tess. She turned away and collapsed into the snow, sobbing, and Hoops moved to embrace her.

"Jesus Christ!" said Blaine. "Jesus-fucking-Christ! That's a hand! That's Cale's fucking hand!"

Wade could feel his pulse quicken. "Okay, okay," he said, trying to rein in his runaway heartbeat. "Look, I know this looks bad. But this isn't necessarily a fatal injury. These freezing temperatures actually help stem blood flow and pain with an injury like this."

"Injury?" Blaire exclaimed. "That's no injury. That's his fucking hand!"

Wade pushed himself to his feet. "We need to pull ourselves together. Cale could still be alive. Surely the producers have seen this entire scene play out on the cameras here"—he tapped the whirring camera on his shoulder—"so I'm sure reinforcements will be on the way. In the meantime, we need an orderly search. We'll start from this spot and fan out. Come on, guys—don't give up. We can still find him."

Wade dropped the glove containing Cale's hand onto the ground. He moved quickly from the spot, hunting north along the rock wall. The others followed suit, dutifully, but any shred of optimism had vanished with the discovery of Cale's bloody hand.

Wade exhaled heavily, watching his breath cloud evaporate.

Where was the rest of the body?

CHAPTER TWENTY-NINE

Team Providence
Kuk Sur: 18,973 Feet

Conner Michaels never considered himself a pioneer. Bonatti, Herzog, Hillary; those were pioneers. Those climbers braved unknown peaks with little more than an adventurous spirit and a pair of mittens. They were trailblazers, ascending peaks that, in some cases, had never seen human footprints. Their accomplishments were rightly honored, and their names would fill mountaineering and exploration history books forever.

Now, as Conner gazed up at the peak of Kuk Sur, he realized that he was about as close as he could get to those luminaries. Here was a mammoth mountain, twenty-two thousand feet of ice and snow and rock. Never conquered. And here he was: Bound in thick alpine gear, a seventy-pound pack on his back, snow blowing mildly over the rocky ridge, ascending single-file up the spine. Despite the fact Team Providence carried no maps, Conner knew exactly where he was.

He had been here before.

Preston led the procession, stabbing the snow pack with his favorite trekking poles. He was hunting for hidden crevasses. In addition to providing balance and weight distribution on solid ground, trekking poles were also useful in testing potentially dangerous faults in the shifting icepack. Like all glaciated mountain ranges, the Himalayas were constantly changing.

All mountains were created in the same way, by the same geological processes. A collision of giant continental plates forced a massive upheaval of the earth's molten crust. This upheaval created all of the earth's great mountains—from the Andes and Rockies in the Americas to the Alps and the Urals in Europe and Asia. The Himalaya was no exception. When the landmass now known as India slammed into Asia over fifty million years ago, the resulting crumple zone lifted from the ocean floor, reaching nearly three miles into the sky. And as the plates continued to plow together, the mountains of the Himalaya grew ever taller. The most recent summiteer of Everest bested Hillary's 1953 ascent by nearly three feet.

Because of these inviolable geological processes, all mountains shared similar characteristics: ridges, couloirs, buttresses, thin air. Even up close, mountains looked the same. But this one, this mountain, this ridge, had burned an indelible image onto Conner's brain.

Team Providence ascended tentatively through the crevasse field. The glaciated ice had shifted, new chasms opened, old ones collapsed. Ice spires six stories tall sprouted from the pack. The landscape was different, but Conner could feel his brother's presence, could sense his spirit hovering over them as they pushed through the field.

Ahead, Team Providence would have to cross a second crevasse field—an icefall nearly twice as large.

The same one that had taken the life of his brother four years earlier.

Conner, trailing the others, moved on, studying the pyramid-shaped peak above. Tried to occupy his mind with thoughts of anything other than that crevasse field looming ahead. To climb such a peak—without maps—he would have to learn as much as he could simply by studying her, listening to her. How did the snow and ice lay upon her flanks? What did the wind sound like as it swept across her ridges? And what did the answers tell him about what lay beyond?

From what he could see, Kuk Sur looked equally daunting on the south and west faces. The south face was steep and coated with ice, meaning ice axes and crampons would be needed to break steps. Slow going, then.

The west face didn't look much better. The slope was dotted with rocky exposure surmounted by an imposing three hundred-foot vertical buttress. The north and east approaches to Kuk Sur would require a time-consuming, exhausting reconnaissance expedition around the perimeter of the mountain. And even once they were able to get a glimpse of the hidden faces, there was no guarantee those routes would prove any more climbable.

The decision was an easy one. He had already experienced the south face. Six years earlier. And now that he was here, far from the comfort and safety of his lakeside cottage in rural Virginia, Conner wasn't about to turn back now. From the moment he had landed on Tibetan soil, he knew he would have to face the southern route again.

And the giant icefall.

"I guess North Face decided on the west face," said Ian, suddenly materializing beside Conner. "I don't see them to the south."

Conner glanced up and across the southern face. Little had changed in the intervening years; the route was still horribly recognizable.

"Unless Wade's taking them around to tackle the north face," Thad said.

Preston had paused a few feet ahead, resting his trekking poles against a large boulder. The rest of the team used the impromptu break for a water stop.

Shandi shook her head. "No way is Wade going all the way to the north face. It's way too far. He'd lose all kinds of time."

Malika wiggled out of her pack, placed it on the snow, and sat on it. She didn't look great. Her dark complexion had turned ruddy. Conner could see watery eyes behind her goggles.

"You all right?" he asked her, pulling away from the others.

"Fine, fine. Just got this pounding headache is all."

"Diamox?"

"This morning." Malika saw Conner frown. "I know what you're thinking, but I'm fine. I don't have any other symptoms."

"A headache is the first sign."

"Don't you think I know that?" Malika snapped. "But I also know that a diagnosis of acute mountain sickness requires other symptoms. I am not feeling lightheaded, I slept well last night, and my stomach feels fine."

"So I don't have to give you the straight-walk test?" Conner said, smiling.

"You can give me any type of test you want, Doctor Michaels," she said, smiling back.

"Just get some extra fluids in you. I'm going to check back on you in a few hours."

"Looking forward to it, Doctor."

The flirty exchange did not ease Conner's concerns about Malika. As they climbed—they were now moving past nineteen thousand feet—the air thinned. Conner knew the inexorable process of oxygen starvation was beginning to affect them all. It was called hypoxia—when the body orders more oxygen to burning leg muscles, leaving less for the equally hard-working brain. Slowly, brain functions would dull and mental acuity would diminish.

During sleep, it was even more dangerous because hypoxia could lead to spells of not breathing at all. Spells long enough to cause permanent injury to the brain. With every step, the oxygen content in the air dropped, and the condition worsened.

He would have to keep a watchful eye on his beautiful teammate. Not an unpleasant prospect.

"This place sure is grim," Ian said between gulps from his water bottle. "I haven't seen so much as a bug since we set foot on this mountain."

"You'd be surprised at how many animals live up here," Preston said.

Conner was surprised at the comment. *All of a sudden, Preston is an expert on Himalayan fauna?*

"Wild yak," Preston continued, "the Tibetan wooly hare, antelope—and probably even a few snow leopards around up here."

"Snow leopards?" Shandi said, looking puzzled. "I thought they were extinct."

"Almost. The last census of those sneaky buggers never actually found any live animals—but did turn up tracks. Probably less than twenty left in the wild."

"And isn't it true that we may not be the only humans ever on this mountain, too?" Thad asked. "I mean, the natives must've wandered up here at some point, right?"

Preston shook his head. "I don't think so. The local tribes hold Kuk Sur in high reverence—the name literally means 'God of All Life.' To tread upon these flanks would surely bring bad luck upon their people. I think they kept a respectful distance."

"I don't believe in all that spiritual mumbo-jumbo," Ian said. "It's just a mountain."

"Don't be so quick to discount the beliefs of the Tibetans," Preston said. "In all of their stories and legends, there's always a heart of truth."

"So Kuk Sur really is the 'God of All Life'? A kind of mystical birthplace or something? Come on—it's a rock!"

"The Tibetans believe that man originally emerged from the highlands surrounded by the tallest mountains on earth. To them, the Kukuranda is holy. The center of the world. That's where the legends come from."

Ian waved off his burly teammate. "There are all kinds of legends. Bigfoot, the Abominable Snowman, the Loch Ness Monster. Are we supposed to believe there's a giant dinosaur swimming around a lake in Scotland just because legend says so?"

Preston paused a few moments before answering. "'The eye sees only what the mind is able to comprehend,'" he said. "Henri Bergson, one of the leading minds of the nineteenth century, said that."

"And that's supposed to mean what?"

"Hey, you guys, hush for a moment—" Shandi interrupted.

"It means, young Ian, that just because you haven't seen something, or don't believe in something, that doesn't mean it's not out there somewhere. Waiting to be discovered."

Ian chuckled. "Preston, I think the altitude is—"

Shandi cut him off. "I mean it, guys. Shut up a minute. I think I hear something."

Conner had heard it, too. In the distance, still far, far away. But the rhythmic thumping was unmistakable.

"Helicopter," he said.

Team North Face
Kuk Sur: 19,449

Nobody from Team North Face wanted to admit it, but they were not going to find the body of Cale Anders.

They had been searching for three full hours. The minutes drained away painfully. With each fruitless step, their collective morale sank even lower. No one uttered a word but simply went about their dreadful task in miserable silence. The image of Cale's right hand and the blood-splattered rocks spread like cancer through any hopes that their teammate and friend was still alive. Without proper clothes—Cale's outerwear was still tucked inside his sleeping bag—he would've frozen hours ago.

There was no trace of him amongst the crumbled icepack. Nor along the ice-strewn slopes that fell away sharply to the south. The others moved listlessly over the barren terrain. Tess collapsed on the ground, head hung low. Wade could practically smell the despair.

Wade wondered what Carlton and the crew down at the forward base camp thought of the grisly discovery, the team's hapless search. Surely the producers were aware of what was happening—they were watching the feeds from their shoulder-mounted cameras, right?

So where was the mountain rescue team?

"I don't think we're getting anywhere here," Tess said finally.

The looks on the rest of the team's faces told Wade they were all thinking the same thing.

"I can't go on," added Blaine. "I don't want to go on. Every time I see something I pray it isn't him. I'm sorry, but I don't want to be the one to find his body."

Hoops nodded. "I'm with Blaine. We're all beat. We need to get back to base camp. Carlton will pull together a proper search party. If Cale is still alive somewhere on the mountain, we're not going to find him in our condition."

Wade studied the graying skies above Kuk Sur. They still had most of the day ahead of them. Turning back now meant that *Darwin's Race* was over for them. The end of the two million-dollar prize. The end of his summit attempt. It was a bitter pill to swallow, and Wade hesitated making the decision. They were so close.

But there was no choice, was there? Even if he wanted to continue—and a big part of him wanted to do just that—the others would surely revolt. They wouldn't ascend without knowing what happened to Cale.

"Should we tell the producers we're coming down?"

asked Tess.

"We're not going anywhere."

The rest of the team turned at Wade's abrupt pronouncement.

"What the hell are you talking about, Wade?" Hoops said. "How can we go on knowing that Cale is probably dead on this mountain?"

The team leader didn't answer immediately, letting the question hang in the cold mountain air. When he did open his mouth to reply, his words were measured and even.

"We go on because that's what we do. We're adventure racers. We're mountain climbers. Every single one of us knows the risks every time we set foot on another mountain or another river. I dare say it's the very reason we do it. The risk, the danger, the threat of something bad happening— that's what gets our blood pumping. And now, when something does go wrong, you want to pack it all in? Quit?"

Wade's teammates shuffled nervously but remained silent.

"It took me five years and three attempts to finally summit Everest. On the second attempt, my team lost a man. Dan Brown. He had been just a few hundred feet from the summit, but he just had nothing left. He sat down to rest and never got up again. I was climbing behind him when a storm blew in. I had to turn back. When I found out he had died up there, I was crushed. He was more than a good climber; he was a friend. The next year, I hit Everest again. I was climbing up past the Lhotse Face, and I came across a body, frozen there in the ice. The face had been ripped away by the wind, but I could tell it was him. No one had brought his body back down. The Sherpas were too superstitious, didn't want anything to do with dead bodies lest the bad luck rub off on them. It would've taken a Herculean effort to pry his body from the ice and haul it back down to Camp II. So you know what I did? I said a prayer for Dan, stepped over his dead body, and pressed up toward the summit."

"Jesus, Wade," Tess said. "You never told me that."

"No, I didn't. But I'm glad I made that decision. Dan knew that Everest was a dangerous place; all mountains are. He knew there was a chance he would give his life upon its slopes. His death was a tragedy, yes. For all of us. But do you think for one minute that he would've wanted me to turn around and go home? Think about it. Do you think Cale, if he is dead, would want us to stop this race on his account? If something happened to me, I know I wouldn't. And I would bet top dollar that none of you, not a one, would expect your teammates to quit this race if something happened to you. Am I wrong?"

More nervous shuffling, but no response. Until Tess finally spoke. "You're right, Wade. If something happened to me, I would expect the rest of you to press on. That's what I would want."

Blaine shook his head. "That's true for me too, probably for all of us. But I just can't go on. My body and my mind are just sick with the thought that I just lost the guy.

And after Powder? No, it's too much for me. I just want to get the hell off this mountain. By myself if I have to."

Wade surveyed the others. "Anyone else? Anyone else want to stop here and turn back?"

Tentatively, Hoops raised a gloved hand. "I'm done, too," he said.

"That leaves me and you, Elizabeth," Wade said. "Good luck to the rest of you. As for me, I will choose to honor Dan Brown, Powder, Cale, and the scores of others that came and fell before us. Because nature may challenge us, may even claim some of us, but she cannot and will not dissuade us."

And with that, Team North Face was down to two.

Forward Base Camp
17,483 Feet

"What the hell are they doing?" Carlton yelled. "They're coming down?"

He didn't need an answer from his crew. The producer had heard enough of North Face's team discussion to know exactly what was happening.

Blaine Reeves and Paul Robeson were quitting the race.

What the fuck was going on here? Did they think they had signed up for a walk in the park? This was no time to declare the race over. Terrance Carlton was the only goddamned person authorized to make that decision. Race over? Not yet. Not when there was still a second team making their way toward the summit. Not when millions of people were watching back home. Not when tens of millions of dollars were pouring into NBC's coffers. And certainly not with Terrance Carlton's own career hanging in the balance.

Race over? Not for one missing racer, it wasn't.

Carlton turned and yelled across the forward production tent, to no one in particular, "Where is my goddamned rescue helicopter?"

"Should be there by now," someone reported back.

The producer turned to his production assistant. He was sitting at the control board, staring into the bank of blank monitors. "Mr. Scott," he said, "let's shift our attention to Team Providence. We've got a show to produce."

CHAPTER THIRTY

Team North Face
19,101 Feet

Team North Face had split into two factions—Blaine and Hoops descending, Wade and Tess pushing on—but were still within shouting distance of each other when the sound of helicopter blades pierced the silence of the mountain. The labored *thwack-thwack-thwack* had Wade Stanley and the rest of Team North face scanning the skies for what was surely a high-mountain rescue team.

Wade saw the chopper first, a tiny speck against the white of the surrounding range. "There."

"About time," said Tess. The team had abandoned their futile search for Cale Anders over an hour before. Now, as Hoops and Blaine made their slow, plodding way down to forward base camp, the arrival of the rescue chopper seemed pointless.

The fire engine-red helicopter climbed steadily up the slope toward them. Then, amid a whirlwind of billowing snow, it soared over their heads, aiming for the team's abandoned camp.

"Isn't this a little high for a helicopter?" asked Tess. "That pilot must have a death wish."

Wade and Tess scrambled down two hundred feet of steep ice to rejoin their teammates. "Looks like a Eurocopter," Wade said. "Older model, but still pretty good. Those babies are designed for high-mountain rescues. With those twin Arriel engines, he can reach nineteen easy."

"Nineteen thousand? In these winds?" Hoops shook his head. "No chance."

"And need I remind you, we're already well above nineteen thousand?" Tess added.

The wind picked up. Wade tugged his cap down over his exposed ears.

"At least they finally sent someone," Blaine noted. "They must've been watching."

The helicopter hovered, apparently searching for a stable landing area in the snow pack. Wade could see someone in the pilot's seat gesturing to the rock wall below.

The engine revved loudly, the pilot asking for more power. The chopper barely moved.

The pilot turned, and for an instant Wade could make out the man's appearance. He was a Tibetan, with a large round face and dark skin. The pilot wore goggles to ward off the snow glare, but in that fleeting moment, Wade would swear he saw something in his eyes.

Panic.

"Something's wrong."

The chopper lurched, pitching dangerously close to the slope. The blades cleared the rock wall by mere inches. The engine roared in protest.

"There's not enough air," Wade said. "They're not getting any lift."

The rescue chopper lurched again. And this time, there would be no recovery.

With a loud *crunch* the chopper crushed into the rock. The blades crumpled away, spraying shards of ice and rock and steel into the air. A large black chunk of rotor careened out of the whirling wreckage, hurtling down the slope, missing Team North Face by mere feet.

"Everyone down!" Wade yelled.

Now bladeless, the chopper plummeted to the slope with a mountain-rattling tumult. It bounced once upon its landing gear, then began to lean into the slope. The nubs of the rotors, still spinning futilely, caught against the mountain, bucking the chopper violently. The Eurocopter tumbled end over end, spewing ice.

Plunging directly toward the men and women of Team North Face.

"Run, run, RUN!" screamed Wade.

The racers scrambled in all directions, fleeing the plummeting steel wreckage. Wade lost sight of Tess as she took off in the opposite direction, toward a steep ice ridge. The helicopter was less than two hundred feet away. Sliding fast.

The tumbling helicopter slammed into an ice-encrusted ledge. The nose of the chopper pushed out over the ice shelf. And then it stopped.

It teetered over the edge, half of the chopper dangling in midair over their heads.

As he scrambled to his feet, Wade could see a splash of red against the cracked cockpit glass.

"Jesus Christ!" someone exclaimed from nearby. "That ridge won't hold for long. We've got to help them!"

It was Tess, on the far side of the slope. She was struggling up the slope through knee-deep snow.

The helicopter swayed in the wind, metal groaning like a wounded animal.

"Tess, no!" Wade yelled. "It's too unstable. We have to go around!"

If his girlfriend heard his pleas, she didn't give any indication. She had dropped her backpack and was moving quickly now, climbing on all fours up the loose snow.

Wade felt a hand on his shoulder. "Where's Hoops?" Blaine asked.

Wade barely had time to scan the slopes when a thundering boom shook the ground. For a second, nothing happened. Then, with a second boom, the ledge supporting the chopper gave way. Boulders of razor-sharp ice the size of desks barreled down the mountainside. As Wade held his breath, he watched the boulders hurtle past Tess. That was too close.

Under his feet, Wade felt the ground rumble anew.

"*No—*"

Freed from its rocky prison, the Eurocopter lurched a few feet down the slope. Then, before anyone could scream, the chopper plummeted down the face, spewing ice into the air. As the craft slid down, gaining speed, Wade could see frantic hands braced against the cockpit glass.

Dear God, he thought. *They're still alive in there.*

A mass of screeching metal and ice and snow collapsed down around him.

The avalanche slammed into Tess Chamniss with the force of a category four hurricane. One desperate last breath was knocked from her lungs. She tumbled, legs and arms thrashing, through darkness. She sensed something heavy and solid over her head—the chopper? In the swirling snow pack, it was impossible to be sure.

Her head smashed against something solid.

Her lungs were on fire, threatening to explode.

She swept down the mountain. Opened her mouth to breathe—only to have it jammed full with a torrent of fuel-laced snow.

Her backpack tore away, ripping from her shoulders in a fierce jolt. She tried to tuck her arms around her legs in a cannonball, as she had been taught in ice-climbing school years before. To avoid having limbs snapped off. But the muscles in her arms and legs were not responding. She plunged down, inside the avalanche, like a rag doll.

And then, everything stopped.

It took a moment for Tess to believe it, but once she was sure the avalanche had abated. She was still breathing; her legs and arms were still attached.

She began to dig. She didn't know where the surface was, but it didn't matter. She had to act now. Snow in a slide was most malleable in the first twenty seconds. After that, the snow would harden like concrete.

And then she would be trapped.

Ignoring the shooting pain in her right elbow and right leg, Tess managed to create a small pocket of air around her body. But the snow was already hardening, and each movement sucked precious oxygen from her icy cocoon. Suddenly, she felt blood rush to her head. And stay there. Her brain began to swim.

She was digging in the wrong direction. She was upside down!

Tess panicked. She flailed wildly against the snow, but it didn't give. An icy tomb had already hardened around her body.

Fighting back waves of hysteria, Tess tried to scream but her mouth was still full of snow. She gagged, spitting up what she could. Felt her head swoon. She had two minutes of air. Maybe.

Unless one of her teammates found their way to the surface, and somehow managed to find Tess buried under God-knew-how-many inches of snow and ice, Tess had two minutes. Two minutes to live.

She closed her eyes.

Crunch.

The strange sound roused Tess from her cataleptic state. She blinked her eyes open. She was wrapped in utter darkness, shivering, disoriented, absurdly tired. Her body felt like five hundred pounds, and try as she might she could not move.

How long had she been out?

Crunch. Crunch.

Blood pulsed at her temples. Everything throbbed. She remembered suddenly that she was wedged upside down. The sound was coming from the surface, above her feet.

The crunching continued above her, but it was so faint Tess couldn't determine if it was real or imagined. The air in her pocket was thinning rapidly. *Oh, God, if there's someone up there, please let them hurry.*

Tess tried to scream, but only a faint whine escaped her lips.

The effort drained her, and she felt the warmth of unconsciousness sweep back over her body.

Just before she blacked out again, Tess felt a strong hand on her leg.

Team Providence
19,247 Feet

Conner gazed through the thin air across the Himalayan valley.

The sounds of the distant helicopter had faded, but the suspicion that something was wrong lingered. He assumed the others had heard the chopper, too, but if they had they were keeping it to themselves. He could understand that. There was only one reason for a helicopter at this altitude. A prospect nobody wanted to dwell upon.

Mountain rescue.

Ian was doing his level best to divert everyone's attention with rambling stories and random jokes. His teammates seemed to be humoring him. Conner even caught Malika grinning at one or two of Ian's best lines. Despite her admitted headaches, she had not slowed the group. He had kept his promise and had maintained a watchful eye over her. She hadn't stumbled—any more than the others, at least—and her breathing was normal. Malika Child was one tough woman, a chip off her old man's block for sure.

Team Providence approached a sharp incline that rose to a saddle between two pinnacles. After a brief discussion, they decided to climb. They roped up in groups of three, Conner and Preston leading the two groups. Traversing in wide swaths across the snow-packed face, Team Providence slowly ascended.

If anyone thought the steep slope would somehow diminish Ian's running monologue, they would quickly be disappointed. Now he spoke even louder so both ascent teams could still hear.

"So the research team was there, on this big-ass lake, when they heard something under their boat. Now this was no small boat—this was a forty-five footer with enough electronic equipment, depth finders, and radar gear sensitive enough to find a minnow—and all of sudden without warning, something big passed under their boat. I'm talking big. *Huge.* Bigger than their entire boat. So the captain, watching on the radar, sees this enormous *something* under his boat and says, 'We're gonna need a bigger boat.' So this other guy goes—"

"This story is starting to sound familiar," Thad interrupted.

Ian plowed on. "So this other guy, a young fisherman named Mac, instinctively throws a harpoon into the water at the shadowy figure under the boat. And he hits it!"

Conner could see Malika shaking her head, smiling.

"A line is already fastened from the harpoon to the boat and that forty-five footer starts getting dragged right across the lake! So whatever it is, it's strong enough to pull a couple thousand pounds of dead weight. The captain orders the engines full forward. Doesn't work. The boat is still being dragged. And then—"

"I mean it, Ian," Thad interrupted again. "I know this story. Bigger boat . . . dragged backwards through the water. *Jaws*, right?"

"This is a true story! My buddy told me this a couple months ago. And he heard it directly from the fisherman."

"Alright, alright. Go on. But does this story end with an exploding scuba tank in the mouth of a great white?"

"And let me guess," Conner chimed in. "The fisherman? He doesn't know how to swim, right?"

"Did you ever notice that all monster movies are always the same?" Thad said, now totally ignoring Ian's protests. "Try to get you to believe that the monster is dead; then—surprise!—the monster suddenly reappears. I think that happened in Jaws, too."

Conner nodded. "And *Jaws 2* and *Jaws 3* and all the *Friday the 13th* movies. It happens in all of them. It's like a rule of monster movies or something."

"Someday, some cool new writer is going to come along and fool everybody by killing the monster—and having it stay dead. Now, *that* would be a surprise!"

"Hey! Hey!" Ian said, throwing up his arms. "I'm in the middle of a story here!"

"Oh, right. Sorry, Ian," said Thad. "Go ahead. I definitely want to hear the rest of your story. It's been like five years since I've seen *Jaws*."

"Hey, Thad?"

"Yeah?"

"Fuck you."

While the others laughed it up at Ian's expense, Conner noticed Malika was not joining in. She gazed up the slope as if she were lost in her own world. Already attuned to her condition, he watched until he caught her eye. Even under her snow goggles, he could see that her eyes were wide.

She was scared.

Slowly—like she was moving in slow motion—Malika raised her trekking pole and pointed. Conner followed her line of vision to the ridgeline above.

And then he saw what she saw.

At first he thought it was a rock jutting up from the ice. But all signs of rock had disappeared a thousand feet below. This was no rock.

It was a body.

Conner quickly untied himself from the safety rope and headed straight up the pitch. He heard shouting from below, but their warnings fell on deaf ears. Using ice axes in both hands and crampons on both boots, Conner moved quickly, breathing heavily in the thin air. By the time he reached the top of the saddle, he was soaked with sweat.

What was left of the body was lying face down in the ice. Head twisted unnaturally. Face obscured by a snow-drift. Giant red streaks ran the length of the back, blood and gristle and skin open to the elements. Frozen. A down jacket was blowing in tatters in the wind that swept along the ridge. Half of the left leg had been torn away. One of the hands was missing completely.

Conner leaned over to scrape the snow from the face.

The nose was obliterated. The left eyeball was sliced in half. The jaw had been torn open to the gums. Conner, no stranger to severe injury, turned away.

Preston had climbed to the ridge. He looked down at the body without flinching.

"Who is it?"

"Cale Anders. North Face."

"How the hell did he get up here?" Preston asked.

Conner considered the question a moment. A dead body at nineteen thousand feet. Obviously didn't get there under his own power. But there was something in the way Preston had posed the question. It had contained no trace of curiosity. It was like he already knew the answer.

Conner looked down the slope. His team was now huddled together. Waiting.

First Powder, now Cale Anders. It was too much.

"The race is over," he said, turning back to Preston. "We're going down."

Forward Base Camp
17,483 Feet

Carlton's world was crumbling.

Courtesy of the shoulder-mounted cameras on Team North Face, the producer had just witnessed the crash of the rescue helicopter. Then, as if that weren't enough, he and his crew had watched in horror as the damaged chopper plunged down the slope, unleashing an avalanche that had barreled right through the team of helpless racers.

That was over an hour ago. Repeated efforts to reach the chopper crew failed. The video feeds from Team North Face were all in failure. The monitors along the far wall of the production tent were all maddeningly black.

And then there was Cale Anders. Conner Michaels had discovered his mutilated corpse on a high ridge, and now the entire team was descending to forward base camp.

Darwin's Race was in shambles. Two racers dead. Four others presumed dead in the avalanche. The two-man chopper crew? Lost, most likely dead. The one team still intact, on their way down, obviously quitting the race. *Darwin's Race*? There was no *Darwin's Race* anymore.

Horace Alger had called three times in the last fifteen minutes, demanding to know what was going on. Carlton refused to take the calls, but his assistant had scribbled out Alger's questions on a piece of paper. All were variations on the same theme: Why were the feeds down? Where was the new footage?

Carlton paced in the production tent at forward base camp. He had to think of something. *Darwin's Race* couldn't die like this.

His communications chief must've been reading his mind. "What do we do now?" Leslie asked.

For maybe the first time in his career, Carlton didn't know. There would be an investigation, of course. And he would have to answer for Cale Anders' death. The helicopter crash, too. And the missing members of North Face? Carlton couldn't even contemplate the prospect of losing an entire team. Men and women with families. Families that would be screaming for answers.

"Terry, what are we gonna do?" repeated Leslie. "We've got racers down out there!"

"You don't think I know that? I'm thinking here! Just . . . give me a minute."

A young production assistant approached. "Mr. Carlton?" she said timidly. "Mr. Alger is on the phone, says it's urgent that he speak with you."

"Give me a minute to think!" Carlton yelled. All activity in the production tent ground to a halt. "Can you give me a fuckin' minute's peace here? One FUCKIN' minute?"

The assistant shrunk away, and the crew slowly and silently returned to their jobs. Carlton slumped into a canvas chair in front of the mostly blank video monitors. He had yanked the feeds from North Face just after the attack on Cale Anders and had kept them off the air. No one back home had witnessed the chopper crash. But that provided little consolation. Now that he had pulled the feeds from Team Providence, too, the calls would be coming into NBC and Discovery Channel headquarters by the thousands. Viewers would soon recognize that all of the direct feeds had been pulled.

You're the producer. Think of something.

"We need to get up there and search for North Face," he said finally. "Is there a second chopper in Lhasa?"

Leslie shook her head. "The closest one is in Beijing. It'll take hours to get here, if we can get it at all. What about a ground team?"

"Ground team? Who do we have with the skills to get back up the mountain? We didn't bring rescue climbers. Remember?"

A blast of cold mountain air swept through the production tent, and Carlton looked up to see Conner Michaels and his teammates stampede inside.

Just what I need. Another pissed-off team.

Conner didn't waste time on pleasantries. "Cale Anders is dead," he announced. The rest of Team Providence stood behind him like an angry mob.

Leslie stepped between Conner and the producer. "We know, Conner. We saw your feed."

"You want to tell us what happened? Because I just dropped what's left of his body in the medical tent! And it ain't much!"

"We don't know," Carlton said. "We think he had a bad fall."

Conner lunged forward, held back by his teammates. "A fall? His face was fucking *clawed off*! Something took a giant bite out of his leg! This was no fall!"

"We couldn't tell anything from here," Leslie said, now looking genuinely frightened. "Whatever happened, it happened in the middle of the night."

"And how the hell did the body end up there on that ridge? Who put him there? Where is the rest of Team North Face?" Conner glanced toward the monitors. Six screens were broadcasting the feeds from Providence's own cameras, interiors of the production tent. The other six screens were black.

"Where are they, Carlton?"

The producer could feel the accusation in Conner's voice. And the collective stares from the other members of Team Providence—and his own crew—weighed heavily upon his shoulders. A phone was ringing in the background; he heard someone say, "No, Mr. Alger, he's still meeting with someone. Yes, I'll give him the message." Leslie shuffled nervously beside him.

Darwin's Race couldn't fall apart like this. There was too much riding on it. If this production crumbled now, all previous successes would fade away, replaced by the spectacular failure of *Darwin's Race*. You only get one shot in the entertainment world—you're only as good as your last show. He would be finished. Already, he could feel the cold grip of obscurity tapping him on the shoulder.

He needed time to think. To come up with a plan that would somehow salvage all this. Save *Darwin's Race*. Rescue his dying career, his life.

Conner demanded again, "Where is North Face?"

"We're having problems with their cameras," Carlton said, swallowing hard. "We're working on it right now, and I expect to be back up soon." He shot a look in Leslie's direction. *Just play along*, it said. She apparently recognized the look and retreated slightly.

"They know about Cale?" Conner asked.

"They know he's missing. They don't know he's . . . uh . . . dead."

"What are you waiting for? You need to get word to North Face. They need to get back to camp right now. Right now!"

"Calm down, Conner. You're getting hysterical. It's a stressful situation for all of us, but we're not going to accomplish anything by rushing to action. Now, you and your team here need rest. I suggest you—"

Suddenly, from the ranks of Team Providence, Preston charged forward, grabbing Carlton by the neck. "Rushing to action? Why, you little piss-ant! That man was slaughtered up there!"

Conner struggled to pull Preston from the producer's throat. "Preston, let go! Let go!" His arms were as thick as a pair of boa constrictors, and just as strong. Conner could barely get a grip around them.

Preston began to shake the producer like a rag doll. "If you don't do something right this fucking second, we're going to have more dead bodies on our hands. Do I make myself clear?"

"Daddy, stop!" Malika screamed. "We've let this go too far. People are getting killed."

Preston released his grip. Carlton fell to the ground, gagging and clutching his throbbing neck. Everyone stopped. The crew halted what they were doing. All eyes were on Malika.

She was staring at her father with pleading eyes.

"What are you talking about, Malika?" Conner asked. "What do you mean 'we've let this go too far'?"

"She doesn't mean anything by it," Preston answered quickly. "We all share the responsibility for what's going on here. I certainly do. It was my idea to bring a second team to this mountain. But now, Mr. Producer, you're going to do the right thing. You're going to recall North Face right away, aren't you?"

Carlton, still struggling to regain normal breathing, nodded. Leslie helped him to his feet.

"We'll take care of it," she said. Turning to Conner, she added, "But you need to control your team. We won't get anything done if we're fighting amongst ourselves."

"Don't dictate terms to me," Conner said. "Just get North Face down. Now."

The members of Team Providence swept out of the production tent. It took a full five minutes for the tension inside the tent to ease.

Leslie waited another few minutes for the crew to scatter before turning to face her boss. "What the hell are you up to, Terry? Why didn't you tell them about Team North Face?"

Carlton rubbed down his bruised throat. "Tell them what?"

"The truth, goddamn it. About the chopper crash.

The avalanche. That they're probably all dead up there. That's what you tell them!"

"But what if they're not dead?" Carlton asked.

"What the hell are you talking about?" Leslie demanded. "You saw the feeds. That avalanche all but obliterated—"

She cut herself off. Carlton was pointing at something on the far wall.

The video monitors for North Face.

They were back on.

CHAPTER THIRTY-ONE

Forward Base Camp
17,483 Feet

"You want to tell me what the hell that was all about?"

Conner Michaels stormed into the small Team Providence tent, red-faced and furious. Ian, Shandi, and Thad retreated to the fruit and cheese platter the crew had left for them. Preston slumped into a chair in the corner, still seething. It was Malika, standing in the center of the tent, who now drew Conner's anger.

"I don't think now is the right time, Conner," she said quietly.

"Oh, that's where you're wrong, Malika. Now is exactly the right time. I'm getting a very distinct impression that you and your dad over there are hiding something. If you're keeping secrets, if you know something about what happened to Cale, now is the time to tell us. There are people up on that mountain!"

Malika gazed to her father. His head was down, staring at his snow-crusted boots. He did not look up.

"No secrets," she said, turning back to the captain. "I'm just feeling anxious about all this. I didn't know Cale the way some of you did, but I'm still crushed by his death. Jesus, I do have feelings here. All this . . . it's just reminded me of my mother, that's all."

"Your mother? I don't understand."

"Mama," Malika said softly. "Her death here in the gorge. And now Cale." Her voice trailed off.

"She was Tibetan, wasn't she?" Conner asked. "That's why you speak the language. That's how you spoke to the children back in Pema."

She nodded. "My father met her in Lhasa, during one of his climbing trips. She was beautiful, and he fell in love with her almost immediately. He pulled out of his trip just so he could travel with her back to her village. He spent the next five months living with her, among her family. But her father, my grandfather, didn't approve of him. Old ways are difficult to break. My grandfather couldn't accept an outsider. If they wanted to stay together—and by now they had pledged their love for one another—they would no longer be welcome in the family home.

"So my father moved with my mother to a small hut on the outskirts of the village of Lugu, at the footsteps of the

Himalaya. When my mother got pregnant, they went back to my grandfather and he finally accepted them back into the family. The day I was born was a day of great celebration for the entire family."

"We named her after her mother." Preston had emerged from the shadows, a look of forlorn happiness on his face. "Malika means queen. Because that's how we felt about her. She looked just like her mother. Exotic. Beautiful."

Conner didn't speak. Malika had already told him that her mother was dead, and as much as he wanted to speed up their story, he didn't interrupt. He couldn't.

Malika continued, "Then one day, when I was eight, my mother went into the jungle to collect fresh water from the creek. In Tibetan villages, children, even younger than I was, were often left alone like that. It is part of the culture—it's what makes us a hearty people."

"I was back in New York on business," Preston said. He shook his head. "There was nothing I could do."

Malika's eyes glistened as she spoke directly to her father. "You had already given up so much to be with us." She turned back to Conner. "He didn't want to take us from our home, so he was making arrangements to cede control of his companies to trusted employees. There were more papers to sign. He had to go."

"What happened, Malika?" Conner asked gently. "What happened to your mother?"

"She was killed."

"Murdered?"

"Yes," she replied. "And no."

She didn't elaborate further.

"And now Cale's death here has brought back those memories, hasn't it?" Shandi had moved forward to comfort the distraught Malika. "I think we can all understand that."

The others nodded with obvious concern on their faces. But something didn't sit well with Conner. She was obviously hiding something . . . but what?

"So what do we do now?" asked Ian. He had been wandering aimlessly inside the tent, his nervous energy palpable. "Just wait around here? Waiting for something to happen?"

Malika looked thankful for the change of subject. "Are we really done, Conner?"

Conner looked up to find a lineup of intent eyes boring down upon him. "What? You want to go back up?"

Malika considered this a moment. "Well, I can't speak for anyone else, but I came here for a race."

Preston nodded his big head. "Malika speaks for me, too. I put up a hell of a lot of money for this. I understand your decision to turn back, but I'd hate to quit now."

"There are two people dead. Doesn't anybody remember that?"

Thad stood. "Hey, we all remember Powder and Cale. They were our friends. But, Con, you know as well as I— it's part of the game here."

Murmurs of assent rose from the team.

"So all of you want to go on? Shandi, even you?"

She nodded. "Two million dollars, even split six ways, is a lot of money."

"I never pegged you to be motivated by money," Conner said, perhaps with a bit too much anger.

"Come on, Conner. That's unfair. Thad and I can't climb forever. It would be nice to get out of this someday, start a little climbing business. Start a family. We need a nest egg to make those things happen."

"Why am I the only one who thinks this is a lousy idea?" Conner asked. Out of the corner of his eye, he caught an exchange of glances between the members of his team. "What?"

Shandi moved close enough to lay a hand on Conner's shoulder. "Look, I hope I'm not out of line here; you know I love you like a brother. We all do. But maybe you're just not ready to go back up. I mean, it's the same mountain—"

A hush descended inside the tent as her voice trailed off. For a moment, everything seemed to stop. Even Preston's raspy breaths grew silent. When Conner finally spoke, his voice was little more than a whisper.

"You think I'm playing this one too safe?" he asked into his boots. "Because of what happened to Tucker?" He looked up. "Is that what you all think?"

No one made a move to answer. Just then, a man swept into their tent, looking intent. He glanced around the tent until he locked eyes with Conner.

"Carlton wants you in the production tent right away," the man said. "Something's happening."

Kuk Sur
18,848 Feet

Wade Stanley blinked his eyes open. Somehow, his goggles had been ripped from his head. He squinted into the sun.

He tried to move, but his bones groaned in protest. A quick mental check of his body revealed a sore right knee, but otherwise all seemed intact.

What the hell happened?

The helicopter. A crash. The avalanche.

He had been climbing toward the downed chopper when the ridge gave way. The last thing he remembered was being knocked unconscious by the crushing front edge of the slide.

He sat up with a bolt. "Elizabeth!" he called out. "Elizabeth!"

There was no answer. He realized his pack was gone, too, but the miniature camera was still strapped tightly to his shoulder harness. He had no idea if it was working or not. He hoped so. Maybe help was already on the way.

"Elizabeth!" he tried again.

Wade dragged himself to his feet, rubbing his tender knee, and scanned the surroundings. He was at the foot of a giant ice wall. It stretched over four hundred feet over his head. Huge chunks of snow laced with hard ice were strewn about. Had the avalanche washed him over the precipice? How had he survived that kind of fall?

He heard a moan.

Scrambling toward the sound, he plowed through a minefield of waist-high snow chunks. "Elizabeth! Is that you?" he called out in desperation.

He rounded the corner of a giant block of snow and saw the body. It was Blaine, lying there, propped up against the ice wall. His backpack lay on the ground beside him. He managed a feeble smile.

"Enjoy the ride?" he asked.

"What I remember of it. Are you hurt?"

Blaine winced. "Not too bad. I think I did something to my shoulder, but I'll survive."

Wade squinted up the ice wall. "What about the others?"

"I haven't heard anything," he said. He paused a moment before adding, "That was a big slide, Wade. We were damn lucky."

Wade knew it. Surviving an avalanche of that magnitude was almost impossible. Still, if they had done it—

"Can you climb?" he asked. "We have to get up this wall, but I lost my pack."

"Climb? Are you nuts? We need to get our asses off this mountain."

"Not now. Not when there may be survivors up there in the avalanche field."

Blaine considered this a moment, then nodded. "I've

got the rope, but only one ice axe."

Wade studied the wall. It looked solid enough, but the avalanche had ripped open fresh gashes in the face. Shards of ice were still tumbling down to the ground. They would have to somehow skirt the unstable sections.

"We're going to have to improvise," he said.

Forward Base Camp
17,483 Feet

Conner burst through the heavy canvas flap into the production tent, his team in tow. Carlton was there, standing behind a wide control panel, waiting for them.

"Before we begin, I believe I owe you an apology," the producer said.

"Where's North Face?" Conner demanded. "Have they been recalled?"

Carlton emerged from behind the panel, whispering a few directions to an assistant before turning his complete attention back to Team Providence. He confidently strode around Conner, weaving through the rest of the team—Preston glaring menacingly—and casually took a seat in his director's chair. He gestured to the bank of monitors in front of him.

Of the six monitors assigned to Team North Face, four were black. Two flickered with activity. Pieces of electrical tape beneath the screens were marked with two names:

Stanley and Reeves. Wade and Blaine.

"Why are they climbing, Carlton?" demanded Conner. "Why aren't they on the way down?"

"This is where the apology comes in," the producer said. "We already sent up a rescue helicopter to search for Cale Anders. You may have even heard it early this morning."

"That was hours ago."

"Let me finish. We sent up the chopper *before* you found his body. But there was an accident."

Conner stared hard at Carlton.

"The chopper lost thrust in the air. It crashed into the south face. We haven't been able to raise the crew."

Sensing Conner was too shell-shocked to speak, Shandi stepped forward. "North Face was on the south face."

"The crash started an avalanche," Carlton said. "North Face was hit."

Conner lunged for Carlton, but this time the producer was ready. A team of production assistants acted quickly to restrain him. Conner struggled against their grip, but when he felt Preston's thick hand on his shoulder, he stopped fighting.

"I'm sorry, Conner. You have no idea how much. We didn't tell you because we didn't want to alarm you unnecessarily. We couldn't be sure about what happened until we reestablished video contact."

Conner couldn't believe his ears. Just hours earlier Carlton had promised to recall the team and end *Darwin's Race*. Now the producer was acting as if nothing had happened. Didn't he remember that Cale Anders had just been massacred on the mountain?

"But Wade and Blaine are *climbing*," Conner whispered through gritted teeth. "Why aren't they coming down?"

"We don't know," Carlton said. "We can't pinpoint their location, and the other two cameras are still not transmitting properly."

"The others," Shandi said. "They could be up there, buried in the snow. And you sit here doing nothing. They could be dying up there!"

"We have ordered a second rescue chopper from Beijing," Carlton continued calmly. "But it will not arrive until this afternoon. We're lucky to obtain one at all."

Conner began to pace. His head was swimming. Tess was up there. *Somewhere.*

"Why haven't you called in the Chinese Army?" Thad asked. "We need to mount a full-scale search and rescue right now. Jesus, Carlton—what you're doing is criminal."

"The fact that Wade and Blaine are still climbing indicates that North Face survived the avalanche and are continuing toward the summit. I have decided to allow them to keep going. Who are we to deny them Kuk Sur now?"

"The race is still on? Are you telling me that the race is still on? While Cale's bloodied body sits in a medical tent just twenty feet from here?" Conner demanded, shaking. "Is that what you're telling me, Carlton? Because if it is, you're going to need more than your entire crew to keep my hands from your throat."

"*Darwin's Race* is bigger than Cale Anders. Bigger than any single competitor," the producer said. "There are millions and millions of dollars in play here. Don't think for a moment that I don't mourn the death of Cale Anders. I do. But I have a responsibility to my crew and the staff back in New York. There are millions of people hanging on every word, every movement our racers make. And I'm not about to let them down. I'm a producer. I'm the head guy out here. I have my obligations." Carlton pounded his chest like a Sunday morning preacher. He gestured to the crew members gathered inside the production tent. "There are literally hundreds of jobs relying on *Darwin's Race*. People who have families to feed, people with elderly parents to take care of. In some cases, they gave up good jobs to come here. To be part of history.

"But the strongest reason to continue is the racers themselves. Everyone who signed up for *Darwin's Race*— the great Conner Michaels included—knew the risks associated with this extreme endeavor. It's a race up an unclimbed peak—across dangerous ice ridges, crevasses, class five whitewater in a gorge populated with tigers, poisonous snakes, and who knows what else. It's the very reason—the essence—of why all of you signed on. The challenge, the danger—that's what makes *Darwin's Race* so popular."

"Danger is one thing," Conner said. "Powder's death was an accident. This is . . . this is something else. It is morally irresponsible to continue this race."

At this, a faint smile flashed across the producer's face.

"Morally irresponsible, eh?" Carlton said. "What if I told you that it would be morally irresponsible for you *not* to continue?"

Conner laughed humorlessly. "That would be a neat trick. There's no way I'm continuing up that mountain. And I know I speak for my entire team. Team Providence is officially out of *Darwin's Race*."

Murmurs of assent drifted up from his teammates. Conner felt a reassuring hand on his shoulder. He turned to see Ian standing at his side.

"I see, I see," Carlton said under his breath. Then, louder, he said: "May I have camera twelve on the main monitor, please?"

Conner turned toward the bank of screens to see a large image flicker to life on the ten-foot screen.

It was grainy, and the image was difficult to discern. Squinting through the static, Conner could make out a smooth wall of ice lining the left edge of the frame. The rest of the screen was too dark to make out clearly.

A cave?

"An hour ago we began to receive this transmission from one of the North Face cameras."

Despite the poor image quality, Conner could just make out what appeared to be the faint outlines of a cave. A cave of ice.

"What you are seeing is a live picture from the camera. It appears stationary now, but we have seen occasional movement suggesting the racer is still active."

Conner shuffled forward, peering into the monitor.

"As you may have already figured out, the image is tilted on its side. What appears to be a wall of rock along the left is actually the ground. Our racer is lying down."

Conner felt his heart pound inside his chest as he posed his next question. "Carlton, whose camera is still broadcasting?"

Carlton paused a moment before answering. It seemed to Conner that the entire conversation had come to this—that the wily producer had orchestrated the entire sequence to lead him up to this exact point, this precise moment. Conner felt trapped, manipulated, but try as he might, he could not do anything but hang on Carlton's every word. He hated himself for it.

"The camera," Carlton said slowly, "belongs to Tess Chamniss. We don't know where she is, only that she is still alive."

Conner's spirit soared. *Tess was alive!*

But Carlton wasn't finished.

"She has not moved from that position. She could be injured, maybe even seriously. But without a rescue chopper, we can't get up to the crash site to look for her. Or any other survivors."

"It looks like she's in a cave somewhere," Ian said, stepping forward and pointing at the screen. "Are there any known caverns in the area? Preston?"

"The Himalayas are filled with natural caves," he replied. "That could be anywhere."

Conner remembered the first time he met Malika. She had presented him with Tucker's red cap. Found near a cave.

"We don't even have an accurate map of the mountain itself," Carlton said. "I'm afraid we have to conduct the search the old-fashioned way. Someone is going to have to go up there."

Conner turned to his team. "Looks like all of you are going to get your wish. We're going back up."

The team brightened at the prospect. "We search for Tess and the others first," Conner said. "We find them, we continue on. We don't, or we find them in bad shape, and this race is over."

They nodded eagerly at this. They wouldn't have had it any other way. But the summit of Kuk Sur—and the two million-dollar prize—was still within their grasp.

They were already heading toward the door when Carlton called after them. "Keep your cameras on. If we can follow your movements, we can direct the chopper to your exact location when it arrives. Taking the camera could save hours."

Conner wanted desperately to tear the camera from his shoulder holster. *Screw Carlton.*

"It could mean the difference between life and death," the producer added.

He was right, of course. Conner would wear the damn thing.

"Fine. But we need to get ourselves to the medical tent," Conner ordered. "We'll need bandages, a few Sam

Splints, an intubation kit, oxy-bags, anything you can get your hands on. We're heading up an unclimbed mountain with injured racers on it. We have no idea what we're going to find up there."

Preston and Malika exchanged glances. Conner caught it, but now was not the time to press them about it. It was ancient history. He was concerned only with the next few hours. Still, an unsettling thought rattled around inside his head. He didn't have to give voice to the terror. Nobody wanted to hear it. Not now.

Something was up there. Something that had already decimated Cale Anders. Something that could be up there still, waiting for them.

Conner shoved the thought away.

"Let's get a move on," he said. "We leave in ten minutes."

CHAPTER THIRTY-TWO

Kuk Sur
19,123 Feet

"Careful here!" Conner Michaels yelled over the howling wind. It had picked up since the rescue team left forward base camp. Dark clouds had moved overhead, dropping the temperature to below zero. Despite thick layers of down, he could feel the cold deep in his bones.

"The snow and ice is unstable. There may be pockets under the surface."

Conner jabbed his trekking pole into the snow. As if to illustrate his point, a patch of snow the size of a manhole cover dropped out, plummeting down into a bottomless crevasse.

Conner stared down into the chasm. "As I said, stay close, take in your slack, and call out if you see anything.

Rescue first."

It had taken the team two hours to reach the lower reaches of the avalanche scree. The ground was torn up, with chunks of broken limestone jutting dangerously through the churned snow. The debris field was dangerously prone to a subsequent slide, another reason for Team Providence to proceed quickly.

Darwin's Race may have turned into a search and rescue operation, but a team was a team. Though the descent to forward base camp had alleviated Malika's headache somewhat, the rest of the team was approaching physical and emotional exhaustion. Four days of racing had left them with sore muscles and aching joints. The prospect of Cale's death had brought them to the brink of despair.

Their participation in *Darwin's Race* still very much alive, all six of them still wore the race-issued shoulder-mounted cameras. They knew that fifteen hundred feet below the producers and crew of *Darwin's Race* were watching each frame of their feed with bated breath.

Though their words would be echoing throughout the production tent, none of them bothered to conceal their disdain for Terrance Carlton. Conversation had escalated from simple name-calling to creative ways of disposing of the producer: "Shove one of these cameras up his *ass*," someone suggested. "Then everyone can see that the prick *is* full of shit!"

Suddenly, everyone became very cognizant of the serious look on Conner's face. He was staring, steely-eyed, up the slope. His bottom lip curled into his mouth, a sure sign of worry.

"What is it, Con?" Ian asked.

Conner pointed. "Rotor blade."

The rescuers dashed up the remaining sixty feet and fell to the ground, frantically digging in the deep snow. The blade wasn't intact, most of it shorn away. Only the jagged nub protruded from the snow. But the snow was clumpy and easy to burrow through.

"There could be pockets of air," Conner called out. "Keep digging!"

After a few minutes, they had tunneled five feet into the snow. Then Conner struck something hard. He quickly wiped away some snow, revealing cracked glass.

"Cockpit," Ian said. Then, "Shit."

It was full of snow.

Working even faster now, they scratched through the snow, slowly revealing the rounded edges of the compartment. The chopper was lying on its side, buried. They swept the snow from the side cockpit door. A long crack snaked down its length.

Conner grabbed the cockpit door handle. "Stand clear," he said.

Bracing himself, Conner yanked hard on the door, pulling straight up. The cabin door opened with a loud crack and Conner swung it all the way open, then dropped and began to dig through the snow inside the chopper.

He didn't have to dig deep.

Just inches under the blanket of white, Conner latched

onto an arm. He gave it a squeeze but got no response. Conner quickly uncovered a shoulder, a neck, then, the back of a man's head. Slowly, he cleared enough snow to rotate the man's head.

"Oh my God—" Shandi uttered, turning away.

The man—apparently the pilot—was dead; that much was certain. His mouth was stretched almost impossibly wide and crammed with snow and ice. A gaping white scream. His eyes were frozen open, dark and cold and unseeing.

They found the copilot a few feet farther down. Neck broken.

Conner stood. "Okay, let's spread out. Work in circles from this spot. Use your trekking poles to probe under the snow pack. If you hit anything, yell it out. Let's move!"

They continued the search, digging deliberately and slowly, as to not miss anything. But with each passing minute, their hopes of finding a survivor dimmed. After a few hours, they had found several items of clothing, a torn pack, and one North Face wool cap. Since all of the members of Team North Face had worn identical sponsor hats, there was no telling to whom it belonged.

And then, a voice called out. "I've got something!"

Thad. His voice was a strange fusion of excitement and dread.

Shandi and Thad had cleared away the blanket of ice from the form by the time Conner dashed to their side. Preston and Malika abandoned their own search to join them.

"It's just a jacket," Thad said, breathing heavily. "I

think it belongs to Hoops."

Shandi started to cry. The realization that her fellow racers had been swept up in a storm violent enough to strip clothing swept over her. "I can't do this anymore. They're all dead. They're all—!" She dropped her face into her hands, sobs wracking her body. Thad moved to comfort her.

Ian put a hand on Conner's shoulder. "She's upset, Con. We all are. I don't think she means—"

"It's alright, Ian. I understand. Look, guys, I realize this doesn't look good. But if it's okay with all of you, I'm not quite ready to give up just yet. We all saw Tess inside some sort of cave. But if it's still buried under all this, she's gonna run out of air pretty fast. Officially, this is still a rescue mission."

Everyone nodded their assent, murmuring comments like "Let's keep going" and "There's still a chance." Preston and Malika hurried off to resume the search. Thad helped Shandi to her feet. She wiped the tears from her cheeks. "Conner, I'm sorry. I—"

"Thanks for hanging in there, Shandi," Conner interrupted. "Let's keep going."

But the enthusiasm had drained from his voice. Over eight hours had passed since the avalanche and even with a pocket of air—

"I've got something here!"

Conner nearly jumped out of his plastic boots. It was Malika who was screaming, pointing toward what appeared to be a gloved finger poking out of the snow. It was right in the center of their search grid—they must have passed over it several times. With barely a half inch sticking out of the ground, the finger was easy to miss.

But now it was moving.

Everyone converged, adrenaline surging anew, shoveling away clumps of snow and ice with bare hands. Four feet down, they uncovered another body.

And could scarcely believe what they were seeing.

Kuk Sur
18,848 Feet

Blaine's face and limbs had numbed over long ago, but he could feel the telltale tightness burning his face. Ice had begun to cling to his cheeks. Frostbite was setting in. A quarter-inch rope and a three-inch screw were all that supported Blaine's one hundred fifty-five pounds as he dangled two hundred feet in the air. If he dwelled on it, he probably would've felt a touch of nerves, but he was too exhausted to feel anything. Even the fierce wind that whipped like a full-force gale over the smooth ice face was not enough to rouse him.

Wade was leading, one-handed because of his injured shoulder, ten feet above his head. He wielded an ice axe in his good hand, stepping with two razor-sharp crampons. He set safety bolts in the ice wall for Blaine as he climbed.

After two exhausting hours, they had only reached the

halfway up the icefall. Two hundred grueling feet left.

"I need a break," Blaine called out. He winced as his frozen face cracked. "I can barely lift my arms."

Wade finished placing an ice bolt, then pulled his ice axe free and pushed away from the pitch, letting the rope and safety belay his weight.

"So we rest," he said. "But we have to keep moving. This face is too exposed. There's no protection here at all. This wind will freeze us up if we stop now."

"I don't know if I can make it," Blaine said. "It's getting dark. We need to think about other options."

"Blaine, listen to me. There *are* no other options."

"You got a sling in your pack?"

Wade shot Blaine a look. "Bivouac?" he said, eyeing him like he was delirious. "Up here? On this face?"

"It's been done before."

"Yeah, sure, on rock. But not on this. Not on strange ice."

That was true. Blaine stretched his leg, testing the knee. It was tight, and he was cold. Maybe all he needed was a rest. But God, they had so far to—

From the ice came a strange sound.

At first, Blaine thought a piece of ice had torn loose from one of the safety bolts. He did a quick check. They were still intact. He looked at Wade, who returned his puzzled look.

"You heard that, too, huh?" he said.

And then he heard it again.

A scraping. A rustling.

Definitely *not* settling ice.

Their precarious position exposed them to the distinctive shrieks of the whipping alpine winds and the slow groan of shifting ice. Together, the wind and the ice created their own macabre symphony.

But this was something entirely different.

"It sounds like it's coming right from the ice," Blaine said. "But how could that be?"

"Ice is a great sound conductor," Wade explained. "Something could be scraping the face at the bottom, and we'd still hear it pretty good all the way up here."

"But you just heard it. It sounds like it's coming from up there." He pointed to a spot just over their heads.

Wade reached up with his ice axe and tapped the face with the steel blade. They listened again. This time, nothing.

"It's probably just a bird flapping against the face," Blaine said hopefully.

"A bird? We haven't seen a bird in five thousand feet. Maybe I should just go and check it out."

Before Blaine could object, Wade thrust his axe into the ice above his head and restarted his single-armed ascent. Suddenly spooked, Blaine didn't want to be left behind. He found the energy to climb.

A few minutes later, they reached the source of the mysterious sounds. The closest approximation anyway. Wade quickly placed a safety and tied off slack so they could hang freely.

A blast of alpine wind whipped across the face, screeching and howling like an angry monkey. The climbers swayed dizzily. Underneath the shriek, Blaine thought he heard the noise again.

"Right here," he said. "It's coming from right here." He pressed the side of his head close to the face.

And listened.

Suddenly, he yanked his head back as if he'd been burned.

"What? What did you hear?"

"Whatever it is," Blaine said slowly, as if trying to believe his own words. "It's coming from *behind* the ice."

Wade was already shaking his head. "Behind the ice? That's impossible. Unless—"

"Ice caves," they said simultaneously.

Suddenly, the presence of ice caves behind the ice made their safety bolt seem incredibly unstable. Caves would mean that the ice was not nearly as thick as they had originally supposed. Ordinarily, ice climbers jam support bolts into feet of ice, not inches. It was dangerous business, and Blaine felt a rush of adrenaline surge through his body.

"We've got to get down from here."

Even as he spoke these words, the bolt moaned. A flake of ice peeled away from the safety. Blaine watched it fall to the ground, two hundred feet down.

"Time to move," Wade announced.

"Where? The ice could be just as thin all around here."

"There's only one way to find out." Wade wielded his ice axe in his right hand. "We'll have to test it."

Tapping lightly at the ice, he listened for an echo, the test for ice thickness. Like checking for a stud in a wall, the sound of firm ice sounded deeper, more solid. Hollow ice echoed—not a good sign.

Blaine watched as Wade continued testing the face, now tapping more strongly. The ice seemed more solid to the right of their position and he decided to test it again, this time with real force. Though he was tied off securely on two safety bolts, he would plummet nearly twenty feet if the ice shattered. *If* the bolt below held. But if that one had been placed in thin ice, too—

Blaine didn't want to dwell on that.

Wade's hack splintered the ice with a loud crack, showering sharp shards below. He looked at Blaine with wide eyes.

His axe had knocked a two-inch hole in the ice.

"It's hollow," he said, peering through the gap. "It *is* a cave."

Blaine breathed in deeply. "Let's get in there," he said. "We're not safe out here."

Tapping on the ice, they slowly chipped away until a body-sized hole emerged. Now large enough for one of them to pass through, the gap beckoned them like a mysterious black hole. Wade was in the better position to climb through first. He pulled his headlamp from his waist pack.

"Okay," he said, pulling himself through the slot. "Wish me luck."

He pulled himself through, released his safety ropes, and flipped on his headlamp. Dropped his backpack at the mouth of the cave. Smiling back at Blaine, Wade disappeared into the cave.

For a few moments, he said nothing. Blaine dangled alone. The wind sounded like a screaming child.

He jumped when Wade returned.

"Blaine, get your ass in here," he said. "This cave is huge. And I can see more, all over the place."

It took less than five minutes for Blaine to pull himself through the hole in the ice. He was instantly relieved to be standing once again on solid ground—even if it was a solid block of ice. The dim beam of light from Wade's headlamp reflected against a far wall. More ice. The cave was maybe ten feet deep, but Blaine had to crouch over to move deeper.

"It gets bigger," Wade said.

Blaine placed a hand on his back as they pushed into the cave. A shadowy recess in the ice led to a second, larger chamber. Wade paused at the threshold, training the light from his headlamp into the cave.

"Oh my God—" whispered Blaine.

In the dead silence of the cave, he could hear the camera on his shoulder whirring into focus.

"I hope you're picking this up," he said for the benefit of the camera mic. "Because you're not going to believe this."

CHAPTER THIRTY-THREE

Kuk Sur
19,215 Feet

The sight was so absurd that Conner blinked twice to make sure he wasn't hallucinating. High altitude could bring on strange visions, and the sight before him was so bizarre and unlikely that Conner looked at his teammates to make sure they were seeing the same thing.

Apparently they were. All eyes were on the four-foot hole they had dug in the snow. On the figure huddled at the bottom.

Paul "Hoops" Robeson. Buried to his waist.

Alive.

He was clutching an emergency oxygen bottle over his lips, the mouthpiece foggy with his steamy exhalations. His eyes were half-opened; vacant.

"We don't have much time," Conner said. "Let's get him out of there."

Moving quickly, he reached down and removed the oxygen bottle from Hoops' face. Taking a whiff of the canister confirmed Conner's notion. It was empty. He had been sucking on an empty bottle. *But for how long?*

"Hoops?" he said, waving his hand in front of a pair of unfocused eyes. "Paul, can you hear me?"

There was no reaction. It didn't even look like Hoops was blinking his eyes.

"He's in shock," Shandi said. "We need to get him out of there. Right now."

Conner and Preston thrust their hands into the snow at Hoops' waist and began to dig. But something wasn't right. They were digging straight down under his waist, but couldn't uncover the rest of his body. *His legs must be bent at a strange angle*, Conner thought. *Broken, maybe, or—*

Preston pulled his hands from the snow. They were covered in blood. He looked up at Conner, puzzled.

Hoops Robeson's legs were gone.

Under his body—where his legs *should* have been— was just more ice and snow, stained crimson, hard-packed up against a mess of bloody entrails. He had been cut in half—probably by a spinning chopper rotor.

"Where are his legs?" Shandi cried. "Where are his friggin' legs?"

Her screams seemed to rouse Hoops. His eyes widened, then blinked. His lips moved ever so slightly.

Conner had to put his ear right up against his mouth to hear him.

"*Chopper . . . avalanche . . .*" Hoops gagged. A series of coughs choked the words out.

"Easy, Hoops, easy," Conner said. "We're going to get you out of here. We're here to take you home."

He was already shaking his head. "*Not . . . going . . . anywhere,*" he gasped. "*Others?*"

Before Conner could answer, Hoops jerked forward, coughing a spray of blood into the snow. His breathing became a series of choked gasps.

"He's hyperventilating," Thad said. "Give him some room."

As Conner leaned back to give Hoops some air, the fallen racer grabbed Conner's sleeve. Conner was surprised at Hoops' strength—his grip was iron-tight. Hoops' body spasmed with a fresh jolt of pain, and his hand tightened around Conner's arm. Conner clasped Hoops' hand, hard, like he could somehow transfer some lifesaving energy to him.

"Hang in there, buddy. Hang in there."

A gargle of gibberish fell from Hoops' mouth. *He's losing it*, Conner thought.

"He's trying to say something," Preston said.

Conner leaned down, pressing his ear close to the dying climber's mouth. Hoops whispered a few words. Conner tried to engage him in conversation, anything to keep him talking, moving, *breathing*. He whispered a few words back, but Hoops had fallen silent.

Under Conner's hand, Hoops' grip loosened. He pulled back his hand. His friend's hand slipped lifelessly to the ground.

He was dead.

They stood for a moment over the fallen racer.

Shandi looked at Conner. "What did he say?"

Conner didn't immediately answer. How could he? Hoops' words were still rattling around in his head, but they still made little sense. Surely his last words were little more than delusional ramblings.

"Nothing," Conner finally said. "Gibberish."

The others accepted this, nodding, and silently stepped away from the body. But Conner lingered. Paul "Hoops" Robeson's words tolled in his head like a church bell.

Tess . . . taken, he had whispered.

Who, Hoops? Who took her? Conner had whispered back.

And then, Hoops' final words: *The white ape.*

A loud *chop-chop-chop* broke Conner's stupor, and he looked up as snow swirled around his head.

The second rescue chopper had arrived.

Forward Base Camp
17,483 Feet

The bloody death scene had cast a pall over the entire

crew of *Darwin's Race*. When Conner Michaels limped into the production tent, he could see gloom in their faces. Even Terrance Carlton looked distressed. The producer was pacing nervously.

Conner had been reluctant to call off the search. Tess, Wade, and Blaine were still out there, somewhere. But his team was dog-tired. Physical and emotional wrecks. Shandi had become despondent, barely able to remain upright. Even Ian had reported a burning, tingling sensation in his toes. Conner recognized the early symptoms of frostbite. They all needed medical attention.

They had put up a valiant effort, but in the end three dead racers, two dead chopper pilots, and five harrowing days in the Himalayas had finally exacted their steep price. For Team Providence, *Darwin's Race* was over.

Conner had also felt an obligation to carry the bodies from the mountain. So they loaded up the bodies onto the second helicopter—three leaden corpses—and watched it soar back down toward forward base camp. The chopper already pushing its weight capacity, Team Providence had to climb down on foot.

Hoops' final words still echoed in Conner's brain. *The white ape.*

Was the injured racer just delusional? Or was there something else going on high on Kuk Sur?

Conner, something's down here with me. I can't see it, but I can hear it breathing. The smell . . . Oh, Jesus—!

As soon as they touched down, Ian, Thad, and Shandi

stumbled to the medical tent. To attend to their frostbite, Preston and Malika followed Conner into production control. Conner made a beeline for the bank of monitors against the far wall where he found Carlton staring attentively at the feeds.

"What's going on?" he said. "What are we looking at?"

"It's Wade and Blaine," Carlton said. "They've found a cave complex behind an ice face."

Caves? Tess was in a cave. According to Malika, Tucker's cap had washed out of a cave. More and more, it was appearing that the answer to this mountain mystery lay deep within its caverns.

Conner quickly found Tess's live camera feed. It was still broadcasting and though it was dark, he could still make out the ghostly features of the cavern, still shown on its side. She hadn't moved.

"We're having trouble with the audio," Carlton reported. "My sound guys say the transmitters aren't strong enough to penetrate the ice. And as they move deeper into this cave, it's getting worse. Video, too."

"Have you seen anything?" Conner asked.

Carlton turned to look Conner directly in the eyes. The producer's dark brown eyes were unusually expressive, Conner saw. For the first time since *Darwin's Race* began, there was a flicker of emotion there. It was the unmistakable face of fear.

Conner turned to the monitors. The feeds from the cameras of Wade and Blaine were barely visible. Their headlamps were dying.

The feed from Blaine's camera was the better of the two. His headlamp seemed to have a bit more juice. Conner concentrated on his movements as he moved about the cave.

And immediately saw what had rendered the producer speechless.

Scraps of clothing and mountain-climbing gear lay strewn about the cave. Bits of cloth, a single intact mitten, a rusted crampon, its straps torn and frayed. Conner's heart lurched at the sight of a torn jacket—red, like Tess's—until he realized it was far too old to be hers.

On the screen, Blaine picked something up and displayed it in front of the camera. It was a boot, frozen stiff. It looked old, made of cracked leather favored by climbers before the invention of protective plastic boots. Rusted metal nails protruded from the peeling sole.

"Hobnail climbing boots," Conner said. "Like the ones Mallory and Irvine used."

Blaine now removed his glove and with the fingernail of his thumb began to scrape away at something on the boot. Dropping the boot, Blaine held his thumb in front of the camera. As the camera whirred into focus, struggling to acquire the closer image, his audio feed gargled to life.

"*. . . on the boot . . . looks . . . all over . . .*"

The camera clicked into focus on Blaine's thumbnail.

The entire assembled crew drew a collective gasp. His fingertip was covered with flecks of red.

Blood.

"*. . . Blaine . . . look at this.*"

Conner turned his attention to the second feed. Wade had trained his camera into the shadows of the cave wall. Something was piled inside a large cleft. The heap was knee-high, haphazard. At first glance, Conner thought it might be shards of broken ice. Closer examination bore a truth much more horrifying.

Bones.

The image jerked across the cave. Bones were littered everywhere, some in piles, others strewn across the ground. The feeds were jerky—Blaine and Wade were moving rapidly now, so it was difficult for Conner to get a good look at the skeletons. Finally, the image slowed enough to make out a critical detail.

Skulls lay amongst the bones. Human skulls.

Wade must've seen them too. He could hear the fear in his crackly voice.

"*. . . must be dozens . . . skulls . . . sweet Jesus . . .*"

The image panned to Blaine. His eyes were wide, trembling. His audio feed scratched with static. "*What's . . . that . . . smell . . .?*"

Suddenly the two images jumped. Moving too fast for focus, the images upon the monitors blurred. Jerked.

"What's going on?" Carlton demanded, shouting at his production crew. "Why can't we focus?"

"They're swiveling their heads," Conner answered. "They're looking for something."

Preston murmured under his breath, "It's too late."

"Too late?" Carlton pressed. "Too late for what?"

Preston stared the producer down. "Too late to survive."

Suddenly, activity burst across the monitors. The cameras jumped, jerked. Garbled sounds erupted from the speakers. Even through the static, it was clear what the sounds were.

Screaming.

Wade and Blaine started to run. Scrambling all over the cave, bumping into each other, shouting, screaming. The cameras struggled to regain focus.

"They're panicking," Conner said.

The *Darwin's Race* crew watched, transfixed. Helpless. Horrified.

Wade's camera blinked out.

"Camera nine is down," someone called out unnecessarily.

"What the hell is going on?" Carlton thundered. "Get that feed back on!"

As production assistants scrambled to reacquire the transmission, Conner turned to Blaine's feed. His image jumped rhythmically up and down in sequence.

He's running, Conner thought. *He's making a run for it.*

The image dropped, as if Blaine had fallen, but still the image moved forward. It appeared as if he was squeezing through a smaller cave. Then, a sheet of ice filled the frame, a boulder-sized hole in it. Through the hole, faint light illuminated what looked like a backpack. Ropes dangled beyond the pack.

He's heading for the ice wall. He's going to try to climb down.

His hand appeared in the frame, reaching through the gap. His fingers grazed the ropes.

Suddenly, the image jerked back violently. *Away* from the ropes. Even without a clear image, Blaine's screams were enough to make several crew members look away.

"No . . . no . . . oh, God, please . . ."

Blaine's cries escalated feverishly as he was lifted into the air by some unseen force. Then he was hurled against the cave wall. His shrieks were replaced with moans of agony. Then he was lifted again. Again smashed against the ice wall. Then again. And again. On the last pass, the camera image cracked and splintered. Streams of blood flew in all directions.

And then it stopped.

Inside the tent, silence fell, broken only by the muffled sobs of a few crew members.

Conner stared at Blaine's feed. He was no longer moving, the transmission grainy, the audio cut off completely. Across the cave floor, Wade's motionless body lay amidst the rubble of bones. Blood spurted through his crushed skull. Even through the garbled image, Conner could see he was dead.

Suddenly, the crew gasped.

Something else entered the frame.

"What . . . *the fuck* . . . is that?" Carlton rasped.

Two legs, thick as tree trunks, filled the screen. They were covered in what appeared to be silvery gray fur, but everything above the knee disappeared off the top of the screen. But the scale was all wrong, Conner thought. *It had to be.* Using Wade's lifeless body in the background as a frame of reference, Conner realized the silver-gray legs were . . . *enormous.*

The legs moved toward the camera.

Impossibly, they grew larger and larger until the hairy limbs blocked everything else. Whatever it was, it was now looming over the body of Blaine Reeves.

Then, with a swift, lethal move, a giant clawed foot rose into the air, pausing momentarily, then drove down viciously, smashing into Blaine's skull. The last piece of audio heard in the production tent was the sickening crunch of his cranium.

Blaine's camera died with him.

The entire room held its collective breath. Conner had to remind himself to breathe. Now, slowly and warily, they all exhaled. The sobbing resumed and now, with nothing to see on the bank of monitors except for Tess's inert transmission, several crew members staggered out of the tent for fresh air.

Carlton stared at the screens, as if he couldn't believe what he'd just seen. As if he expected the images to miraculously come back to life.

"Can somebody tell me what just happened?" he screamed, his voice cracking. "What the hell just happened?

What was that thing up there? Can somebody please tell me just what the FUCK is going on here?"

And then, a voice from the back of the tent. "I can."

Whirling around to the sound of the voice, Conner was stunned to see Malika Child step forward.

"Malika?" Conner said. "What's going on here? You know something about this?"

Behind her, Preston reached for his daughter. "Malika, wait," he implored.

"No, Daddy." She pulled away from his thick hand. "Not this time. It's time to finish the story."

Conner grabbed Malika by her shoulders, stared hard into her eyes. "Malika, if you know something about this, you have to speak up."

"We never meant for any of this to happen," she cried. "This wasn't supposed to happen this way."

"Malika, come on. Pull yourself together, and tell me what's going on."

"*Oh, God, Mama—*" Sobs wracked Malika's body, choking out her words. Preston shuffled uncomfortably behind her.

"Your mother? What does this have to do with your mother?" Conner turned to Preston. "I'm only going to ask this one more time, Preston. And you better start talking, or God help me, I will tear the life out of you. What is going on here?"

Preston swallowed. "Go on, Malika. Tell them."

"You said your mother was murdered," Conner said

to her.

"I told you that wasn't exactly true."

"No more games," Conner said through gritted teeth. "It's time for the truth."

"There is something up there. Something that tore apart Cale Anders. The same thing that just slaughtered Blaine and Wade."

Conner was stunned. "How is that possible? What are we dealing with? What kind of animal could do this? Snow leopards only—"

"Goddamn it, this is no snow leopard!" Preston yelled. "This thing we're talking about? It eats leopards for breakfast. You are dealing with an animal that has survived for generations in the most inhospitable place imaginable. Keeping to itself, killing only to feed. Leopard, yak, sheep."

Preston paused to take a deep breath. "But now, all of us have entered its province."

Conner's head was spinning. *What kind of creature could possibly live at these altitudes?*

"The creature goes by many names," Preston said. "*Gin-sung. Nguoi Rung.* The tribes of the Tsangpo call the creature *Meh-Teh.* The savage white ape. But the rest of the world knows the beast by a different name."

Conner's head ached. Malika's murdered mother. Cale's mutilated body. The blurry image on the monitors. The pieces were coming together.

A final piece slid into place.

Tucker . . .

"Conner, something's down here with me. I can't see it, but I can hear it breathing. The smell . . . Oh, Jesus—!"

Preston's words echoed inside the tent like thunder. "We have entered into the killing zone of the Yeti."

PART FOUR

CHAPTER THIRTY-FOUR

Forward Base Camp
17,483 Feet

We have entered into the killing zone of the Yeti.

The pronouncement hung in the air like a ghost. Everyone in the production tent stood stock-still. Unable to move. Or afraid to. Ian, Shandi, and Thad had entered just in time to hear Preston's impossible pronouncement.

Silence descended. Outside, even the wind died.

Conner met Preston's glare. Those dark, brooding eyes bored a hole in his forehead. Something in the man's eyes made him shiver. Like Preston already knew what Conner was thinking.

Something's down here with me. I can't see it, but I can hear it breathing. The smell . . . Oh, Jesus—!

"What the fuck are you talking about?" Carlton had

regained his composure. His shouts cut the tense silence inside the production tent. "Don't bring that crazy shit in here."

Preston stepped forward aggressively. "You think I'm crazy? You've got seven dead bodies on your hands. What do you think is killing them? The cold?"

"It was the chopper accident—" Carlton began lamely. Then, apparently thinking the better of it, he let his voice fade. Even the producer had realized they were dealing with something extraordinary here. Cale Anders' body was testament to that.

And those enormous legs captured on Blaine's dying camera haunted them all.

Carlton swallowed hard, turning to one of his production assistants. "Jamie, get security in here. Let's get this nut job escorted out of here."

The assistant scurried out, giving Preston's thick frame a wide berth. Carlton himself retreated to the control board, a safe distance from the menacing man. Tried to appear busy.

"I think we should listen to what he has to say," Conner said.

"He's a crackpot!" Carlton yelled. "We have a serious issue on our hands here, and we're supposed to stop everything to listen to absurd stories about the Abominable Snowman? This is ridiculous!"

"If you've got a better idea, I'd love to hear it."

"Come on, Conner. The notion is preposterous. We've

all heard the legends about the Yeti, but that's all they are. Legends. Are we really supposed to believe that some giant ape has been roaming the mountains all these years? Without anyone ever seeing it? Without any proof of its existence?"

"What did you just see on that monitor? Because I saw a pair of legs that can't possibly belong to any animal I know of."

"What I saw—what we all saw—was a blurry image of something we couldn't explain. I hardly think that jumping to the conclusion that it's some kind of snowman will help any of us."

"You've got another explanation?"

Carlton pointed to Preston. "I'd like to know why, during the night Cale was killed, Preston was nowhere to be found. We saw it on the monitors, Conner. He wasn't in his tent."

Conner cast a suspicious eye toward Preston. That was new information.

The producer sensed momentum. "You didn't know that, did you? Suspicious, don't you think?

"You think Preston had something to do with Cale's death?" Conner asked.

"I'm just saying, it was a raging snowstorm. And Preston decides it's time to go for a stroll? Right when Cale Anders is killed?"

"It's true I was out of my tent," Preston said calmly, eyes fixed on the executive producer. "Though I didn't realize it then, it did have something to do with Cale Anders."

A smug grin appeared on the producer's face. "I told you. Something's not right with this guy."

"I went out into the storm because I could smell it."

"Smell . . . what?"

"The creature. It has a distinctive scent. Musty. Bold."

The smell . . . Oh, Jesus—

Preston recognized the puzzled look on Conner's face. "You're wondering how I'm familiar with the scent of a Yeti."

"I think I'm beginning to understand. Your wife. Malika's mother. She was killed by the Yeti, wasn't she?"

Out of the corner of his eye, Conner saw Malika bury her face into her hands.

"I didn't believe it at first," Preston said. "I thought it was a rival from the village. Someone who didn't approve of me. I received the news of her death on the phone. I was in a rage all the way back to Tibet. Malika was so upset she could barely speak. Her grandfather had smartly shielded her from her mother's body, but when I saw her, I saw that the woman I loved had been torn apart. Gashes across her face, her throat. Claw marks gouged her exposed bone. I thought, no man could have done this. I began to look at other options."

Malika had composed herself. She dabbed at wet eyes with her glove, listening intently. Now she exploded. "When they found her . . ." Her voice cracked before she could finish. Her soft sobs echoed in the cold tent.

Conner waited silently for her to regain her composure and continue. "When we found her, we barely recognized her. She was all cut up, torn open. Like someone had taken a knife to her body, over and over and over."

"Torn open?" Conner probed. "Like—?"

Malika nodded. "Yes. Like Cale Anders."

"The villagers were sure about what had happened to her," Preston said. "I had listened to their stories of the Yeti for years. They say the creature lived in caves, sleeping during the day. Moved with preternatural stealth. Ventured out only at night. They had seen its tracks showing that the creature walks on two legs. They also said the Yeti can kill with a single punch. And they told me about his smell, the strong stale stench, the only warning that the beast was near."

"But your wife . . . that was twenty years ago."

Preston burst to his feet. The color had returned to his face with a vengeance, and his eyes bulged from his head. He drew to within a few inches of Conner's face, his breath stale and hot.

"Some monsters never die," he said. For a flicker of an instant, Preston's bottom lip trembled. "There are things that can live forever."

Conner let the silence linger. By the expression on Preston's face—desperate anguish—he sensed there was something the man was ready to let go of.

"You think this kind of suffering ever ends? There *are* monsters that live forever. They're demons. They haunt us, hunt us, until the pain overwhelms us." Preston swallowed hard, his resolve firming. "There comes a time when enough is enough. When it's time to end the suffering. That time has come. It's time to kill the monster."

Some monsters never die. In that instant, when he looked deep into the soul of Preston Child, Conner knew in his heart that they had much more in common than he had ever believed.

"This is crazy," Carlton pleaded. "He's basing all this on some old legend."

"I looked into the eyes of those storytellers," Preston said, "and I saw that they believed in what they were telling me. Truly believed. And grasping for some explanation of what happened to my beloved, I devoted myself to discovering the truth. And I was shocked at what I found."

Preston waited a beat before continuing. "The legend of the Yeti is hardly a new phenomenon. According to the Greek philosopher Plutarch, Alexander the Great pushed his army of Greeks into the Indus Valley three hundred years before Christ was born, encountering people who told him of a great beast that could not breathe at low altitudes. The first mention of the Yeti in print came one hundred fifty years later, when a Roman high priest scribbled a cryptic note in his book *Animal Stories.* I've read it so many times, I can quote it from memory: *"If one enters the mountains neighboring India one comes upon lush, overgrown valleys. The Indians call this region Koruda. Animals that look like Satyrs roam these valleys. They are covered with shaggy hair and have a long horse's tail. When left to themselves, they stay in the forest and eat tree sprouts. But when they hear the din of approaching hunters and the barking of dogs, they run with incredible speed to hide in mountain caves. For they are masters of mountain climbing."*

Conner interrupted. "This valley, the one the Indians call Koruda, they're talking about the Kukuranda?"

Preston nodded before continuing. "In 1942, a Polish cavalry officer named Slavomir Rawicz escaped a Soviet prison camp in northern Siberia and made his way along the shores of Lake Baikal, across the Gobi Desert. As he and his fellow escapees traversed the Himalayas through the Kukuranda, they came across strange animals they didn't recognize. Hungry, Slavomir followed. They observed a pair of creatures for nearly two hours. Later, in his book called *The Long Walk*, Slavomir wrote of giant creatures— half bear, half ape—nearly eight feet tall, with fur that looked gray in the fading daylight."

"Oh, I get it," interrupted Carlton, waving his hands in the air. "This is the bit where you try to convince us that for hundreds of years science has somehow overlooked the presence of an unknown species of giant monkey. These so-called eyewitness reports are hardly credible."

"Science?" Preston replied. "You want science? How about the Chinese Academy of Sciences' discovery of hands and feet of a 'wild man' in the province of Zheyang inside a den surrounded by staves and insulated with leaves and branches that obviously belonged to a group of hominids."

"But that was—"

"How about documented photographs from Sir Edmund Hillary himself, detailing footprints that stretched for over a mile along the snows near the Sherpa monastery of Khumjung? Prints that proved that whatever made them was enormous and heavy, that it walked on two feet and that it lived in glacial regions."

"Photographs can be doctored and—"

Preston plowed on, ignoring Carlton's fading protestations. "In 1984, a University of Montana researcher wandered into a Chinese medicine shop while on an expedition down the Yangtze River. Alongside shelves of remedies ranging from dragon-teeth to flying lizards, the researcher was drawn to a row of jars filled with different kinds of teeth. He found there a massive jawbone, a fresh specimen brought in just days earlier, and immediately took it back to his lab. His new acquisition dwarfed the jaw of a gorilla, and he quickly scanned other samples and databases for a match. To his astonishment, he found one. His new jaw matched that of an ape species known as *Gigantopithecus blacki*. Problem was, *Gigantopithecus blacki* roamed Asia during the Middle Pleistocene period. It had been extinct for over a hundred thousand years."

This, finally, seemed to capture Carlton's attention. "This researcher, he published his findings?"

"The official journal of the American Anthropology Society. Peer-reviewed."

Conner consulted his memory of evolution. A million years ago, there were many species of hominids in Africa.

One of those species developed into an ape that walked upright, *Homo erectus*. This new species—apes that harnessed the power of fire and used axes as weapons—spread into Asia and Europe, eventually evolving into modern humans, *Homo sapiens*.

So where did the Yeti fit in?

"What are you suggesting then?" Conner asked.

"I believe we're dealing with the remnant of a breed of hominids with an incredible capacity for survival."

"But what is it exactly? Last I heard, apes don't walk around on two legs."

"The Yeti is an intermediate stage between *Giganto-pithecus* and *Homo erectus*," Preston answered.

Conner swallowed hard. "You're talking about the missing link."

Carlton threw his hands up in the air again. "The missing link? What are you talking about now?"

Preston said, "If you accept Darwin's theory of evolution, you believe that human beings are descended from apes through a process of gradual change over a period of millions of years."

Carlton sighed heavily. "Of course; everyone knows that."

"But there's something missing. The fossil record contains ample specimens of *Homo erectus* and *Gigantopithecus*, but nothing in between. Despite decades of searching for this so-called missing link, nothing has ever been found."

"And now you're saying that this Yeti may be the missing link?"

Conner shook his head. "I'm not saying anything. I'm just telling you the facts."

"Facts?" Carlton snorted derisively. "The only thing I've heard here is speculation. Do I have to remind everyone that we have racers still up on that mountain? We need to plan a search and rescue operation."

Preston drew up to within a few inches of the producer. "And I'm telling you that you can't send anyone else up there until we're all damn well clear about what we're dealing with! You want more blood on your hands? I know this creature! I've seen what it's capable of! I've seen yaks with their spines broken. I've seen footprints as wide as tree trunks. And I've found broken claws that could slice your head off with one swipe." Preston removed an object from his jacket pocket. "Look at this. I found this embedded in a fresh tiger carcass just a few days ago. Feel it. Feel how strong it is, how sharp. Imagine an entire hand filled with these claws. It could lop your head clean off with one swipe. Now you want to act like you're still in control here, go ahead and live in that world. Because in this world, here on this mountain, we all have to accept that something else is in charge."

Conner watched the producer take a step backwards before turning back to Preston. "But if what you're saying is true, that the Yeti is some kind of preliminary stage to *Homo sapiens*, then you believe it's at some lower stage of intellectual development, right? I mean, we are smarter than this thing, right?"

Preston considered the question. "I have searched for this creature for nearly twenty years. I've tracked it through the jungle, through the gorge, and up to the valley of the Kukuranda. I neglected my stateside businesses, devoted everything to my search. But the beast eluded me, just as it had eluded dozens of researchers before me. We're dealing with an alpha predator, a man-eater. So I think it's dangerous to believe we can outsmart this thing."

More pieces slipped into place inside Conner's brain. "When the Chinese closed the Kukuranda, you lost the trail of the Yeti."

"Just when I thought I was closing in on it—just when its scent was thick in the air—they snatched it away from me. I tried repeatedly to skirt the army outposts to continue my quest, but each time I was forced by the guards to turn back. The last time, a few months ago, I was warned in no uncertain terms not to return under threats of incarceration."

"But when you heard about *Darwin's Race*, the opening of the Kukuranda, you jumped at the chance."

Preston nodded. "Maybe my last chance."

"So you knew what was up here."

Preston didn't answer. He glanced at Malika.

Conner glared. "I'm going to forget for a moment that the two of you knowingly placed the rest of us in harm's way to settle a twenty-year-old score. I'm going to put it aside only because there are people up there, maybe still alive. Now that I know what I'm dealing with, I'm prepared to go back up that mountain by myself. I don't ask or expect anyone else to join me." Conner shot a reassuring look at Ian, Shandi, and Thad. They were in no shape to continue. They smiled back, silently grateful.

Conner pointed at Preston and Malika. "I do, however, expect the two of you to come along. Whatever distorted motivations you may have, I understand a little about searching for truth. It's a powerful force. But that's not why I want you up there with me. I want you up there because you know this creature better than anyone. When we come face to face with this monster—and I assure you, we will— we're going to need all three of us to bring it down."

Carlton had one more protest: "Great. All three of you are going off half-cocked on some wild goose chase. And for what? The Abominable Snowman? I'm sorry, but nothing I've heard here has convinced me we're dealing with anything quite so dramatic."

"Still not convinced, huh?" Preston said. "I think I can take care of that. You have an Internet connection somewhere in your equipment, I believe?"

The producer pointed lamely to a workstation.

"Pull up www.cryptozoology.com, please. Click on *Cryptids* at the top. Can we have the image on the main monitor?"

Carlton nodded to an assistant, who made the appropriate connection. The large screen popped to life, displaying a dozen or so sub-headings.

"Click on the box labeled *Yeti*," Preston ordered. "Good; now scroll down. You may be surprised to learn that the field of crypto-zoology, the scientific study of hidden animals, is a certified discipline of study at over two hundred colleges and universities in the United States alone. Commonly mistaken as a group of crackpots searching for the Loch Ness monster, crypto-zoologists are actually responsible for some of the biggest discoveries of the last fifty years. There; stop there."

Two large black and white photographs filled the screen. The first image showed a series of prints, stretching off into the distance across a field of snow. The second picture was a close-up, more detailed. The blade of an ice axe had been placed next to the print for scale.

The print extended beyond the blade. Nearly two feet long.

"An explorer named Eric Shipton sought out the creature's tracks on an expedition in 1951," Preston narrated. "The tracks he found were located within the *Gauri Sankar* range, not far from Everest itself, where Shipton had previously attempted to climb five times.

"The tracks stretched for about sixteen hundred meters, dodging about and between crevasses, and eventually ending in a moraine. For comparison, Shipton laid down his pickaxe adjacent to one of the prints and snapped one of the most famous photographs representing the Yeti."

Preston surveyed his audience. They were enraptured, staring alternately at the images of the screen and at Preston himself. Conner, for one, could not tear his eyes from the image of the print beside the axe. *Whatever had left the track, it was huge.*

Preston turned to Carlton's production assistant. "Might I get you to pull up Blaine's footage from the attack in the ice cave? Just as the beast is about to smash down on your racer's *camera.*" He spit out the final word, as if it were poison.

The assistant pushed a few buttons at the control panel—Conner noticed she did not even pause to ask Carlton for permission—and the image appeared upon a small monitor. The tape played through the sequence again, the clawed foot smashing down with a cringe-inducing crunch.

Calmly, the assistant spun a dial counterclockwise, re-winding the sequence frame by frame until the beast's foot was clearly visible, poised just inches above the camera.

Conner studied the image. Glanced at the photograph of Shipton's prints from 1951 on the main screen.

They were a perfect match.

Everyone else must have come to the same conclusion, because murmurs filled the tent. Even the armed members of the Chinese Army still patrolling the grounds erupted into an agitated conversation. Preston slowly looked over the crew, meeting the eyes of each member, as if to assure them that what they were seeing was, in fact, real. The color drained from Carlton's face. He lowered himself slowly into his chair and pinched his temples with the fingers of his left hand.

"I assume that means we have satisfied your doubts," Preston said to the producer. Then, turning to Conner, he said, "We need to go now. Soon it will be dark, and we'll be blind up there on the mountain."

Conner turned to Malika. "You ready?"

"I've waited twenty years for this," she said. "You couldn't keep me off that mountain if you tried."

"We need to travel light and fast," Conner said. "Alpine assault. Take only what you need to climb. I'll carry some medical gear, but this is a rush evac—up and down. We all may have business to attend to with the Yeti, but the search and rescue come first. We'll take the chopper up to eighteen thousand, then go on foot across the crevasse field up to the ice wall. Understood? We don't have a lot of time."

"There's one more thing," Preston said.

"Yeah?"

"This thing we're going up against? He's a big motherfucker. Strong as an ox. Smart, too. Had to be to stay so elusive all this time."

"Make your point, Preston."

"I know this is a rescue mission, not a hunting expedition. But what happens if we run into the Yeti up there? We're going to need more than a couple of ice axes to bring him down."

Conner considered this a moment. "You're right. Suggestions?"

"Firepower," Preston answered. "Lots and lots of firepower."

"And where do you think we are going to get that? Look around; we're in the middle of nowhere."

Preston smiled and gazed across the tent. Conner followed the line of sight. And then he smiled, too.

If the Chinese soldiers were surprised by the rather abrupt demand for their weapons, or by Preston's flawless use of their native tongue, they didn't show it. They handed over their rifles without comment. Even the soldiers realized the grave consequences of what was about to happen.

"Kalashnikov AK-74s," Preston said, inspecting the weapons. "Standard Red Army equipment. You know how to use one of these?"

Conner shook his head.

"Listen up, then. The magazine, here, holds thirty rounds. Five-inch bullets. To unlock the bolt, release the safety here. Careful; it's always been stiff on this model."

"You know a lot about this."

"I tried to sneak into the Kukuranda; remember? I've been on the wrong end of one of these too many times. Now look here. See this lever? Switches the gun from regular fire . . . to semi-automatic . . . to automatic. With what we're up against, I suggest we keep it locked to automatic."

"You got it."

Conner watched Preston sling his rifle over his shoulder, and he followed suit. "I have reason to believe that those climbers are still alive," Preston said.

Conner looked at him curiously.

"Not now. Every minute we waste down here is another minute one of those survivors will come closer to death."

The crew parted to make a path to the tent flap.

"Wait!"

It was Carlton, back on his feet, color back in his face, scrambling after them. He looked downright giddy. "Need I remind you that you are all still under contract to *Darwin's Race*. That means to me. And therefore, I am going to have to insist that all of you wear the remote cameras back up the mountain."

"What the fuck for?" Preston spit back. "I thought you said we were chasing ghosts."

"Well, I've had an epiphany of sorts. If there is something up there, I want to be the producer that brings it to the rest of the world. If they thought the ratings for *Darwin's Race* were high? Wait until they get a load of this!"

The producer's eyes were practically sparkling.

Preston and Conner looked at each other as if to say, *Who wants to take this one?* It was Conner who eventually stepped toward Carlton.

His fist smashed into Carlton's jaw, sending the producer sprawling to the ground. A thin line of blood appeared in the corner of his mouth.

"Consider our contracts terminated," Conner said.

With that, he ripped the camera from his shoulder harness and dropped it to the ground. Malika and Preston quickly did the same, dropping the cameras onto Carlton's prone body. Somewhere behind them, someone clapped.

Conner, Preston, and Malika dashed from the tent into the cold Himalayan air.

There were monsters to slay.

CHAPTER THIRTY-FIVE

Kuk Sur
19,011 Feet

Tess Chamniss was surprised to be alive.

A flash of pain flared from her eyeballs to her skull, from her temples to her shoulders, down her back, out her arms, and down to her legs. She clenched her eyes shut, wincing. She couldn't actually feel her fingers or toes, but she was silently thankful that at least *something* didn't hurt like hell.

She was lying on her left side; that much she could determine. Even with her eyes closed. Gingerly, she tested each body part, slowly flexing each joint, starting with her wrists then proceeding slowly to her elbows, shoulders, waist, knees, and finally ankles. Her right knee throbbed when she moved it, though at least she could move it. It probably wasn't broken.

Her eyes popped open, and she bolted upright. The furious scene of the avalanche suddenly flashed before her, thrusting her back to the terrible moment. The helicopter crash. The momentary lull of silence. Then, the riotous tumult of snow and ice caving in around her. Over her. Relentless and unstoppable.

The last thing she remembered was being swept up in the maelstrom, tumbling, tumbling, like a toy boat on a raging ocean. Somewhere in the maelstrom, Tess thought she had died.

The pain in her knee told her otherwise.

Tess peered at her surroundings. It was dark, but she could see she was in a cave of some sort, surrounded on all sides by walls of ice-covered limestone.

It was a pit.

What the hell is this place? she wondered, a touch of panic creeping into her thoughts. *And how did I get here?*

She reached up instinctively to snap on her headlamp. It wasn't there. Her hat was gone, too. *Probably torn off in the avalanche.* Tess fumbled through the pockets of her red down jacket. Empty, except for what was left of a partially frozen Clif Bar. She hungrily devoured the last few bites and felt strong enough to try to stand.

On wobbly legs, Tess climbed to her feet and was rewarded with a fresh bolt of pain in her knee. Still, it seemed strong enough to support her. Maybe even strong enough to climb. But the pit was deep. At least fifteen feet, she estimated. She ran her fingers over the ice walls, searching for fissures, cracks, anything that could accommodate a jammed finger. The walls were smooth, featureless, solid ice tinted blue. There was no way to climb. A whimper slipped from her lips. There would be no escape from this icy prison.

How had she gotten here? Somebody must've put her into the pit purposefully. But who? And why?

Tess heard another whimper coming from somewhere in the darkened pit. She jerked her head toward the sound. A huddled shape lurked in the shadows.

"Hello?" she whispered, fear gripping her vocal cords like a python. "Is someone there?"

Another whimper.

Tess inched closer. In the darkness, the form became clearer.

A body.

"Hello? Are you alright?"

Close enough to reach out and touch the shape, Tess could see the person was pressed up against the wall, curled in the fetal position. Shaking uncontrollably.

Another racer, Tess realized with a rush.

Emboldened, she reached out and grabbed the body by the shoulder. The form cried out in surprise, jerking spasmodically at her touch. A moan like a dying animal filled the pit.

"It's alright," she said soothingly. "My name is Tess Chamniss; I'm not going to hurt you."

There was a moment of silence, and Tess left her hand on the person's shoulder. Slowly, tentatively, the body started to turn over. It was an older man, nearly bald, with a brown moustache caked with ice and dried blood. There was more blood, too. Across the forehead, down the cheek, his face was covered in cuts and scratches. Most of it was frozen in red rivulets. Despite the carnage, the man looked vaguely familiar.

"You're alright," she repeated. "What's your name?"

The man lifted his head slowly. His eyes were red, streaked with tears. His voice trembled as he spoke.

"My name is Bill Greenback."

HH-60G Blackhawk
17,665 Feet

The *thump-thump-thump* of the HH-60G Blackhawk kept its four occupants in silence. A young Tibetan captain named Ang Tshering piloted the rescue helicopter, on loan from the hospital in Lhasa. Apparently he had detected the somber mood inside the chopper, because he didn't attempt to engage the others in any conversation.

Not that any of them particularly wanted to speak. Preston Child sat in the copilot's seat, scanning the frozen tundra of Kuk Sur below. Conner sat back inside the stripped-down cabin, staring into the floor. He hated helicopters—particularly because he knew that with each meter of altitude, the chopper would become less stable, more likely to give in to the lack of air and the power of gravity and plummet back to the unforgiving earth. The Blackhawk was a powerful machine, better than the crashed Eurocopter. But it still made Conner nervous.

They climbed past seventeen thousand feet.

He glanced at Malika to see how she was holding up.

She didn't appear nervous, but she wasn't looking outside either. Deep in thought, she held her trekking poles close to her chest.

Probably thinking of her mother, he thought. *Just like I'm thinking of Tucker.*

"How well do you know your Bible?" she asked out of the blue.

"Probably not well enough. Why?"

"In Job, God brings forth a terrifying beast, a monster with teeth as long as pitchfork tines, claws like sharpened steel. He calls the beast Leviathan."

"I don't know that one."

"God's telling Job that as a sensible person, he should take note of Leviathan's ferocity and invincibility and maintain a safe distance. He's reminding us that there are creatures that are above humans in the natural order. It's God's way of reminding us to stay humble."

Conner gazed into Malika's eyes. "Why are you telling me this?"

"I don't know about you," she replied. "But I'm feeling

pretty humble right about now."

Something about the way she spoke those words, her aching vulnerability, suddenly made Conner want to comfort her. He leaned over and pressed his lips against her cool cheek. She returned the kiss with a fleeting smile.

"You know what they say about humility," he said. "Keeps you humble."

The joke drew another smile, as Conner had hoped.

He patted Malika on the knee and leaned forward into the cockpit. Preston looked up immediately.

"Back at base camp, you said something about believing that people were still alive. What makes you so sure?"

"First, why don't you tell me something about the missing racers?"

"Blaine and Wade? I've competed against both of them. They're good racers, good climbers. Wade would be the first to tell you he's probably one of the best out there—and he'd be right." Conner reflected a moment before adding, "But you saw the footage. They're both gone."

"We'll see. But there's one more, right?"

"Elizabeth Chamniss," he said over a lump in his throat. "Tess. Experienced climber. Eco-Challenge, Beast of the East—she's done them all. She's done all the Seven Summits without supplemental oxygen. She's a tough girl, remarkably immune to cold temperatures. If anyone could survive that avalanche, it would be her."

Conner saw Preston frown. "Something's bothering you. Out with it."

"I have searched for the Yeti for over twenty years. I've lived in these lands, catalogued tracks, collected scat, listened to countless stories, investigated every sighting. Most of them pure crap. So through it all, there's been this nagging sliver of doubt in my mind about the Yeti. Maybe somehow I had it all wrong. Maybe something else killed my wife. Maybe, for all these years, I've wasted my time chasing a ghost."

Preston paused and gazed down at his feet, as if pondering something deep and vital to his soul. "You can't imagine what it felt like to finally catch a glimpse of that . . . creature. Finally, I know. Conner, I *know*. Do you have any idea how that feels?"

Yes, Preston. I know exactly *how that feels.*

"There used to be many of them, you know," Preston said, abruptly changing the subject. "There had to be, of course. I've seen the tracks, collected hair follicles. But over the past few years, the trail has dried up. I almost started to believe they had died out completely. The Chinese, when they invaded these lands and set up mining operations, I think it affected the Yeti's natural habitat. The deforestation in the lowlands of the Himalaya forced them into smaller and smaller territories. The yak population is a quarter of what it once was. Its food sources have dried up. The species is dying."

Conner considered this before replying. "There's still one left."

"Yes, one left. One lonely soul, high up on Kuk Sur,

probably living in the caves, staying out of sight. But consider the Yeti's predicament. His habitat has been squeezed by the Chinese. Populations of wild prey are dropping. The situation is getting dire. Without a new food source, the creature must realize he's doomed to the same fate as the others."

Conner felt the helicopter bank sharply. He glanced at the altimeter. Eighteen thousand feet.

Preston looked Conner in the eyes. "I think we're the new food source."

"Cale Anders?"

"You saw it. Half his leg was gone. I think the Yeti was feeding."

An image of Tess popped into Conner's head. She was in some kind of pit, surrounded by walls of ice. That's when it hit him: *That's why Preston believes there are survivors.*

"The Yeti isn't killing them," Conner said. "It's storing them. For food."

Preston nodded slowly. "He's just trying to survive. He's turning to his most basic natural instincts."

"Shelter. Food."

"That's right: Darwin's stuff. The biological essence of a species. The soul of nature. To survive. And if this one knows it's the last, its nature is going into overdrive. It'll do anything to survive and to ensure the survival of its species."

"What are you saying?" Suddenly Conner didn't like the direction of the conversation.

"I'm saying that our little friend down there," Preston said, pointing to the glacier below, "isn't going without a fight."

Conner leaned back into his chair. From his jacket pocket, he pulled out a tattered red wool cap. Tucker's cap.

"It doesn't have to worry about a fight," Conner said. "Because we're about to bring the fight right to its doorstep."

CHAPTER THIRTY-SIX

Kuk Sur
19,011 Feet

Bill Greenback was whimpering. Tess had finally calmed him enough to stop his crying, but he still recoiled at every touch like a whipped dog. Sensing his fragile state, Tess kept her arm draped around his shoulders, whispering soothing words into his ear. The engineer remained mute. Every few minutes, strong shivers wracked his body. It was still cold enough in the pit to chatter teeth, and he was obviously still in a state of shock. Who knew what had happened to this guy?

But one thing was certain. He was scared. And looking around at her ice pit prison, Tess didn't blame him one bit.

"Is . . . it . . . gone?"

The sudden question surprised Tess. They were his

first words in nearly an hour. "Is what gone?"

Greenback rolled his bloodshot eyes up to meet her gaze. They quivered with fear.

"The monster," he said.

Tess swallowed. *He's hallucinating. Just need to get him calm.*

"It's just the two of us," she said, dabbing some blood from his forehead. A three-inch gash was still bleeding. "You're safe now."

Greenback shrugged her off and scrambled to the far wall. He pushed his back against the wall, drawing his knees to his chest protectively. "No, no. It's not gone. It's not gone. I can hear it. CAN'T YOU HEAR IT?"

Tess gave the ranting man space. "I don't hear anything. I haven't heard anything since I got here. In fact, I'm not even sure *how* I got here. The last thing I remember is the chopper crash. Then there was an avalanche. After that, nothing."

Tess's dialogue seemed to settle him somewhat. His breathing slowed, though he still exhaled sharply through his mouth. "IT brought you here."

"Who? Who brought me here?"

"The monster."

The memory came back to Tess in a flash. It was after the accident, after the avalanche. She was buried under the snow and ice. Running out of air. She had blacked out.

Something had grabbed her leg.

The image cut off abruptly.

She turned back to the engineer. "There's no such thing as monsters."

Greenback looked up with quivering eyes. He began to laugh, mirthlessly, the laugh of a deranged man. The laugh of a man who was losing touch with reality. He mumbled something Tess couldn't make out.

"Bill, you have to slow down," Tess said. "I can't understand you. *Meetah?* Is that what you're saying?"

He shook his head. "Not *meetah. Meh-Teh.*"

Tess did not recognize the word.

"Meh-Teh," he repeated. "The savage white ape."

Suddenly, a scream echoed inside the cavern. Tess jumped at the sound. It was so close. Greenback immediately began sobbing again, burying his head into his folded knees, rocking from side to side. An awful smell filled her nostrils. Like rotted meat. She scanned the rim of the pit above for any sign of the source of the screams. Though it sounded otherworldly, like the shriek of a hundred vampire bats, there was something vaguely familiar about that scream.

It was human.

A split second later, something plummeted into the pit. Something large. Tess scrambled out of the way as it landed with a sickening thud. It was enough to send the engineer into another bout of hysterics. Tess recovered quickly, realizing with dread what it was.

A body.

Slowly, the form rolled itself over.

❂ ❂ ❂

HH-60G Blackhawk
18,439 Feet

"There they are," Conner announced over the roar of the Blackhawk. "I can see the ropes."

The pilot followed Conner's pointing finger and banked the chopper sharply toward the icy slopes of Kuk Sur. The thin purple climbing ropes lined an otherwise featureless ice wall. A narrow ridge extended from the base of the face to a large expanse dotted with clefts and fissures. Even from high above the terrain, Conner recognized the spot.

The crevasse field.

A few hundred yards below the field was a surface large enough and flat enough to land on. The chopper swooped.

If it was a Yeti high on Kuk Sur that was responsible for the carnage of *Darwin's Race*, Conner knew that he, Preston, and Malika would be going up against a beast many times stronger and more resilient than human beings. The very fact that the creature had survived in these hostile mountains was testament to that. But that's not what filled him with alarm. What horrified Conner down to the marrow of his bones was the possibility that the creature was somehow accumulating racers for food. Including Tess. If he was reading the grainy broadcast image correctly, she was trapped in a giant ice cave.

Perfect for storage.

The thought made him shudder.

An animal will resort to anything to protect its own species, Preston had said. *We are dealing with a truly desperate animal turning to its natural, inborn instincts. A Yeti is a dangerous beast. A Yeti struggling for its very existence is something else entirely.*

The only consolation from this whole maddening mess was the belief that Tess and the others were still alive, somewhere inside the ice pyramid below. If the Yeti was keeping them for food, the animal would have to keep them alive. At least for a while.

A cloud of snow billowed around the chopper as the pilot touched down roughly on the expanse beneath the crevasse field. Once the cargo of the three-person rescue team had been offloaded, the rotors revved up once more. Shielding their faces from the icy exhaust, they watched it lift up and soar down the valley until it blinked from view.

Silence returned to the mountain.

Conner looked across to the crevasse field. It was dotted with towering spires and towers. It looked like the skyline of a brilliant ice city. An Oz of snow. Conner allowed himself a quiet moment.

But only a moment.

"Cross the field, up the ridge, climb the ice wall into the caves," he said. "Any questions?"

There were none.

Kuk Sur
19,011 Feet

Tess immediately recognized the huddled shape that had just plunged into the pit. The long loose blond hair gave it away immediately.

Wade Stanley.

Brilliant red blood pooled under his prostrate body. Tess moved quickly to examine him for the extent of the injury. Greenback crouched in the corner of the ice pit, moaning, rocking on his heels.

"Get yourself together, man!" Tess yelled at him. "And get your ass over here. Help me stop this bleeding!"

Blood spurted from a large slash in the back of Wade's left thigh. Tess frantically applied pressure just above the wound. Greenback was moving now, but too slowly. "Hurry up! Find something to tie this off, or he'll bleed to death right here!"

Finally roused, Greenback stripped off a black balaclava and with trembling hands fastened it tightly around Wade's thigh. Tess released the pressure. Blood still oozed from the wound. She looked up at the engineer and shook her head.

Wade wasn't going to make it. Not unless they got him some serious medical attention right away. All that blood. And who knows what other internal injuries he might have. Jesus Christ, what had gone so wrong?

Had they only turned back when they had the chance, none of this would've happened.

Wade moaned. Tess moved quickly to place a comforting hand on his arm. "Wade, it's Tess. Come on; you've got to wake up now. Please, Wade. It's Elizabeth."

A few moments passed before Wade's body stopped shaking. Slowly, he began to roll over. When Tess could finally see his face, she had to squeeze her own leg to prevent herself from screaming.

He had been torn to shreds. Blood flowed in bright red ribbons from three parallel gouges that gaped open from his forehead down to his chin. His left eyeball oozed pus and blood in a pink stew. Skin hung in limp flaps. His clothes were in tatters. A climbing harness clung to his hips by a thread.

A choking sob escaped before Tess clamped a hand over her mouth.

"It's the monster!" Greenback yelled. "The goddamned monster! That's a claw across his face. It tore his face off!"

The outburst forced Tess to push aside her own distress. "Shut the hell up, Greenback," she whispered harshly. "Keep it together, man. We all need to keep it together." Then, turning to Wade, she continued in low, comforting tones. "You're alright now, Wade. Nobody's going to hurt you anymore."

Wade's eyes suddenly filled with fear, trembling in their sockets. His body started to tremble anew—then uncontrollably, as if in the grips of a powerful seizure. He was going into shock. Tess held him tight.

Greenback slammed the wall with his fist. "It's coming for us; *IT'S COMING FOR US!*"

"Shut up, and calm down!"

We need to get the hell out of here. Now. Think of something!

She didn't know about any monsters, but Wade's injuries sure as hell weren't from a fall. Greenback may have been losing it, but he had seen something. Something that had him exceedingly spooked.

"Wade, honey, what did this to you?"

Wade met Tess's gaze, and she had to fight back another wave of revulsion. Wade's face had been . . . *ravaged*. He tried to open his mouth to speak, and a spurt of fresh blood erupted from a slash in his jaw. Only then did Tess realize Wade's jawbone was probably dislocated. She thought for a moment about trying to reset it, but decided against it. Monster or no, Tess didn't want to stick around for another minute. It was time for her to take charge.

"Okay, here's what we're going to do," she said, rising to her feet. "We need to get out of this pit. Wade, I'm not going to lie to you. You need a doctor. We're not going to be able to stop that bleeding for long."

Wade steeled himself with a deep breath. Nodded.

"The only way out is up these walls. We're going to have to form a human ladder. Bill, with Wade's condition, you're the strongest. You're the bottom rung. Brace yourself against the ice right here."

The engineer, revived at the thought of escape, placed his back against the wall, and cupped his hands together at his knees. "Alright, Wade. Get up on my shoulders."

Tess helped Wade to his feet. The injured racer grimaced, grasped for his bleeding thigh. "I know it hurts. But this is the only way."

Whimpering in pain, Wade put his good right leg into Greenback's hands. He hoisted him up, and he climbed onto his shoulders. He teetered, his thigh bleeding profusely once again, but managed to brace himself against the ice wall.

Here comes the tough part, Tess thought.

"Okay, you're both going to have to lean forward a bit. Into the ice. Give me some angles."

Holding on to Greenback's neck, Tess stepped into the back of his knee. He groaned, but she didn't slow down to apologize. She placed her other foot into the small of his back, while simultaneously stepping quickly onto his shoulder. It was a move only a seasoned rock climber could make.

"That hurts like hell," Greenback said. "Keep going."

"Wade, this is going to hurt," Tess said. "Are you ready?"

He nodded. Braced himself.

Tess lifted her foot from Greenback's shoulder.

"Wait."

"Bill, we need to hurry. You need to suck it up."

The engineer shook his head. "It's not that. I think I hear something."

Tess froze. She felt him sway beneath her.

And then she heard it.

Footsteps. Something heavy. Growing closer.

A shadow appeared on the cave wall. An awful stench settled into the dank air.

"This is it," Greenback breathed. "We're all gonna die."

CHAPTER
THIRTY-SEVEN

Kuk Sur
18,789 Feet

Head bowed against the scouring winds, Conner dashed across the glacier. The ice field spilled down the mountain in a crumble of ice and snow, with crevasses and crests the size of tractor trailers. He barely looked up as he passed under a series of ice towers and spires, the peaks spewing snow like frozen smokestacks. He didn't wait to make sure Preston and Malika were keeping up with his frenetic pace. Tess was up there somewhere. Alive.

And Conner knew she was not alone.

He wasn't about to slow down now.

The terrain resembled a vast frozen ocean, with troughs and ridges and waves of ice. Conner surfed the ground with ease—he was running now as quickly as the thin air and his plastic climbing boots allowed. The rapid ascension was surely wreaking havoc inside his body. His blood was already thinning, and his pounding heartbeat was not delivering enough energy to his limbs. He ignored a faint tingling in the tips of his fingers and toes. No time for that.

Without breaking stride, Conner hurtled a deep but narrow rift in the ice. He glanced over his shoulder to make sure that Preston and Malika were still following. They were right on his heels. He waited for them to clear the crevasse before turning back upslope.

And then he stopped.

It was the angle of the peak that caught his attention. The way it appeared through a two-foot cleft in one of the giant ice towers. From Conner's position deep inside the canyon of snow, only the topmost five hundred feet of Kuk Sur were visible. It didn't look so immense from here, though he knew it was one of the biggest mountains on earth. He remembered having this same thought once before.

At this exact location.

The landscape surrounding him had changed, shifted with the ice. Giant crevasses that had once gaped open like hungry mouths had now closed to thin cracks. New chasms opened in their place, beckoning.

Conner got his bearings. Just to the right of the tower, the peak up at ten o'clock. That would mean the crevasse would be just about—

It wasn't there. The crevasse that had consumed his brother had vanished. Another victim of the crushing ice.

Malika emerged beside him. "What is it? Why are you stopping?"

Breathing heavily, Preston arrived in time to hear her question.

"It's not here anymore," Conner said flatly.

Malika scanned the field. "What? What's not here?"

"The crevasse. Where the snow bridge collapsed." He looked to the ground. "The place where I lost my brother."

"Conner," she said softly. "I'm so sorry."

A brittle ridge had formed where the glacier had pressed the chasm out of existence. The ice crumbled under Conner's boot.

"It's been six years," said Preston. "This glacier is constantly shifting. You must've known it would be gone after all this time."

"I'm not sure what I expected. But a part of me wanted to see it again."

Malika touched his arm with a thick expedition mitten. "What if it was still here? What would you do? Would you abandon the others, climb down into the hole? To look for what? There's nothing down there anymore. It's been too long."

"I'm surprised to hear you say that. You and your father, of all people, should know what this is like. You've been there. To have someone you love snatched away from you. To feel that hole, right in the center of your being. And that awful feeling that nothing can ever fill that hole. Except, maybe, just maybe, coming to grips with what happened. For me—I'm trying to fill that hole—because I helped dig it."

Conner's breaths had become heavy, ragged, and he paused a moment before continuing. "I wanted to see it because I thought it might help me close that hole. Aren't the two of you here for the same reason?"

Preston rammed his trekking poles into the ground. "I was away on business when my wife was killed . . . killed by that thing. I know all about the pain. Twenty years' worth. And you know what I learned? I learned that the only thing that's gonna take away my pain is to inflict some of my own."

"That was your motivation from the beginning. The reason you pushed for a second team, the reason you put up the second million. You came here to kill the Yeti."

Preston yanked his poles free of the ice and adjusted his snow goggles. "We all came here for the same reason. It just took you a little longer to figure it out."

"What's that supposed to mean?"

"Don't you get it yet? The Yeti killed your brother. Not that snow bridge, not you. The Yeti. And I think you knew it all along. When we found your brother's hat, there was no doubt in our minds that you would want to return to this mountain. To discover, once and for always, the truth. And now that you've found it, you want to kill the creature as much as I do."

Conner shook his head. "I'm no killer. This is a rescue mission. That's why I'm here."

The only reply from Preston was a shrug, which Conner took to mean the discussion was over. He stepped toward the ridge, wondering if there was any truth to Preston's words.

The ridge was a narrow spine, perhaps eighteen inches wide, forcing the climbers to place their boots cautiously one in front of the other. The razor-thin arête rose sharply—sixty degrees—toward the ice wall. Steep slopes fell away on either side. Despite the bitter cold, it felt like a stairway to hell.

Wind and snow scoured the ridge as the trio ascended single file. More than once, Conner was nearly blown off the ridge by the wind gusts. He reached the base of the ice wall thirty breathless minutes later, thankful for some respite from the gale.

"Hope we don't have to down-climb that sucker," he said as Preston and Malika caught up.

The purple ropes that belonged to Wade and Blaine dangled from the face. Frozen stiff.

"I don't trust these ropes," Conner said. "Their anchors were set before they knew about the brittle wall ice. We'll have to start over." He waited for nods from the climbers. "I'll lead."

The sun had passed its midday zenith and was falling behind the peak of Kuk Sur. A dark shadow was creeping across the east face toward the rescue team like an inexorable ocean tide.

Six hours of daylight left.

They climbed for an hour, stopping only to place safety bolts, moving in a carefully orchestrated, and silent, ascent. They were connected by ropes that crisscrossed through a series of metal hooks, leaving behind a spider web of nylon.

"I can see the opening," Conner called out. "Just thirty more feet."

He scampered up the final distance without placing another anchor bolt. Risky—a fall now would result in a harrowing sixty-foot plunge—but it saved precious minutes. At the mouth of the cave, he jammed redundant bolts into the ice, noting that Wade and Blaine had done the same.

Preston and Malika, now using only the tips of their crampons to avoid shattering the ice with their axes, ascended to Conner's position and quickly tied off.

"I'll go first," Conner said.

"Wait," Preston cautioned him.

"Preston, what?"

"You are about to enter the lair of the Yeti. I just thought you'd want to know what we're up against."

"I know what we're up against."

Preston's eyebrow rose. "Do you? Are you familiar with Bergmann's Rule?"

"Come on, Preston. We don't have the time to—"

"Bergmann's Rule states that body size is larger in colder regions than in more temperate ones. Greater body mass conserves heat better."

"Why are you telling me this? The Yeti is big? I already figured that. If this thing is halfway between gorillas and human beings on the evolutionary scale, it's pretty damn big."

"Not just big," Preston said. "The Yeti have thrived in the coldest place on earth. A common gorilla couldn't survive here, nor could we. We're too small. That means the Yeti evolved to cope with its environment. He *grew*."

"So how big are we talking?"

Preston nodded toward the porthole. "We're about to find out."

Conner pulled himself through the gap into the cave and unclipped his harness. He felt cramped in the small opening, trapped. The air was stale and frigid and smelled of spoiled food. A backpack was there, probably belonging to Wade or Blaine. He moved it out of the way to make room in the small alcove for the others. Another minute, and the rescue team was together again on solid ground.

"Leave the gear here," he said. "And keep conversation to a minimum. No headlamps. I don't want to draw any unnecessary attention."

Preston dropped his small pack of carabiners, bolts, and rope. He fastened his trekking poles and an ice axe to his back and ran a finger along the roof of the cave.

"The Yeti is not here," he said.

"How can you be sure?"

"Because we're still alive."

A gust of wind whipped through the cave, showering the climbers with millions of tiny ice particles that glistened in the light.

"We have entered the lair of the Yeti," he continued.

"If he knew we were here, he would already be upon us. Protecting his territory."

"He? You think we're dealing with a male?"

Preston nodded. "I tested fecal matter for the presence of estrogen. There was none. It's a male."

Conner stepped deeper into the cave. "Well, then, he it is. Let's take a look around while he's out. If we hurry, we can be in and out before he ever returns."

The adjacent cave was large enough for them to stand fully upright. It was much larger, cast largely in shadow, as cold and stagnant as as an icebox. The ceiling rose to twenty feet, framed on all sides by notched ice and exposed rock.

"Man, what is that smell?" Malika wrinkled her nose. "Smells like dead skunk."

Preston sniffed the air like a bloodhound. "You're half-right," he said.

Even in the darkness, Conner could see other passages tunneling off in all directions. *Probably an entire subsystem of caves*, he thought. *This is how the Yeti has stayed out of sight for so long.*

Moving slowly, the rescue team inched their way through the cavern, feeling their way along the wall. It wasn't nearly as dark as it should've been, this deep within Kuk Sur. The opening in the ice couldn't cast this much light into the inner chamber. Conner glanced up and saw several long vents yawning up to the surface. Natural windows.

The light cut angular shadows across the cavern, and Conner surveyed the rock walls. They looked wet, slippery.

He slipped off his mitten, feeling its rough contours with a bare forefinger.

"Conner."

He glanced up at the sound of Malika's voice, ready to reprimand her for speaking. But she was kneeling beside some rocks in a corner of the cave, motioning him over.

"Bones," she whispered. "Human bones. Look—there must be dozens of bodies here."

The bones were stacked haphazardly along the edges of the cave. The same bones they had seen on the monitors down at base camp. There was no sign of Wade or Blaine.

Some skeletons were more or less intact; other bones were strewn about randomly. The damp air had permitted some semblance of decomposition. Dried and decayed flesh still covered several skeletons. Conner counted six skulls before his stomach lurched. Judging by the bleached appearance of some of the bones, the bodies had been here for ages.

Preston was on the far end of the cave, picking through the rubble. He lifted a small pale bone, held it under a shaft of sunlight.

"What is it?" Conner asked.

"Medial metacarpal, from a female *Hemitragus jemlahicus*. A common Himalayan tahr."

"But there's no way a sheep could've climbed up here."

Preston leaned into the shaft of light. "Not on its own."

Conner's pulse quickened, suddenly remembering that Tess may be in this labyrinth somewhere. He resisted the urge to call out to her.

That's when he saw it.

A snatch of red amongst the bones.

It was an expedition backpack. Faded, pale with frost. Unmistakable.

Malika materialized beside him. "Is that—?"

"Yes."

Conner fell to his knees beside the backpack that had once belonged to his brother. It was a Kelty Red Cloud 6650, black and red. The lid had been ripped off, and Conner fingered a torn harness. The shoulder straps had been slashed, too. The pack reeked of violence.

A nylon daisy chain that vertically lined the bag still held a series of chocks, cams, and carabiners. Conner pulled one from the strap and examined it.

It was a Black Diamond spring-loaded camming device. A big one. Double axel, serrated teeth, rated to fifty Kilonewtons, able to displace almost ten thousand pounds. He recognized it immediately. It had been a Christmas present to his brother just months before their final climb together.

He triggered the stainless steel lever, and the cam blasted open. From its coiled position, the serrated teeth exploded outward. Designed to be inserted into a crack in rock or ice and then released, the cam's teeth extended until they filled the space. It could then support a climber's weight. Without resistance, however, the cam would burst open like a reverse bear trap.

Conner pushed it back to a closed position and hooked

it to his climbing harness.

Suddenly, this mound of bones surrounding him had taken on a personal meaning. These skeletons belonged to real people—fathers, sisters, friends. Brothers.

One of these skeletons could be Tucker. Somehow, his body—or at least his backpack—had been transported from the crevasse below. The chilling thought that Tucker had been carried to this lair for—

The prospect was too horrible to consider.

"Conner, I'm sorry," Malika said.

Before he could respond, a sound echoed in the cavern.

"What was that?" she asked, eyes darting.

Preston sniffed the air again. He pulled the rifle from his shoulder. With a flip of his wrist, he released the safety. "We've got company."

CHAPTER THIRTY-EIGHT

Kuk Sur
19,011 Feet

Tess resisted the temptation to call out.

Just as Tess, Wade, and Greenback had formed a human ladder, an ominous shadow loomed on the cave wall above the ice pit. Not moving. She prayed that it belonged to a rescuer, but a sinking feeling instructed her to stay quiet. There was something different about the shadow.

It was huge, for one thing. Far too large to have been cast by a person. She suddenly remembered the footprint she had discovered in the jungle far below. For all his fevered ranting about monsters, Greenback may have been onto something.

Standing atop his shoulders, Tess couldn't see his eyes, but she could feel the waver in his knees.

"Easy now, Bill," she whispered. "Just stay still."

The only response was a muffled whimper. Tess felt Wade's grip on her arm tighten.

And then the shadow was gone. It vanished so quickly and quietly, she hadn't even seen it go. She waited a full minute before daring to move.

She dropped to the ground, then helped Wade down. His leg wound was pulsing now, badly, and he had turned pale as a ghost.

"Now what?" Greenback asked, rubbing his shoulders. Desperation filled his voice.

"If that's your monster up there, something just got its attention. If someone else is up there, we need to draw some of our own."

Kuk Sur
19,007 Feet

Heavy footfalls echoed in the cavern. Approaching fast.

Conner, Preston, and Malika scrambled for cover. If they had any chance at all against the creature, they would need to have surprise in their arsenal.

A series of tunnels led from the main chamber. Dark, impenetrable. No way to know where they led. But Conner would have to choose. And quickly.

If his ears could trust the odd acoustics in the caverns, the creature would be approaching from the tunnel directly to his left, the widest of the five passageways that led from the chamber.

"This way," he called.

Conner dashed into the middle passageway, Preston and Malika following at his boot heels. The tunnel was narrower and the ceiling lower, forcing them to crouch single file down the corridor.

Thirty yards farther, the tunnel split into two sweeping passages.

"Which way?" said a breathless Preston.

Conner peered into the darkness. Both passages disappeared around bends in the rock.

Then, faintly, the sound of a voice wafted down the tunnel. It echoed past, bouncing off the cave walls, then back again, making it hard to pinpoint the source.

Conner exchanged glances with his team and flipped a mental coin. He dashed down the left passageway. Though he wouldn't admit it to the others, Conner was sure he recognized the voice.

Tess.

They almost raced right past the pit. Tucked away in a shadowy recess, the pit was hidden well. It was only the sound of a whimpering cry that brought Conner to an abrupt halt.

"I heard that, too," Preston said.

They backtracked to the pit and peered over its precipice.

The bottom was shrouded in shadow.

"Is anybody down there?" Conner whispered as loudly as he dared. "Hello?"

A voice rose from the pit. "Conner?"

Conner's heart soared. "Tess, oh, thank God. Tess, it's me. I'm here with Preston and Malika. We're here to get you out of there."

"I'm not alone," Tess murmured.

"I was hoping you'd say that," Conner said. "Blaine and Wade?"

Another pause, then a weak reply, "Just Wade. And Bill Greenback."

"The engineer," Preston whispered.

Conner leaned over the rim. "Are they alive?"

"Conner, please just get us out of here." Her voice cracked, on the verge of a sob.

"Hang tight, Tess. We'll be right down."

Preston and Malika were already uncoiling rope from their shoulders. There was nothing to anchor the ropes to, so they quickly established a human winch. Preston braced himself against the far tunnel wall, wedging his crampons into the hard floor. Malika did likewise, a few feet away, and fed the belay ropes through both harnesses. Conner clipped in and tested the line with a sharp tug. Preston nodded, and Conner rappelled into the inky darkness of the pit.

The temperature dropped noticeably inside the pit. It was like descending into a freezer.

Conner's boots hit the bottom. He quickly tugged on the line to signal that he was off belay. Then, he turned to Tess.

Her face was caked with dried blood. Her trademark red jacket was ripped at the shoulder, and she was missing one boot. Nonetheless, his heart soared.

Tess flung herself into his arms, but only for a moment. "Wade's bad, Con. Real bad. Something's wrong with his jaw; he can't speak. We need to move him right now. Greenback's losing it, but physically he's okay."

"What about you?" For a moment their eyes met.

"I'll be fine. Just get us out of here. There's something up here, in the caves. Some kind of—"

Conner stopped her. "I know, I know. Let's get out of this pit; then I'll tell you what we're up against. Okay, Wade, let's get you clipped in. When you get to the top, throw it back down to us."

Nodding, the bloody racer stepped into the harness, tightening the too-large straps the best he could. Tess was right. Wade looked horrible, hemorrhaging blood. He didn't have much time. Eyes quivering, he nodded he was ready.

"Up," Conner called. Wade lifted off the ground in spurts as Preston and Malika hoisted him toward the rim.

Greenback emerged from the shadows like a shot, grabbing Conner's arm roughly. "It's coming back! For us! I need to get out of here! It's coming!"

"Calm down. Right now. We're going to get you out of here, but if you make one more sound, you will jeopardize all of us. You have to stay quiet if you want to get out of here alive. Show me that you understand what I am saying to you."

Greenback nodded slowly.

The harness fell to the pit floor, momentarily startling them. Wade had made it to the rim. Conner helped the engineer climb into the harness and gave a tug on the rope.

"Up."

Greenback rose. Tess gestured toward him. "He kept babbling about a monster. And then there was Wade. You saw him. He couldn't tell me anything—but, Jesus, something did that to him."

"Tess, I'm going to tell you something now. Something that you're not going to want to believe."

On the lip of the pit, Preston helped Greenback unclip himself from the harness while Malika tended the best she could to Wade Stanley. He was in bad shape, his face was a bloody mess, and a deep slash in his leg exposed pale bone. The injuries were unmistakable.

The Yeti had done this.

Sharp memories of his own wife roared into his head. He had seen her body, but only after the blood had been wiped away, the lacerations closed. Had his beloved looked this bad, too? The thought brought up an anger that smoldered like hot lava. Soon, he would face the terror that had taken his wife. And vengeance would be his.

"Which way outta here?" Greenback stammered.

There was a vacant look behind the engineer's eyes. *He's checked out completely*, Preston realized. *I'll have to keep a close watch on him.*

"Which way outta here?" he repeated loudly. His shouts attracted stares from Wade and Malika.

"Easy, there. We've got two more people to get out of that pit. Then we're going to make our way back down—"

"It's coming! It's coming back for us! I've got to get out of here now!"

Before Preston could move, Greenback turned and sprinted full-bore down the tunnel. Unable to give chase because he was still serving as an anchor for Conner and Tess, Preston watched helplessly as the engineer disappeared into the darkness.

Malika began to untie herself from the belay.

"Don't bother," her father said. "He's already dead."

"A Yeti?" Tess said, trembling. "Is that what we're dealing with? A real Yeti?"

Conner had told her everything. The discovery of Cale's mutilated body. The dramatic footage of the attack on Wade and Blaine. The fleeting glimpse of a strange animal. He told her about Preston's astonishing story about his wife, and his twenty-year quest to find—and kill—the predator.

The annunciation of the name of the beast hung in the

air. What had been shrouded in mystery and myth for so many years had suddenly become very real.

"It looks that way," Conner said. "I saw it myself. Not the whole thing, but enough to know that we're dealing with something no one has ever seen before."

"And Preston *knew* about this?"

He nodded. "He thinks we're dealing with the final remnant of the species. The last Yeti on earth."

Tess looked at Conner warily. "But there's still one thing I don't understand. Why did the creature put us in this pit? Why not just kill us?"

"The monster is getting desperate. The Yeti is just like any animal; just trying to stay alive—survival of the fittest and all that."

"But we were the predator, right? Humans? We're the ones responsible for the extinction of their species. So why keep us alive?"

"Tess, the Yeti is running out of food. That's why you and Wade and Greenback were spared. We're not the predators anymore. We're the *prey*."

"*My . . . god*," whimpered Tess.

From above, the harness descended to the floor between them.

"Your turn," Conner said.

As Tess lifted out of view, he tried to think ahead. She didn't have an extra harness, and he hadn't thought to bring extras. Wade's had been destroyed. Even if they managed to get all six to the ropes on the ice wall, there was no way for everyone to rappel at once. Perhaps he could fasten a Prusik sling, but that would be one hell of a ride—nearly two hundred fifty feet of vertical ice—with little in the way of protection. *Too dangerous.*

Maybe there was a way through these caves. There must be another entrance. The Yeti certainly wasn't using the hole in the ice wall to access the lair.

But how could they negotiate the cavern complex without bumping into the Yeti?

The harness fell again from the rim.

"Alright, let's move," Conner said once he had reached the top. "Where's Greenback?"

"He bolted," replied Preston.

He didn't even hesitate. "Then we can't do anything for him. We need to go now, quickly and quietly."

He led the others down the tunnel to the fork, then down the right tunnel toward the main chamber. He paused at the precipice of the bone-filled cave, listening for signs of occupation. Everything was quiet.

"Okay, we have a decision to make," he said, explaining the harness predicament. Three harnesses. Five people. "Risk the descent, or chance the caves."

"Not exactly a win-win," muttered Tess.

"What about the pack at the mouth of the cave?" Malika suggested. "Maybe there's an extra harness."

"Good thought. Let's check it out," Conner said. "I don't like the idea of trekking blind into these caves. If the system's as large as I think it is, we'd get lost for sure."

Agreed, the five moved stealthily through the chamber toward the smaller cave beside the ice face. Daylight peeked through the hole, glistening with the purple hues of dusk.

With room for only two, Tess and Malika ducked into the smaller cave to check the packs. Any bad blood between them had evaporated in the face of threats on their survival.

"Anything?" Conner called in after them.

A second later, both scrambled back into the larger chamber. "We got one," Tess said. "Still one short."

"Ah, guys? I think we've got bigger problems."

Conner turned at the sound of Malika's voice and followed her gaze across the cave.

A shadow appeared along the wall of the tunnel.

Moving toward them.

Without taking his eyes off the looming shadow, Conner breathed his instructions to Tess through clenched teeth. "Malika and Preston still have their harnesses on. Help Wade get into that one; you take mine." He shoved the British climber into the cave and stepped out of his harness. He handed his harness to her.

"But Conner, what about—"

"Do it now," he said forcefully. Then, softer, "Put it on. I'll free climb."

"Free climb? Down a two hundred-foot ice face? That's suicide. Even for you."

"It's the only way. We're one harness short. And we're out of time for discussion."

Malika lifted a shaky finger toward the shadow. Everything stopped.

"It's here."

A figure appeared at the entrance of the tunnel, its form obscured by shadow.

Conner turned back to the small cave. "Tess, you and Wade go now. Malika, get ready. You and your father will rope up as soon as they clear—"

Preston Child slowly unbuckled his harness, letting it drop to the ground.

"What the hell are you doing?"

"It's the only way. You need a harness."

"But you'll be stuck up here," Conner protested. "How will you—?"

Preston shook his head. "I've been looking for this thing for over twenty years. You think I'm going to turn back now? When I'm so close? This is the reason I'm here. This is where my journey ends. And I've got my friends here." He gestured to his rifle and his taser-equipped trekking pole.

"Daddy, no!" cried Malika. "You have to come with us."

"I can't leave you here alone," Conner said.

"Don't think about it anymore. Just go. And live."

A voice came from the small cave. Tess. "Roped up and ready."

Preston nodded toward the opening. "Go."

Conner hesitated. It wasn't in his nature to turn his back on anyone. Even for all the man's underhanded dealings to get him in this damned race, he couldn't leave him now.

He wasn't about to abandon another person to the Yeti.

"Go now!" Preston commanded.

Conner extended a hand, and Preston took it; held it for a long moment. And then, without another word, Conner ducked into the smaller cave, pulling a sobbing Malika with him. Tess and Wade dangled on ropes outside the hole in the ice.

"Tess, go right now. Go quickly, and don't look back. We're right behind you."

As Tess and Wade fell away from view, Conner helped Malika attach her harness to the safety ropes left behind by Wade and Blaine. They were dicey, but there was no choice. She had to climb on separate ropes from Tess and Wade. Certain she was secured tightly, he pushed her through the gap.

But he made no move to follow her.

"What are you doing?" she asked.

"I'm going back," he said, pulling the rifle from his back. "Your father's gonna need the help."

CHAPTER THIRTY-NINE

Kuk Sur
19,011 Feet

Preston stood stock-still. His exhalations formed frosty clouds that hung in the air like dark spirits. Despite the subzero temperatures inside the cave, a line of perspiration swept across his forehead. He did not blink.

On the far side of the cave, just inside the tunnel no more than forty feet away, the shadow loomed. Unmoving. *Goddamn, it was big.* He trained the barrel of his AK-74 on the mouth of the darkened passageway.

"Come on, you bastard!" he yelled into the cavern. "You think I'm afraid of you? I've been waiting for this moment for twenty years!"

He heard his own voice echo down the tunnels before fading away to nothing.

Preston turned abruptly at a noise behind him.

"I thought I told you to go."

Conner Michaels slapped him on the shoulder. "Figured you could use some help."

He didn't argue. "You come with a plan, too?"

"I figure it's the same as yours. Strafe the motherfucker as soon as he shows his big ugly head." Conner pointed to Preston's trekking poles. "The Yeti will bite those in half like matchsticks."

"Maybe, but these things bite back."

Just then, the shadow moved.

For a split second, Preston thought it merely a trick of light. The ice reflected the dusky hue of the Himalayan night like crystals. Light danced with the shadows. And then it moved again, and this time there was no mistaking what was coming.

Something was moving in the tunnels. They could hear it now: heavy footfalls, otherworldly grunts of exertion. Approaching fast. Hurtling toward them.

"Showtime," Preston said.

The creature exploded into the cave.

Preston and Conner loosed their weapons simultaneously, spraying rounds into the gloom. The cave erupted in a cacophony of sound and smoke. Bullets shattered the walls of the cave, unleashing shards of ice that rained down upon them. Through the blizzard, Preston could see the darkened form jerking violently with each round. The ground shook beneath his feet, but he didn't let up.

Couldn't let up. Not now.

Only when he felt an arm on his shoulder did he lift his finger from the metal trigger. The din slowly subsided.

"The cave is becoming unstable," Conner said. "No more shooting."

It took a full, heart-pounding minute for the smoke to dissipate. Only then could they see what their barrage had wrought.

The body had been completely blown apart. Blood covered everything. Bits of arm and leg and God-knew-what-else were scattered all over the cavern. The smell of burnt flesh scoured their nostrils.

Preston surveyed the carnage. "Bastard never even had a chance. Man, that felt good."

But Conner didn't share the sentiment. He was kneeling on the ground, fingering a bloody body part.

"What is that?" Preston asked.

"An arm. Or at least, a part of an arm."

"Yeah? So why do you look so glum?"

Conner held up the arm. "Because I don't figure your Yeti was wearing a jacket with fleece sleeves." The charred remains of black cotton were unmistakable.

Preston felt a tightness in his chest. "Jesus Christ, who did we just—?"

He didn't finish the thought.

Something had moved into the room. The smell of rot was unmistakable. But it was more than that. Preston could sense a new presence.

It was close.

But the smoke from the earlier barrage still obscured the shadowy recesses of the cave. They couldn't see anything.

And then the murk cleared.

"*Jesus*—" Conner said.

"—*Christ*," Preston finished.

The creature emerged like a phantom from the shadows.

It was impossibly huge. The top of its skull grazed the ceiling of the cave—over eight feet. And almost as wide, the Yeti was as solid as a truck. Broad shoulders bulged with thick muscle. Its legs were as wide as tree trunks and looked almost as strong. The Yeti circled along the perimeter of the cave, stalking, each footfall shaking the ground, unleashing more ice shards from the cave ceiling.

Preston was too transfixed to even think about the rifle still clenched in his near-frozen hands. The Yeti's face resembled that of a mountain gorilla: dark, leathery, with a set of flared nostrils that seemed to spew smoke, though Preston knew it was only its frozen exhalations. Its mouth was agape, lined with a razor-sharp series of long yellow fangs. Bits of blood and flesh hung in flaps from its massive jaw. It had been feeding.

Except on the face—that hideous contortion of simian countenance—silver-gray fur covered the Yeti's body down to his extremities. Each hand was as large as a dinner plate, with long fingers, thick and rough. Dagger-shaped claws jutted menacingly from the tip of each. The Yeti's raw feet were likewise armed with dangerous talons.

Altogether, Preston guessed he was looking at an eight hundred-pound beast that had somehow learned to adapt in the most frigid and unforgiving place in the world.

One tough son of a bitch.

The creature eyed Preston warily, as if surprised its prey had not yet fled. Perhaps twenty feet separated men and beast, a distance Preston knew the Yeti could close in a single heartbeat.

Slowly, he raised the rifle to his shoulder. Aimed. Felt for the steel trigger with his bare finger.

And then he hesitated.

The Yeti made no move to flee. Didn't even flinch.

"What are you waiting for?" Conner asked. "I'm empty. You have to take the shot."

For a fleeting instant, a strange and unexpected emotion welled up from somewhere deep inside his soul. This was an animal—just an animal—not even intelligent enough to fear a weapon. No matter how fearsome its appearance, though, didn't the Yeti deserve to survive, too?

"Preston. Take the shot."

With Conner's impassioned plea, all vestiges of sympathy vanished. Preston aimed for the beast's heart. *You took mine,* he thought, *when you took away my beloved. Now I'm taking yours.*

He fired.

The bullet exploded into the Yeti's chest, dead-center. The beast staggered backwards, grasping awkwardly at his wound. A round hole gaped open, spilling a thick ooze of blood down its torso. For a moment, it looked like the creature was going to fall.

But before Preston could react, the Yeti charged. He scrambled to loose another shot, but the creature was too fast. The Yeti slammed into the climbers with outstretched arms, knocking them across the cavern like plastic toy soldiers. Preston smashed into the wall shoulder-first. His rifle clattered out of his grasp.

Before Preston could rouse himself, the Yeti pounced.

A giant calloused hand gripped Preston around the neck. Claws burrowed into his flesh. He was lifted off the ground, kicking and gagging for air. He flailed at the Yeti's hand, fighting to free his windpipe. His blows had no effect. His lungs threatened to explode.

And then the creature crumpled to the ground, releasing Preston. He scrambled away from the Yeti, gulping ragged air into his starving lungs.

What the—?

Conner was wrapped around the beast's left leg. He must've rolled the leg—an old wrestling technique—exerting enough force to buckle the Yeti's knee. Seizing the opportunity while the creature was down, Preston attacked. He rained blows down on the Yeti's broad chest.

The creature roared. Kicking out with his legs and up with his arms, the Yeti flung the climbers across the chamber. Preston landed roughly again, felt something crack in his shoulder.

He recovered quickly and pulled his ice axe from his back sling. Gestured for Conner to do the same. "Circle around. Our only chance is to hit him from two angles."

The Yeti did not immediately attack. Its enormous head swiveled on a thick neck, darting from Preston to Conner. It seemed to be studying its adversaries.

Preston spit blood to the ground. "Not used to a fight, are you?"

The Yeti lunged forward, just as Preston slashed his ice axe through the air.

The beast plowed into Preston's shoulder, before the axe found its target. Preston screamed as the bones in his shoulder crumbled. Lifted off his feet by the force of the blow, Preston was launched backwards, crashing into the ice. The blade skittered harmlessly across the ground. Stunned, he vigorously shook his head, trying to revive himself. His shoulder felt as though it were on fire.

Leaping with bent knees like a long jumper, the Yeti flew through the air, landing like an avalanche beside Preston's prone body.

As he awaited the death blow, Preston caught movement from the corner of his eye. Conner, brandishing his own ice axe, charged the beast. With a smooth slice through the air, he plunged the blade deep into the Yeti's shoulderblade.

The creature cried out—a sound like a thousand shrieking bats—and whirled to face its attacker. Conner never even had the chance to extricate the axe. The axe handle tore out of his hands, still lodged in the Yeti. He stood helpless before the beast. He craned his neck to look up into its wild eyes.

Roaring, the Yeti struck Conner with the back of his arm, sending him sprawling across the cavern floor.

Taking advantage of the Yeti's sudden change in focus, Preston rolled onto his elbows, regained his feet. His ribs throbbed mightily, and he wrapped his arms around his torso for support.

The handle of Conner's ice axe flashed tantalizingly just a few feet away. Preston reached out. His fingers grazed the aluminum handle. Before he could grasp it, the Yeti reached up over its own shoulder and grabbed the haft. With a sickening tear of flesh, it pried the axe free.

The beast studied the blood-streaked blade, touching it with a leathery finger. Brought it to its broad nose. Rapped it against the wall. A cascade of ice fell to the floor. The Yeti's head tilted quizzically.

He's learning, Preston realized. *Not good.*

He scrambled to find his own ice axe, knocked loose in the initial struggle. There, resting near the mouth of the tunnels. He scurried after it, recoiling in pain at his crushed ribs. He wielded the blade over his head. Turned back to the injured animal.

Let's see you deal with an axe in the head, you furry bastard.

Preston charged, swinging with all his might.

Just as the axe was a mere two feet—and closing fast—

from the Yeti's skull, the monster whirled and swung the other axe up in defense. The blades collided in an eruption of sparks. Preston's axe wrenched from his grip. This time, he didn't see where it landed.

"Quick learner, huh?"

Using the momentum of the blow as extra force, the Yeti swung the ice axe back. It slammed into Preston's shattered ribcage with a loud *crack*! He crumpled to the floor, unable to breathe. He clutched his side, miraculously found it was not bleeding—then his brain caught up with his pain. The Yeti had struck him with the blunt side of the axe.

The Yeti roared in disgust at the apparent lack of blood. Looming over the prostrate body of its attacker, the creature reared back with the ice axe, the muscles in its shoulders rippling with rage. Snarling with exertion, the Yeti brought the axe down.

Preston closed his eyes.

The blow never came.

When his eyes reopened, he saw what had happened.

Conner had revived himself and somehow managed to grasp the axe over the Yeti's head. Holding on, he was being lifted clear off the ground, tossed around like a puppet, but his weight was slowing the axe on its path. Preston scrambled out of harm's way.

With a second bone-crunching blow, the Yeti swung its free hand toward Conner's head, smashing him in the temple. Ricocheting from the blow, Conner smacked into the wall with an audible *thwack*. He twitched once, then was still.

A thin line of blood leaked from his skull onto the ice floor.

"Conner!"

One foe vanquished, the Yeti turned back toward Preston.

He was still down on one knee, his arm pressed protectively against his cracked thorax. He saw Conner's lifeless body, cried out to him again. "Conner!"

No answer.

Preston rose slowly to face the creature. He reached for the object lashed to his climbing harness and pulled it free. The Yeti tilted its massive head.

"That's right; it's just me and you now. Come to Papa."

The Yeti obliged, hurtling across the cavern, the axe held high over its head.

The axe sliced the air like a scythe on a dead angle for Preston's forehead. Rising up to meet the blow, Preston lunged forward, thrusting the sharp end of his trekking pole up and into the Yeti's solar plexus. And when Preston felt the steel point lodge deep inside the creature's stomach, he pressed the trigger button.

The Yeti's flesh rippled with electricity.

A rush of ecstasy coursed through Preston's body.

Simultaneously, the Yeti's axe blow continued its deadly arc downward, slicing cleanly through Preston's left temple.

With his final breath, Preston felt the pole pulse with electricity. Even as the Yeti howled in agony, Preston heard the *crunch* of his own skull splintering apart.

The last thing he felt was warm Yeti blood as it spilled out over his hands.

CHAPTER FORTY

Kuk Sur
19,011 Feet

"Preston!"

Conner couldn't stop himself from crying out. As he watched the Yeti lodge the axe blade into the side of Preston's head, grief exploded out of his mouth. He had roused himself just in time to see the old climber's lifeless body crumple to the ground, his hand still clutching the handle of his trekking pole. Preston's face was contorted in an odd grimace. It resembled, Conner thought, a smile.

The Yeti turned at the outburst, slowly as if the creature couldn't quite believe its quarry was still breathing. It made no move to attack. The beast looked down to its midsection, to the trekking pole still stabbed into its flesh. Dark blood spilled forth. The Yeti staggered to one knee.

"Not used to getting hurt, are you?" Conner said. "It doesn't feel so good, does it?"

With a quick flip of its wrist, the creature wrenched the pole from its stomach. Without so much as a whimper. Conner had seen Preston's trekking pole deliver a near deathblow to a six hundred-pound tiger, and the Yeti had just tossed it aside like a nuisance.

He studied the creature's face. For the first time, he could see a series of furrowed lines across its leathery skin. Wrinkles creased the animal's eyes. A three-inch scar marred its jaw line.

It's old, Conner realized. Maybe the last in what was once a proud line of hominids. Who knew? For a brief moment, he felt something for this old creature bleeding before him. It was, after all, just a creature struggling to survive. Not so different from Conner himself.

The beast rose to its feet.

Conner swept the ground beside him, looking for anything to fight off the Yeti—a rock, anything. He saw the charred remains of the body he and Preston had shot up just moments before. He now recognized the body— Bill Greenback. If only the engineer hadn't run off on his own—

Another remnant of Greenback's body caught Conner's attention. What was left of his head had come to rest against the wall of the cave. The back of his skull had been completely shorn away, revealing a pulpy mixture of blood, pink brain matter, and scalp. A series of deep gouges cut across his soft brain tissue.

Fang marks.

The Yeti had gnawed the back of Greenback's head off.

In all likelihood, the engineer had already been dead when the shooting started. With a shock of comprehension, Conner realized that the Yeti had pushed Greenback out of the tunnel as bait.

Jesus Christ. What chance did he possibly have against something so monstrous and so clever?

Conner's hands brushed against Preston's second trekking pole. He stood and jabbed the air with the steel tip as menacingly as he could manage in the face of the towering creature. The Yeti glowered, but made no move to attack.

Conner jumped at the hesitation. He took off like a shot, sprinting toward the ice wall as fast as his legs would carry him. The opening in the ice was just visible, the safety ropes dangling just outside. He ran harder.

He dared not look over his shoulder for fear of slowing himself down, but he could feel the Yeti on his heels.

Conner dove into the smaller cave and dragged himself toward the opening. He grabbed Preston's harness and in one smooth motion slung his shoulder through the cloth straps. The Yeti was crawling through the cave, a sharpened claw snapping at Conner's boot.

Conner took a deep breath—

—and jumped through the gap in the ice.

He fell through thin air.

And grabbed the safety rope with his bare hands. The

frozen nylon burned his skin, but his grip somehow held firm. Holding on with one hand, he snapped a carabiner through his harness and clipped it to the safety bolt. He dangled two hundred feet above the ground.

He glanced down and saw Tess rappelling far below. Malika, descending solo, had caught up to Wade on the ice field. They were little more than colored dots against the silvery ice below.

Don't stop now. Whatever you do, don't stop now.

Suddenly, the ice wall over Conner's head exploded.

The Yeti burst through in an eruption of ice shards. Roaring with rage, the beast soared through the air, claws outstretched, crouching like a pouncing ape. It plunged past Conner, falling fast.

With a wide swipe of his impossibly long arms, the Yeti slammed its talons into the ice wall. A shower of ice rained down as the creature gouged deep into the face. A second clawed hand thrust into the ice, and the creature came to a stop. It clung to the wall halfway between Conner and Tess.

"Don't look up," Conner silently admonished her. "Do *not* look up."

But the uproar had already captured her attention. She looked up, and Conner could see her eyes widen with fear. She kicked off from the ice, moving frantically now, feeding the rope through her harness as fast as she could. She fell ever faster down the face.

The Yeti paid her no mind. Instead, the beast lifted its head to look up at Conner.

And began to hack his way *up* the face.

Shards of ice cleaved away as the beast jammed its claws into the wall, ascending like the tree-climbing lions of the Masai Mara.

Conner was trapped. He tried to weigh his options, but there were none. If he rappelled, he would descend right into the approaching Yeti. He could cut away from the ropes and take his chances back in the caves. He would have a few minutes' head start, but the array of tunnels could lead to dead ends at any turn. It would only be a matter of time before the Yeti hunted him down in the dizzying passages.

He stole a look down the ice face. The Yeti was climbing quickly, spraying ice with each clawed step. And then Conner glimpsed something glistening in the ice.

An ice bolt.

It was about thirty feet down, just below the approaching creature.

As far as options go, it wasn't very promising. But he didn't have much of a choice.

Using Preston's trekking pole, Conner smashed the tip into the ice encasing his supporting ice bolt. Shards chipped away from the screw. But it was a deep one, four inches. He smashed the tip again into the ice.

The Yeti clawed its way to within five feet of Conner's dangling boots.

The steel tip slammed into the ice again. The bolt creaked loose. Still holding.

Something seized his boot. He kicked out without looking down.

Last chance . . .

Sharpened claws dug into his calf, causing Conner to scream out in pain. This time, he couldn't shake the grip loose. But the Yeti was in no position to do anything; it needed to climb higher to get leverage. The beast let go. Jammed another talon into the ice, grasping upwards . . .

It was the break Conner needed.

With all of his remaining energy, he slammed the point of the trekking pole into the ice.

The ice bolt fell free.

Conner kicked out from the ice face—

—and soared in a giant arc over the outstretched arms of the Yeti.

Conner hurtled through the air, tumbling. He plunged sixty feet in seconds. Then the slack tightened. He swung back toward the ice wall.

He braced for the impact.

Conner crashed into the cliff—shattering through the wall in an explosion of razor-sharp ice. He landed with a thud behind the wall. Rousing himself quickly, he found himself inside another cave. He scrambled back out to the ropes to see that the safety bolt had been dislodged by the force of his plunge. There was no sign of the Yeti above, but the beast would be coming. With no time to lay new bolts even if he had some, which he didn't, Conner was out of options.

He untied his ropes and let his harness fall to the ground. Glancing around the ledge—much like the one seventy feet above his head—he saw a passage disappear into the darkness.

Conner dashed down the murky tunnel.

CHAPTER FORTY-ONE

Kuk Sur
18,522 Feet

Tess was in free fall. Her anchor had been wrenched out by Conner's frantic descent. Luckily, at the moment the bolt came free, she was only ten feet above the ground. She landed on her back, her breath knocked from her lungs. Looking up, Tess could see the dark shape of the Yeti ninety feet up the face. The terrifying image spurred her to her feet. Her back groaned in protest.

Malika and Wade had already reached the ground and were waiting for her with anxious eyes.

"What just happened?" Tess demanded. "Where's Conner?"

"I'm not sure," Malika replied. "It looked like he went through the wall. Probably inside another ice cave."

"We can't go without him. We have to go back."

"There's no way to—"

A tug on Malika's jacket stopped her. Wade was pointing toward the ice wall. He was trembling.

Tess looked up. "*No*—"

The Yeti was careening down the ice face, using its crampon-like claws in a furious descent. Sparks of ice rained down on the climbers.

"Move!" Tess yelled.

She shoved Malika and Wade toward the ridge.

Jutting from the base of the ice wall like a knife blade, the narrow crest descended at a dangerously steep sixty-degree angle. Rock cut through the crest like a stony spine. Stretching from the ice wall above to the front edge of the glacier below, the ridge cut between two deep valleys, stretching hundreds of vertical feet on either side.

Any fall here would be a fatal one.

Tess tried not to look down as she stepped onto the ridge. Her crampons grated against the bare rock. Malika took the lead, half-running down the ridge. Wade followed, limping badly now. Tess stopped him and quickly fastened a safety rope between their two harnesses.

"Run as fast as you can," she told him. "If you fall, I will hold you."

Wade nodded and moved quickly down the knife ridge.

Tess chanced a glance back over her shoulder. She couldn't see the Yeti, but sensed it was there. Racing closer.

Wade's foot slipped on the frozen rock, and Tess felt

the support rope tighten around her waist. The injured climber recovered quickly and, without a look back, dashed down the ridge.

Farther down the ridge, Malika reached the crevasse field. She turned and began to scream for the others to hurry.

Wade, perhaps trying to move too quickly, slipped again. He fell to his knees, barely clinging to the rock to stop himself from plunging off the cliff. This time he rose a bit more slowly.

"Come on, Wade!" she called out. "You can make it! We've got to get to the ice fall!"

Even as she yelled her encouragement, Tess felt the Yeti's hulking gait upon the ridge. Closer. She quickly judged the distance to the field below.

It was too far. Though she couldn't see the creature, she knew it was close. And she had witnessed the Yeti's startling speed.

That was when it dawned on her.

We're not going to make it.

Tess stopped running and turned back to the ridge. A plume of snow billowed off the crest, obscuring her view beyond twenty feet. But she sensed the beast there. At any moment, the Yeti would bound down upon her. It was hopeless.

She glanced down the ridge. Malika had turned back to the crest and was now staring anxiously up at Tess and Wade from the icefall. And screaming.

Tess whirled just as the Yeti burst into view. It was loping on all fours—more ape-like than human—hurtling through the air between its muscular strides. Jaws snapping, claws extending.

Ten feet away.

Tess pressed her eyes closed.

And prayed.

And then a strange sound echoed across the mountain. For a moment, Tess dared not open her eyes, but when the sound grew louder, more insistent, she risked a look.

The Blackhawk rescue chopper rose from the valley like a phoenix, hovering just off the ridge. Its rotor wash blasted Tess with a bone-numbing rush of air and snow and ice. She crouched down to regain her balance. The din was deafening. The crest filled with a maelstrom of snow. Visibility plummeted to nothing.

And then Wade materialized beside her, pulling her. At the rim of the crevasse field, Malika had stopped screaming.

Tess peered up the ridge through the billowing snow.

The Yeti had disappeared.

CHAPTER
FORTY-TWO

Kuk Sur
19,342 Feet

Despite all intentions to the contrary, Conner Michaels was climbing.

After his trapeze-like ride over the Yeti and the crash through the brittle ice wall, he had found himself with few options. His safety bolts had ripped from the ice, so rappelling down the face was not an option. Without an ice axe, a free climb would be suicide.

After watching the Yeti force-slide down the ice wall after the fleeing forms of Malika, Wade, and Tess, Conner had lost sight of the action. They still had a healthy lead, but the creature was moving fast. Not knowing their fate drove him crazy. He felt helpless and cursed. But there was nothing he could do for them now. He could only take care of himself, get down there as fast as he could.

Get to the rescue helicopter—that was his only objective.

And so he had turned his attention to the passage that led directly into the mountain.

Conner had followed the tunnel as it wound its way through the ice, down to the rocky core of the peak. Smaller caves and passages branched off the main artery, but he quickly determined they led nowhere. He searched the shadowy recesses for any chamber that led down, but it was as if he was on the ground floor of a towering building. Nowhere to go but up.

The tunnel arched steeply, but the rocky ground made the going easier. After just thirty minutes, Conner guessed he had ascended nearly five hundred feet.

Five hundred feet? he realized suddenly. *That would put me above the Yeti's lair.*

He stopped to consider the predicament. He was confident he had explored all of the other passages, but it was obvious that he had somehow missed the entrance to the Yeti's lair. But with his brother's bones somewhere inside, Conner didn't mind sidestepping that den of death.

All he wanted was to find another way out. He needed to get off this fucking mountain, wanted to make sure Tess and Wade and Malika had eluded the Yeti and made it down to the rescue chopper. The pilot had promised to wait on flat ground somewhere around seventeen thousand feet. He could deliver them back to base camp, where they would be safe.

Until he could see for himself they had made it, Conner wouldn't stop. He had to get down to base camp.

But without equipment of any kind except a battered climbing harness and some cams and chocks—hell, he wasn't even wearing crampons anymore, and his ropes had long since been discarded—getting back down the mountain would be a serious mission. But Conner didn't want to concern himself with that just yet.

Find a way out of the caves first; then worry about getting down.

His purpose reestablished, Conner continued his solo ascent.

Kuk Sur
18,664 Feet

Tess and Malika clung to each other like reunited sisters as the rescue chopper settled onto a flat expanse amidst the broken crevasse field. Ducking instinctively, more against the whipping ice particles than the rotors themselves, Tess and Malika followed Wade up to the helicopter. They clambered in, assisted by the pilot who had moved into the main compartment to help. He identified himself as Ang Tshering, a pilot in the Chinese Army, and pointed to a thermos of hot coffee and a small pile of dry blankets. He quickly conducted triage evaluations of the climbers' various injuries. By his reaction at the sight of Wade's mangled face, Tess guessed the pilot was concerned. Tshering practically jumped back into the cockpit.

Just as quickly, the chopper lifted off again, jerked in the thin air, and banked down the mountain, soaring down the glacial valley.

Tess glanced down for one final look at the crevasse field.

And remembered.

She was lying upon the icefall, on her back, clutching a frozen nylon rope with both hands as if in a tug-of-war. The end of the rope was affixed tightly to her climbing harness. The heels of her crampons dug into the icepack. Her knees wobbled with strain.

On the other end of the rope, Conner dangled helplessly inside the crevasse. Below him, Tucker Michaels clung desperately to life. Snatches of frantic conversation rose up to the crevasse rim.

"Can you brace yourself? You need to use your axe!" Conner screamed down to his brother.

"Arm's . . . broken. Can't . . . hold—"

"Tucker, can you see the bottom?"

"No. Too dark. But there's a ledge. If I can swing a little, I may—"

"Okay, Tucker, do it. I'm going to help you swing."

Tess's crampon slipped through the ice. The combined weight of Conner and his brother yanked her toward the precipice. Two inches from the rim, her crampon caught again. She struggled to maintain balance, felt herself losing.

"Cut him loose!" she screamed down the chasm. "Cut him loose!"

Conner called out to her, desperation filling his voice. "Hang on, Tess! Just a minute longer!"

But she couldn't do it. She couldn't hold on for one second longer. The weight was just too much. One more moment and she would go tumbling into the deep crevasse, Conner and Tucker with her. She had to do something. Fighting against every screaming fiber of emotion in her body, she knew that if she wanted to live, she had to cut them loose.

With her elbow, she managed to loose her ice axe from her waist. It fell to the ground beside her.

Her eyes filled with frozen tears. "I'm sorry, Conner."

In one smooth motion, Tess released the rope and reached for the blade. Her equilibrium momentarily interrupted, she felt herself falling forward. Clutching the haft of the axe, she swung it down. The blade sliced through the nylon rope—

—and she cut them free.

But the rope held. The blade had only pierced the mantle, leaving the inner core of the braided cord intact. She readied herself for a second blow.

And then she felt the crushing burden ease. She grasped the rope with both hands. She heard Conner's voice drift out of the chasm. "Tucker! Tucker, can you hear me? TUCKER . . .!"

"Tess?"

Reality came rushing back at her. She was back on

the chopper, Malika staring anxiously at her. She smiled weakly; turned back to the window.

Everybody had their own reasons for entering *Darwin's Race*. Wade wanted glory. Conner was searching for salvation from years of guilt-induced seclusion. Tess, too, had come to Kuk Sur with a specific purpose. Redemption. Six years ago, she had made the gut-wrenching decision to save herself. To abandon Conner and his brother. It had been a twist of fate that only Tucker had perished. But that's not what mattered to her. In that singular moment, Tess saw what was in her own soul. And she didn't like what she found there.

After they returned from Tibet, she could hardly bear to watch Conner writhe in his grief. But even as he suffered, she was battling demons of her own. What role had she played in Tucker's death? First, she had insisted they cross the snow bridge—*It's silly to go around*, she had argued. *We'll waste hours. There's a perfectly good bridge right in front of us.*

It was not, as it turned out, a perfectly good bridge. Had she missed the warning signs? Had she been so hell-bent on reaching the summit that she had ignored the thickness of the ice? The streaks of black that warned of internal fissures?

And then, when the snow bridge collapsed and all hell broke loose, what had she done? She had tried to save herself—at the expense of the man she loved and his brother. Just to look into Conner's anguished face was pure torment.

In the end, she could stand it no longer. The guilt was too great. While Conner was out kayaking on the water, she had packed and slipped away, never to return.

She had let him down once. She wasn't about to do it again.

Tess immediately climbed into the cockpit. "We can't go down!" she yelled over the roar of the rotor blades. "There's still one more up there. Conner Michaels is still up there!"

The pilot stared at her through a black faceplate. "Up? Up?" he asked in heavily accented English.

"I don't know. Somewhere up on the ice face. Maybe nineteen thousand?"

The pilot shook his head. "No nineteen, no nineteen. Only here. No higher. We go higher, and we crash for sure."

"We have to go back!" she screamed. "He's up there!"

"No higher," Ang Tshering repeated. "No nineteen."

"So what can we do?"

"No nineteen. He come down here," the pilot said. "We circle here, wait here."

Tess slumped back in her seat. This time, it was Malika that comforted her, wrapping a thick wool blanket around her shoulders and forcing her to sip from the thermos. Though the coffee warmed her body, her stomach turned at the thought that somewhere, somewhere up there, Conner Michaels was all alone.

CHAPTER FORTY-THREE

Kuk Sur
21,694 Feet

Conner stood at a gaping hole in the side of Kuk Sur.

After climbing for what had seemed like an eternity, he had finally stumbled upon a tunnel that extended to the outside world. Anxious at seeing sunlight—the purple-hued light of dusk—Conner raced to the mouth of the cave. He closed his eyes and breathed in the fresh air.

He opened them again to find he was standing at the precipice of a giant abyss. Over five hundred feet of vertical ice and rock yawned open at his feet. The entire Himalayan mountain range stretched out before him.

Another dead end.

This time, Conner began to worry. Was there any way off this mountain? All of the tunnels seemed to lead up. He knew to backtrack through the maze of chambers searching for a passage that would lead to lower elevations would be fruitless. The only other choice was to take his chances upon the dangerous slopes of the mountain—with no equipment. In the dark.

He was trapped.

He leaned out from the cave and craned his head toward the summit. It was surprisingly close. The snow-covered peak was no more than two hundred feet above his head. An exposed ridgeline rose from just outside the cave mouth directly to the peak, practically begging to be climbed.

Conner pulled his fleece collar up around his ears and zipped his down jacket up to his chin. He stepped from the cave mouth into a fierce alpine gust. Clambering on all fours, he climbed onto a narrow ledge, and pulled himself up to the ridgeline. Ignoring the five hundred-foot drop below his boots, he pushed higher, hoping the summit would afford him a three hundred sixty-degree view of the mountain. Then he could make a survey of all possible routes of descent. There might be a clear way down the north face. Mother Nature had not defeated him just yet.

Approaching the summit, Conner suddenly felt the cold and the altitude rush at him like a hurricane. He had climbed nearly three thousand vertical feet in a single day. Dangerously fast. Though he didn't feel affected, victims of pulmonary edema rarely did.

He deliberately slowed his pace. *Step-inhale-exhale. Step-inhale-exhale.*

The elements battered him. He had to hunch over to avoid being blown off the mountainside. His lungs that had grown accustomed to the relative warmth of the cave air now burned in the sub-zero Himalayan air. The dizzying lack of oxygen robbed his muscles of fuel. His legs wobbled with fatigue, his head ached like it was being squeezed in a vise, but through all that a familiar feeling washed over Conner's body. It was, he realized with surprise, exhilaration.

Conner hadn't felt the exhilaration of a summit attempt—he called it the "elation of elevation"—for over six years, and he was stunned by the acuteness of its return. If they could bottle this feeling, the utter euphoria of stepping on the top of a mountain, the world would be a far better place. This feeling was the reason Conner Michaels had become a climber.

He could see the summit, a sharp pinnacle of wind-blown rock surrounded by a narrow plateau of packed snow. Just a few feet more.

With a surge of adrenaline, he placed his right boot atop the summit of Kuk Sur.

For just a moment, he forgot everything that was going on below him. In the back of his mind, Conner knew there was nothing he could do for Tess. Or Wade. Or Malika Child. So, as he had done on so many summits before, he gave himself over to the feeling.

And it happened again. The superfluous elements of his life slipped away. All thoughts of mortgage payments, loose planks on his dock, and sore knees evaporated into the thin air. Even his arguments with Terrance Carlton were forgotten. And when everything else had been stripped away, Conner was left with only one thing.

The essence of his life.

Powder was dead. He had struggled mightily to rescue her from the clutches of the mighty river, but it was not to be. There was nothing he could've done to save her.

Tucker was dead, too. And there was nothing he could do to change that. No amount of solitary grief was going to bring him back to life. No amount of solitary guilt was going to resurrect his brother. What had happened on the blustery slopes of Kuk Sur six years before was not his fault.

Not his fault.

The guilt that had churned within his heart for so long now lifted up toward the heavens.

And he was free.

Standing there atop the mountain, Conner felt his spirit soar. Like God himself had reached down and lifted a great weight from his shoulders. He remembered a favorite passage from the Tibetan Book of the Dead and recited it aloud.

"When I am chased by snow, rain, wind, and darkness, may I receive the clear, divine eye of Wisdom."

And then he began to cry. For a full minute, he sobbed unabashedly, his cries rising up to the clouds. Tears of grief, of guilt, of joy, streamed down his face, releasing what had consumed him for so long. The tears froze upon his bare cheeks.

And then it was over. A biting gust of wind swept over

the peak, blasting Conner. The freeze brought his attention back to the predicament at hand. He was standing twenty-two thousand feet above sea level, with no ropes, no climbing harness, and no crampons. All he had was a handful of chocks and the old camming device he had removed from Tucker's backpack. A lot of good that would do him now.

Kuk Sur stretched out beneath him like a giant pyramid, with sheer slopes on all four faces. Even with proper gear, those routes would be extremely technical. Without gear, they were all but impossible. Conner quickly ruled them out.

He was left with two options.

The first was to retrace his steps through the caves and search for another way down. Perhaps he could find his way back to the Yeti's lair. Take his chances with the frozen ropes left by Wade and Blaine.

There was one other alternative. To the northeast, a narrow ridgeline fell away from the summit like a bent saddle. It was not steep, angling down toward a distant peak of another mountain in the Kukuranda. Conner did not relish traversing the exposed crest in this wind, in the dark; plus it did little to get him down to base camp. Wrong direction.

So there really was only one option. The caves. He *must've* missed something. Certainly the Yeti did not enter his own lair through the portal near the peak.

Conner shook his head. Of course he had missed something. In his state of fatigue, he shouldn't have been surprised. It was the only practical way down—and besides, inside the caverns he could escape the elements and the footing was more stable.

Still he hesitated. Backtracking would mean he would have to reenter the lair of the Yeti.

Taking a deep breath, Conner surveyed the view one final time. He could see the curvature of the earth from here, as if he were standing on the top of the world. A final surge of elation coursed through his body as he realized he alone had reached the summit. That was, if nothing else, something. He turned back toward the cave.

And stopped dead in his tracks.

The Yeti was there, standing atop the ridge. A mane of silver fur fluttered in the wind. Frozen blood lined its stomach and legs like crooked lightning strikes. The creature's left arm hung limply at its side as if broken.

Conner stared ahead. "You look like shit."

The Yeti took a step forward. Conner could see its leg was injured, too. *So you're hurt, huh? That evens things up a bit.*

As if suddenly sensing its place on the mountain, the Yeti paused and gazed to the horizon. The creature took in the entire view, rotating his head all the way to take in every side of the mountain. The creature drew a hand up to its bloodied chest.

Conner recognized the gesture.

"All this is yours; I know. Mother Nature crowned you King of the Mountain. Top of the food chain, right? But then something happened. Someone else came along to challenge you. Someone else encroached on your territory. *Us.*"

The Yeti tilted its massive head.

"That's right. *Humans.* And I almost feel sorry for you, under siege up here on your mountain. But you had to live; you had to eat. So like any other animal, even like us, you had to kill. But then you killed my brother."

The creature took a thundering step forward.

Conner stood his ground. "You killed my brother, and now you're coming to kill me. And you'll probably do it, seeing as how I have nowhere to go. But there will be others after me. Now that they know you exist, they will come. But I'm not going to lie down. You killed my brother and for that, you earned yourself a fight. So come on, let's see what you've got."

The Yeti began to run. It dropped to all fours, loping like a charging gorilla.

"Come on!" Conner roared.

The beast leaped.

With an ear-splitting roar, the Yeti soared impossibly high into the air, claws and feet extended. Aiming directly at Conner's chest. Eight hundred pounds of brute attack force. He would not survive a direct hit.

But he was ready. As the Yeti arced closer, Conner hurled himself from the peak—

—into a free fall!

He crumpled to a narrow ledge he had spotted just beneath the summit. Scrambled quickly to avoid slipping off into the cavernous abyss below. The Yeti soared overhead, landing like thunder atop the summit. The creature wobbled momentarily on its injured leg.

Conner seized the opportunity. Grabbing the injured leg with both hands, he yanked with all the strength he could muster. The leg swept out from underneath the creature. The Yeti toppled backwards, plunging out of sight on the far side of the summit rock.

Conner stood for a moment atop the ledge, listening. His heaving gasps for air abated; his racing heartbeat slowed to normal. There was no sign of the creature.

"That was for my brother."

With both hands, Conner hauled himself to the summit.

He peered over the edge.

"You gotta be kidding me."

The Yeti was clinging with one hand to an inch-wide spit of exposed rock, its body dangling helplessly five hundred feet above the glacier floe below.

Conner loomed over the creature, placing his boot over its thick fingers.

"It's better this way," he said.

Conner reared his foot back, ready to kick the creature into oblivion.

"Welcome to extinction."

But then the Yeti's flailing foot found purchase. With staggering strength, the beast reached up with his free hand, grabbed the ledge and, kicking up with its massive leg muscles, hurtled itself up into the air.

The Yeti soared clear over his head, landing on its feet along the ridge behind him.

Conner whirled in awe.

"Okay," he said. "*That* was cool."

The Yeti charged, fangs bared. This time, Conner wasn't prepared. He absorbed the brunt of attack into his chest. He was knocked flat to his back atop the summit. The beast pounced, straddling his prostrate body. Slowly, the Yeti leaned over and ran a leathery finger across Conner's cheek.

The creature reared back with a clawed fist for the deathblow.

Then stopped. The Yeti jerked erect, ears perked.

For a moment, Conner could hear only the screaming wind. And then, something else.

Conner followed the Yeti's gaze.

There, silhouetted against the setting sun, was something impossible.

A helicopter.

It was the HH-60G Blackhawk. And it was shooting straight up the mountain! The chopper climbed at a sharp angle, hugging the sheer slopes, rotors screaming.

He can't maintain that climb, Conner realized. *There's not enough air.*

Using its speed and momentum to fight gravity, the chopper surged higher. But it was a battle it could not win.

The chopper would plummet at any moment.

Conner had one final chance.

While the Yeti was still transfixed by the approaching helicopter, Conner scrambled away. Climbed to his feet.

The chopper's rotors groaned, straining the metal to the breaking point.

Come on. Another forty feet.

Conner's sudden movement broke the Yeti's reverie. The beast seized him with both arms, crushing out what little air he had in his lungs. The crack of bone echoed. Lights and stars danced before Conner's eyes. Consciousness blinked.

Out of the corner of his eye, Conner saw the rescue chopper rise level with the peak. Then, in a cough of exhaust, the engine sputtered. The rotors stalled. The chopper struggled to hover just above the summit.

This is it.

With the last ounce of energy in his being, Conner slipped a hand to his waist, fumbling for his harness. He felt his ribs implode, popping one by one in the beast's vise-grip. Conner's fingers found what they were searching for. Working feverishly now, he managed to unclip the object from his harness.

And then, as blackness threatened to overtake him, Conner shoved outward, thrusting the camming device—Tucker's bloodied camming device—deep into the Yeti's open stomach wound. The beast howled in agony. Released Conner from its death hold.

"This time," Conner rasped. "My brother gets to end it."

He released the trigger.

The camming device exploded outward like an erupting volcano. Serrated gears tore through the Yeti's abdomen, obliterating flesh and bone, spraying hot entrails into Conner's face.

The Yeti clutched for the cam, desperately trying to tug it free. But it wouldn't budge. The steel trap held fast. Just like it was designed to do.

The creature fell to its knees—blood flowing now from its mouth— and collapsed forward, crumpling in a lifeless heap upon the summit rock. The creature's fur—matted with ice and snow and blood—fluttered in the helicopter's rotor wash.

Conner took a deep breath, felt his rib bones jut in unnatural places. Every bone in his body wailed in agony, but somehow he managed to climb up to his knees, then to his feet.

The chopper hovered just off the mountainside. The pilot was unable to maneuver close enough for Conner to reach the cabin door. It was miracle enough that the chopper was still holding at this altitude. From the main cabin, Tess gestured towards the landing rods.

Reaching out with both hands, Conner grabbed hold and, with a kick, threw his legs around the struts. The helicopter banked slowly away, drifting down into the valley, towards lower—and more stable—altitudes.

Squinting against the wind, Conner turned his gaze

up toward the summit. It was now hundreds of feet above his head, and awash in swirling snow. The snow concealed the pinnacle rock, obscuring the Yeti's lifeless corpse.

But it was over.

Conner was too exhausted to shout out in exultation, but inside he was screaming like crazy.

He laid his head on the landing strut and took a deep breath.

A hand reached down from the chopper's cabin.

CHAPTER
FORTY-FOUR

Forward Base Camp
17,483 Feet

The HH-60G Blackhawk touched down a few yards
from the production tent at forward base camp. A crowd of
crew members gathered, shielding themselves from the icy exhaust, carrying blankets and medical supplies. Anxious faces
waited to see who would emerge from the rescue chopper.

Wade was the first to disembark, and gasps rose up from
the crew at the sight of his mangled face. Exhausted, he staggered from the cabin. A trio of medical technicians sprung
to action and quickly ushered him toward the medical tent.

Conner climbed out next, flanked by Tess and Malika.
Scattered applause rose from the crew, but was quickly ex-
tinguished as they realized there were no others.

Another med tech approached Conner and began to

dab at the various cuts on his face.

"I'm fine," he said, shrugging her off. "A couple of broken ribs, maybe. No big deal. Go take care of Wade. He needs all the help he can get."

The young woman sprinted away, Tess following closely behind. Conner watched her go.

He hoped—genuinely—that Wade would pull through. There had already been enough death in these mountains.

Someone called out to make way, and they were swept into the production tent. He lost sight of Malika in the throng, but it felt good to escape the harsh elements outside. He immediately stripped out of his heavy jacket. Someone handed him a hot thermos. He took a deep pull. Relished the burn in his stomach.

Terrance Carlton pushed his way through the crowd. "What the hell happened up there? Where are the others?"

"Others? There are no others," Conner said somberly. "Preston, Blaine, Hoops. They're all dead. Your engineer, too."

"Greenback? How—?"

Conner drew up to within an inch of the producer's face. "Never mind how. They're gone." Out of the corner of his eye, he noticed a young crew member approach, a small video recorder perched on his shoulder.

"And the creature?" Carlton pressed. "Was it a Yeti? Was it real?"

Conner pointed toward the cameraman. "You're still

recording?"

"Of course. This is a television show."

"No, Carlton. That's where you're wrong. This is life."

"If you don't talk, there's no prize money. That's in your contract."

Conner shook his head. "Prize money? Carlton, I don't want your prize money. I expect you to pay the entire two million dollars in equal payments to the families of Cale Anders, Bill Greenback, Powder Freyer, and Paul Robeson."

"And why would I do such a thing? There's no contractual reason—"

"Because if you don't, I'm going to call a press conference the second I get back home to explain to the world how you knowingly manipulated this race to put the competitors in harm's way. That ought to put a damper on your ratings success."

"But that's not true!" Carlton yelled. "I didn't know. I didn't know anything."

"By the time you convince everyone of that, I'm pretty sure your television career will be in shambles. So I'm betting that you'll do exactly as I say: honor the families of the racers who died during your race, and pay them the prize money. You'll come across as a caring guy, and you'll get to reap the benefits of *Darwin's Race*. If you do this, Carlton, I suspect the offers will come rolling in. The networks will be fighting each other for your next project."

The notion seemed to mollify the producer somewhat.

"But what about you, Conner? You said from the beginning that you wanted to take care of your brother's family. What about them? If you don't get any of the money, how are you going to help them?"

Conner smiled. "Leave it to a television producer to believe that money solves everything. But now that you mention it, Malika Child has agreed to set up Melanie and Jake so they don't have to worry about money anymore. Now that Malika controls her father's empire, she has that kind of clout. And the best part? The only thing she asked for in return was my silence. No interviews, no magazine articles. We're going to honor her father's death by staying out of the press. Going on television to talk about it would cheapen everything; don't you think?"

Carlton hung his head. He knew when he was beaten. "You've got it all figured out; don't you, Conner?"

"No," Conner said. "But I'm getting there."

He turned and walked out of the tent. He could hear Carlton yelling after him.

"You're a fool, Conner! It was a Yeti up there. I know it! And I'm going to prove it. I'm not just going to sit back and walk away from the story of the century!"

The producer's words faded into the cool breezes of the Tibetan dusk. Conner continued across the courtyard and into the medical tent.

Wade Stanley was lying on a cot, an oxygen mask strapped across his nose and mouth. A stream of tubes snaked from his arm into bags of fluid. Tess looked up at

Conner's approach. Her face was streaked with blood and tears.

"How's he doing?" Conner asked.

"He's going to make it."

They had cleaned up most of the blood on Wade's body. A thick gauze bandage wrapped around his jaw. "He's going to need you. Now more than ever."

Tess rose from Wade's side and wrapped her arms around Conner's body. He squeezed back, feeling years of bitterness drift away. They held each other for a full minute without speaking.

"But what's going to happen to us?" Tess asked. "Are we good?"

Conner smiled. "We're good. I guess a piece of me will always love you, but I realize I was hanging on to you because you represented someplace safe for me. A place that existed before Tucker died. I just didn't want to let go of that."

"And now?"

"I'm still not sure if I'm ready. But I'm at least ready to try."

"And Malika? Am I wrong to think that there might be something there?"

Conner chuckled. "I'm not sure if I'm entirely comfortable discussing this with you, but if you must know . . . Yeah, there might be something there. But not now. I'm not sure she ever properly grieved for her mother, and now she's got Preston's death to deal with. She needs time. We both need time. Who knows what will happen down the road. But for now, I need to take care of myself first, too."

"You're going to do fine, Conner Michaels," Tess said. She placed her head against his chest.

Conner kissed her forehead and broke from her embrace. She knelt down beside Wade and dabbed a wet cloth to his forehead. His eyes blinked open, grateful to see her there. Conner slipped from the tent, leaving the two to their moment.

He emerged into the purple twilight of the Himalayas. He could barely see the summit amidst the descending cloud cover. Atop that peak, a clear vision had appeared to him—a new basis for proceeding. He knew it would be difficult—accepting the death of a loved one always was—but this time he would turn to others for help. His brother's family, Melanie and Jake, needed him—maybe as much as he needed them. And now he was ready for that.

But for all his progress, Mother Nature had once again exacted her toll. And this time, he doubted if he would ever be the same. It would be a long time before he challenged her again. It just wasn't worth it anymore. If it had ever been.

Mother Nature couldn't be beaten.

Malika emerged from the production tent and joined Conner as he stared up at the peak of Kuk Sur.

"What are you thinking about?" she asked.

"Not a thing," he said. "And it sure feels good."

Malika gestured back toward the studio. "You know Carlton's inside talking about another race. Can you imagine?"

"Not me," Conner said, smiling. "I'm retired."

CHAPTER FORTY-FIVE

Kuk Sur
19,215 Feet

Ang Tshering and his copilot Dawa wrestled with the wreckage of the Eurocopter EC 145. Four other members of the cleanup crew had been gathering up the remnants of the chopper for the past four hours.

The bodies of the crew had already been taken to Lhasa for a proper Buddhist burial. That left only two tons of twisted steel to clear. The crumpled helicopter would have to be dismantled piece by piece to get it off the mountain. It certainly would never fly again.

It had been four days since the crew of *Darwin's Race* had departed, removing even the smallest scrap of base camp. A fleet of UH-1 Huey helicopters had carried the crew and equipment toward Lhasa, where Tshering knew they had continued overland to the international airport in

Katmandu.

They would be landing back in the United States soon.

The Chinese Army had sent a full mountain detachment into the mountains to retrieve the body of the *Meh-Teh*. After two weeks they returned, claiming they had found no trace of the creature. The wind had blown the creature from the summit, they announced. The veteran pilot knew better; he had lived with the Chinese since they invaded Tibet. They had discovered the *Meh-Teh*, all right, and now they would keep it for themselves. The world would hear nothing further of the great beast.

"Hey, Dawa, throw me that wrench!" he called in Chinese to his copilot. The fuselage was giving him trouble; he would have to wrestle with its frozen bolts. It was grueling work, but he wouldn't want to be anywhere else. He certainly wouldn't want to be with the crew of *Darwin's Race*.

There would be tough questions to answer. From the families of the dead racers. Tshering counted nine dead, including a chopper crew he had known since birth. And it could've been much worse. For them, Tshering had tied a prayer flag to a shabby *mani* wall he and his crew had erected at the site of the abandoned base camp.

And there would be questions from the authorities, though the pilot didn't know for sure how the American justice system worked. Justice would've been swift here in Tibet, but perhaps the Americans would show leniency. After all, the producers hadn't known of the existence of the *Meh-Teh*, had they?

Dawa handed over an adjustable wrench and surveyed the damage. "We'll be here all week," he said dejectedly.

Tshering nodded. "All this snow will make our job difficult. Just pray we don't get any more."

The entire Kukuranda range had been covered with a fresh blanket of snow just two days earlier, forcing the salvage crew to dig through two feet of snow to get to the wreckage. Giant piles of snow ringed the chopper but helped to break the whipping mountain winds.

Dawa suddenly pointed toward the half-exposed rear rotor. "What do we have here?"

"What do you see?"

"Ang, come look at this."

Leaving the stubborn fuselage for a moment, Tshering tromped through the snow toward his copilot. Dawa was kneeling beside a twisted piece of metal.

"What is it?"

Dawa pointed to the ground, and Ang gasped.

It was a giant print in the snow. Larger than a human footprint, the impression clearly showed five distinct toes jutting from a central depression. Whatever had left the print had been barefoot. And huge.

Tshering scanned their immediate surroundings. There were no other prints.

"What do you think it is?" Dawa asked.

"It could not be the Meh-Teh. I have seen its dead body with my own eyes. Perhaps this print is old."

"But it snowed just last night," Dawa pointed out. "An old print would have been covered just like our chopper here."

Tshering pondered this a moment and could think of no reply. He turned from his copilot and the strange footprint and walked back to the fuselage in silence. He had seen the *Meh-Teh* upon the summit, he reminded himself. Survival was impossible. This must be the print of something else, or a trick of the snow and wind. He had seen such things before—shapes in the shifting snows that looked like faces, bodies, or perhaps, even footprints.

Yes, Tshering thought, applying the wrench to the frozen bolts on the fuselage. *A trick of the snow.*

Just then, the wind picked up and gusted over the bank of piled snow. It swept across the strange footprint, forever concealing it beneath a blanket of freshly blown flakes of white.

Want to know what's going on with
your favorite author or what new releases
are coming from Medallion Press?

Now you can receive breaking news,
updates, and more from Medallion Press
straight to your cell phone, e-mail, instant
messenger, or Facebook!

Sign up now at www.twitter.com/MedallionPress
to stay on top of all the happenings in and
around Medallion Press.

For more information
about other great titles from
Medallion Press, visit

m e d a l l i o n p r e s s . c o m